Cycle of Coincidence

by

Debra Birdwell Winkler

This is a work of fiction. Names, characters, places, and incidents are either the product of the author's imagination or are used fictitiously, and any resemblance to actual persons living or dead, business establishments, events, or locales, is entirely coincidental.

Cycle of Coincidence

Cover Art by *Tina Lynn Stout*

The Wild Rose Press, Inc.
PO Box 708
Adams Basin, NY 14410-0708
Visit us at www.thewildrosepress.com

Publishing History
First Edition, 2023
Trade Paperback ISBN 978-1-5092-4545-1
Digital ISBN 978-1-5092-4546-8

Published in the United States of America

As Roy walked out through the hotel's revolving doors, Daan said to his wife, "You are beautiful."

"Thank you, darling," Francine said. "You have the opera tickets, of course."

Daan tapped his empty jacket pocket. "Oh my gosh. We got to talking, and I forgot. What would I do without you?"

Roy was pulling up in the front.

"Go, join Roy. I'll get them from the concierge, and I'll be with you in a minute."

Daan watched as his family exited the hotel, and Roy opened his rear car door for them. He hurried across the lobby and picked up the tickets from the hotel agent at the concierge desk. He then turned back towards the front of the hotel when he heard the rumble of an explosion. Shards of sharp broken glass from the front windows filled the air.

The concussive force knocked Daan and everyone else in the lobby off their feet. He was propelled across the marble floor, where he hit the concierge desk. Metal, furniture, rugs, and lamps flew past, accompanied by the screams of his fellow victims.

Before Daan passed out, he forced his eyes open and was left with the image of Roy's car totally engulfed in fire. Red, orange, yellow roaring flames billowed out from the car, with bits of debris still crashing to the pavement from the portico above. In an instant, his family was gone, and his life was a smoldering pile of ash.

Dedication

To my dear husband, Elliot,
who encouraged me to follow my writing dreams.

BOOK 1: The Past

Chapter 1

And so, the cycle begins: Fall 1653, The Caribbean Sea.

Emanuel de Sylva opened his eyes, startled. He had been awakened by strange noises outside the cabin door of the *Zilveren Morgenster (The Silver Morningstar)*, the ship he and his brother owned. He shook his wife and jumped out of bed, pulling on his britches and boots.

"Hide in the secret compartment," he told his wife as he pulled back his sleep-tousled, curly, auburn hair from his light brown, weathered face. "Don't come out for anyone but me."

Turning, Emanuel tucked his pistol in his waistband and drew his sword. He glanced back to make sure his wife and son were hiding, then left the cabin.

Securing the door behind him, Emanuel faced a skirmish of men and weapons before him. Through the smoky haze, he could see his men were battling with unknown marauders, clashes of blade against blade resonated like crashing cymbals along with the roaring sounds of pistols being fired.

Emanuel shifted his sword to his left hand and drew the pistol from his waistband in his right. He thanked his father under his breath for teaching him and his brother, Dominik, to be ambidextrous with weapons, a quality that was important to have in a fight to the death, and he was sure this was such a fight.

Someone ran towards Emanuel. He shot the stranger, who slumped hard to the wooden deck. Emanuel dropped his weapon, swearing at its inability to shoot more than once. He grabbed the knife from his boot, to face the next assailant.

Emanuel, an expert swordsman, plunged his sword into the chest of the second attacker. He pivoted towards a third's charge, cutting the man's neck with his knife, blood spewed forth dousing Emanuel. Turning, he sliced his sword across the back of another. Then, he raced up the stairs to the poop deck, stabbing one more who flipped over the banister and crashed below.

At the top, Emanuel found his blue-eyed first mate, Van Dyk, flat on his back fighting off a large, heavy man. Next to Van Dyke, the dead helmsman had collapsed against the whipstaff that guided the ship. Emanuel ran across the deck and plunged his sword into the attacker. He then sensed someone behind him, so he jerked his elbow into the aggressor's gut, whirling around to slice this one's face with his knife, kicking him over the taffrail into the sea.

Emanuel was pushed from behind by another enemy. As he swung around, he was sliced across his back. The wound would have been deeper had not the sword of Van Dyk found its way through the man's abdomen, bowels spilling out. Emanuel pulled Van Dyk from the deck, and they stood back-to-back fighting off several invaders. Emanuel's men soon had the upper hand, and it only took a few more minutes before the pirates were either dead or scurrying off the *Zilveren Morgenster* to another vessel tied alongside.

"Van Dyk, what happened here?" Emanuel asked,

breathlessly.

"We were boarded, sir," Van Dyk said wiping sweat from his brow. He steadied the whipstaff and yelled an order for a sailor to take over.

"And why were the cannons not fired?"

"The lookout saw a Dutch ship in distress. It was listing and seemed to be taking on water, so the captain had us heave to." Van Dyk pointed in the haze to the other ship. "You see, it's still flying a Dutch flag, so we had no idea it was a trap. Before we knew what was happening, we were boarded and fighting for our lives."

"You sent no one for me?"

"There wasn't time, sir."

Emanuel looked around. "Where's the captain?"

Van Dyk spat out, "Captain Ziebach is one of them, sir."

"What?"

Emanuel now noticed the other ship's flag was being hauled down, and Captain Ziebach—*his* Captain Ziebach—was ordering the other ship away.

"De Sylva, are you listening?" Ziebach called out as he flipped his golden white mane back from his sunburned face.

Emanuel took a deep breath but did not respond.

"Your other two ships brought a good price on the open market. The *Morgenster* is too good a prize, and I'll have it as my own. No one has ever gotten away from me! And I'll follow you, mark my words!" Ziebach saluted and grinned. "That lovely wife of yours will be mine as well, you watch and see!"

Emanuel looked at Van Dyk. "Fire the starboard cannons and show me the talent of your men. You told me they were good, now prove it. Then turn our ship into

3

the wind."

Van Dyk gave the order and in just a few minutes, cannons roared, releasing their load towards the pirate vessel, and sending a shiver through the *Zilveren Morgenster*. A cracking of timber echoed as cannonballs hit their mark through the side of Ziebach's ship. A second volley echoed, and cannonballs hit the three masts of the pirate ship. Then, the *Zilveren Morgenster* was veering away as her sails caught the wind.

Emanuel heard a slew of colorful obscenities from Ziebach followed by, "You think you have destroyed me, de Sylva, but think again. I will get you, your brother, and all your family. I will erase you thieving Jews from the face of the earth. This I promise. Maybe not in this lifetime, but me and mine will take you down. You'll have nothing in the end. Do you hear me, de Sylva? As God is my witness, you will end up with NOTHING!"

Emanuel turned his back on Ziebach and smiled, imaging his former captain's fist waving in the air. The pirate vessel faded from view in the early morning light and Ziebach's words waned, ignored.

For over a century, the de Sylva family's Silver Fleet Shipping Company of Amsterdam had transported goods throughout Europe and the Mediterranean. It was Dominik and Emanuel who had convinced their father and uncle to expand into the Americas. For the last decade, they had been delivering precious sugar and Brazilian wood to European markets, returning finished products to Recifé, Brazil. During that time, they had surprisingly never lost a ship. They had done well but things were changing. He and Dominik could feel it in the wind that the Portuguese were going to take Recifé, so they decided to move their trading routes to the

Caribbean Dutch Islands and New Amsterdam.

Pirates looted ships in Caribbean waters, and they had lost two ships in four months. Now, with this ship being their last to leave Recifé, Emanuel had put his faith in his new captain who came well recommended. However, he swore to himself for taking on Ziebach as captain, but it was too late to worry about that now. Luckily, the brothers had commissioned the *Zilveren Morgenster* with the latest equipment, including twelve cannons which those at the Amsterdam shipyard thought was too great an expenditure for a merchant vessel. But with those cannons, Van Dyk and his men had protected the ship and all its contents, including his family.

Emanuel stood on deck as the wind tangled his hair while the *Zilveren Morgenster* glided along swiftly through the whitecaps. He knew he and his brother would succeed. They had not lost everything like the family had so many years ago when they were forced to leave Spain. He couldn't wait to get word to Dominik. They were still solvent, still a company, still a force to be reckoned with in the marketplace.

And Ziebach's threat?

Emanuel and Dominik would take down Ziebach together, if need be. But that was for another day, another time.

Chapter 2

February 1781, Dutch Island of Sint Eustatius.

That morning, Amos de Sylva was surprised to see a British battle fleet off the coast of Sint Eustatius surrounding the one Dutch Navy ship moored in the harbor along with several American, French, and Spanish vessels. He heard the cannons of Fort Oranje fire two shots into the bay and knew it was a gesture of resistance because Governor de Graaff would have no choice but to surrender in front of such overwhelming odds.

Amos knew the British had it out for the governor and the Dutch island for being the first to give international recognition to the young United States as a free and independent country back in November 1776. There was no doubt the island would be plundered and de Graaff imprisoned along with many others.

News spread fast throughout the town that Great Britain and the Dutch Republic had been at war since December. Not exactly a surprise with the Dutch supporting the Americans in their war for independence from Great Britain. This Dutch island was an open port where French, Spanish, and Dutch ships bought and sold goods, many bound for the new United States.

The de Sylvas agreed with the rights of liberty the Americans were fighting for, so they had been busy shipping guns, ammunition, and other supplies to the new nation for several years. Being a Dutch merchantman in a world ruled by Great Britain was becoming increasingly more difficult. Nevertheless, de Sylva ships were adept at evading the British King's fleets on the high seas in captured British merchant vessels, masking the fact they were Dutch. It was the best way to hide from the British, out in the open. Dominick's ship, the *Queen Anne*, was one such vessel that had left early for Amsterdam just last week, evading the invasion.

Amos' own ship was due any day from Curaçao loaded with supplies bound for the Americans. The *Elizabeth's* return in the middle of this fiasco would deal a devastating blow to the de Sylvas since the British would take possession of the cargo and Amos and his crew would be hanged as pirates.

As the days passed, few islanders left their homes as the British took over the island. The enemy patrolled the streets and those, who dared to venture out, were manhandled by soldiers as they exerted their strength and authoritative tactics against the Dutch population, as well as the French, Spanish, and American residents.

On the tenth day, the British broke into Jewish homes, rounded up all the Jewish men including Amos, and dragged them to the town square. People were standing in the streets yelling and screaming at the British and a few were struck down.

A British officer in full dress red military uniform and powdered hair, braided down his back, appeared and stepped on a box with lesser officers on either side of him. He carefully unrolled a proclamation and announced, "You, Jewish scum, are ordered to be imprisoned for your treasonous actions of aiding and abetting the enemies of the British government."

A Frenchman shouted from the spectators gathering around, "You're not my government!" Several people laughed, but the closest soldier hit the rabblerouser in the head with the butt of his rifle, and he fell, bleeding to the ground.

The officer, ignoring the scuffle, continued, "For these criminal actions, you are being transported to St. Kitts Island to be incarcerated until the Crown decides to execute you."

Rolling up the proclamation and placing it under his arm, the officer shouted to the junior officer before him, "Do your duty and get these swine loaded onto ships."

The British officer looked at the crowd and shouted, "All who are not British citizens will be dealt with very soon!"

Soldiers brought out balls and chains to shackle the feet of the prisoners. As a soldier pulled him forward, Amos heard a familiar voice. At least, he thought the sound of the voice was familiar, but the man was speaking with a British accent.

"Albert! Albert, is that you?"

He turned to face the blond-haired, blue-eyed captain of his ship, Harrison Van Dyk, who grabbed him in a hug. "Where have you been, Albert? I've been searching all over for you!"

The officer who had read the announcement came over to Van Dyk. "Who are you?" he demanded. "Why are you hugging this criminal?"

"Say nothing and act dense, sir," Van Dyk whispered, then pushed Amos away, winked, and turned to face the British officer. "Criminal? Are you kidding?

This is my brother Albert. He can't speak, and he's not very smart, you see."

"And you are?"

"Jedidiah Harrison of York." Van Dyk vigorously shook the man's hand. "And how may I address the man who saved my brother?"

"I'm Colonel Arthur Ziebach."

The last name seemed familiar to Van Dyk, but he dismissed the thought and smiled broadly.

"Colonel Ziebach, thank you so much for finding Albert." Van Dyk wrapped his arm around Amos' shoulder and ruffled his auburn hair. "Come on, Albert. We must be going."

"Why are you here on this island?"

Van Dyk nonchalantly stopped and looked out to the bay. "Do you see that British merchant ship lying there, just behind our fleet?"

"What ship?"

Van Dyk proudly pointed to the British schooner he and Amos had captured two summers ago. "The *Elizabeth*. Isn't she a beauty?"

In disguise, the *Elizabeth* had already made runs between Philadelphia and Sint Eustatius. While Amos was here on the island organizing freight with his brother for their ship heading for Amsterdam, Van Dyk had picked up cargo in Curaçao. They had returned to pick up the rest of the shipment for the Americans but were surprised to sail right into the hornet's nest of the unexpected British fleet.

"I see her," the colonel said. "Now, why are you here?"

"I've been here for nigh on four months now, observing St. Eustace for the British foreign office," Van

Dyk answered using the British name for the island. "It was a surprise to see the fleet here. I thought you'd be off the coast of Virginia supporting our troops there."

Ziebach looked at the fleet and said, "Admiral Rodney wanted to shut down this God-forsaken supply depot to stop anyone helping the rebels."

"The admiral is wise," Van Dyk agreed. "But no one has struck the Dutch flag and raised our colors to confirm we're here."

"A ploy to bring in enemy ships so we can capture them as pirates," Ziebach said.

"Ah." Van Dyk nodded.

"Where are the de Sylvas?" Colonel Ziebach demanded, changing the subject. "I heard they were established here on the island."

"The de Sylva brothers loaded a consignment of goods onto their ships and left a few days ago," Van Dyk lied.

"They're gone?"

"Yeah," Van Dyk said and pointed to the docks. "Their warehouse is down there with the others full of cargo. One ship was heading for Amsterdam, the other headed south to trade for more goods. I'm sure the second ship will return here in a few days to grab what's left in their warehouse and sail north."

"That warehouse will be mine," the colonel said. "Admiral Rodney said we'd all get a piece of the loot found here. That de Sylva cargo will be mine because the de Sylvas owe me."

Amos was unsure what that meant. He knew there was a Dutch Ziebach family. They had caused trouble for his grandfather when Amos and Dominik were lads and attempted to sue his father and uncle a few years back.

But he didn't know this British Colonel Ziebach. He didn't want to stand around and wait for someone to recognize either Van Dyk or himself. He hunched over to tug on Van Dyk's arm and gave a low moan.

"Thank you again, Colonel." Van Dyk tapped Amos' hand. "You can see why I must get him out of this crowd."

Ziebach stepped back. "Let these men through. They are British citizens."

As Van Dyk and Amos jumped into the boat with two sailors waiting to row them to their ship, Amos tried not to pay attention to the men in chains being loaded onto British ships. But for Van Dyk, he would have been joining his Jewish brethren.

A while later, they stood on the *Elizabeth's* deck, and Van Dyk smiled at Amos. "Can't believe that colonel fell for me being from York."

"Your mother is from York, right?" Amos asked.

"Yes, but I've never been there!" Van Dyk paused. "Ziebach? Why is that name familiar?"

"That's a family who works in the shipyards at home. They're a sorry bunch," Amos said. "They have caused trouble for my family over the years."

"Right."

Amos noticed smoke rising from the warehouses. "Van Dyk, our warehouse is on fire."

"Of course, it is, sir." Van Dyk nodded at the crew as they prepared the ship for sailing. "These men are loyal to you, sir. That cargo belongs to us and not the British!"

A few minutes later, the *Elizabeth's* sails billowed full as she picked up the trade winds that carried her away from the island. Amos stood on the poop deck, watching the flames engulf his warehouse and spread to others, as British soldiers ran to put out the fires.

Well, the de Sylvas had survived another almost defeat. His brother, Dominik, was returning to the Old World. But maybe his destiny belonged in the New World with the new American nation. He smiled at the thought.

Chapter 3

December 1864, Savannah, Georgia.

It was late afternoon when Phoebe opened the door to the knock, letting in the cold.

"Yes?" she said to the tall, weather-worn, scraggy-bearded Union officer in a heavy army overcoat standing in front of her. "How may I help you?"

He began, "Miss, I am to quarter here while General Sherman's army is—"

He stopped abruptly as he looked at the dark-haired woman before him. She was thin and underweight, looking rather defeated and downtrodden in her faded dress with no hoop in her skirt and a worn shawl wrapped around her shoulders. This woman was dreadfully pale. But her eyes, her hazel eyes. He knew those eyes.

Could this be the bright-eyed girl he had met in Philadelphia six years ago, the girl he had fallen in love with when he first saw her, when she entered the room, when he danced with her?

"Phoebe?" he asked. "Phoebe Van Dyk?"

She stared at the rugged, hard-looking man standing at her door. She waited before responding. "Oh, my God," she whispered. "You can't be Emanuel de Sylva?"

He smiled. It was the girl he remembered. "Manny de Sylva, in the flesh." He took his hat off, revealing a head of unruly, curly auburn hair and bowed low.

She laughed.

He remembered her laugh. A sweet laugh that reminded him of bells tingling.

"Ah, I'm supposed to be at the—" He looked at the paper in his hand. "—Abner Johnson home."

"You are. That's my husband."

He sighed. "Ah, yes. Your husband."

"I'm a widow, Manny. My husband died at Antietam in '62."

"I'm sorry."

A cold wind whipped around her, and she opened the door wider. "Come in."

"Stables are behind your house?" he asked.

"It's not much of a stable now. I haven't had horses there for a couple of years."

He turned to the stout, scruffy soldier in mismatched uniform waiting at the bottom of the stairs holding the reins of two horses. "Take the horses to the stable in the back, Sergeant Ziebach. I'll be right there."

Manny followed Phoebe through the door and hung his coat and hat on the wall hook. He watched the sergeant guide the horses around the side of the house, and then shut the door behind him.

"That man's just been assigned to me, and I find he's not much of an asset."

Phoebe shivered.

"It's as cold in here as it is outside, Phoebe." He investigated the parlor on his right. "There's no fire lit."

"Not much wood available, so we only have a fire burning in the kitchen stove," she said and motioned for him to follow her down the dank, barren hall void of pictures or decor of any kind.

The house was long and narrow with the kitchen at

the very back. From the window Manny saw the sergeant quartering the horses in a dilapidated building that looked like it was once a grand stable.

A chocolate-skinned woman came into the kitchen. "Manny, this is Patience," Phoebe said.

"Hello," he said. "Is she your house slave?" Patience looked as thin and shabby as Phoebe.

"Oh, no, sir," Patience spoke in much better English than slaves he had come across as Sherman's army had marched through Georgia. "I am no slave to Miss Phoebe. She freed me when she married Mr. Johnson."

"When Abner was killed, all the slaves left. Here and at Johnson Hill, his cotton plantation." Phoebe smiled at Patience. "Only Patience stayed with me."

"I see."

"Please sit down, Mr. Manny," Patience said, pulling out a chair from the table. "We don't have much, but I can fix you some eggs. We still have a couple of chickens in the back. And, we have a little bread. Will that be okay with you?"

Manny looked around the sparse kitchen. "I'm not hungry, Miss Patience. Just coffee."

Phoebe looked at him with sad eyes that had lost the sparkle he remembered. "We haven't had coffee for months. The pump's broken so we must go to the well in the backyard for water."

"Water will be fine, Phoebe. Tomorrow I'll have Sergeant Ziebach requisition some rations for our stay here."

Patience left for the well and Phoebe sat down at the table opposite him.

He began, "Phoebe, in Philadelphia, we had just gotten to know each other when you suddenly disappeared. My mother said you were engaged or something. Why didn't you tell me?"

Phoebe said nothing.

"Do you know how much in love I was with you?" he asked. "Do you?"

She waited and then said softly, "Philadelphia was a long time ago." Tears flowed down her cheeks. "I married Abner to save my father who was in debt, Manny." She pulled her hands to her face. "After we were married, my father sailed home for Amsterdam, but his ship went down in a storm."

"Oh, Phoebe," he said and took her hand. "I would have—"

She quickly pulled away from him and walked over to the wooden cabinet with a metal sink basin next to the pump. "It's what I had to do, Manny. My feelings for you meant nothing to my father. So, I married Abner and came to Savannah. The war started not long after, and then he was gone, too."

Manny moved to Phoebe and touched her shoulder. "I tried to forget you," he whispered. "The war allowed me to drive you out of my mind. My brother took our ships into Federal service. I had to get away from Philadelphia and everything we knew together. I joined the army and served in the western theater. I thought I was okay until you opened the front door." He wrapped his arms around her and pulled her into his chest. "Ah, Phoebe, it's like a dream come true holding you in my arms again."

Then, the back door flew open and hit the wall. Manny and Phoebe jumped. There stood Sergeant Ziebach holding his revolver at Patience's head.

"Well, now, it looks like we're going to have a little

party." He pushed Patience into the room and kicked the door closed. "You know, Major de Sylva," the sergeant spit out, "I have been waiting and watching you all the way through Georgia trying to get near you."

Manny stepped in front of Phoebe. "Me?" he asked the soldier. "Why?"

"That's why I'm here. To destroy all de Sylvas. You have tormented the Ziebachs long enough!" Ziebach's eyes were full of hatred as he showed a wicked, toothless grin. He waved the gun at Manny. "When I'm finished with you, I'm going to have fun with these two before I shoot them." He moved the gun back and forth between the two women, laughing. "In the morning, I'll report that they were attacking you, and I had to kill them. In the scuffle, you were mortally wounded. A terrible accident that couldn't be avoided."

"But why kill me? I haven't done anything to you and neither have these women."

"Just a curse made against you many years ago when your ancestor tried to destroy mine," Ziebach claimed. "I've already taken care of every de Sylva in America. Your Philadelphia family was the last. You are the only one left."

"My parents, and my brother and his family died in a fire that destroyed my home last January."

"Who do you think started the fire?" Ziebach smirked. "I have to protect the honor of my family!"

"You killed my entire family." Manny's voice was thick yet controlled as he emphasized each word. Both of his hands made fists as he inched towards the murderer.

"It was so easy." Ziebach roared with laughter. "It took me a while, but I finally found you."

Manny contained his rage as he continued to slowly edge forward while Ziebach kept the gun focused on him and held tight to Patience.

"A curse? To destroy all de Sylvas? Sounds medieval and a bit melodramatic." With great effort, Manny controlled his voice. "Come on, sergeant, let's put down the gun and discuss this logically." By this time, Manny was close enough to touch Patience. "Why don't you let go of the lady."

"She's no lady. She's nothing but a lowly—"

Manny pulled Patience away from Ziebach's grasp, knocking the gun out of the sergeant's hand. Patience fell to the floor, and Ziebach pushed against Manny as he lunged for the gun. Then, Phoebe had a knife in her hand and stabbed it into Ziebach's neck, blood squirting all over as he tumbled down hard on top of Manny.

Patience sat up and cried. Manny forced Ziebach off him. Phoebe just leaned into the sink, ferociously cleaning the knife with a cloth. Manny reached over and gently took the knife from Phoebe, dropping it into the sink.

"It's going to be fine," he whispered and turned her to face him.

"I've just killed a member of the United States Army, Manny. I'll be taken away and shot." Phoebe began to shake.

"No, you won't." He wrapped his arm around Phoebe, pulling her to him.

"I may have saved you, Manny, but I'm the enemy here who just killed your sergeant.

"I was going to kill him myself when he said he had murdered my family. You just beat me to it." Manny kissed the top of her head. No one was taking Phoebe away from him now, no one. But he had to think of something and fast. Finally, he stood back from Phoebe.

"First, we must get rid of the body before anyone knows," he said. "We'll wait until night falls and dig a grave in the backyard under the bushes."

Patience spoke confidently. "No, Mr. Manny. Not in the backyard. The ground is too hard in the winter. Under the house."

Phoebe nodded. "The dirt under the house is softer. That's where we buried the silver and other valuables for safekeeping from Yankees."

"You've buried valuables under the house because you were afraid of Sherman's army?" He laughed. "You were afraid of me?"

"Well, not you, exactly. We didn't know you were with Sherman," Phoebe answered.

"But you buried everything under the house?"

"Best hiding place ever, Manny."

Both women nodded.

He paused, then said, "So that's where we'll bury Ziebach."

"What will the army say?" Phoebe asked.

"I'll tell them he disappeared in the night. He'll be one of the many who have deserted so they can loot homes." He held her hands in his.

"They won't question?"

"No."

"What was he saying about a curse?"

He kissed her forehead. "God only knows. He's dead, and we may never find out. But don't worry."

Patience secured a quilt from upstairs, and Manny and Phoebe wrapped the sergeant in it. Then, they cleaned up the kitchen, throwing bloody rags in with the blanket. It was after midnight when they completed burying the dead man.

"Miss Phoebe," Patience said when they returned to the kitchen.

"Patience, how many times must I tell you that it's just Phoebe?"

"But you saved me a long time ago, Miss Phoebe."

Phoebe hugged Patience. "You saved me, Patience."

Both women laughed.

"I'm going to set up my bed right here under the table as usual. My lips are sealed about that sergeant. He was a bad man, a very bad man."

"Set mine up, too, Patience," Phoebe said. "We'll light the fires in the parlor and the major can sleep there."

"Oh, no, Miss, I mean Phoebe. You and Mr. Manny must go upstairs. I have a fire lit in your bedroom, so y'all will be warm."

"Patience," Phoebe said, astonished. "Manny and I aren't married."

"You would've been if you hadn't taken care of your daddy."

"You know, Miss Patience, you are a smart woman," Manny said sincerely and winked.

To Phoebe, he said, "Phoebe, the war will be over soon, and I'll be back to marry you. I promise."

"But what if someone comes looking for you, Manny de Sylva?"

"All the de Silvas are gone, according to Sergeant Ziebach. Let's make it so." He smiled and lifted her in his arms. "I'll return as Emanuel Silva and we will be married right here in Savannah, and no one will know otherwise."

"What if I say no?"

"You won't," he said confidently as he carried her up the stairs.

Chapter 4

August 1950, Amsterdam.

Two men sat on a bench on the River Amstel, watching the construction of a building across the way. Both men were smoking as they concentrated.

The older, white-haired man took a final drag on his cigarette and flipped the butt into the water. "It's too bad the Nazis didn't win the War, Son. We would have been a very rich family."

The younger man was clean-shaven with neatly trimmed golden hair. "Perhaps, Papa. Perhaps."

"No, perhaps. We had almost everything. It would have just been a matter of time before we would have had it all."

The son inhaled and blew cigarette smoke in the air. "Our construction company handles a lot of contracts with the rebuilding here and in Rotterdam. We've been very successful since the War."

The elderly man pointed across the river. "That contract should have been ours as well."

"The de Sylva home was ours, Papa, until the Nazis left," the son complained. "It was good our cousin let us know the old woman and the boy returned, allowing us to torch the place before they arrived."

"We did get a lot out before we started the fire and made money on its contents." The father had a fit of coughing and then lit up a cigarette from his son's pack. "I don't understand how the de Sylvas escaped the Nazi trap," he said. "The rest of the family were captured and sent to Germany. No one was supposed to come back. We were promised Germany would destroy all the damn Jews!"

There was silence between the two men as they continued to watch the progress of the construction. The young man walked over to the river's edge and cast the butt of his cigarette into the dark water.

Turning to his father, he asked, "How do they do it, Papa? They continue to exist no matter what we do." He walked over to his father, shaking his head. "Did they make a deal with the devil?"

"Them and all their kind are evil through and through." The old man lit another cigarette and looked directly at his son, determination in his eyes. "There's only a few de Sylvas left now, and this time we are going to do it differently. You and me and little Luther, here."

The old man reached into the pram and touched the hand of the three-year-old sleeping soundly.

"Four hundred years ago, our ancestor cursed that filthy de Sylva bunch, to wipe them off the face of the earth because they took what was ours. So, we will watch, plot, and scheme to become the most powerful entrepreneurs on the face of the planet. It'll take a while, but soon we will control everything. They will know nothing until we destroy them."

The father pounded his fist on the bench. The son took his father's hand and sat next to him.

"Sounds like a plan, Papa. The de Sylvas and their kind don't have the right to be here. They're not Dutch, anyway."

"So, we are saving our nation from Jewish vermin." The old man smiled sadistically and leaned back to inhale smoke from his cigarette, held it in his lungs, and then released it slowly. "The three of us, together, will destroy the de Sylvas. Every one of them!"

The two men smiled at each other as the noise from the new hotel's construction filled the air and they watched without comment.

BOOK 2: The Present

Chapter 5

Daan de Sylva, a chief inspector with the Dutch Police, had been in San Francisco for a week participating in a cooperative international law enforcement training. He enjoyed learning tactics from police departments in different countries, and during the past week, he was relishing comparing notes with these Americans who seemed an easy lot to get to know. They were jovial to a fault yet determined to close a case with energetic fortitude.

Roy Sanderson, his assigned liaison, was a couple of inches shorter than Daan and had a ruddy complexion and large grin but looked disheveled in his worn-out trousers, plaid sports coat, and striped shirt with a stained tie. When he greeted Daan, Roy had a cigarette in his left hand which he ran through his orange-red hair, dropping ashes along the way. Daan looked at the grimy-looking hand being extended to him and decided he might need to wash up after the handshake. However, Daan found Roy to be quite a competent detective. They performed well as a team, tackling each assignment thrown their way with meticulous precision, and they were good friends in a couple of days.

On Daan's last night in town, Roy and four other police detectives from the training had taken him to their favorite bar to say goodbye.

Roy took a puff on his cigarette. "Are you always so

formal in your attire?" He took a step back from Daan. "You're a tall and handsome Dutchman, who looks more Mediterranean with those dark eyes and hair. You have a sharp, debonair look about you, man." He laughed and his fellow police officers joined in.

Daan was getting used to the playful ribbing from this boisterous group. They were all dressed in jeans and t-shirts and there he was in his standard attire. He nodded at his colleagues.

"What? These old trousers and shirt aren't formal," he responded, chuckling. "This is nothing. You ought to see me when I'm heading for the opera."

As he spoke, the waitress brought their next round of drinks.

Roy snuffed out his cigarette in the ashtray. Pointing to the drinks lined up on the table before them, he said, "He dresses formally for work, goes to the opera, and drinks vodka with a lemon twist." Roy elbowed Daan. "Gentlemen, this man is a hoity-toity foreigner. What next? Dressing us all up in tuxedos as we chase the bad guys?"

A roar of laughter echoed through the bar.

The rest of the evening was spent in much the same way, bantering back and forth while relaxing after a week of heavy training. One eventually looked at his watch and commented that it was after eleven.

"Damn, my wife's gonna kill me for staying out so late, even on a Friday night."

There was a grumble of agreement as the waitress brought the bill to the table, and everyone scrambled for their wallets.

"What's my share?" Daan asked.

"Your money's no good here, friend," Roy said,

"even if you are a foreigner."

The group laughed. The man to Daan's left slapped his back. "Our treat. When we visit Amsterdam, it's your turn."

They were tipsy and a bit unsteady, but not drunk as they strolled out of the bar and headed down the street to Daan's hotel, a mere three blocks away.

They had not made it far when they heard a commotion as they crossed in front of a darkened alleyway. Shouting, and then a gunshot. The six officers froze, suddenly sober. Training kicked in as the group backed up to assess the situation.

Daan instinctively reached behind him where he normally kept his service weapon holstered, but he wasn't home. As a foreign policeman in America, Daan wasn't carrying his gun. He watched as Roy and the others drew their pistols with expertise and moved forward, hugging the worn brick wall. Roy motioned Daan back, then reached down and pulled a small pistol from his boot.

"Daan," Roy whispered before tossing it to him. "Just in case."

Daan caught the gun but stayed back, hunkering down behind the huge garbage dumpster up against the wall. He watched around its corner as Roy and his colleagues inched along in the shadows.

Daan could make out four—no five men under the light above an entranceway cut into the brick wall. Four were in suits but one was dressed in a chef's getup. The only thing missing, Daan noticed, was the *toque blanche* from his head.

Two of the men held the stout cook steady, while the third man punched him in the stomach, with alternating fists. The cook would slump forward with each hit, but he'd be lifted back up for the next attack. Periodically, the hitter aimed for the face, leaving blood drooling from the chef's mouth and face cuts, mixing blood with the dried food coating on his uniform.

Daan eyed the fourth criminal hovering against the wall of the dead-end lane. There was just enough light for him to see the man was rather large, standing over six feet tall with broad shoulders and weighing around 240 pounds. Immaculately dressed in a tailored linen suit, his matching Panama hat was lowered to hide his face from view. He was chewing on a toothpick and artfully rolling a coin across his knuckles, staring at the ground. The rhythmic sound of the chef's beating was disturbed only by his intermittent breathless screams, "It wasn't me!" But the big man seemed to be uninterested in the scene before him.

Then, in an unexpected burst of speed, the fourth man spit out his toothpick and tucked the coin in his pocket. With his back to the police officers, he withdrew a gun and screwed a silencer into place. He nudged the three thugs out of the way as he grabbed the terrified victim by the collar and forced the cook to his knees, mumbling words Daan could not decipher. The cook shrieked and suddenly he collapsed in a heap on the cobblestones.

Roy shouted, "Police, drop your weapons!"

He and his colleagues ran forward. Startled, the big man jerked his gun back into his jacket and his group scattered. But they were boxed in at the end of the alley and, with policemen blocking their escape, they had nowhere to run. Roy and his friends quickly had everything in hand. One of the detectives called an ambulance while the others grabbed the men in suits and handcuffed them.

Roy dropped to one knee next to the injured man, blood oozing out onto the cobblestone pavement. "Call the coroner instead. This guy's dead."

Daan was surprised the whole incident had only taken a few minutes. He stepped from his hiding place to help, but Roy gestured him away, not allowing him to be involved. So, as Daan made his way to his hotel, the shooting scene played over and over in his head.

He smiled as he realized the guy in the Panama hat was Luther Ziebach, the notorious mobster, who was wanted by the Amsterdam police and several other European agencies for racketeering, money laundering, human trafficking, and selling illegal drugs. There was a rumor the mobster was spreading his tentacles to the United States. This was proof.

Daan and Roy discussed the arrest of the infamous Ziebach the next morning.

"As a foreign national, you know you couldn't be a part of the arrest team," Roy explained, taking his gun from Daan. "The San Francisco Police Department handled everything." Roy laughed. "Besides that, with Ziebach being Dutch, it was good you weren't involved."

At the airport, Roy said, "I know you told me you went to law school and passed the bar and everything. But Daan, you became a policeman and, as a policeman, you must bring in the perps. As I've been telling you all week, leave your law training behind or become a god-damned lawyer yourself."

"Thanks, Roy."

Roy shook Daan's hand. "Have a safe flight back to Amsterdam, my friend, and don't worry about last night."

Daan kept up with the trial proceedings from afar. Although he witnessed the crime, his testimony wasn't needed. The case had been air-tight, and the jury convicted Ziebach and his associates of the murder. Ziebach received twenty-five to life.

In open court, Ziebach made a vow. "I will bring down all the American and Dutch law enforcement officers who lied to take me down," he yelled as he was dragged out of the courtroom. "All of you!"

His words were repeated in the media. When interviewed, Ziebach explained he was innocent, and the crooked police had created trumped-up charges. He promised his conviction would be overturned on appeal, and he would be free.

In a phone call after the trial, Daan cautioned Roy about Ziebach. Similar threats had been carried out before in Europe and witnesses had either died or disappeared while others refused to testify.

"I told you everything would work out and it did," Roy told Daan on the phone. "The policemen did their jobs and the lawyers put Ziebach and the others away."

As Daan hung up the phone, he felt relieved that Ziebach was in prison.

Chapter 6

Daan and Roy had stayed connected over the next five years. They discussed police business, of course, but mostly Roy kept Daan up to date on what was going on with Ziebach.

In June of that year, Daan let Roy know he and his family would vacation for a few days in San Francisco and stay at the Benjamin Franklin Hotel. Roy was testifying in court when Daan and his family arrived, but Roy promised to meet Daan at their hotel on Friday evening. The family had tickets to the last section of Wagner's *The Ring Cycle*, his wife's favorite opera.

Daan had never liked Wagner and felt *The Ring Cycle* was too complicated and much too long. But he bought the opera tickets as a surprise for Francine and his daughters. The evening was going to be spectacular, and his wife was ecstatic when he told her. He promised no work and he purposely left his work cell in their home in Rotterdam to keep his word. On the plane, Francine couldn't stop talking about *The Ring Cycle*. Their twin girls were sitting between them as she explained the love story between the characters and that Brünnhilde would die for love.

"Like Juliet and Romeo," Ilsa said happily.

"It was Romeo and Juliet," Anya argued.

Francine smiled at them and said they were both correct. Then, she leaned over them and took Daan's hand and said, "But, I am luckier than anyone because I love your father very much and, together, we'll watch the two of you grow up, go to school, marry, and give us grandchildren."

"Get your degrees, first, like your mother." Daan grinned and then kissed his wife's hand. "You know, I'm going to love your mother forever."

"And what about us, Papa?" the twins asked together.

"I'll love you both forever as well!" And he kissed their hands and they giggled.

Daan told himself a few hours enduring an opera he did not like was worth the happiness it brought to his wife. Their six-year-olds would not be able to tolerate the long opera, so he planned on them ending up asleep on his lap. He would have the best of both worlds with his wife and daughters happy and content.

They arrived at the hotel on Thursday evening and spent the next morning relaxing by the pool, vegetating after the long flight from Amsterdam. Then, the girls took naps allowing Francine and Daan to rest in each other's arms before enjoying an early dinner.

"Must you meet that policeman?" Francine asked back in the room as Daan prepared to meet Roy in the lobby. "This is our vacation, and you promised you would not be doing work!"

"Sweetheart, this isn't work," Daan said. "Just two friends seeing each other for the first time in years." He gave her a quick kiss. "I'll see you in about twenty minutes, okay?"

"Fine," she pouted as he left their suite.

Roy was in the lobby waiting when Daan stepped out of the elevator a few minutes before 6:00 p.m. The guys greeted each other with a handshake and slaps on the back.

"Hey, man," said Roy, "you always make me look out of place." Roy was dressed in his typical mismatched outfit. "So, this is how you dress for the opera? You look spiffy in that tuxedo. Like James Bond."

"Wait until my ladies come down," Daan promised. "Hold on a minute and let me have the hotel call a taxi to take my family to the opera."

"Don't call a taxi. Let me take you."

"Roy, that won't be necessary."

"Hey, man, it's only a few blocks away," Roy insisted. "I'm going that way anyway."

When Francine and the girls joined them in the lobby, it was twenty minutes to seven and they only had a few minutes to reach the opera house on time.

Roy whistled. "Daan, your ladies are dressed to the nines. Very lovely."

Francine was wearing wine-colored silk with sequins and lace and matching heels. She floated across the lobby with her straight blonde hair cascading down her back like a waterfall. His identical twin girls were dressed in white with one wearing a pink satin bow sash around her waist, while the other wore blue.

Daan beamed as he introduced Francine. "I'm a lucky man, Roy."

"Daan, you certainly are," his friend agreed. "I'll get the car and meet you out front. I may not be dressed as grand as you, but I can do this."

As Roy walked out through the hotel's revolving doors, Daan said to his wife, "You are beautiful."

"Thank you, darling," Francine said. "You have the opera tickets, of course."

Daan tapped his empty jacket pocket. "Oh my gosh. We got to talking, and I forgot. What would I do without you?"

Roy was pulling up in the front.

"Go, join Roy. I'll get them from the concierge, and I'll be with you in a minute."

Daan watched as his family exited the hotel, and Roy opened his rear car door for them. He hurried across the lobby and picked up the tickets from the hotel agent at the concierge desk. He then turned back towards the front of the hotel when he heard the rumble of an explosion. Shards of sharp broken glass from the front windows filled the air.

The concussive force knocked Daan and everyone else in the lobby off their feet. He was propelled across the marble floor, where he hit the concierge desk. Metal, furniture, rugs, and lamps flew past, accompanied by the screams of his fellow victims.

Before Daan passed out, he forced his eyes open and was left with the image of Roy's car totally engulfed in fire. Red, orange, yellow roaring flames billowed out from the car, with bits of debris still crashing to the pavement from the portico above. In an instant, his family was gone, and his life was a smoldering pile of ash.

Chapter 7

Phoebe Silva and her friend, Vanessa Auerbach, had entered the Opera House in downtown San Francisco early. They were jabbering as they leisurely strolled through the lobby. As usual, Phoebe thought they looked like the cartoon characters, Mutt and Jeff. Except they were real live people. Phoebe smiled at herself.

Vanessa was black, almost six feet tall, short black curly hair. Phoebe believed that Venessa's willowy physique was a dead giveaway that she was a long-distance runner. She had almost won the Boston Marathon several times. Vanessa's fireplace mantle was lined with several trophies winning Bay area races over the years. Vanessa always liked to make an entrance and tonight was no difference. She had on red flats with a multi-colored, geometric patterned dress and a red silk wrap. She wore gold dangling earrings with a long gold chain necklace with which she was constantly fiddling.

Phoebe was not quite five feet five inches tall with shoulder-length, curly, auburn hair which she wore up this evening, clamped with a black velvet clip. Her black chiffon dress and shawl were topped off with a pearl necklace and matching drop earrings.

Phoebe and Vanessa had attended Emory University in Atlanta together, earning graduate degrees (Vanessa had a master's in finance and advertising; Phoebe, history and geography). Afterward, Vanessa had returned home to San Francisco and became an advertising executive in her father's firm while Phoebe moved on to Brandeis for her Ph.D. Vanessa had never married because she admitted she liked playing the field. But she was Phoebe's maid of honor at her wedding to Dominic.

When Dominic died in a boating accident off the east coast of Florida, Phoebe had moved her family to southern Utah to be near her parents in Nevada. She joined the faculty of the University of Zion as an assistant professor of history because she wanted a simpler life. Vanessa tried to get Phoebe to apply at a California university to earn more money, but mostly because Vanessa loved Phoebe's girls. She was Aunty Vanessa to Charlotte and Lucy, ages six and three. Since she had no children of her own (and didn't want any she had to admit to herself), she was attached to these two and wanted them nearer to her.

Vanessa was clearly not happy that Phoebe seemed content in southern Utah where she lived across the street from her school. She had only visited once, and it was enough for her. The scenery in southern Utah was quite breathtaking, but she preferred the liveliness of San Francisco. Vanessa found her friend's fascination with the podunk college and its podunk village quite tedious.

Phoebe hadn't been to California in years. However, when Vanessa called to let Phoebe know she had bought tickets to the final section of Richard Wagner's *The Ring Cycle*, Phoebe was delighted to join her. Vanessa certainly enjoyed *The Ring Cycle* and had dragged Phoebe to see the other three opera sections over several years, attending the first section in Los Angeles, the second in Seattle, and the third in New York. Vanessa knew that Phoebe would want to join her to see the last segment of Wagner's famous opera.

So, Phoebe had driven to her parents in Las Vegas and dropped off the girls so she could fly to San Francisco. She was spending the weekend with Vanessa, seeing the opera that night, driving down to Monterey the next day, and returning for a late dinner on Fisherman's Wharf before flying to Las Vegas on Sunday.

As Phoebe and Vanessa were standing in line at 'Will Call,' there was a roaring sound not far away. Car alarms were going off, and people were running out of the building. No one knew for certain what was happening. A guy next to them said his car was parked just up the street so he ran to check on it. Many were just looky-loos talking and staring up the street. Vanessa had told her it was probably a truck backfiring, but Phoebe didn't think so. When they heard emergency vehicle sirens, Phoebe knew something terrible had happened. Then someone told them a car had exploded and was on fire in front of a hotel a few blocks away. Vanessa and Phoebe stayed in the lobby, tickets in hand, watching out the windows.

Even with it starting thirty minutes late, the opera was fantastic, and the next day was delightful. They drove down to Monterey, ate an early lunch in a bistro where they could watch the seals playing in the surf, and visited the magnificent aquarium. The day ended with Vanessa and Phoebe returning to San Francisco and sashaying around Fisherman's Wharf where they picked up gifts for the girls. They ate a late dinner at Vanessa's favorite restaurant around the corner from Union Square and then returned to Vanessa's penthouse apartment.

At the airport the following day, while she was waiting at her gate, Phoebe saw the newsfeed on the television about the explosion at the Benjamin Franklin Hotel on Friday evening. The reporter said several people were killed, including four in the car. In addition, it was reported that police were in the process of linking the explosion to a defendant on trial who allegedly killed a witness who was testifying against him in court. Nothing more was mentioned.

Phoebe thought the incident was horrible, but it was soon forgotten as she boarded her plane for Las Vegas with the anticipation of seeing her daughters.

Chapter 8

Across the street, about a block from the Benjamin Franklin Hotel, stood a man leaning against a building with his right foot propped behind him against its wall. He wore a double-breasted, chocolate brown trench coat with a matching fedora pulled down well over his eyes. He was of Hispanic heritage with no distinguishing features. Just an average looking man with dark hair, dark eyes, and of average height. He had strived many years for a look that was perfect for his profession.

Others around him had jumped at the noise of the car explosion. He had not. He knew it was coming.

Behind dark reflective sunglasses, he focused on the bombed-out car engulfed in flames. With a large crash, the hotel's fractured portico crushed the car. Fire began spiraling up the side of the hotel as black smoke curled its way into the darkening sky.

Now, he casually pocketed his cell phone and walked in the opposite direction. Several blocks away, he pulled the phone out and dialed a number as sirens echoed in the distance.

"Yeah, it's Nick."

Short wait as he listened to a voice.

"As ordered, four destroyed."

Another short wait.

"No, he's still alive as you requested. Probably injured and shaken, but he's not dead."

A few seconds passed.

"No one can trace it back to you. Someone else will be blamed, I made sure of that."

Silence.

"On the way out of the country. You know where to reach me when you need me again. Not in the States, though."

Nick listened.

"I speak several languages, you know that."

He nodded his head.

"The Middle East? That's fine. Send me the details."

Nick hung up the phone and walked another block and, turning a corner, he dropped the phone on the ground and smashed it with his foot. He picked up the sim card, dropping it in his pocket to get rid of later. The individual chunks and fragments were discarded into various dumpsters as he meandered along city streets and headed towards Fisherman's Wharf where he dropped the sim card into the saltwater.

After a while, when he guaranteed no one was following him, Nick hailed a taxi. He had completed the hit he was paid to do. No one would be able to track him or his employer because he was excellent at his job.

There was only one more thing he had to do before he vanished into the proverbial puff of smoke he was known for.

Chapter 9

Daan woke up two days later in the hospital. He had a concussion, several broken ribs, a collapsed lung, his left arm broken in three places, and he was covered in cuts and bruises. Assistant District Attorney Ricardo Diaz visited him on Monday morning and told him the doorman, two hotel employees at the front desk and the concierge, three hotel guests, and two passersby had been killed in the explosion. Many others had been injured.

"You were fortunate, Chief Inspector," Diaz said. "Very lucky indeed."

Daan didn't feel lucky.

Diaz, who had been part of the prosecution team who convicted Ziebach, was a short man with large framed glasses. He happy to give Daan all the details of the bombing.

"The police have traced the dynamite used in the bomb to the construction company owned by the defendant who's been on trial this last week. The most prevalent theory is that the defendant arranged for Roy to be killed so he couldn't testify." Diaz shook his head and then adjusted his glasses. "Your family, unfortunately, was collateral damage."

"How comforting."

"By the way, I was told to let you know Luther Ziebach's case is scheduled to come up on appeal on

Thursday."

"Roy told me."

"Well." Diaz took a breath. "The case is being dismissed, and he will be released from prison."

Daan was suddenly alert. "Why?"

"You are the only witness who is either not dead or has disappeared."

"Fine, I'll be happy to testify."

"You don't understand," Diaz continued taking his glasses off and cleaning them with a glasses-wipe from his pocket. "In addition, the evidence box at the police department vanished. Probably misfiled somewhere but gone. There is nothing to back up your testimony."

"You've got to be kidding?"

Diaz carefully put his glasses on and pocketed the wipe. "Chief Inspector, there is nothing we can do."

"Great." Daan slumped further into his pillows.

"It's a hard blow, I know."

Daan focused on the clock on the opposite wall.

"Is there anything I can do for you?"

Daan shook his head.

"I suppose you'll be returning home to Europe soon."

Daan said nothing.

"Here's my card," Diaz said, dropping a business card on the side table. "Call me if I can help you in any way." Diaz picked up his briefcase and walked out, not looking back.

Daan had listened to the district attorney in bewilderment. Ziebach's case would be dismissed, and the man would be walking the streets of the world again causing havoc. Men like Ziebach had the means to run criminal organizations from inside prison. Within days, though, Ziebach would be free to continue his diabolical doings just like before.

The hands of the clock across from him ticked the minutes by.

He had no proof against Ziebach, but Daan knew the gangster had been responsible for the deaths of his wife and children. Daan vowed he would find a way to get Ziebach. It would take time, but, somehow, he would do it.

Daan's only question was why Ziebach let him live. Roy was dead. Francine and his girls were dead. Why had he been left alive? He would rather have been in that fiery car.

The doctor advised Daan to stay at least two more days in the hospital, but Daan refused. Francine's parents had convinced him to let them bury his family in Francine's hometown in Napa Valley so they could visit their only child's grave.

Daan endured the funeral in his stoic manner and shed not a tear as he stayed glued in his place beside the joint grave, which held only fragments of his family. He didn't respond to the attendees who filed past him and Francine's parents and slowly left. He was still in shock, his feelings numb, his heart empty. Declining his in-laws' invitation to stay with them for a few days, he requested a ride to the airport after the funeral.

Daan couldn't tolerate another moment in California. However, he promised himself that he would return to lay a wreath on his family's grave in remembrance on the anniversary of their deaths and in their memory attend any performance of *The Ring Cycle* whenever it was in Amsterdam.

Chapter 10

Nick stood next to a large, branched tree across the lane between the gravestones, separating himself from the funeral attendees. He blended into the tree beside which he was standing in his brown trench coat as he watched Daan de Sylva slowly get into his father-in-law's sedan, nursing his broken arm in a sling. The next plane to Amsterdam was due to leave in four hours, Nick surmised that the chief inspector was on his way home.

As Nick watched the car head toward San Francisco, rain began to fall, and he drew his belt tight about his waist and pulled his Fedora lower down on his face.

Nick's employer had been especially specific about making sure not to hurt the chief inspector. The contract only stated the San Francisco police officer and the family be killed. Nick knew his employer was a cold-hearted bastard. Killing the chief inspector's family, but not the chief inspector, was just plain mean. Nick never left witnesses. He was uncomfortable with this strange request.

But the man paid well, and Nick never asked questions. Completing assassinations for him had become routine. Phone call. Do the job. Money transferred to his Swiss bank account. Move on until he was called for another contract.

Nick walked towards his rental car. He was booked on the night flight to Hong Kong. Confirming the burial of de Sylva's wife and children was the only reason he was here. As Nick got into the car and started the engine, he felt slightly sorry for the chief inspector.

There was a reason why Nick no longer had a wife or children. And now, neither did Daan de Sylva. Oh well, life sucks and then you die.

Chapter 11

Years later, Phoebe Silva and her two daughters, Charlotte and Lucy, boarded the shuttle from St. George in front of the University of Zion at 10:00 A.M. heading for the Salt Lake City International Airport. Their eleven-hour flight to Amsterdam was scheduled to leave at 9:00 P.M.

The journey from their home to Salt Lake would only take five hours, but Phoebe wanted to check in and then take the girls on the train into Salt Lake City for a leisurely late lunch and then meander around the downtown malls before returning to the airport for their flight.

Timewise, her plans were scrapped when the shuttle broke down on Interstate 15 more than ten miles south of the city of Beaver. There was nothing to do but sit inside the van on the side of the road with all the windows and doors open in the 100-degree temperature waiting for the relief shuttle. Everyone was relieved when it finally showed up forty minutes later. Their journey continued only to be caught in traffic near Springville due to a seven-vehicle pileup when a pickup truck crossed traffic, causing a tractor-trailer to jackknife, blocking the highway.

The shuttle finally arrived at the airport at 6:30 P.M. and there was not enough time to go into Salt Lake. Phoebe shook her head as they unloaded their suitcases from the shuttle on the airport departure level. She wished she had just driven up and paid for a week's worth of parking at the airport instead of taking the shuttle.

Well, hindsight is 20/20. Take a deep breath and move on.

Her girls, fourteen and eleven, were cranky, tired, and angry about the trip to the airport. But they seemed more upset at Phoebe because she couldn't take them to the malls. Phoebe didn't blame them. She was exhausted herself. But there was nothing she could do except wonder if this vacation was doomed to be racked with problems.

They checked in and made their way to their gate, stopping only for a hamburger supper on the way down the concourse. But the girls continued to bicker.

If we can just make it to the plane in one piece, I'll sit between them after we board to help eliminate this unfriendly banter between them. Maybe they'll go right to sleep, and I won't hear a peep for several hours. I should be so lucky.

Phoebe had planned the trip to the Netherlands for them to visit where their ancestors had lived five hundred years before. They were also going to attend Richard Wagner's *The Ring Cycle* at the Amsterdam Opera House, scheduled to be performed over the course of four nights. She was told the opera was sold out but, as a professor, she was able to purchase three student tickets on the last row on the main floor of the auditorium.

Their five-day vacation consisted of the four evening performances of Wagner's opera with their days full of sightseeing. They would arrive in Amsterdam late on Tuesday afternoon. On Wednesday, they would visit the Anne Frank House, Dam Square, the Royal Palace, and Madame Tussauds Wax Museum. Thursday, taking a river cruise around the city and a walking tour of the Jordaan district was on the agenda. Friday, she had planned to visit the homes of their ancestors in Amsterdam and Rotterdam. Saturday, they would tour Keukenhof Gardens, home to Holland's famous tulips. The whirlwind visit would end on Sunday with a leisurely morning walk along the River Amstel before heading for their evening flight for home.

Well, at least that's what Phoebe had planned. She just hoped that their vacation trip would be better than the last few hours.

As she looked over at her girls at the airport, Phoebe was afraid she had lost the ability to inspire Charlotte and Lucy. Though she had encouraged them to read about the Netherlands and Wagner's opera, they seemed lukewarm about everything except the wax museum and the tulips.

She sighed deeply.

If I can't inspire my own daughters, how can I expect to inspire the students in my classes?

She was deep in thought when she heard an announcement made over the loudspeaker at their gate. Their flight to Amsterdam was being delayed for about two hours because of a medical emergency on another flight. The diverted plane was taxiing towards their gate, and the agent asked for everyone to move to the side to make room for the ambulance attendants meeting the plane.

Delayed? Another two hours? It was almost one hundred degrees outside according to the television monitors at the gate and the area was hot and stuffy. Phoebe wasn't sure she could handle another couple of hours intervening between the girls' squabbles.

People were moved back as emergency medical personnel made their way down the concourse corridor towards their gate. Outside a plane docked at the jet bridge. It took about thirty minutes for the medical personnel to go down the jetway and transfer the injured patient from the plane. The medics pushed the gurney with the injured man towards the front of their terminal, followed by a wailing woman, who held the hand of a weeping boy about Lucy's age.

Around her, sounds of people oohing and aahing with a few tsks tsks and shaking heads as they watched the medical entourage pass by were intermixed with indistinguishable conversations that buzzed with speculation. Did the man fall? Did he have an allergic reaction? Was he suffering from a stroke or a heart attack?

Phoebe looked over to check on her girls when someone tapped her shoulder. She hadn't noticed that one of the gate agents was Angelina Ortiz, a former student.

"Hello, Angelina," Phoebe said. "It's good to see you."

"Professor Silva, would you and your daughters come with me, please?"

"Yes, of course, Angelina." Phoebe motioned for Charlotte and Lucy to pick up their things and follow. "Is everything okay?"

When they were at the counter, Angelina said, "Professor, we have a proposition for you. The plane diverted to Salt Lake for the medical emergency was on its way from San Francisco to Amsterdam. We now have three empty seats available, and we would like to put you and your daughters in those seats if that's okay with you."

"Angelina, are you sure?"

"Your flight is overbooked and, since I know you, I thought of you first with these open seats," Angelina said with a smile. "The aircraft will be leaving in a few minutes. Your luggage will be on your original flight to Amsterdam. If you give me your hotel information, the airline will have it delivered to you there."

Phoebe looked at the bored faces of her daughters and made the decision. "That would be great, Angelina."

"Please hand me your boarding passes so we can get you on this plane as quickly as possible."

A few minutes later Angelina walked Phoebe and the girls down the jetway. Angelina proudly said, "Professor, you three have seats in first class. I hope this is okay for you."

First class, what a godsend. Maybe things are changing in my favor and the trip wouldn't be so bad after all.

Phoebe said aloud, "That's wonderful, Angelina. Thank you."

"This is to let you know how much I appreciate everything you did for me in class, especially when my father died."

"Angelina, all I did was give you extra time to turn in your work and take your final. You had an emergency, and it was the least I could do to help you through a trying time."

"Well, this is an emergency, and you are helping us right now."

Phoebe hugged Angelina. "Thank you."

Before taking her leave, Angelina introduced them to the flight attendant who met them at the end of the jetway. "Here are your three new passengers. Dr. Phoebe Silva and her two daughters, Charlotte and Lucy."

To Phoebe, she said, "Have a fun time in Amsterdam, Professor."

Angelina smiled and then turned around, heading up the jetway.

Chapter 12

The flight attendant greeted them with a smile. "Hello, ladies. My name is Sally. If you follow me, I'll take you to your seats."

Sally showed Charlotte and Lucy to the two first class empty seats side-by-side. To Phoebe, she indicated the empty aisle seat behind them next to a man reading a newspaper.

"Hello," she said, but he did not respond.

Sally whispered to her, "He hasn't said anything since we left San Francisco, except to alert me his seat companion was having a heart attack. That is why we had the emergency landing here. He pulled the passenger to the floor and was pumping his chest and giving him mouth-to-mouth. He must be an EMT or something."

"I see," Phoebe said to Sally. "He's a hero. I'll let him be."

"May I get you anything, Doctor Silva?" Sally asked.

"I'm sure my two daughters would love Cokes. I'll take a glass of water." Then, after a second of hesitation, "Please, I think I'll have a vodka on the rocks, instead. Thank you."

Phoebe was not one for drinking, especially during the day. But at this point, Phoebe felt she deserved it as she prepared for the long, overnight trip to Amsterdam.

As they took off and settled in at a cruising altitude,

the guy next to Phoebe slowly closed his paper and began to carefully fold it. He then placed it in the seat pocket in front of him.

"Did I hear the flight attendant say your last name was Silva?" he questioned with a foreign European accent, but she couldn't place the country.

"Dr. Phoebe Silva." She held out her hand to shake his, but her gesture was ignored.

"Hmmm," he pursed his lips. "Medical doctor?"

"Ph.D., in fact."

"Ph.D. of what exactly?"

"American and European History."

"Interesting," he said flatly.

"And you?" she asked. "The flight attendant said it was you who saved that poor man's life. What do you do?"

He ignored her question. "I prefer vodka with a lemon twist myself."

"I save lemons for lemonade."

"I'd be careful. Vodka can be more potent in the air." He mumbled something as he turned towards the window.

Phoebe thought she heard, "You Americans." She couldn't be sure but sensed he was rolling his eyes. *You Europeans,* she whispered under her breath as she looked the other way. She was no stranger to arrogant Europeans. Her university often hosted visiting foreign professors.

Last year Dr. Juan Gonzalez, a history professor from Spain, was insistent on telling her a woman could never be as good a teacher as he. Two years before that, Vladimir Aleksandr, a science professor from St. Petersburg, often mocked her because he obviously knew more about European history than she ever would. Neither seemed to understand why she didn't want to date them, especially when they'd gone out with just about every other single woman on campus yet been so arrogant towards her. American professors were also challenging as well with their conceit, but the egotism and condescension from those two left an impression about obnoxious Europeans.

Who in the hell was this obnoxious European who felt entitled to school her about the potency of vodka in the air? This wasn't the first time she drank vodka. Then, she admitted to herself that it was, in fact, the first time she had taken a drink while flying. With a second sip, Phoebe side-glanced the know-it-all.

Her mind drifted to Wagner's *The Ring Cycle*. Which character would he be? He definitely wasn't an ancient German-looking hunter. No beard and no long scruffy hair. He didn't look like a Wall Street executive type, more casual really. He slumped down in his chair with his legs extended under Lucy's seat in front of him. Maybe six feet, give or take. He had curly dark hair, a classic face with high cheekbones, and a firm chin. Italian? Greek, maybe? He'd obviously taken the lifesaving attempt in stride because he wasn't unnerved by it. In his blue long-sleeved shirt, open at the neck, and nice blue slacks, he was well-groomed, smartly dressed, almost stately, she had to admit. Even in his arrogance.

Her attention was drawn away by Charlotte and Lucy, who were bickering over a book. Phoebe thought about moving one of them to her seat so she could separate them then, almost as quickly, ruled out that option. She was not going to subject her children to the insufferable guy next to her. With a sigh, she undid her seat belt and casually moved forward to her girls, spiriting the book away from them both.

"If I must come up here one more time, as soon as we get to Amsterdam, we will take the next flight home, do you understand?" she half-whispered.

Both seemed more upset by the removal of the book than her chiding.

"Please, Mom, we'll be good," Charlotte promised not too quietly.

Lucy crossed her arms and refused to look at her mother.

"Either find a movie on the monitor there or go to sleep!"

"Yes, ma'am," the girls said in unison.

"At least pretend that you are excited about our trip."

Phoebe really did want this trip to Amsterdam to be an exciting time for her girls. If they could just focus on the trip instead of trying to pick at each other, her life would be better. Phoebe knew it was Lucy who was usually the instigator. She was younger and enjoyed arousing Charlotte's dander.

Give me strength!

Phoebe returned to her seat and tried to get comfortable. She was restless now. She looked out the window over the man next to her, deciding he was more like a devil than a god from Wagner's opera. While sleeping, the Devil wasn't so nasty-looking. In actuality, he was fairly handsome, reminding her of Apollo, the god of love. But she didn't think this Devil played the lute or used a bow and arrow. No. In this day and age, if anything, he was probably better with an AK 47 than a bow and arrow. And hate, not love.

She dragged her bag from under Charlotte's seat in front of her. She dropped in the book the girls were fighting over and pulled out a notebook with an article about *The Ring Cycle*. She knew it all by heart but reread the synopsis of the four opera sections.

Wagner's opera was full of conflict. It was a mythical story about gods and jealousy, a battle of the sexes, and lots of infighting dealing with hate and love, good versus evil, death and survival, and the ring everyone wanted. However, for this saga there was no happily ever after ending.

It was a long opera, but Phoebe was excited to see the presentation of the entire performance in Amsterdam. She'd never seen all four sections, one night after another. This was a treat for her. She enjoyed opera, although this one was not her favorite. She preferred Verde. But comparing Wagner to Verde was a great historical teaching tactic.

Sometimes, Phoebe felt that her life was in turmoil much like *The Ring Cycle*. But her life wasn't total tragedy. She had lost her parents three years ago and her best friend Vanessa had moved to Australia a year later after she met her dream partner who made her happy.

Phoebe took a deep breath and leaned back in her seat.

Losing her parents and Vanessa within a two-year span was really difficult to handle. But her job was good since she made tenure last year. Her salary was decent, but not as high as the male professors and she was working on that.

The fact she hadn't had a date in several years wasn't really a big deal. She was busy with her girls and teaching. However, it was lonely, sometimes, as a single mother and widow. Her major conflict was her girls' lack of restraint and self-discipline. Phoebe just wanted them to master the ability to be kind to each other. Did it make her sound like an ogre to suggest they just relax and enjoy the moment?

Originally, she had saved up to visit Vanessa and her beau in Australia this summer, but they were on safari in Kenya. So, instead she booked this trip to Amsterdam, a trip Vanessa would have loved.

Phoebe knew her daughters were disappointed to not see Aunt Vanessa, but she hoped they would enjoy themselves. She leaned forward and returned the notebook to her bag.

Phoebe listened and, hearing nothing from the girls, decided to leave well enough alone. She pulled out earbuds and reclined her seat, engrossing herself in a movie before falling asleep.

Chapter 13

When the plane came to a stop at the Amsterdam-Schiphol Airport, Phoebe stepped into the aisle and pulled out their carry-on luggage from above Charlotte's and Lucy's heads. Her seatmate pushed past her quickly, reaching into the adjoining overhead for his beige sports jacket, and pulled out his dark blue soft garment bag with the initials, DDS.

"Goodbye," he said tersely as he donned his sunglasses and headed for the exit door.

Neither of them had spoken the entire trip except for his comment about her name and her vodka, and now his farewell. Before he'd slipped on his sunglasses, she'd noticed his eyes were a deep shade of brown, but his gaze was flat and unfeeling. To Phoebe, it was as though he didn't even see her as he spoke. Phoebe assumed the DDS on his bag certainly did not indicate that he was a dentist. Perhaps his first initial was for David or Donald. What about Dennis or Dylan? She shook her head and then laughed to herself. Wasn't it funny that her D for him was Devil?

She pushed him out of her mind and turned her attention to her daughters. After all, she would probably never see him again, and that was for the best. She returned her thoughts to this wonderful vacation which, unexpectedly, had begun with a first-class trip to Europe and now tours of the Netherlands and attending a world-famous opera was on the agenda. She was determined to return home with copious photos and joyful memories.

They waited with others to go through Customs, the girls finally behaving like young adults. Even though the Devil was one of the first ones off the plane, he was inexplicably standing right in front of them in the line to which she and the girls were directed. Wearing his sports jacket, he didn't look like he had just been on an overnight, trans-Atlantic flight. He looked...how had she described him earlier? Stately, that was it.

Conversely, Phoebe decided she did look like she had been traveling for hours, her clothes creased and unkempt. She tugged at her blouse and sweater, attempting to uncrumple them a bit before admitting it was a lost cause. She'd shower and change when they arrived at the hotel.

When it was the Devil's turn at the customs counter, he handed the agent his passport and declaration documents. As they were conversing in Dutch, she watched other booths on either side of them. Passengers passed through with little difficulty and departed through the Customs Hall door to the corridor beyond.

But not the Devil. After a couple of minutes, the agent questioning him motioned another agent to join them. They spoke briefly, examined his passport, and then the Devil was escorted out of line by the second official and down a narrow hall to their right.

Phoebe wasn't surprised. Maybe he was the Devil she thought him to be. But his manner was dignified as he followed the official. Regal, without a care in the world. She glanced down at herself and shook her head. *Not like me*.

Her family was next.

"You speak English?" the agent asked.

She nodded.

"Passports, please."

He examined their documents thoroughly.

"You have come from America?"

"Yes."

He reviewed another paper on his desk.

"You did not board the flight in San Francisco?"

"No. Salt Lake City."

"Hmmm."

As he had done with the Devil, he turned around and motioned to a uniformed agent, this time a woman.

He handed the new official their passports and documents. "Please follow this young lady." His expression was firm.

"But sir…" Phoebe began.

"Please, miss." He dismissed them as he called for the next passenger.

Though concerned, Phoebe motioned her girls forward to follow the lady agent out of the large hall. Phoebe couldn't imagine why they were prevented from passing out to the freedom of the corridor with others. No other passenger was asked to go the way she and her daughters were going, the same way the Devil had gone.

Why? They were carrying no drugs or contraband of any sort. They weren't on any watch list, God forbid. It must just be a random check, she decided. Unless this was all because they had been transferred onto that rerouted flight from San Francisco.

The woman led them down a long institution-type hallway, opened a plain plywood door on the right and pointed to a table that stretched along the far wall.

"Place your bags over there and open them up for

inspection," she demanded with a heavy accent.

Phoebe recognized the dark blue garment bag with the DDS initials already open on the table. Everything had been taken out, and all its contents were lined up neatly next to his bag. The Devil obviously knew the drill. Since she had never had to do this before, she would take her cue from him.

"Girls, place everything from your bag out on the table just like that." She pointed to the Devil's neatly arranged articles.

"But, why, Mom?" Lucy was confused.

"This is just a random check, little loves. Let me help you, Lucy."

It only took a few minutes to open their three carry-ons and organize their articles like the Devil's.

"This way, please." The woman officer led them back into the dreary hall opposite from Customs. A few feet further, she showed them into a small, dimly lit room. Four metal folding chairs were lined up against the wall to their right and four opposite them as they entered the room. A large mirror adorned the left wall.

"Sit here," the customs officer directed before closing the door.

The only person in the room was the Devil himself.

Chapter 14

The Devil was seated in a chair at the end of the room. He seemed relaxed and unconcerned as he leaned his head against the wall with his arms criss crossed over his chest and his legs stretched out, crossed at the ankles. His beige jacket was nicely folded on the chair beside him.

When the door closed, the man at the end of the room lifted his head up briefly, his reflective glasses hiding his eyes so Phoebe couldn't tell if he was staring at her. Who wore sunglasses in a dimly lit room? But there he was, all suave and sophisticated like he had nowhere else to go and could care less.

"Girls, have a seat and please behave," Phoebe warned. "I'm sure this is just a routine check. As soon as Customs sees everything's okay, we'll be allowed to go on to the hotel."

"Fine," Lucy snapped and plopped herself onto a chair.

Charlotte sat next to her in a huff and growled, "What are we supposed to do in the meantime, Mom?"

"Figure out a way to entertain yourselves with your phones."

Without moving his head, the Devil said, "This is Security not Customs."

"Security?" Phoebe asked exasperated, looking directly at him and sitting next to Charlotte. "Why are we being held by Security?"

"Only you can answer that."

"Well, we've done nothing to warrant being held by Security."

He remained in his original position as though nothing phased him. Her chair definitely wasn't comfortable, but he sat in his with no hint of discomfort. His serenity annoyed Phoebe, who glared at him with contempt. Maybe he was used to such treatment, but they weren't.

She casually stood up and studied herself in the mirror that ran the length of the far wall. She looked frazzled and ran her fingers through her auburn hair, trying to look more presentable. Her curls looked chaotic but that wasn't unusual, considering the humidity. Neither comb nor brush could tame her ringlets. She took lipstick from her purse. Puckering her lips, she applied some color then decided it didn't matter and tossed the lipstick back.

She remembered in the movies that security rooms always featured a two-way mirror. So, in her imagination, she decided there was probably a security guard watching them from the room next door, studying them to see how they were reacting to their captivity.

She waved and smiled. *Take that, guys!* Then she tried to be calm as she returned to her chair and pretended to appear composed.

How could the insufferable man at the end of the room be so tranquil? She decided to take a page out of his playbook, leaning her head against the wall and closing her eyes. She listened as the girls laughed and talked together, playing games on their phones.

Thank goodness I added more games when I

upgraded our phone plan to the international mode for this trip.

The door opened. Phoebe was startled and jerked open her eyes, sitting up straight in her chair. She looked at the Devil, but he did not react. He maintained his position without moving a muscle. At least, she did not detect any movement. A uniformed male officer entered the room. She assumed he was a security guard rather than a Customs agent because of what the Devil had said.

"Chief Inspector de Sylva?"

She watched him curiously as he slowly and patiently stood up, picking up his jacket. He walked fearlessly across the room with what she decided was a military bearing. Maybe that's because he was with the police.

"It's Mr. de Sylva," the Devil remarked as he casually put on his sports jacket. "I'm no longer with the police, and you know that."

As he passed by Phoebe, he looked directly at her and bid them farewell with a nod. "Ladies."

The guard allowed the Devil to leave the room and then closed the door, leaving Phoebe and her daughters alone.

The minutes ticked by slowly after the Devil left. Phoebe feigned a sense of calm for the girls' benefit, but when the agent didn't reappear after a while, she became concerned. She looked at her watch and saw they'd been in the room for over an hour. Finally, the door opened, and the same male security guard appeared.

"Mrs. de Sylva," he said, "please, follow me."

"It's Doctor Silva," she corrected, a bit agitated. "My name is Dr. Phoebe Silva."

As the Devil admonished earlier, Security should

know my identity, so why add the 'de' before my last name?

They were led back down the hall to the room where they had left their bags. The Devil's bag was gone, and so was he. Good, maybe their release would be soon. The guard told them to pack up everything.

Phoebe quickly examined their things. Nothing seemed to be as they left them.

Would I even notice if something were out of place? And, what on earth would they be looking for in our luggage?

She hurried the girls up and closed their bags quickly.

The guard had them follow him towards the Customs area with their bags in tow. Phoebe saw the doors of the large Customs Hall just beyond them. A few more feet and they would be outside. She took a deep breath of relief as she focused on those doors.

To her dismay, the guard stopped.

In her head, Phoebe could hear the Devil's voice echoing, "This is Security not Customs." That was when she realized they weren't going anywhere.

Chapter 15

The guard opened the door to a furnished office with glass windows which they had passed earlier. They were told to leave their carry-ons outside the closed door and wait.

An older uniformed officer was on the phone, hanging it up when they walked in. As he walked around his desk to open the door, she noticed he was taller than she, graying hair and a mustache, chipmunk cheeks, and a paunch belly over which his uniform jacket pulled tightly. Smiling at Phoebe, he took her elbow and guided her and the girls to chairs in front of his desk.

"Mrs. de Sylva," the officer began as Phoebe sat down and reflected that this chair was only a little bit more comfortable than the other one. His accent was so heavy she could hardly understand him, and she had to listen carefully.

"My name is Dr. Phoebe Silva." Phoebe was slow and specific as she corrected him. "There is no 'd e' in front of my last name."

"Really?" the man sounded confused. "Ah, then it's Mrs. Silva, no?"

"No — Yes." Phoebe was flustered. "It's just Dr. Phoebe Silva."

"Ah. So, you are not Mrs. de Sylva," he said, emphasizing the 'de.'

"Yes."

He raised his left eyebrow now. "Mmmm—"

Phoebe was unsure how to respond to this. The man was obviously a high-ranking officer. She didn't know much about military attire and such things, but he had bars and ribbons on his uniform and his own office, which probably meant he was the officer in charge of the security section here at the airport. Wouldn't you think he would know her correct name? After all, he had their passports right there on his desk.

"My name is Captain Hans Vanderburg," the officer said. He waited for her to respond.

She nodded her head. "Captain."

He moved around his desk and dropped down in his plush chair, which creaked under his weight. He settled himself and picked up a paper from his desk.

"There seemed to be a problem when your names did not appear on the airline's original passenger manifest."

Phoebe said nothing. She had read books and seen the movies where the victim says something innocent, which was construed to be something different.

"So, the airline just confirmed that you joined this plane as passengers in Salt Lake City, Utah."

Phoebe smiled at the captain's pronunciation of Utah which came out as 'ŏŏh tah.' She thought about correcting him, but decided it wasn't worth it.

The captain took their passports from his desk, shuffled them in his hands, then looked up at her. "Very pretty names for your daughters, Charlotte and Lucy." He pronounced Charlotte's name with a hard "CH" like Charles.

"Thank you." She figured that was safe enough.

"Mrs. de Sylva," he began, then stopped and tapped

67

the passports. "Oh, well. Mrs. Silva, if you insist."

"I do."

Then, he put the passports down and picked up another paper. Without looking up, he said to Phoebe, "Please forgive our intrusion on your privacy, but in this day and age with rampant terrorism, we had to check out everything."

She wasn't happy he was insinuating she might be a terrorist, but what could she do?

He showed a plastic smile.

Phoebe was concerned for their well-being as minutes ticked by. She looked out the glass window to the doors beyond that would take them out of this area. She gathered her wits about her to confront this Dutch official and tried to sound calm by using her firm teacher voice.

"Well, Captain, I hope you found everything satisfactory with my daughters and me. Are we free to go now?"

"A few more minutes, please."

"But, sir, we've taken so much of your time." Phoebe was trying not to sound confrontational. "We should have boarded the hotel shuttle over an hour ago and—"

"Oh no, Mrs. de Silva," Captain Vanderburg interrupted. "Please do not be concerned about your shuttle." He looked up from the paper in his hand. "We understand you have reservations at the Inn on Amstel near the Opera House?"

"Yes," Phoebe remarked, annoyed he had returned to calling her Mrs. de Sylva.

Captain Vanderburg picked up another paper and then compared the two with interest. Phoebe's apprehension heightened. If this were not a civilized country, she supposed that in a minute or so they would be on their way to some dark and distant cell. She had no idea what they had done for this captain of security to hold them. She decided she would treat him like he was a troublesome student questioning her authority. She sat straight in her chair and squared her shoulders, waiting for him to speak.

The captain placed the two papers on his desk. He looked intently at Phoebe and then shifted his eyes to her daughters.

No, you don't. Not my daughters.

Phoebe stood, standing in front of Charlotte and Lucy. "May I answer any other questions for you? We really do need to get to our hotel."

"Hmmm." His focus returned to her for a moment. "Please sit."

Irritated, she sat back in her chair, and he looked at her again. Now, he lifted another paper from his desk that looked like a form. Then, from his right desk drawer, he took out what appeared to be a stamp of some sort. He took his time examining the form, signed the bottom of the sheet, and slammed the stamp on the paper, causing her and the girls to jump. He observed the paper again and then dropped the stamp back, closing the drawer.

"Do not think we are barbarians here in Amsterdam, Mrs. de Sylva."

She decided it would not be good for her to correct his pronunciation of her name and felt his smile was more forced than sincere. He stood up and clapped his hands. A lesser officer appeared at the door. Captain Vanderburg handed Phoebe their passports which she promptly placed securely in her purse.

"To let you know how sorry we are for the delay, please allow Lieutenant Voss here to take you directly to your hotel, courtesy of my department."

Phoebe immediately stood and tried to exhibit an aura of confidence. "That's okay, Captain Vanderburg. We can find our own transportation to the hotel. We wouldn't want your government to be put out with such a trivial thing."

"But I insist." The captain moved around his desk to stand next to Phoebe. "And, to show how saddened we are to have inconvenienced you so much, we have upgraded your suite at the hotel."

Phoebe smiled sweetly. "Again, Captain Vanderburg, that really won't be necessary."

Captain Vanderburg said, "You are here to see Wagner's operas, ja?" He was leaning quite close to her, and she could smell the onions and garlic he had for lunch.

Phoebe nodded then placed her purse strap on her shoulder and stepped back a bit.

"I understand you are a teacher and you have arranged to have student seats in the back of the auditorium, true?"

"Why, yes." She motioned for her girls to stand.

Captain Vanderburg extended his hand towards his office door like he was ready to let them leave. But he stopped between them and the door. Phoebe was a little worried that he would not let them go.

The captain reached for her hand with his rather fat fingers, raised it to his lips and kissed it.

"We cannot have such special guests in the back of the Opera House auditorium, can we, Mrs. de Sylva?"

"Please, Captain Vanderburg, I'm Phoebe Silva."

"Well, then, Mrs. Silva," Captain Vanderburg said as he held her hand in both of his and cleared his throat. "We have upgraded your seats to show our appreciation for your understanding of our mistake in keeping you in custody."

Phoebe looked at him in disbelief, wondering why he would change their seats without her permission. When did he have time to do this? Why? But she just wanted to leave and decided not to ask questions.

"Thank you, Captain Vanderburg," Phoebe managed to say and gently pulled her hand back from the captain. It was all she could do to not wipe the moisture off her hand on the back of her slacks.

"Good, then it is settled." He seemed pleased with himself. "Your special opera tickets will be waiting at the theater tomorrow evening." He stepped back and held the door open for her and her girls. "Please enjoy your stay in my country and have a nice trip home on Sunday evening."

Phoebe did not turn around as she and the girls left Captain Vanderburg's office and followed the lieutenant through the Customs Hall doors into the corridor beyond.

Chapter 16

As he shut the door behind his guests, Hans Vanderburg watched them follow Lieutenant Voss across the Customs Hall and out the doors to the large corridor beyond, dragging their luggage behind them. They soon disappeared into the throng of people making their way through the maze of hallways in the airport to their destinations.

As they were swallowed up by the crowd and out of sight, he walked around his desk and dropped back in his chair, grabbing his phone. He dialed a number he knew by heart.

When a familiar voice answered, he said, "Sir, they just left."

He listened to the person on the other end of the receiver.

"No, sir, she insisted that her name was…"

He was interrupted by the voice and the captain remained silent, listening to his instructions.

A few minutes later, Vanderburg replaced the phone receiver in its cradle. He collected the papers before him, enclosing them neatly in the file on his desk. He unlocked the credenza behind him and placed the file in its place, closed the drawer, and relocked the credenza. He dropped the key in his pocket.

The name on the file label: *de Sylva, Daan.*

Chapter 17

After his visit with Captain Vanderburg at the airport, Daan de Sylva made his way quickly through the throng of people in the corridor and then downstairs to the train for the Amsterdam Centraal Station. Daan always enjoyed this way into the city. He didn't have to drive and worry about traffic. A bus just wasn't efficient enough for him and a shuttle meant he had to speak to other passengers. Although the train was the fastest way to the city, it allowed him to view the countryside as it faded into the city. As a teenager, Daan thought he would like to live in the country, but he had chosen a different path. He smiled.

Oh, well. a slower way of life isn't going to happen for me at this stage of the game.

In a little over fifteen minutes, Daan stepped out of the train car at the Amsterdam Centraal Station. If he were going home, he would have boarded the train for Rotterdam at the airport. However, he was in Amsterdam because he had tickets to Wagner's opera, *The Ring Cycle.* He was attending the next four nights in honor of his beloved Francine and his children. It had been eight years since their deaths. This year, Francine's favorite opera was being performed over four nights, one right after the other.

For you, I'm doing this for you, Francine.

It was drizzling as he left the station. It was only a

ten-minute walk to the hotel where Daan was staying. Where he always stayed when he was in Amsterdam. His family's hotel, or at least the family corporation's hotel. Every time he and Francine visited the city, they stayed in the two-bedroom suite on the top floor. It was just a couple of blocks from the Opera House. And now it worked for him as well, even though he was alone.

He hurried along the streets he knew so well. As he made his way through Dam Square, his mind drifted back to when he first met Francine. She and two friends were visiting the city for the first time. They asked him for directions, and he was infatuated with her dancing blue eyes, long blonde hair, beautiful full mouth, and the fact she was almost as tall as he. Daan was in Amsterdam for a security class and was only on his lunch break, but he quickly walked them to their hostel and promised to meet them for dinner after he was free. As they ate together, Daan knew he was in love and that was the beginning of their romance.

They were married a year later at Francine's home in Napa Valley. She had been an art major and easily found a job at the Kunsthal Rotterdam. Their love for the opera was one of the things that drew them together. So, they were in Amsterdam at least twice a year to see an opera dear to Francine. He enjoyed opera, always had. And he preferred her opera choices to his.

After their twin girls were born, it was difficult to get to the opera until they were older. Daan smiled as he remembered the hours he spent listening to Francine explain the opera stories to Anya and Ilsa. It was their love of opera that had taken them to San Francisco so many years ago. It was their love of opera that caused him to lose his family. On that note, he quickened his pace and was soon at the hotel.

Daan walked in and addressed the desk clerk in Dutch, "You must be new." Daan decided the boy was maybe eighteen or nineteen.

"My name is Ty, sir," the boy responded. "I only started a few days ago."

"Well, I need to check-in, Ty."

"Your name, sir?"

"Ah, Mr. de Sylva," came a deep voice behind Ty.

"Lars," Daan stretched his hand across the counter to a tall, fair gentleman with graying hair.

"Ty, Mr. de Sylva is a long-time guest of our hotel. Only the best for Mr. de Sylva."

Lars Van Dyk had known Daan since he was a kid, running around in the lobby and playing soccer with him in the halls of the hotel. There was no longer anyone on staff who remembered this, so now Lars kept his link to Daan and his family confidential.

"Yes, sir, Mr. de Sylva," Ty said and stepped to the side, allowing Lars to help Daan.

Lars smiled broadly and nodded his head to Daan. "Your regular suite is ready and waiting for you, Mr. de Sylva." Lars handed over the registration card for signature and gave Daan a room key card.

"You have my box in the safe?" Daan addressed Lars.

"One moment." Lars left the reception area through the door behind them and returned in a couple of minutes. "Here it is, sir." Lars handed Daan a plain black metal box with a lock.

"Thank you, Lars," Daan smiled as he took the box from the man and tucked it under his arm.

Lars nodded and walked around the registration

75

desk. "Do you need help with your bag, sir?"

"No, I've got this." He smiled at Lars, ignoring the kid.

Lars fell into step with Daan as he left the registration desk.

"Just to let you know, Lars, I have an appointment this evening, so I won't be back until late."

"Very good, sir," Lars responded as they crossed the lobby. "I understand congratulations are in order."

"Congratulations?" Daan stopped.

Lars nodded at Daan. "It's about time, you know."

"For what?"

"I'm sorry. I guess I wasn't supposed to say anything."

"I don't know what you're talking about."

"No problem, sir. I understand." Lars winked and started back to the reception desk.

Daan was confused as he watched Lars walk away. Perhaps it was the jet lag.

On the top floor, the elevator opened to a short hall. This had been the penthouse suite where he'd grown up. He smiled as he felt the ghosts of his great-grandmother, his grandparents, and his parents welcoming him home, even though it wasn't his home any longer. After his parents died, the hotel had been sold, and Daan moved to Rotterdam with his uncle.

Daan used his key card to open the door and he walked into the dark suite, closing the door behind him. As he stood in the foyer with his eyes closed, he allowed more memories to flood back to him.

And there she was. Francine. Coming towards him from the shadows with her long blonde hair cascading over her shoulders and dressed in her long white silk robe, motioning him forward to join her.

Ah, my love. I miss you so much.

Yet, he couldn't see her face. That's what was bothering him. It was like her face remained in the shadows, her lovely blue eyes and luscious mouth hidden behind a veil. She had become almost ghostlike, He reached out to her.

Suddenly, a clunk sound invaded his thoughts as he dropped his garment bag on the floor. He still held the black box under his arm. Awakened from his reverie, reality set in.

Before him was the sitting area with two bedrooms on either side. The one to his left was set up with two double beds and the one to his right had a king-size bed with a canopy over it. He took a deep breath, switched on the light, and picked up his bag, making his way into the sitting room.

The hotel had renovated the place since last year, but Daan was unprepared for this and didn't like the change. Instead of purples and golds, the suite had been redecorated with a black and white motif. The original colors had provided a softer appeal and seemed more comfortable. The black and white was stark and sterile. The canopy bed in the larger bedroom had been replaced by a more modern, sleek mattress design which was covered by a geometric black and white material that matched the curtains and was adorned with black and white pillows.

Daan moved over to the center of the room and dropped the metal box on the bed. Then, he walked to the closet and hung up his garment bag. He pulled out his tuxedo and allowed it to hang on the rack. He would need that pressed for tomorrow night and made a mental note to tell Lars. Then he added his other clothes to the rack while pulling out an outfit of nice slacks, a golf shirt, and his blue windbreaker. The evening was going to be chilly, especially with the rain. He laid out his clothes on the bed, then slipped into the shower. He only had a few minutes before he had to get out. He was meeting his friend and former partner, Piers Vogel, in thirty minutes, so he had to hurry.

He always prided himself on being punctual, even early when possible. This was one thing he and Francine argued about. He wanted to be on time, and she was always late. Even that night so long ago in San Francisco. She was late coming downstairs with the girls and maybe if they had been on time, maybe—

He let the thought drop.

As he showered, he thought about that Silva woman who had sat next to him on the plane. She worried him. She was a relatively nice-looking woman with luscious deep auburn hair that smelled of lavender, lovely hazel eyes that a man could get lost in, and a delightful set of lips with a provocative smile.

Wow, where did that come from?

Daan cursed as he remembered the woman from the plane. He hated to admit it, but he was a bit drawn to her. For the first time in eight years, he was attracted to a woman. Phoebe Silva was nice looking with a with a petite nose and an intoxicating smile he noted on the plane and in the security room. She seemed intelligent enough and he figured it might be interesting to get to know her better.

Daan paused. This one he should not get involved with because God only knew how deep she was with Ziebach. He knew the Silva woman was involved somehow. She had to be.

Stepping out of the shower a few minutes later, he grabbed a towel from the shelf and quickly dried himself.

As he shaved, he found himself thinking about Francine, the love of his life, who would be here with him now if only he had stopped his family from getting into Roy's car. His razor fell into the sink and his chin dropped to his chest. Why couldn't he have stopped Ziebach or made sure he was arrested for killing his family? But most importantly, why could he not see her face anymore?

Daan slammed his hand on the bathroom counter and was very still for a few minutes trying to remember. But it was no good. He wiped the condensation off the mirror with his open hand and finished shaving.

As he dressed, he found himself comparing Francine and the Silva woman. They were complete opposites. Just two inches shorter than he, Francine was tall, fair, slender, and stunningly beautiful. This woman just didn't compare to his wife. She was darker, shorter, good-looking while not being overly attractive. He smiled. She was nowhere near the beauty his wife had been. So, why was he so interested?

Both wore their hair loose but, while Francine had long straight hair, this woman's hair was curly and shoulder length. A bit unruly, he remembered from the security room. His twins were blonde and looked like their mother, but they had his eyes. The Silva daughters were not twins. The younger one looked about eleven or twelve probably; the older one was fourteen, maybe? They, too, looked like their mother with her auburn hair and hazel eyes. She didn't wear a wedding ring, but not all married women these days wore them.

What am I doing? There's no comparison between Francine and this woman.

No one had ever made him feel like his wife did. And when she died, he had shut down his heart, surrounded it with a high wall to protect himself from further hurt.

As he washed his face and brushed his teeth, he wondered where Ziebach had found this woman and her daughters. How could Ziebach have that man feign a heart attack on the plane so that the Silva trio could board and be seated with him? He didn't believe in coincidences, so the 'chance' meeting had to be something more.

Another thing, what about the sharing of the interrogation room at the airport? Ha! On the surface, it looked so innocent. But did she not think he saw her waving to Ziebach's guy on the other side of the mirror. He was not an idiot!

And a third thing, what was it with the similar names? Had Ziebach purposely arranged that just to irritate him? Daan felt he had to always be on his toes with Ziebach. Since he left the police department to become an attorney with the Public Prosecution Service (Staande Magistatuur), he was watching Ziebach, just waiting for him to make a mistake. At the same time, he knew Ziebach was watching him for the same reason.

What was that American baseball term? Three strikes and you're out? Well, Ziebach had his three strikes. Daan had to be more careful this time. He had to admit he was certainly frustrated by today's chain of events.

Daan knew Vanderburg was in Ziebach's pocket. That was why Daan was detained every time he came back into the country when Vanderburg was on duty. They pulled him into that same room and watched him for fifteen to twenty minutes on each arrival. Then he was escorted to Vanderburg's office where the plump captain reminded Daan of Dutch regulations and the importance of detaining possible terrorists. The captain would apologize for the inconvenience and Daan would smile without saying a word. Then, he was allowed to go. He was always alone in the security room when detained. Only, this time he shared the room with the Silva woman and her children.

Why?

Daan walked back into the bathroom and pulled a small key from the lining of his travel kit, dropping it in his pocket. He hung his wet towel on the rack on the back of the bathroom door. Then, he packed his things in his travel kit which he hung up next to his clothes in the closet. Daan knew Ziebach was watching him and this way he would know if something was touched.

Walking over to the bed, he unlocked the black box. He removed the white linen cloth around his small Beretta, then inspected the gun and magazine. Everything seemed to be fine, nothing to indicate someone had handled his gun. Giving it a quick wipe down, he popped the magazine in place. Daan never questioned Lars' integrity when he left his gun in the safe. In fact, since the car bombing that killed his family, Daan trusted only two people. Lars, who he'd known all his life, and his best friend and former partner, Piers.

Daan carefully placed the gun in its holster on his belt in his back, placing the cloth back in the box and locking it. He dropped the key in his pocket again and dialed the front desk. After Daan asked Lars for his tuxedo and shirt to be pressed for the next evening, he hung up the phone and placed the box on the shelf over his garment bag in the closet.

Returning to the bathroom, Daan put his watch on his wrist, noting the time. Grabbing his jacket from the bed, he hurried out the door. In the elevator on the way down, he thought about Phoebe Silva.

What is your connection with Ziebach, woman? Was it just a coincidence you and your daughters boarded the plane in Salt Lake City? Just a fluke? He shook his head. *Nah, I don't believe in coincidences.*

But what bothered him the most was how Ziebach staged that heart attack. It was enough to make anyone frustrated.

When the elevator doors opened on the main floor, he crossed the lobby with ease. Another might think he wasn't paying attention to those in the lobby, but out of the corner of his eye, Daan had noticed two things. Two men were still in the lobby from when he went upstairs. Both were dark with jeans, t-shirts, and leather jackets. He also noticed that the new kid, Ty, was watching him as well.

As he walked out of the hotel, Daan laughed out loud. So, he was being watched.

Ziebach, Daan decided. *Why, this time?*

Night was setting in as Daan made his way through the crowd of people on the street.

Chapter 18

As the phone call immediately went to voicemail, the caller hung up. He released several obscenities and paced up and down in his office. This was the sixth time he had called the assassin in the last few hours, and it was the sixth time the call had been sent directly to voicemail.

Where is that son of a bitch? Why is he not answering?

The assassin had been paid handsomely for a specific job eight years ago. Facts had now come to light that the assassin had not done his job as reported. And now, he wasn't answering his phone. Was the assassin hiding from the caller?

A seventh call was made but the caller slammed down the phone almost immediately.

"No one betrays me!" the caller screamed.

Chapter 19

After the eleven-hour plane trip from Utah and their long sojourn in security, not to mention the interrogation by Captain Vanderburg (whom she didn't like at all), Phoebe felt she didn't have the energy to fight for a place on the train or a bus or a shuttle to get them where they needed to go. Her daughters were tired and hungry, and so was she.

Phoebe was glad Lieutenant Voss drove them to the hotel, and she found his English easy to understand as they exchanged pleasantries in the car. The sun was going down as they pulled up in front of the *Inn on Amsel*, and he helped them take their carry-ons inside. A young boy about nineteen greeted them at the reception desk.

The boy asked in English with a heavy accent, "How may I help?" Then, he glanced behind Phoebe to smile at Charlotte and Lucy.

Before Phoebe could say anything, Lieutenant Voss began speaking to the kid in Dutch. The kid nodded and handed the Lieutenant a check-in card.

"Please sign here, Mrs. de Silva," the Lieutenant told her. "This is Ty who will take you to your suite."

"Lieutenant, we just really want our original room. Can you make arrangements for that, please?"

"I anticipated your question and, I'm sorry to say, your original room has been rented already." He smiled at her. "However, even if it had been available, Captain Vanderburg would have been pretty upset had his orders been disobeyed."

"Then, could you please ask Ty if our luggage has arrived from our original flight?"

The Lieutenant turned and spoke Dutch to the boy, who shook his head no.

"Thank you, Lieutenant, for checking. I assume they will take our luggage to our room when it arrives?"

"Yes," he said.

"Mom, I'm hungry," Lucy whined.

"Lieutenant Voss, can you tell us of a nice place where we can eat?"

"The small hotel restaurant closed about ten minutes ago. I suggest you take a walk along the Amstel — that's the river there." He pointed out the front of the hotel. "Several nice restaurants are down to the right."

"Thank you, Lieutenant, we just may do that."

The kid, Ty, came out from behind the desk. He smiled at both girls and loaded their carry-ons onto the luggage trolley he brought with him.

"Enjoy your stay in Amsterdam, Mrs. de Silva." The Lieutenant tipped his hat as he headed for the front door.

Phoebe was annoyed with the name confusion but followed Ty and her girls to the elevator. They were jabbering with Ty all the way up to the top floor. He opened their suite door with the key card, which he promptly gave to Phoebe. Then, he wheeled the luggage trolley through the entryway.

"You are here," Ty told the girls and directed them to their bedroom. He took the girls' two bags and had them follow him.

Phoebe looked around the space. It was rather

modern with a black and white scheme, firm lines, and very little other color. Even the curtains had a geometric black and white pattern.

Not that there was anything wrong with their suite. It was too bleak for Phoebe's taste, and she would have added a bit of color. A couple of bright yellow throw pillows, maybe, or a hint of lavender would have added something to the starkness. The Inn wasn't even a five-star hotel, yet it did look expensive. Phoebe dreaded how much the suite would cost them when they checked out on Sunday.

Lucy came running out to Phoebe. "Wow, Mom, our room is gorgeous!"

"Are you sure we can afford this?" Charlotte exclaimed.

Ty then picked up Phoebe's bag. "This way, Mrs. de Silva."

"Doctor Silva, actually," she corrected him.

He directed her to the other bedroom with a king-size bed. He placed her carry-on bag on the suitcase holder and looked at her.

"Will there be anything else, Mrs. de Sylva?" he asked.

"Doctor Silva," she corrected him again, but he wasn't listening. He was watching the girls—well, really Charlotte—as he edged his way through the sitting room.

"No, I think that will be all." She opened her purse and pulled out her wallet, looking for a tip.

"Oh, no, Mrs. de Sylva," he told her. "Please call downstairs if you need us."

Both girls waved at Ty as he pulled the luggage trolley out to the hallway and closed the door firmly behind him.

"Mom, are all the guys in Amsterdam that cute?" Charlotte asked dreamily.

Phoebe looked at both girls and laughed, "Can you not think of anything but boys right now, Char?"

Phoebe walked across the sitting room over to the large window. Amsterdam's lights were twinkling below them. "Come look at the city, girls. This is a gorgeous place at night, isn't it?"

Charlotte stood next to Phoebe and said, "Mom, you're right. It is beautiful."

"Let's go eat, Mom." Lucy was always the one who was hungry.

"Mother, you didn't answer my question," Charlotte said with concern. "How can we afford this wonderful suite? It must be costing a fortune!"

It was as though Charlotte was beginning to pay attention to things, Phoebe thought as she continued to stare out the window to the city that lay before them.

"Char, you heard the captain at the airport. His department wants to make sure we are compensated for the detention we endured this afternoon. And, I might add, for no reason!"

Phoebe turned around and headed towards her bedroom. "I'm going to take a quick shower. Why don't the two of you do the same? Then we can go to supper fresh and clean. Hurry now."

"Let's do it," Charlotte said.

About thirty minutes later, the Silva women walked arm-in-arm out of the hotel's front door, made a right, and walked down the sidewalk along the Amstel looking for a nice place for supper.

Chapter 20

Daan met Piers at the door of the bar.

"How was your trip, Daan?" Piers asked his friend as he put out his cigarette in the ashtray inside.

"It was hard, but I handled it. Like usual."

"You look good, Daan."

They followed the waiter to a table in the back corner.

"How do you do it, though?" Piers slapped Daan on his shoulder.

"Do what?"

"You've been on an overnight flight across another continent and the Atlantic. And you come back still all suave and sophisticated looking while I stand here in worn-out jeans, t-shirt, and denim jacket."

"I am neither suave nor sophisticated, Piers."

"Look again, my friend," Piers told him as he slid in the booth with high back seats. "Even outside of a courtroom, you have an air of elegance about you from the top of your head down to the tip of your toes. Always dressed impeccably in your picture-perfect outfit with every hair in place."

"It's amazing what a quick shower and a comb will do." Daan laughed as he sat across from Piers.

"No, I mean it," Piers said, lighting up a cigarette. "You and I are about the same height but with that dark wavy hair of yours and those—how to they say it in the movies—bedroom eyes, I think they call it. Every female we ever questioned as cops only responded to you. Next to you, no one even notices I exist."

"Ah, come on, stop teasing about how I look, Piers. I'm just a plain man dressed in simple clothes." He let his windbreaker rest on the seat beside him.

Piers observed the menu without looking at Daan, "You're dressed in Ralph Lauren, aren't you?"

"Okay. I like this outfit. It makes me look good," Daan said, smiling.

"You always look good, Daan." Piers looked up and laughed. "I'm nowhere in your league and being a Nigerian doesn't help."

"Nigerian, my ass. You're only half-Nigerian, Piers. Your other half is European!"

Piers laughed. "True, but we are pretty much opposites, you know."

"That's why we made such a great team as policemen, my friend." Daan laughed. "I was the good cop, and you were the tough cop."

"Right. You never made it as the tough cop next to me. No one believed it." Piers laughed. "We did have a great record apprehending the bad guys."

They ordered drinks, and Piers teased him about his vodka with a lemon twist, like always, before sharing some laughs and finally ordering sandwiches. Shortly after which, they went back to having more drinks.

Piers looked at his friend after a while and smiled, "So, you were telling me you had more paperwork you wanted to go over on Ziebach."

Daan was pleased that Piers remembered their conversation before he had left for San Francisco. "You know I've been collecting evidence to nail Ziebach on human trafficking."

"We've discussed this before. Many times," Piers said as he extinguished his cigarette butt in the almost full ashtray. "We just never seem to have enough evidence. He's just too slick."

Daan bent forward over the table between them and said quietly, "I stumbled on some more information in another file at the office when I was investigating my latest immigration case. We now have two specific dates when trafficking occurred, and there was a mention of a container from the *Ziebach Berenice*."

"That makes how many possible trafficking testimonials now? Ten? Twelve?" Piers commented and pulled out his pack of cigarettes.

"This is number thirteen, to be exact." Daan slapped the table, took a sip of his drink, and leaned against the high seatback. "Lucky thirteen."

"Daan, you won't find anyone who will corroborate the information. They're too scared." Piers lit up a cigarette and placed the pack back into his pocket. "Remember two years ago? The witnesses just disappeared."

Daan sat forward and kept his voice low. "I did speak to this family the Friday afternoon before I left. They are willing to discuss the information with you and no one else."

"Why?"

"I told them I would trust you with my life, that's why."

"Dammit." Piers chuckled and leaned back against his seat. "You are walking a thin line, my friend, if they believed you."

"No, I lie with conviction when I must." Daan

smiled at him. "However, I am even more convincing when I tell the truth."

"Okay, then," Piers nodded. "You are returning to Rotterdam when?"

"The opera ends Thursday night, so I'll get a good night's sleep and return Friday morning. We can get together maybe Friday noon at my place. We need to get our facts straight before we talk with the family together, and then we can take it to my boss and yours."

"I'll be there," Piers said. "Guess I'll bring the pizza since you will have just returned, and there will be nothing in your fridge except sour milk, I'm sure."

"Ha!" Daan laughed. "Sour milk, hell. I don't think there's anything in my fridge except maybe ice in the freezer trays."

"I don't think there's ever much in your fridge," Piers said.

They laughed and Piers smashed his cigarette in the ashtray.

"Have you noticed there may be a reason why we haven't had much traffic in the Ziebach files lately?" Piers took a sip from his glass. "He might be going legitimate. What do you think?"

"Ziebach? Legitimate? No way!" Daan drank the last of his drink and then slammed the empty glass on the table. "With all the illegal money he's made over the years, there's no reason for him to become legitimate."

"Maybe. Maybe not."

"We can get him on this. I really believe we can."

Piers ordered another round and decided to change the subject. "So, anything fascinating happen in America?"

"As a matter of fact, yes." That was when Daan

began his rendition of what had happened on his trip from San Francisco. The guy with the heart attack. The Silva woman. The security room at the airport. He discussed with Piers how he knew Ziebach was behind it all. Daan had found it interesting that Piers didn't agree with him.

"Daan, this is pure conjecture, old friend." Piers said and chuckled, "Ziebach doesn't have as much power as you think."

"No? There's no way all this could have happened out of the blue," Daan said firmly.

"You are being paranoid, my friend. You are seeing things that aren't there."

Daan shook his head. "I don't think so."

The waiter brought another round of drinks to the table, taking Daan's glass. Piers waved the man away, nursing his old drink while pulling his new drink to the side.

"Come on, Daan, no one can stage a heart attack. Didn't you just say you rendered first aid to the poor guy?"

"True," Daan agreed. "I think I may have saved that man's life." He smiled now and took another mouthful from his new drink. "At least that's what the flight attendant told Phoebe Silva when they thought I wasn't paying attention to them."

Daan felt they were both a bit tipsy by this point. Possibly it was hitting him harder than Piers because of the long trip from the States he had just taken. He had always been able to hold his liquor. He was never drunk. Well, hardly ever.

Daan emptied his glass and laughed. "What do you think about that? I may have saved his life." Piers gave

Daan his full glass, taking the empty one away.

"So, what was she like, this Phoebe Silva?" Piers asked.

Daan smiled. "You know, Piers, she was a rather handsome woman, I'd say. Auburn hair that smelled like lavender. Gorgeous hazel eyes. Small little nose and wonderful-looking lips. She's a doctor, you know. Not a medical one, a Ph.D." Daan took another drink. "She might be someone I could, well maybe would like to get to know better."

"Handsome, you say?" Piers teased as he took another drag from his cigarette. "Not beautiful or lovely?"

Daan pursed his lips together. "Well, okay, she may have been more than handsome."

Piers smiled. "I think maybe you might be onto something, Daan. It has been a very, very long time since I've heard you speak of a woman like that."

"It doesn't matter, anyway, Piers. I'm never going to see her again." Daan took a long drink of his vodka.

"You sound almost sad, my friend."

"Sad? Who me?" Daan laughed and drank some more. "She's got to be a plant of Ziebach's."

"Don't think so. There's no way Ziebach could have figured out a way for the guy to have a heart attack, so your plane landed in Salt Lake City so she could join you." Piers took a sip of the drink he'd been nursing. "And she had two daughters?"

"So, you really think it might be just a coincidence?"

"This was not a plan to reel you into something sinister," Piers said. "Just coincidence."

Daan shook his head. "You know I do not believe in coincidences." He was beginning to visibly slur his words.

Piers motioned for the waiter and paid their bill. Then he crushed out his last cigarette and stood up, reaching for Daan.

"Come on, my friend, let me take you back to the hotel while you can still walk."

Chapter 21

When Phoebe, Charlotte, and Lucy returned to the suite later in the evening, they were happy to find their luggage waiting for them in their bedrooms. The girls promptly began discussing who was taking what bed.

Phoebe started to unpack when she heard the beginnings of an argument between the girls. She casually walked over to the other bedroom and watched the girls bicker.

It was Charlotte who noticed her mother first. She stopped talking immediately. She hesitated and then turned to her sister. "Luce, if you really want the bed next to the window, that's fine."

Lucy exclaimed, running and jumping on the bed she truly wanted. "That's great, thanks!"

Phoebe stood at the door in amazement. She was not even sure if Lucy knew she was there. But Charlotte did. She turned back to her suitcase, happy to avoid a fight.

After getting ready for bed, Phoebe checked on the girls. Both were sound asleep, so she closed their door. She turned out all the lights in the sitting room except for the lamp next to the sofa. She walked to the window and gazed out into the night watching the lights of cars and boats on the water, admiring Amsterdam in all its night glory.

With a deep yawn, Phoebe meandered back into her bedroom. She refused to look at the time, deciding she was too exhausted to even speculate the hour. It had been a long day and the week was going to be longer. She turned off the light and sank in under the covers, falling into a deep sleep almost immediately.

Chapter 22

Daan had allowed Piers to walk him back to his hotel after their evening of eating and drinking. It was midnight when they parted at the front door. Daan assured his friend he was fine but was a bit unsteady as he made his way across the lobby to the elevator. Waving at Piers, he hit the up button and leaned on the wall, realizing he probably had more drinks than usual.

As he stepped into the elevator, Daan realized Piers had him convinced that everything that happened on his return trip was, in fact, coincidence. He was leaning on the elevator wall when it reached the top floor. He fiddled around in his pocket for the key card, and it took a minute for him to open the door.

Thank goodness he had left a lamp on in the sitting room, he told himself as he gently shut the door behind him so the noise wouldn't hurt his head. Now, he made his way to his bedroom.

Chapter 23

Phoebe didn't know how long she had been asleep, although when she heard an unfamiliar noise, she sat straight up in bed. A dark figure, outlined against the sitting room light, was walking quite unsteadily through the open bedroom door and slowly meandering towards the bathroom.

Caught off guard, Phoebe was unsure what to do. Being in a strange hotel in a country not her own with someone in the room that had been assigned to her was unsettling, to say the least. She didn't know this person walking around her bedroom but figured the element of surprise was obviously her best option.

Turning on the bedside lamp, she said loudly, "Excuse me. I think you might have the wrong room."

"What?" A familiar voice responded as the figure turned around and faced her. "Why are you in my bed?"

It was the Devil from the plane and the security room at the airport. She didn't think she would ever see him again. How can he be here?

"Mr. de Sylva, I presume? What are you doing in my room?"

"No, m'lady," he began and gave a deep bow, grabbing the bathroom door frame for support, "it is you who is in my room."

"No, no, no!" Phoebe wanted him to know how agitated she was. "This is our suite!"

What in the hell is the Silva woman doing in my room, my suite?

Even though Daan wasn't thinking very clearly, he knew this was his room. He suddenly realized he was about to fall, so he leaned on the doorframe for support. He looked over at her and decided he now faced an incredibly angry Phoebe Silva. And he was trying to concentrate enough to respond to her question.

So, he decided to answer her question with his own, "And you think this is your suite because…?"

The sound of her voice was so shrill it hurt his ears. "This is my suite because Captain Vanderburg upgraded our room to this suite after he held us in detention at the airport for over an hour! And mind you, we have done nothing wrong!" She emphasized the last five words.

Daan began laughing and slowly slid to the floor. He was no longer capable of standing on his feet.

"Why are you laughing?" Phoebe demanded, getting out of bed. "This is no laughing matter." She stood in front of him with her hands on her hips.

"Vanderburg put you here in my suite to hassle me," he stated aloud and rubbed his forehead. "

"Why?" she sounded confused.

"Ziebach sent you here on a mission for him, right?"

"Who in the hell is that?"

"The man who arranged for you to be here."

She walked back to the bed, sat down, and picked up the phone, dialing the front desk.

"Hello, front desk?"

A woman's voice answered.

"Yes, this is Phoebe Silva," she told the night clerk.

"Mrs. de Sylva, let me be the first to congratulate you and Mr. de Sylva," the voice was soft, and Phoebe could understand her much better than the boy, Ty. "How may I help you tonight?"

Phoebe was confused but she was too tired to ask why congratulations were in order. "There's a man in my room who must be removed."

"The only man who is supposed to be in your room is your husband, Mr. de Sylva."

"Mr. de Sylva is not my husband!" Phoebe accentuated each word.

"Mrs. de Sylva," the girl said, "I understand your frustration since I noticed your husband was intoxicated as he went to the elevator. However, the hotel is full and there is no place else for him to go tonight."

Phoebe could say nothing. She just hung up the phone and looked at the Devil on the floor across from her.

"You don't look happy." His speech was slow, and he slurred his words. "What did they say to you? Did they confirm the suite is mine?"

Phoebe didn't know what to say. She was baffled, angry, distressed, and wondered what exactly had happened since she got to Amsterdam. In front of her on the floor, leaning against the bathroom's doorframe was the man she called the Devil. And she had just been told by the night clerk he was her husband. She didn't have a husband anymore, hadn't had one in quite a long time.

"So, what did the night clerk say?"

"Well, she says you're my husband," she told him. "But since we know that is not true, you must leave!"

"Isn't that something?" he groaned, leaning his head back against the wall with eyes closed. "I wonder who came up with the idea that we're married?"

"I have the same question. Did you set this up?"

The Devil opened his eyes and stared at her. "Are you out of your mind, woman? I had nothing to do with this!"

She was exhausted but tried to work her way through a haze of sleepiness as she reviewed everything that had happened since they boarded that plane in Salt Lake City. Today? Yesterday? No, it was already Wednesday, and they had boarded the flight to Amsterdam Monday evening.

One thing after another had transpired since then, and now she felt she was whirling on a merry-go-round going nowhere. The Devil didn't seem to understand what was going on either because he thought she worked for someone named Zaybach or Zerback or whomever. She didn't know anyone by that name. At this time of night, she wasn't thinking too clearly and wasn't sure what to do.

Didn't he know this was not something she cooked up? But someone did. Perhaps if I go over everything aloud, it will make more sense.

"Okay," she tried to sound reasonable and stood up. "So, your name is...what is your full name, by the way? You know mine." Then, she began to pace, waiting for him to respond.

"Yes, I remember that you are Phoebe Silva from Salt Lake City." His speech was slow and slurred.

She stopped and looked at the inebriated man, crumpled on the floor.

"It's Dr. Phoebe Silva to you. And you're Mr. de Sylva?"

"Daan de Sylva."

"You live here in Amsterdam?"

"Don't be foolish, woman. It would be silly for me

to live in Amsterdam and stay in this hotel." He laughed.

"True. Otherwise, we would not be in this predicament."

He was still laughing.

She stopped in front of him. "That's okay. You can stop laughing, now."

He stopped but smiled.

"You can wipe that evil smile off your face as well," she said and began pacing again. "My name is Phoebe Silva, and your name is Daan de Sylva, right?"

He didn't respond, so she turned around and saw he was shaking his head in agreement.

"Since we landed here, I have been addressed as Mrs. de Sylva and I have been trying to correct everyone to say, Mrs. Silva or Doctor Silva. Even Captain Vanderburg. What is wrong with everybody?"

"So?"

"Don't you find that strange?" she questioned as she continued to pace back and forth. "Even here at the hotel. Ty called me Mrs. de Sylva even after I corrected him. And, just now, the front desk clerk called me Mrs. de Sylva."

"Perhaps, it is because the suite is in my name."

Still pacing, she said, "But why would the captain place my daughters and me in your suite?"

"That is the question of the hour." Daan raised his right hand in the air and pointed his forefinger to the ceiling. Then, dropped his arm to his side.

She stood and faced him. "Mr. de Sylva, you seemed quite comfortable in that detention room at the airport. Is it normal for you to be pulled into that room when you return home from out of the country?" She was curious if her assessment of his calmness this afternoon was because of his frequent visits to that security room.

"Every time Vanderburg is on duty. Every time. I've just learned to accept that it will happen and make the most of it."

"Even though you are a police chief inspector?"

"Was," he said emphatically. He attempted to stand but couldn't.

"Okay, was," she said and began pacing back and forth in front of him. "But you did seem quite comfortable in that room this afternoon."

"Please stop pacing. You're making me dizzy."

He reached out and grabbed her foot, pulling her down on the floor next to him.

"And you're drunk." She sat up carefully.

"Not yet, but a few more drinks will head me that way." He leaned his head back against the doorframe.

"You know, that hurt," she complained, rubbing her backside.

"What did?"

"I'm not a rubber doll who can be manhandled and thrown to the floor."

"You were making me woozy with all that pacing. It was hard for me to concentrate."

"That's because you're drunk."

"Like I said, not yet." Then, he smiled. "Wanna pour me a drink from the fridge in the next room?"

"No."

"Ah, come on. You keep saying I'm drunk so let's make it so!" he slurred his words to the point it was hard for her to understand him.

She decided she would again try to find a reasonable explanation for what was happening. "So, I know you are a policeman, or were. At least, that's what you told the security guard this afternoon."

"You got that, did you?"

"Yes, I did. Why are they constantly harassing you?"

"Don't you know?" he was beginning to fade now but needed to know what was going on and who she was, really. He wondered if he would even remember this entire conversation in the morning. Maybe he did have more alcohol than he thought.

"No. You seem to think I'm an employee of this Zeebat character, which I am not, by the way. I am a professor of history at the University of Zion in southern Utah, and Zeebat is not my employer." Phoebe stopped for a moment, then continued. "This whole day is turning into a fiasco and I'm uncertain what to think." She was still sitting on the floor next to him, her foot resting in his lap, and trying to figure out what had happened.

Daan shook his head and tried to review what she told him. The American was so close that he could smell the lavender in her hair. Things were confusing enough to him with all the liquor he had consumed and now her luscious lavender scent. Concentration was difficult, and nothing was making sense anymore. Then, he passed out and leaned against her, nestling his head in her shoulder.

Phoebe listened to his slow breathing and realized he was out for the night.

It seems strange that you are held in security every time he enters the country. And, for no reason? Really? A former police chief inspector? Wonder who you've rubbed the wrong way to be detained by Captain Vanderburg? That being true, I imagine I'd be drinking as well.

Pushing him against the wall, she stood up and went

to the closet to look for a blanket. There was nothing on the side she was using, so she opened the other sliding door. Sure enough, there was a blanket, but it was on the shelf above a familiar garment bag which was hanging next to men's clothing with shoes on the floor. How she had missed that earlier was beyond her reasoning right now.

Daan had slid down the wall and was sleeping on the carpeted floor. Phoebe couldn't move him, and he was too drunk to move himself, so she gently wrapped the blanket around him. Pulling one of the pillows off the bed, she carefully placed it under his head. Then, she closed and locked the bedroom door. She would just find another hotel for them to transfer to in the morning.

She yawned and closed her eyes.

I'll deal with all this tomorrow just like Scarlett O'Hara.

She slipped under the covers of her bed and was asleep just a few seconds later.

Chapter 24

Piers Vogel had met Daan de Sylva on the first day of training at the Police Academy. That was over twenty some odd years ago. They had been stationed in Rotterdam as partners and made a great team on the force. That's why the brass had never separated them.

Piers was a little over six feet with the dark complexion of his Nigerian mother and the blue eyes of his European father, weighing in at 220 pounds with broad shoulders and a muscular frame. Colleagues described him as being strong as an ox and always bet on him in an arm-wrestling contest.

Daan was an inch shorter, average build, athletic, and 190 pounds. He was slim but muscular and could outrun Piers. It was said that Daan could chase down the criminal while his partner beat the bad guy into submission as needed. Piers used to say he was the brute of the team with Daan, the brains.

Piers was good with his weapon, but Daan was a crack-shot marksman with pistol and rifle. His expertise had saved Piers more than once. They had each other's back and over the years thought alike. Piers believed that was why they were so good together. The two of them had finalized many cases over the years and became best friends doing so.

That's why, in the early morning as the sun came up, Piers was on a bench across the canal from Daan's hotel, adjusting his sunglasses and mulling over in his mind the conversation the two of them had at the bar last night. Daan told him he had found something else in another immigration file that led him back to Ziebach and, Piers believed, that was putting Daan in danger again.

Piers had called the Rotterdam station a few minutes ago to say he was sick, which was unusual for him. The desk sergeant was curious, but Piers explained he had a bug of some sort and didn't want to pass it around. Piers had called in, not because he had had too much to drink last night, but because he was concerned about Daan.

The night before Piers kept filling up Daan's glass with his vodka. Piers didn't drink vodka. He was more of a whiskey man. But he needed to pump Daan for information but didn't get much. If Ziebach was after Daan again, Piers needed to find out. So, he had appointed himself to be Daan's watchdog at seven on Wednesday morning instead of being at his job in Rotterdam.

Something else bothered him as well. Piers really did believe it was an accident, a coincidence, or just one of those things that the guy on Daan's plane had a heart attack which forced the plane to make an emergency landing in Salt Lake City. Although it seemed strange that Phoebe Silva and her daughters boarded his flight there, Piers felt that, too, was a coincidence. What bothered him more than anything was that the Silva women had been put in that security room with Daan.

Piers knew Vanderburg liked hassling Daan by placing him in that room for fifteen to twenty minutes each time Daan flew back into Amsterdam. All on Ziebach's orders, he was sure.

Over the last few years, Daan had only left the

country on his annual trip to San Francisco and business to London, Berlin, and to Malta once. This detention started over seven years ago. Daan complained, but then it became a game for Daan to casually sit in that room without comment. Piers knew the experience had helped Daan to be more observant and less stressed about the little things. Piers did not have the same kind of patience.

Piers ran his hand over his bald head and pulled his shoulders back, looked at his watch and then back at the hotel. Something caught his eye. A black Fiat was making a second trip around the hotel. This time it moved more slowly, stopped in front for a couple of minutes, and then pulled around the corner and parked a few spaces down the street where he had a good view of the car and its occupants.

The two men inside didn't get out but sat still. They were acting like a surveillance team. Why? was the question. The driver glanced in Piers' direction, and Piers noted he had a swarthy skin tone with dark curly hair gathering on his collar. The only thing Piers detected from his companion in the shadows was that he had a cigarette hanging out of his mouth. They were not from northern Europe, he surmised. Maybe from somewhere in North Africa, Morocco or Libya, maybe.

Piers shook his head. *Maybe, they're just waiting for a friend.*

Coincidence was something he accepted in life. Although he also believed it was good to keep an open mind and be observant. He'd be vigilant and keep an eye on those two.

As he carefully surveyed the area across the canal, his mind drifted back to Daan. He had listened with interest as his friend described the specifics about the

Silva woman. He knew that for the last eight years Daan was in the habit of shutting himself off relationships, usually seeing a woman once or twice and then moving on. This was the first time since his wife had been killed that Daan discussed a woman as though he might enjoy getting to know her. This pleased Piers but, in line with protecting his friend, he needed more information.

After he left Daan last night, Piers spent time investigating Phoebe Silva. He could find nothing sinister or wrong about her. She was squeaky clean. However, Piers found that intriguing because in police work that was seldom the case.

He went over in his mind what he had found out. Dr. Phoebe Emanuella Silva was a professor of history at the University of Zion in southern Utah, which was in the western United States. She and her husband, Dominic Thompson, had married but he had added her name to his, rather than her taking his. Piers could find nothing to say why.

The woman's husband had disappeared on a boating trip out of south Florida shortly after the younger child was born. He and a couple of friends sailed out on a fishing trip. There had been some rough weather and the boat capsized. The United States Coast Guard's official report stated that Dominic's friends had been picked up by one of their ships, but he was never found and was presumed drowned. Phoebe had never filed the papers to have him declared deceased, and that was over ten years ago. There was no death certificate and no record of her filing for insurance. She wasn't listed on any paperwork as a widow, only that she was still married. Yet, nothing for Piers to see as a red flag.

Perhaps she was still in love with her husband and

didn't want him out of her life just yet. The situation reminded him of Daan.

Piers had determined there was no connection between the Silvas and Daan. It was strange, but only one thing stood out; their last names: Daan de Sylva and Phoebe Silva.

Chapter 25

Piers still sat quietly across the Amstel, watching and waiting. Then, he was at full alert when the door to the hotel opened, and Daan walked out sporting those reflective sunglasses of his, glancing one way and then the other before heading north. Piers knew his friend completed a daily morning run and varied his routine every day. This morning he veered in the opposite direction from where they had met at the bar last night.

Typical Daan.

To confirm Piers' concern, the two in the Fiat slowly swung into position to follow Daan about a half-block back. Piers rose and walked quickly down the way to the next bridge across the canal. He would pick up his pace and catch up to Daan, pretending to accidentally bump into him so they would talk for a few minutes. While speaking to Daan, Piers would find out another piece of the puzzle and figure out what was going on. Maybe.

"Hello, friend," Piers addressed Daan as he turned the corner.

"Well, where did you come from?" Daan sounded a bit out of breath.

"How are you doing, my friend?" Piers knew Daan wasn't himself. In fact, his friend seemed a bit disheveled, which was terribly unusual for Daan.

"Not as well as you, I see," Daan said and then smiled. "You're awfully vibrant this morning."

Daan was anything but. His head hurt when he woke up on the floor across from Phoebe Silva a little while ago. He struggled to get up and hurt all over because of sleeping on the floor. He decided he needed a long run this morning to get himself together. Bumping into Piers was not on his agenda, but he concluded Piers was here for a reason.

"Slow down and walk, my friend." Piers was in no mood to run and wasn't dressed for it in his jeans and a light jacket.

Daan slowed down his pace to stay in line with his friend. "Are you saying that you are in no condition to run this morning? We did drink quite a lot last night." Daan slapped his friend on the back. "Sure, if it makes you feel any better, I'll walk with you."

"I wanted you to know," Piers began, "that I checked out Phoebe Silva in Google, the international police database, and her university website. I can't find anything menacing about her, so I wouldn't worry about any connection with Ziebach. She was born in the American state of Georgia and attended two colleges there, Georgia Southern University and Emory University. She received her Ph.D. in American and European History at Brandeis University in Massachusetts, USA."

"A pretty smart lady."

"Looks like it." Piers took a drag off his cigarette. "Daan, I'll tell you again, what happened on your return trip was a freaky thing and nothing to bother yourself with."

"Maybe."

"She is a history professor at a university in southern Utah."

"I know," Daan agreed. "She told me."

"When?"

"Last night."

Piers stopped and grabbed Daan's arm. "What?"

"Yeah, she told me last night." He shook his head and ran his finger through his hair. "I'm surprised I remember the conversation."

"Where did you have this conversation?" Piers was surprised.

"In my room."

"Your room?" The two of them were standing right in the middle of the sidewalk, blocking people. So, Piers pulled Daan over to the railing along the canal.

"She's staying in my suite."

"Not possible," Piers stated. "How?"

"Vanderburg."

Piers leaned over to his friend, "Vanderburg?"

"Did you know he kept Phoebe and her daughters in that interrogation room for over an hour? I was only there my usual twenty minutes. I think Vanderburg was trying to see if we knew each other."

"Preposterous!" Piers threw his cigarette in the river.

"I'm beginning to feel the same way. He put her up in my suite, and everyone at the hotel seems to think we are married."

"Strange." Piers leaned on the railing and looked across to the other side of the canal.

"I agree." Daan took off his sunglasses and began cleaning them with his t-shirt. "Now, I want you to slowly turn around and look towards the Opera House. Be casual."

As Daan put his sunglasses on, Piers turned around

as requested. Seemingly ignoring the guys in the Fiat, he concentrated on pulling out the pack of cigarettes from his pocket, taking one out, lighting it, and returning the pack to his pocket.

"Do you see the man leaning against the black Fiat?"

"I do." Piers took a puff and calmly looked around as he blew smoke in the air.

"There's one still in the driver's seat. They drove up next to me as I crossed the street at the hotel and then pulled over there and parked."

"And?"

"Is it possible that I'm being followed?"

"Probable. I saw them earlier, just before you walked out." Piers speculated, "Could be from North Africa or the Middle East."

"My thoughts exactly." Daan casually turned around. "You know you're going to kill yourself with those cancer sticks."

"Perhaps, but it gives me a reason to observe my surroundings without looking suspicious." Piers took a long drag on his cigarette and smashed the butt under his foot into the concrete.

"That's what these are for," Daan touched his sunglasses. "I can see them, but they can't see my eyes."

"Well, I've always thought they were spiffy," Piers commented comically. "They're your signature, you know."

They said nothing for a minute or so before Piers continued the discussion about Phoebe.

"Phoebe's parents died several years ago."

"Siblings?"

"A brother, but he died in a hit and run after a college dance and years before Phoebe married," he remarked. "Did she tell you she was married?"

"I assumed with the two children, Piers," Daan seemed cross, but Piers chalked it up to last night's drinking.

"By the way, did she tell you her husband disappeared off the coast of Florida after the younger child was born?"

"No, we didn't talk about much, Piers," Daan let the information settle in his mind.

"I'm sure, especially in your condition last night." Piers snickered which Daan chose to ignore.

"He was never found?"

Piers gave the official specifics on the death of Phoebe's husband.

Daan turned back to the water, again, and thought to himself, *Poor Phoebe.*

"Also, he took her name. She didn't take his."

"Why?" Daan asked.

"Don't know."

"What was his original name?"

"Dominic Thompson, with a 'c' not a 'k,' by the way. And, she never had him legally declared dead."

"Well, Piers," Daan said, "I'm not sure that I wouldn't do the same thing if Francine had disappeared instead of being blown up right in front of me."

"By the way, he was born here in the Netherlands. His father was an American diplomat at the Hague."

Daan nodded at this information.

The two now walked along the canal towards the Opera House. The Fiat guys were definitely watching them. They were so intent on pretending to not watch the Fiat guys that they didn't notice someone coming up behind them.

"Hello, Mr. de Sylva."
The two men turned around and faced Phoebe Silva.

Chapter 26

Phoebe Silva stood on the sidewalk facing the two men. She was dressed in a pair of sweats and had her hair drawn up in a ponytail.

"How did you find me, Mrs. Silva?" Daan asked bluntly. "Oh, I'm sorry, Doctor Silva?"

"Don't be so damn rude, Daan," Piers reprimanded him. "Doctor Silva, my name is Piers Vogel. Daan here is my friend, and we used to be partners." Piers reached out his hand, and Phoebe shook it. "Please join us in our walk."

"The name is Phoebe. You are so much kinder than your partner, here."

"We're no longer partners with the police force." Daan was brusque. "I'm with the prosecutor's office in Rotterdam, now."

"Well, maybe that's why you are so impolite all the time." She scrunched up her face. "Being a prosecutor could make you growl when you don't convict the criminal."

"I'm in the immigration office, if you must know."

Piers stepped between the two of them and took their arms. "Shall we walk away from the Fiat guys, please?"

"What Fiat guys..." Phoebe began.

"The ones we don't want you to look at, woman," Daan groaned.

"So, let's get out of earshot," Piers laughed as he

hauled his two reluctant companions down the sidewalk a bit by placing his arms around their shoulders. "So, I understand the hotel thinks the two of you are married, right?"

Phoebe said in a low tone, "That's what I was told last night."

"That's rich. I think we must keep up this charade." Piers laughed aloud again.

Daan stopped and yanked himself from Piers' grip. "No! That's not going to happen!"

Piers pulled Phoebe over to Daan and laughed, "Please, my friend. We must put on a show for the Fiat guys."

Phoebe tried to draw away, but Piers held her close to him.

Daan looked directly at Piers, "What are you talking about?"

"Well, Daan, it's obvious the Fiat guys are watching you and your wife here." Piers nodded at Phoebe. "We don't know why yet. But it looks like we need to find out."

"Tell me, how are we going to do that?"

Phoebe was still trying to get out from under Piers' grasp.

Piers took Daan's right hand and, after letting go of Phoebe, he put it in Phoebe's left hand. "Okay, you two. We must put on a show. Daan, please meet Phoebe, who is your new wife. Phoebe, this is Daan, your new husband. They think you're married; therefore, you must act like you're married until we can figure out what's going on."

Phoebe smiled at Daan. "I think the night clerk thought we were having an argument since you came to the suite intoxicated," she let them know.

"I wasn't intoxicated!"

"Yes, you were."

Piers looked at Daan. "You were a bit smashed, my friend."

"See," Phoebe said.

Daan didn't respond.

"Now," Piers said, "as typical newlyweds, you must act like you are making up and back together."

"But we're not together," Daan was trying to explain. "We've never been together."

Phoebe concurred.

Piers just shook his head. "You have been together. You were on the plane together. You were in that interrogation room at the airport together. And you slept in the same room last night together, right?"

"That's right," Daan admitted reluctantly.

"But nothing happened between us," Phoebe insisted.

"They don't know that," Piers informed them and nodded casually towards the Fiat guys. "For some reason, someone thinks you two are married and, until we can figure out the reason, you must keep up this pretense."

"Piers, I don't like this," Daan said between clenched teeth.

Phoebe nodded her head in agreement.

"Unfortunately, I don't think you have a choice," Piers advised them as he started them back to the hotel.

Daan was trying to piece everything together. "So, my friend, where do you fit in right now?"

Piers smiled and slapped Daan on the back, "I am here right now helping you two work this out, as far as they are concerned. Who but your best friend could help you lovebirds get back together?"

"I don't like being a puppet. I brought my daughters here for vacation. We're going to see the opera and tour Amsterdam and Rotterdam, that's all. This was not supposed to be a complicated visit. We were supposed to have just a few days of culture and then go home. Now I find out I must act like your wife. What am I supposed to tell my daughters?"

"Woman, I'm in the same predicament. I must pretend that you're my wife and take care of you and your children in the process."

"Well, Bozo, I really do believe I can take care of my girls and me." She stood firmly and crossed her arms across her chest. "So, don't worry about me!"

Piers was perturbed. "Stop being such idiots. It's only for a few days until we can figure everything out." He looked at Daan and then at Phoebe. "We may all be in danger, especially if this is being orchestrated."

"It's Ziebach I know it," Daan said.

"Maybe," Piers responded.

"Danger? What kind of danger?" Phoebe focused on that one word.

"The kind that can get you killed," Daan hissed with disdain.

They were almost at the hotel, and Piers felt like they had to finalize as much as possible before this walk was over.

"What plans did you have for today?" he asked Phoebe.

"My plans were to take the girls to the Anne Frank house and then to Dam Square to visit the Palace and Madame Tussauds. Then, we have the opera tonight."

"You're going to Wagner's opera tonight?" Daan was beside himself. "You're going to see *The Ring Cycle*? Tonight?"

Phoebe answered him with a hint of sarcasm, "Of course, we're going to the opera tonight. And tomorrow night. The night after and the night after that! I told you that was one of the reasons we are here in Amsterdam."

"Well, that's quite fortuitous," Piers said and smiled at the two of them. "You're going to go sightseeing and then to the opera together. How grand!"

"What do you mean?" Daan asked.

"It seems like the two of you have your day planned." Piers tugged on the two and forced them towards the hotel. "Each of us has our jobs to do. You must stay together today and pretend to be married. I will go to Rotterdam and figure out who's trying to pull our strings."

"Great, I am so very excited to be involved with this charade." Daan was being sarcastic now.

"And you think this is going to be fun for me?" Phoebe's anger was obvious.

Piers walked between them as they crossed the canal towards the hotel. "Ah, you are both going to make me proud. We must do this to figure out what is really going on. Can I depend on you to at least be civil to one another?"

Phoebe was not happy with the situation, but she agreed with Piers that they had to get to the bottom of who was pulling the strings. There was only one thing that concerned Phoebe at this point. "Just tell me what we're supposed to tell my girls."

Piers smiled, "Just tell them that Daan is your lover."

"That is not funny, Piers," Daan barked at his friend.

"Well, I guess we can tell them you're our security guard. What do you think?" Phoebe was pulling at straws. "We can set you up in the sitting room, I suppose."

"It is my suite, you know." Daan was bothered but, when he looked at Piers, he relented. "Okay, fine. I will sleep on the sofa until we can figure out what's going on."

"Fine," Phoebe said.

"Children. Children. Please control yourselves," Piers cautioned as he laughed again for show. "I don't want you to look behind us, but the Fiat guys have moved closer and are still watching."

Daan was serious now, "I still think it's Ziebach."

Piers said, "'Why'? is the question, Daan. I am going to be researching this all day. Could be someone from the States looking for Phoebe. Who knows? Therefore, you must protect Phoebe and her girls. Don't let them out of your sight. I don't know what's wrong, but if you are protecting them, I can investigate to protect you both."

They were near the front door of the hotel now. Piers put on a show of hugging each of them and said, "I think Phoebe's right about this. Daan, you will play their security guard. If the girls ask bigger questions, you must be the one to calm them down." He then looked at Phoebe. "Seriously, you must behave as well. I know it will be difficult for you, but you must treat him as a friend and as a lover, if necessary."

Phoebe was shocked, but she agreed. "I don't like the lover part because I don't like you, Daan."

"The feeling's mutual, woman. You just play your

part and I'll play mine."

Piers looked at them both and started to walk away, then turned around to observe what was happening between these two.

Daan looked back at Piers, smiling deviously. Then he pulled Phoebe to him and held her tight, giving her a kiss on her lips. It was supposed to be a simple kiss, but it lasted much longer when Phoebe responded and didn't pull away. After a few moments, he released her but held onto her because he felt she would fall. Then she pushed him from her.

"Go ahead, lovebirds," Piers said softly. "That was a good beginning."

Then, the two of them left him and walked through the hotel doors together. They were not holding hands, Piers noticed, but they were together. That's a step in the right direction. He watched them for a minute to make sure they weren't going to kill each other. They moved into the elevator with Daan attempting to wrap his arm around her which Phoebe pushed away. She definitely didn't seem happy. Daan waved at Piers then flipped him the finger before the elevator closed.

Chapter 27

Piers stood for a minute after the elevator door closed. He smiled, then swung around and started walking back the way they came so he could cross the canal again to his car. He grabbed a cigarette like before and glanced towards the Fiat guys. They were just passing by, but he pretended to not see them.

He now knew someone was watching Daan and Phoebe, and there was probably more than just one surveillance team. He agreed with Daan that it was probably Ziebach behind this, but he wasn't sure why. He could speculate several scenarios, but he needed facts. Before he went back to Rotterdam, he would make a few phone calls. He'd contact a couple of police friends right here in Amsterdam who could watch out for the two unwilling lovebirds.

Piers knew Daan would take care of Phoebe and the girls despite the argumentative display a few minutes ago, thus leaving Piers to beat the bushes for information. He was afraid Daan was in deeper trouble than either one of them wanted to admit. Or maybe it was the woman. Piers didn't know yet, but he was going to find out.

The Fiat guys had disappeared, so Piers crossed the river and went to his car. There was something else he was thinking. This Silva woman was an interesting character. She was quite lovely with that auburn hair faintly smelling of lavender, had expressive eyes that could laugh at you or set you in your place without a word, and a mouth could smile sweetly or breathe fire at the drop of a hat. He found her smart and delightfully intelligent. Phoebe Silva was exactly how Daan had described her.

However, Piers saw more. The woman's interaction with Daan was almost explosive, an undercurrent of attraction pulling them together, a magnetism so overwhelming the two of them didn't see it. Piers observed his friend's ability to be so busy trying to deny his fascination with Phoebe that Daan was ignoring the fact that he was already enchanted by her. She made him think, defend himself, look under the surface of a thought or idea. Piers knew his friend and was delighted that, for the first time in eight years, Daan seemed interested in a woman beyond a simple one-night stand.

Piers started his car as he looked across at the hotel.

"But, my friend," he whispered to Daan under his breath, "I think you have met your match with this woman, and you may find that she is exactly what you need."

Daan needed a strong woman and Phoebe Silva was perfect. Then, he thought about another woman; a woman he had learned about in school and racked his brain for the name. Finally, he remembered. Helen of Troy, the woman who could launch a thousand ships with her beauty. Perhaps Phoebe was Daan's Helen because it was certainly looking like he was her Paris.

Piers was glad to see the Fiat was nowhere to be seen. As he pulled his car away from the curb, he pondered on the things he had to do in the next twenty-four hours.

Chapter 28

Daan and Phoebe exited the elevator on the top floor, with Daan allowing Phoebe to walk in front of him. Then, they were at the suite door, where both pulled out their key cards, but neither reached to open the door.

She turned to him. "I don't think it's a good idea if we go in together."

"Perhaps, you're right." Daan's face was solemn. "You go in and take your girls down for breakfast. Then, I'll wait here in the stairwell while you take the elevator down. I'll then go in, take my shower, and dress. Afterwards, I will meet you in the restaurant and introduce myself as your security detail."

Phoebe quickly turned her back to him and fiddled with the key card.

"Well, thank goodness that meets with your approval."

She whipped her body back around and poked her finger into his chest a couple of times as she spoke. "Don't push me, Bozo. I am not happy about this little farce either, you know."

He jerked her hand from his chest. "Good. That makes us even." He dropped her hand like a rock.

As she stepped into the suite and closed the door behind her, Daan wondered what he had gotten himself into. She was a formidable woman, and he admitted that, in different circumstances, he might be tempted to take her out on a date. But, my God, she was insufferable!

Woman, you're driving me crazy! Who do you think you are to force me to sleep on the couch in the sitting room when it's my suite? Damn! Why did I agree? Well, as soon as Piers and I have figured out what to do about Ziebach, I will be putting you and your girls somewhere else!

He was standing in front of the door when he heard Phoebe shaking the doorknob. He quickly moved over to the stairwell door and opened it, allowing the door not to close completely so he could view Phoebe and her girls in the hallway.

"Mom, must we go to breakfast now?" the younger girl was saying.

"Yes, my little loves," Phoebe responded. "Breakfast is the most important meal of the day."

"That's what you always say," the older one said. "But we're supposed to be on vacation, and we just want to watch television."

"You can watch television at home, girls."

"Fine," the younger girl grumbled.

"I hope it's not just oatmeal and toast like at that Holiday Inn last summer. That was a horrible breakfast," the older one was rambling.

The elevator bell rang.

"Time to go down now," Phoebe stated, and he knew that was his cue.

He stepped out of his hiding place as the elevator doors closed.

A few minutes later, he was in the shower. As the hot water cascaded down his back, he began reviewing the details they had discussed with Piers.

It was not going to be easy pretending to be Phoebe's

husband. He had not been a husband for a very long time, and it was hard for him to imagine being with someone other than Francine. He had been so much in love with her. She was the mother of his children. The center of his being. He never questioned that. But, in the last year especially, he felt she was fading, like he was losing her. She was more like a shadow in his dreams, and he was finding it harder and harder to conjure up her face. Maybe that's why he had been so difficult as he prepared for his annual trip to San Francisco. He hadn't realized how much she was slipping out of his life, and he found he was feeling guilty.

As he switched the shower to cold and shook himself, Daan said aloud, "This is not good."

Bringing himself into reality, he dried himself and dropped the towel on the floor and prepared to shave. On second thought, perhaps he'd better wrap the towel around his waist. It wouldn't be good if one of the girls were to rush in and see him naked in her mother's bathroom. Daan smiled. He had to remember he was pretending to be a married man with a wife and children roaming around in his life again.

Fifteen minutes later, he was dressed, with his gun tucked into his belt holster as usual. Watching out for Phoebe and her girls was not a problem. That was what a husband, even a fake one, would do without question.

Daan was almost out the door when he thought about something. Returning to the closet in the bedroom, he reached up for his travel kit. Tucked into the lining next to the key for his pistol box was something he thought he'd never, ever use.

It was his mother's wedding ring, the one that had been passed down from generation to generation in his family. His ancestor Dominik had purchased it on a trip to the New World when he and his brother, Emanuel, had set up their business in Recifé.

It was just a simple gold wedding band, beautiful in its simplicity. Francine wore the wedding ring set that she picked out in San Francisco. She had never worn this one because it was still with his mother when he and Francine married. When she died the year after Francine, his mother had made him promise to use her ring, the family ring, when he married again.

"Francine was my life. She meant everything to me. I have no plans to marry anyone else."

"Come, my Daan, sit next to me." She patted the bed beside her. "Open your hand." She placed her ring in his palm and closed his fingers around it. "One day, you will find someone with whom you will gladly share your heart."

"But…"

"Francine will always be a part of you, always." Her whisper was almost undetectable. "However, your heart is still yours, but one day…" She coughed, and he felt her hand hold his a little tighter. "One day, you will need this ring, the family ring. You must keep it with you until one day you will realize your heart no longer belongs to you alone."

"My heart will always be mine."

"Promise me, Daan. Please promise." Her voice had trailed off, and her eyes were sad as she smiled at him, then she coughed again.

He brought her hand up to his lips and kissed it gently.

"I promise, *Moeder*." He held her hand in his for another few minutes, and then he realized she was no longer breathing.

That evening, he had placed his mother's ring in the lining of his travel kit next to the key to his pistol box. It had been there ever since. He used the pistol box key all the time but had never taken out the ring...until now. As he held it in his hand, he could still hear his mother's words ringing in his ears.

Let me be clear about this, Moeder. I need to borrow this temporarily so that Phoebe and I can convince others that we are together. He sighed. *Phoebe Silva doesn't share my heart, I promise you that! My heart belongs to me!*

Daan went to the bathroom, picked up the towel he had just used, and shined up the ring. If they were pretending to be married, then Phoebe must have a ring. Examining the ring towards the light in the bathroom, he decided it would do. He placed the ring in the left trousers' pocket of his jeans, agreeing with himself that it would be a nice touch to their pretend marriage.

Viewing himself in the mirror of the elevator, he decided he looked pretty sharp for a husband on vacation with his family with a simple loose t-shirt to cover his gun, dark trousers, and the windbreaker he'd worn last night. One temple of his sunglasses was tucked casually into his shirt to secure them. The only thing missing was a camera around his neck. The cell phone tucked in his t-shirt pocket would work but he thought a real camera hung around his neck would be better to pull off his role today.

As the elevator doors opened at the lobby, Daan skimmed the area. He saw Lars behind the registration desk with a girl he was training. Daan made his way over.

"Mr. de Sylva," Lars began, "I —"

Daan interrupted Lars impatiently, "I need to speak to you in private about something urgent."

"This way, sir." Lars led him to the back office.

As soon as the door closed behind him, Lars said, "Is everything okay with your suite, sir? I could have had some flowers or something delivered to your room."

"Lars, it's okay."

"Well, sir, you were lost when your wife and children were killed so long ago," Lars stated sympathetically. "I knew you were coming back from your annual trip to America, last night. Usually, your reservation is just for you. When I came in after being out for the weekend, I was surprised when Ty told me you were checking in with a wife and children. But, sir, I am so happy for you."

Daan started to say something, but Lars continued, "Who knows what one does when one is out of the country? Or even what one does when one is here." Lars grinned cunningly.

"No, Lars, it's nothing like that. Phoebe is a delightful woman, but there is nothing between us."

"Sir?"

"It wasn't until early this morning that we figured someone had purposely made a change to add Phoebe and her girls to my suite."

"So, she is not your wife?"

Daan shook his head.

"I can remedy that if you wish. The suite next to you is under renovations but I think I could arrange for —"

"Please don't."

"But sir?"

Daan gave a reassuring smile and then asked, "Do

you know who made the reservation to add Phoebe to my suite?"

"I was informed that you called and made the change."

"Someone else made that call."

"Sir, I'm sorry. I should have checked further."

"Lars, don't worry. But now, we must continue the pretense that Phoebe is Mrs. de Sylva for the time being."

"She is not Mrs. de Sylva, but we are pretending that she is?"

"Yes. It's confusing, I know, but someone is making a great effort to throw us together, and Piers and I are trying to figure out who and why."

"You can count on my discretion, sir."

"I appreciate that." Daan turned towards the door and then looked back. "We will be attending the opera for the next few evenings."

"You and the woman?"

"Interesting, don't you think, that she has tickets to the same opera?" Daan's voice was low, almost like he was speaking to himself and not to Lars.

"Just let me know what I can do for you."

"Right now, please watch Phoebe and her girls, so no harm comes to them when I am not around." Daan looked seriously at Lars. "And, as usual, I'll need you to watch my back.

"That is always my honor, sir."

Daan rested his hand on Lars' shoulder. "Thank you."

They went out to the reception desk with Lars saying, "Consider it done, sir."

They shook hands, and Daan crossed the lobby, smiling. He knew his secret was safe with Lars. As he crossed in front of the elevator, he made note of the Fiat guys sitting in the corner next to the fireplace, reading newspapers. He pretended not to notice as he headed for the restaurant.

Scanning the room as he walked in, he spotted Phoebe and her girls over in the corner and waved. Phoebe waved back. Well, he thought to himself, at least he had a pretty wife for this role play. And the two daughters weren't so bad either. He would make sure to take lots of pictures of them in front of the Palace in Dam Square today.

That's what a real father would do, right? he thought as he snaked his way between the tables of guests.

Phoebe's voice was just a little above a whisper. "Girls, let me introduce you to Daan de Sylva," Phoebe pointed to the older girl first and then the younger. "Daan, this is Charlotte and Lucy, my daughters."

"Hello, it is nice to meet you," he said and, at the last second, decided to kiss each girl's hand instead of shaking it. If they were his children, he would not be shaking their hands. It would be better this way. More intimate.

Both girls giggled as he kissed the hand of one girl and then the other.

"Wait, a minute. Weren't you at the airport yesterday?"

That's Charlotte, he thought. *The older one's name begins with C at the beginning of the alphabet.*

"You sat next to Mom on the airplane, didn't you?" the other child inquired.

The younger one is Lucy. L comes after C. That's how I'll remember them.

133

"As a matter of fact, I did." He sat next to Phoebe and decided she was brilliant because she placed him facing the door like she knew his preference.

The server asked if Daan wanted to order breakfast, and he asked for coffee only.

"Remember girls, I told you there was an incident at the airport yesterday. Someone made a threat against Americans, and that's why we had the escort to the hotel," Phoebe was letting him know what she had told the girls concerning his presence with them. "Daan has graciously volunteered to stay with us for a couple of days in case there was additional trouble."

"Yes, I told your mother this morning that I used to be a Chief Inspector with the Dutch Police."

"You were a policeman?" Lucy wanted to know.

"Yes, I was a chief inspector."

"You're no longer a policeman?" Charlotte asked.

"No, I work in the prosecutor's office in Rotterdam."

"So, you are an attorney," Charlotte confirmed.

"Yes," he answered. "I'm on vacation as well, so I am excited to show you around."

"You were in the United States on vacation?" Charlotte asked.

"Yes."

"And you're still on vacation?"

Before he could answer, Lucy interrupted, "You met our mother this morning? But we didn't meet."

"Not officially."

Charlotte took over the interrogation, "And you saw her this morning? Where did you meet her this morning?"

"We met up as we were running."

"You run every morning, too?" Charlotte was putting on the screws.

"Just about every morning."

"Wow, Mom does that, too," Lucy commented. "And she wants us up at the crack of dawn to run with her. She says it's good for us."

"Well, it can be quite exhilarating," Daan responded. "There is something about getting out into the fresh air at the beginning of the day."

"Do you expect us to run with you?" Lucy sounded horrified.

"No."

"Good," Lucy was relieved.

The server came over with Daan's coffee, giving him a chance to catch his breath. These American girls certainly asked a lot of questions, and he decided they would make great prosecutors.

"Mom says breakfast is the most important meal of the day, so you must eat something," Lucy said.

Phoebe passed him a plate of toast and he graciously took, grabbing a piece in hopes of delaying additional questioning from her girls.

"Char, Luce," Phoebe begged, "please be nice to Daan because he has volunteered to show us around and watch over us while we are here in Amsterdam."

"We're going to the opera tonight," Lucy groaned. "Will you be there?"

"Yes," he said, after swallowing another bite of toast before answering.

"We must go every night for the next four nights," Lucy grumbled dramatically.

"Well, it is a long opera," Daan agreed. "But there are four major stories, one for each night."

"That's what Mom said." Charlotte sounded amazed, then looked over at her mother. "Did you plan this, Mom?"

Phoebe shook her head, no. Then, slowly took a sip of her coffee.

"Do you know what my favorite musical piece is?" he asked both girls, taking control of the conversation.

"No," they responded in unison.

"On the second night at the beginning of the third act, there is a piece of music called the *Ride of the Valkyries.* It is a victory song where Brünnhilde and her sisters, the Valkyries, descend upon the battlefield and take the souls of the dead heroes to Valhalla. It is one of the greatest pieces of music ever written, some say, and several modern movies have that piece as a part of them. For example, it was played in *Apocalypse Now,* a couple of *Star Wars* movies, and even *Rango.*"

"And, the World War II saga *Valkyrie,* as well as *2001: A Space Odyssey,* and even *Grand Theft Auto,*" Phoebe added.

"Mom!" Lucy cried out. "I can't believe that you told him what your favorite piece of music is from this stupid opera!"

"What?" Daan looked at Phoebe nonsensical. "It's not?"

"It is."

"Duh," Lucy exclaimed.

"Really?" he responded with a smile.

"You didn't know that you liked the same piece of music from the opera?" Charlotte squinched her eyes and stared at her mother, then Daan.

"We didn't speak about the opera this morning," he admitted. "I just knew the three of you were going."

"That sounds lame," Lucy told the two of them.

Charlotte chuckled. "I can't believe that my mother didn't discuss her favorite music from the opera."

Daan leaned forward and focused on the girls. "Well, you see, it is hard to have a long discussion when you're running. It's hard to breathe, run, and talk at the same time."

Phoebe decided to change the subject. "Since the three of you are ready for a sightseeing excursion, why don't I go upstairs to shower and change."

"Mom, are you leaving us down here with a strange man in this strange restaurant in a strange country?" Charlotte asked disagreeably.

"I won't bite, I promise," Daan confessed. "I only eat little girls on Thursdays, and that's tomorrow."

"You wouldn't do that," Lucy said cautiously.

"Of course not," Charlotte assured her sister.

Daan snickered. "Are you sure?"

Phoebe laughed and then said, "Well, if you don't stay here, then I'll need to take you upstairs with me if you wish. I trust Daan to not eat all of you." She smiled sweetly at Daan. "Just leave me their hearts so I can cover them with syrup. They taste better that way."

"Mom," Lucy said. "That doesn't work on us anymore."

Lucy and Charlotte giggled, and Phoebe smiled at them.

"I'll tell you what, girls, why don't we walk along the canal until your mother returns all fresh and less smelly." He waved his hand back and forth in front of his nose like he was offended. The girls tried to contain their laughter.

"Will that be okay for you, Char? Luce?" Phoebe

asked.

"Sure, Mom," Charlotte smiled.

"We'll be good," Lucy agreed as well.

"Fine." Phoebe looked thankfully at Daan.

"Phoebe, would you see if they have delivered my stuff to the suite?" he asked. No reason to alert the girls' that his things were already in their mother's room.

She nodded her head. "I'll only be about 18 minutes, promise." She waved goodbye as she turned the corner towards the elevator.

"Is she always that precise?" Daan inquired.

"Always," Charlotte answered. "And she will be looking for us outside in exactly 18 minutes. You can set your watch to my mother's time."

Lucy nodded her head.

"Then, I guess we'd better get going," Daan said as he signed the bill with their suite number, "if we only have eighteen..." He looked at his watch. "...well, seventeen minutes now before she gets back."

The girls followed him out of the hotel as Daan lifted his sunglasses from his shirt.

"I can see myself in your glasses, Daan," Lucy stated.

Charlotte remarked, "That's because they have lenses that look like mirrors to us."

"Can you see me?" Lucy asked as she tried to wave her hands in front of his face.

Daan smiled at her. "I tell you what, you try on my sunglasses and see for yourself."

He placed them on her face over her eyes and she *oohed* and *aahed* for a minute or so. Then, he offered them to Charlotte.

"Wow," she said. "I like your sunglasses."

"Me, too!" Lucy agreed.

Daan replaced the glasses over his eyes and guided the girls down the sidewalk next to the railing as he pointed out the different milk box style houses along the canal.

"They look like they are leaning over and about to fall down." Charlotte said.

"Why don't the owners fix them?" Lucy asked.

"There is a state historical preservation law that won't allow it. Some of these houses have been here for hundreds of years."

"Where do you live?" Charlotte wanted to know.

"In Rotterdam."

"Do you live in a house like this?" Lucy asked with concern as she pointed across the canal. "I wouldn't want your house to fall down with you in it."

Daan laughed, "I live on the top floor of a brick house that is almost 250 years old, very similar to those houses across the way."

They looked at him in disbelief. "Really?" they asked in unison.

"It's called a canal house, and it doesn't lean like these houses here, although there are some homes in Rotterdam that have the same problem." He smiled at these lovely girls who looked so much like their mother. Both seemed enthralled with learning more about his house in Rotterdam. "It belonged to my great uncle. When he died, he left the house to me."

"Didn't he have any kids?"

"No, they died in the Holocaust." Daan stopped and was concerned whether to continue.

"You lost your family in the Holocaust?" Charlotte asked.

"Most of my family, in fact."

"That's sad," Charlotte remarked.

"But that was long ago."

"World War II and the Holocaust ended the same year," Charlotte said.

"1945."

"1945 really was a long time ago," Lucy exclaimed.

They were quiet for a few minutes.

Charlotte broke the silence. "Daan, you have a house in Rotterdam. So, you grew up there?"

"No, I grew up right here."

"In Amsterdam?" Lucy asked.

Daan turned around and pointed at the hotel. "Right there."

"You lived in our hotel?" Lucy asked.

"On the top floor."

"Where we have our hotel room?" Lucy was amazed.

Daan nodded.

Charlotte inquired, "Has it always been a hotel?"

"Over four hundred years ago, my ancestors built a four-story red brick home that had blue shutters and trim. From the time it was built, the house passed down to the oldest son and his family ever since it was built. It sat right here on the waterfront because my family owned a shipping line that traded with the rest of Europe and the Americas."

"Four hundred years ago?" Lucy asked. "But America is not four hundred years old. It was born in 1776"

Daan laughed. "You are a smart one."

Charlotte said, "Lucy, before there was the United States, America belonged to the Native Americans, and

England, France, Spain, and Portugal built colonies."

"And the Dutch, too," Daan let them know.

"Your family sent ships to America before you were born?"

"Yes, Lucy. My family sent ships to America before there was a United States."

"Wow!" Lucy exclaimed.

"Why did you live in a hotel when you were growing up, Daan?" Charlotte asked. "What happened to your home?"

"It burned down during World War II."

"And the hotel was built on top of it?"

"After the War," Daan explained, "my family built the hotel."

"So, this hotel belongs to you?"

"Not anymore. My parents sold it."

Charlotte's questions continued. "That's why you live in Rotterdam."

"It's a really boring story," Daan commented.

"Tell us, please," Lucy begged.

"Well," he began. "We lost our home here in Amsterdam. But my great uncle was lucky he didn't lose his house when the Germans bombed Rotterdam in 1940. Most of the city was in ruins afterwards."

Charlotte remarked, "The whole city?"

Lucy's mouth flew open in disbelief. "Everything?"

"Almost," Daan said. "But after the war, Rotterdam was rebuilt, and the city is better than it was before."

"But your house is still there?" Charlotte asked.

"Sure. There are five floors, and the top two floors were converted by my uncle into two apartments. The top-floor apartment was for him, and the one just below was for me. That's where my wife and I lived."

"You're married?" Charlotte asked curiously.

"Was," he told them. "My wife and daughters died in a car accident eight years ago."

"Oh, we're so sorry, Daan," Charlotte said sadly.

It was then that Phoebe joined them. "Why are you sorry?"

"Mom, Daan lost his family in a car accident eight years ago," Charlotte explained.

"Oh, Daan, I didn't know."

He said, "It was a long time ago."

"When we visit Rotterdam, can we see your house?" Charlotte asked.

"Well…" he began.

Phoebe cut him off. "Rotterdam is on Friday, precious ones. We have places to go today."

Daan looked at his watch and tapped it a couple of times. "You know, girls, you are correct."

"About what?" Phoebe questioned.

"I think it was eighteen minutes on the dot."

"We told you," Charlotte said.

Both girls snickered, and Phoebe was left to guess what had happened.

"Where to first?" Daan asked Phoebe as he took the girls' hands and started to walk away from the hotel.

"We want to see the Anne Frank house," she told him.

"Do you have tickets?"

"I had trouble buying them online, so I thought we'd buy tickets there," Phoebe stated matter-of-factly.

"Wow," he stopped in the middle of the sidewalk. "You can't buy tickets today for the Anne Frank house to see it today."

"Why not?" Phoebe scrunched up her face.

"Woman, you must buy those tickets months in advance," Daan claimed. "Not even I can get into the Anne Frank house without purchasing tickets in advance."

"What are we going to do?"

The girls moved their heads back and forth like they were at a tennis match, moving to whoever spoke next. It was a new experience for them because usually, their mother was always right, but she seemed very exasperated in this conversation. However, so did Daan. Now, there was silence between them.

Finally, Charlotte broached the subject of going downtown. "We could go to—what's it called—Dam Square. Isn't that the center of town, Daan?"

Even Lucy didn't argue with Charlotte on this one. She had never seen her mother so flustered.

"Fine, if that's what you want," Phoebe conceded, throwing her hands up in annoyance.

Chapter 29

Daan led his pretend family down the street along the canal towards Dam Square, all the while casually watching for the Fiat guys. He led Phoebe and the girls into the historical center of Amsterdam, describing the history of his capital city and how there was a dam on the Amstel River which is where the square and the city got its name.

He bought a camera and film at a nearby shop and draped the camera on its strap around his neck. He smiled at Phoebe and the girls, feeling like they were on a family vacation.

When they entered Dam Square, he allowed them to walk in front of him into the open space alone while he held back. He wanted to see their first impression of what he felt was magnificent. There were people all over the place, which was usual for The Dam, so he paid careful attention to the three of them. He began taking pictures, trying to capture their expressions.

Charlotte was the first to speak, "The buildings are so old and beautiful! We don't have anything like this in Utah, except the old Native American ruins."

"It's not a square," Lucy complained as she turned in a circle a couple of times. "It's more of a rectangle."

"You're right, Lucy," Daan said. "A long time ago, two to these five streets that come together to form the square originally followed the course of the River

Amstel."

"It's wonderful," Phoebe remarked as she turned around and looked at him. "Nothing has changed much in twenty years!"

"You've been here before?" he asked, surprised.

"I was here doing research on my thesis," she said.

"Didn't realize that."

"Yeah. I really enjoy being here, again."

He watched her and the girls as they took it all in.

Then, she reached back and slipped her arm in his. "Come, show us more."

Well, this works perfectly for our watchers, he thought as he looked around. The Fiat guys had stopped across the way, but Daan wondered who else in this crowd were shadowing them. He tapped Phoebe's arm as he drew her closer.

"Such a beautiful city," she whispered. "I love Amsterdam."

Leave it to a history professor to fall in love with his favorite city. He loved his country and was so proud of being Dutch. Smiling brightly, he knew the Netherlands would always be his home and nothing could change that.

"You probably already know about all this," he said, waving his free arm around.

"I didn't have my own personal guide then."

He pointed at buildings around the square. "There's the Royal Palace and the 15th Century Gothic *Nieuwe Kerk*. That's New Church in English," he explained. "Over there is the Grand Hotel and the De Bijenkorf Department Store. Here is the National Monument to remember the victims of World War II."

"Mom, look," Charlotte called out. "I see Madame

Tussauds Wax Museum!"

"We'll get there, Charlotte, I promise," Daan said.

He had the girls and Phoebe stop at several places along the way so he could take pictures of them. He asked a uniformed policeman to take a picture of the four of them in front of the Royal Palace. Phoebe noticed he even took off those horrid sunglasses as they posed.

"Now, the Museum," he said.

Daan escorted them through the exhibits. He took pictures of the three of them in front of Albert Einstein, Angelina Jolie, Julia Roberts, Michael Jackson, and several others. He had a museum employee take pictures of the four of them beside the Dutch Royal family and the British Royal Family and Anne Frank. Lucy and Charlotte were delighted to have their picture taken with Shrek and Princess Fiona.

"I think I'm hungry," Lucy finally grumbled. Phoebe was surprised the girls lasted more than an hour in the museum.

"You're always hungry," her sister complained.

"Sounds like it's time to leave," Phoebe said.

"I know the perfect place to take you. My favorite bakery is nearby."

A light drizzle began to fall as they left the museum. Daan hurried them around the corner and showed them down one of the narrow side streets. He directed them into a bakery that displayed wonderful snacks in the windows, including sandwich cookies of various colors of pink, green, yellow, blue, and white with chocolate cream inside.

"These are my favorite cookies in the whole world," he proclaimed happily. "My mother used to bake these for me when I was a little boy."

"They kinda look like colored Oreos," Lucy was excited.

"They're better. They're called macarons."

"No, thank you," Lucy wrinkled up her nose. "I don't like coconut."

"These are not macaroons," he explained. "Macarons. They are almond cookies, and they taste delicious."

"I like almonds," Lucy said.

"Me, too.

The place was packed and full of noise, but Daan maneuvered them around the crowd, and soon, they were at the front of the line.

He pushed the girls in front of him and pulled Phoebe close to his side. "What colors, ladies? I'm ordering two dozen."

"Daan, that's too much," Phoebe complained.

"Shhh," he put his finger on her lips. "They're concentrating."

The girls chose a few of each color, and the clerk placed them in a bag.

"We have sweets for the girls," he confirmed. "What about you, Phoebe?"

She observed him closely and decided this was a different side of him she had not seen.

Was this the same obnoxious man I dubbed the Devil? The same arrogant drunk man who had slept on my bedroom floor last night. The same uppity man who was full of complaints earlier with Piers?

"I like brownies," she stated simply. "Good, old-fashioned brownies."

"The brownies here are the best in Amsterdam." The clerk added two large brownies to a second bag.

147

He paid for the treats and gave them to Phoebe for safekeeping. He wasn't sure he could trust the girls to not devour them before they stopped for lunch. The drizzle had turned to a soft rain while they were in the bakery.

"There is a delightful little café just a few doors down," he told Phoebe.

"Okay."

"Let's go," he called to the girls, and off they went to the café with outdoor and indoor seating. Those sitting outside were covered by an awning, but Daan escorted his ladies inside to an open table in the back.

He cleaned the rain off his sunglasses and returned them to their place in his shirt when they sat down. Phoebe was relieved because, without his glasses, she was able to see his coffee-colored eyes which dominated his classic face that she decided was more Mediterranean looking than northern European. She had to admit that he had a great, warm smile especially when he spoke to the girls. Now, she saw he was looking at her, so she tried to concentrate on the menu.

After they ordered, the girls trotted off to the bathroom. Daan picked up his camera and took a picture of Phoebe who complained. He laughed and turned to the window, snapping several pictures of the Fiat guys across the street. In between taking family pictures in the Square and the museum, he had been able to sneak a couple of pictures of them as well. He would turn over the camera to Piers who might be able to identify the guys. Chances were they were not on any database, but it was worth a try. Now, he tucked his camera into Phoebe's bag situated between them as he shifted in his chair.

"Daan, you are spoiling Char and Luce," Phoebe

objected gently.

"They are on vacation. Children should be allowed a bit of freedom on vacations." He was sitting close to her, and he leaned over to whisper. "You know that we are being followed, right?"

"Where?" She started to turn around, but he held her still.

"Don't move. We're supposed to be married, so let's give them a show. Just pretend that you are very interested in what I am saying, okay?"

Phoebe smiled and found herself glancing into his deep brown eyes and could hardly believe she had just met him on Monday. Daan was being so attentive to Char and Luce, and now he was acting like her real husband. She felt herself letting her guard down without even realizing it.

Daan moved back and carefully took the ring out of his pocket. "Give me your left hand. I have something for you," he said as he pulled her closer. In the shadows of her sweater and his windbreaker, he gently placed his ring on her left ring finger. He tried to be casual about it but was honestly astonished that it was a perfect fit. She was a bit startled, but he took her hand into his and brought it up to kiss the inside of her palm.

"Why?" she asked in a whisper.

"A married woman should have a ring." He caressed her hand against the side of his face as if to exhibit the ring for all to see. As he kissed her cheek, he felt her pulling away. "Remember, we are pretending to be a married couple."

"Uh-huh," she said.

He drew her a little closer to him. "You're supposed to be enjoying my lovemaking, you know."

She smirked. "Obviously, it's been a while since you made love to a woman," she whispered. Then, she forcibly pushed him away in a playful manner.

He was a little taken aback by her actions. "Let me tell you something," he leaned into her again and was murmuring so only she could hear. "When I make love to a woman, she knows that she is being loved." He then nibbled on her ear.

Phoebe drew in a quick breath. This was the closest any man had been to her in years. The last date she had was with that math professor that Vanessa had set her up with several years ago in San Francisco. When he kissed her good night, it was like kissing a fish. But not Daan. His kiss, which had startled her this morning on the way into the hotel, was a real kiss.

Daan now brought his arm around her and began nuzzling his face into her hair. Her heart was racing, and she felt like she could hardly breathe.

Then, he said softly to her, "See, I can make you feel a little something, can't I?"

She stiffened. "You bastard," she jeered under her breath and tried to push him away. At that point, she didn't care who was watching.

He sat up in his chair now because the girls were coming towards them.

"I think I'll go freshen up," she said as they joined them at the table.

Daan stood and helped her out from the corner where she was. "I'll be waiting with bated breath for your return," he said aloud as she eased by.

She said nothing but hurried away. "So, girls, how are you doing so far?" she heard him say to her daughters.

In the bathroom, it took her a few minutes to compose herself. She was furious that she had almost fallen for his charm. She decided that she had named him correctly. He was the Devil incarnate, as far as she was concerned. How could he treat her in such a manner?

Then, she looked at the expensive ring he had just placed on her finger. It seemed to be real gold. It was no simple trinket, this. And, she had to agree that a ring would secure the belief that they were married. Where did he get the ring in such a short time? And it was a perfect fit! How did he do that?

She gently removed the ring from her finger and read aloud the Hebrew inscription inside, "*Ani le dodi ve dodi li.*" She took a breath. "I am my beloved's, and my beloved is mine." She was astonished and wondered if the ring had belonged to his wife. But how could he have found the ring so fast when he lived in Rotterdam.

She placed the ring back on her finger. She had to admit he certainly was resourceful. It was like he was prepared for anything. Like he had a plan for any and every possibility in life. What was she going to do with this man? This Devil?

She washed her hands and splashed water on her face, reaching for paper towels as a blonde woman with short, curly hair entered the room.

"You are English?" the woman addressed Phoebe in the mirror.

"American," Phoebe admitted.

"That man of yours is quite something, isn't he?" she commented to Phoebe in a German accent. "I thought he was going to ravish you right there on the table if your daughters had not returned. Oh, if only my husband was as passionate with me. You are a lucky woman. Yes, you are."

Phoebe gave a small smile and patted her face dry. Then, the woman went into the stall behind her. From her shoulder bag, Phoebe reached past the camera and brought out her makeup kit. She found her lipstick, and reapplied some color to her lips, dropping the kit back in her bag. Observing herself in the mirror, she breathed in deeply.

As she headed back to the table, she contemplated what to do now. Daan was in make-believe land for the ones who were watching them, expecting her to do the same. She would smile and be kind to Daan because she had agreed to. However, she had not expected him to push so many of her buttons that she thought she had hidden away. So, no more of the closeness that he had exhibited a few minutes ago.

By the time she returned to the table, their meal had come. Phoebe smiled at Daan but decided that was all he would get right now. She ignored him and paid more attention to the girls. She was their mother and only his make-believe wife.

Phoebe looked across the room, and the blonde German lady nodded her way. The man with her was big and reminded her of a wrestler; he also looked dark and sinister. Phoebe felt a chill go down her back and quickly turned away. Were they watching her, Daan, and the girls?

As she leaned in closer to Daan, who was talking with the girls, he touched her hand without stopping his conversation and she felt a little better.

Chapter 30

The rain had stopped by the time they left the café. Daan looked at his watch and then proceeded to put on his sunglasses. He needed to see who was watching. Hmmm, the Fiat guys were standing inside a store across the street, and he looked to see if he could spot any other watchers as he turned around to Phoebe and the girls.

"It's time to go, ladies," he wrapped his arm around Phoebe. "We must get back to the hotel so we can have a leisurely afternoon preparing for the opera."

"Must we go to the opera?" Lucy asked painfully as they walked back towards Dam Square.

"Yes." Phoebe was firm.

Daan laughed and let go of Phoebe, linking his arms into the girls'. "I tell you what, we will discuss the opera this afternoon. Then, I'll ask you two questions, and you must find the answers during the show."

"Two questions for me?" Lucy asked.

"And two questions for me?" Charlotte didn't want to be left out.

"Okay, we can do that," Daan agreed. "Two questions for each of you."

"But it's all in German," Lucy complained again. "How will I find the answers to your questions?"

"I'm sure your mother will help you."

"Mom doesn't know German," Charlotte let him know.

"You don't speak German?"

"Nope, I speak English and Italian," she admitted. "I must tell you that my Italian is rusty."

"That's okay. My mother was Italian, and I speak the language fluently. I also speak German." He looked deep into her eyes and hesitated for a few seconds. "Ah, thank goodness you have me with you here to be your interpreter."

"I do know all about the opera, you know." Phoebe felt his eyes lock onto hers, and it was with much effort that she turned away.

The girls seemed to ignore her comment.

"Do you speak any other languages, Daan?" Charlotte asked.

"As a matter of fact, I speak Dutch, English, German, French, and Italian," Daan was sensing Phoebe's annoyance. He wasn't sure what had caused her sudden frosty attitude. All he was doing in the restaurant was treating her like she was his wife and showing her some attention. He would need to think on this a bit, because she was certainly cold as ice right now and falling back behind him. He couldn't allow her out of his sight.

"Where are the cookies?" Lucy questioned as if on cue.

"Your mother has them in her bag." He let go of the girls to reach back and grab Phoebe's hand. "Come on, let's have the loot."

Daan was making sure they took their time to walk casually back to the hotel, letting the Fiat guys see a happy family on vacation. He wanted these guys to be bored following them everywhere.

Allowing the girls to walk in front of them, he struck

up a conversation with Phoebe.

"So, you're a real doctor?" he asked, although he already knew the answer.

"Yes," she answered.

"Your degree is in European and American history, you said."

"Yes."

"Both?" he commented. "That seems rather intense. Did you have time to eat and breathe?"

"Sure, and I typed, too." She was rather curt in her answer. "I even had time to visit Amsterdam, London, and New York to do research."

"You said you were here a long time ago."

"I was."

"For how long?"

"Three days."

"Three days isn't enough time to visit Amsterdam."

She rubbed her right thumb against her fingers. "College student. No money."

"Right."

"Spent a lot of time in libraries studying and researching."

"I see."

Then, she stopped and looked directly at him. "I even got married before I finished my Ph.D."

"While you were in Amsterdam?"

"No." She was flustered. "We got married later."

"Wow!" he exclaimed. "And you can walk and chew gum as well?"

She ignored him.

"I figured you were probably divorced or a widow," he said.

"Why would you think that?"

"No ring."

"I'm a widow."

"The girls are his?"

"Of course."

"Who were you married to?"

"What's with the third degree?"

"Curious." He wanted her to confirm what Piers found out and fill in the gaps of what they didn't know.

"His name was Dominic, if you must know." She was brusque.

"Dominic Silva?"

"Yes."

"I thought your maiden name was Silva."

"It is."

"Your husband's last name was Silva, too?"

"No."

"He took your name?"

"Yes."

"I didn't think they did that in America."

"Usually not. My father convinced Dominic to take my name when we married so that our children's last name would be Silva, to carry on the family line. I am the last in my family, you see."

They walked silently for a few minutes, then Daan called to the girls. "Hey, ladies, let's sit here on this bench for a few minutes so you can eat a cookie while you rest."

"Okay," Lucy said and ran back with her sister right behind her. "I'm thirsty."

There was a little shop across the sidewalk. "Here," he handed Charlotte a twenty Euro note. "Select something for you two and waters for your mother and me."

"Do you have siblings?" he asked of Phoebe, pretending he didn't know her history.

"My brother, Joel, was killed in a hit-and-run just before I graduated from high school. He was attending Georgia State in downtown Atlanta, and a car sped through a crosswalk hitting several students. He was the only one killed."

"I'm so sorry."

She paused, taking a deep breath. "It was a long time ago."

"I'm sure it was very painful to lose your brother."

She was looking down at the concrete under her feet. "We were only sixteen months apart and were very close. So, yes, it was extremely painful."

The girls came running up to them. Charlotte gave him the change, and Lucy handed them the bottles of water they had purchased. He opened the bag and allowed them to take two cookies each.

"Too bad we don't have a blanket," he said. "We could have spread it out on the lawn and have a mini picnic."

"Yeah, picnics are fun," Lucy squealed.

"But the ground is so wet from the rain," Phoebe said.

Daan was watching Phoebe and decided not to acknowledge her foul mood. To the girls, he said, "Well, then, you can share our bench or sit on the bench across the sidewalk."

"We're not babies anymore, so we can sit by ourselves," Lucy said, and the sisters sped across the sidewalk to the other bench.

Now, back to you, grouch. He handed Phoebe one of the waters and continued, "And, your subject?"

"For my Ph.D.?"

He nodded.

"My family," she stated indifferently, wondering if he even cared.

"Tell me about it."

"None of your damn business."

"Ah, come on," he bent in front of her and pulled up his glasses. "Tell me a little bit."

Despite herself, she smiled. "Well, my ancestors moved to Amsterdam from Spain during the Inquisition. They settled here, starting a bank and a shipping company. Then, a century later, two brothers decided to take advantage of shipping opportunities in the New World. One stayed in the Netherlands, and the other went to…"

"Mauritsstad in South America," he interjected.

"Recifé," she said.

"Mauritsstad was the Dutch name," he corrected her.

"You're right."

"And then what happened?"

"Just before the Portuguese took the colony back, Emanuel de Sylva moved his family to New Amsterdam and then back to the Netherlands after the British took over."

"Why were you investigating the de Sylva family?"

"For my dissertation."

"But you said that you were researching your family."

"I was."

"Your family?"

"Yes."

He listened for a few minutes as Phoebe discussed

the de Sylva family history. Her family history? She was discussing his family history. What connection did they have? If any?

"Hmmm…" he said, looking at his watch.

He stood and called to the girls. "Come on, rest time is over." Then, he took Phoebe's hand, leading them down a residential street. "We're going down this street for a few blocks so you can feel the nuances of Dutch residences without the fear of them collapsing on you."

"So, houses not on the canals do not lean?" Charlotte asked.

"Not in this area."

The girls laughed, and he allowed them to lead the way, tucking Phoebe's arm in his.

"Okay. Who were the two brothers?"

She looked at him, puzzled. "What?"

"What were the brothers' names?"

"Dominik and Emanuel de Sylva."

"Dominik with a 'k' and de Sylva with a 'y'?

"Yes," she responded hesitantly.

"And Dominik de Sylva stayed in Amsterdam while Emanuel moved to the New World."

"I just told you that," she said.

"And then the family returned to Amsterdam after the British took over and named the city New York."

"Yes."

He smiled at her. "Well, Dominik de Sylva is my ancestor."

She stopped. "Your ancestor?"

"Yes," he said but pulled her forward to keep close to the girls. "But in 1780, another of my ancestors named Daniel Dominik de Sylva lost his brother, Amos Emanuel de Sylva, during your Revolutionary War. He was killed fighting for liberty with the Americans."

"You say Amos Emanuel de Sylva died?"

"Yes."

"But Amos didn't die."

"No?" This time it was Daan who stopped.

"After the Revolution, Amos de Sylva moved to Philadelphia and opened up a trading company there."

"Your family's name was 'de Sylva' with a 'y'?"

"Well, yes. The name changed after the War Between the States when Emanuel de Sylva lost his family in a fire. He moved to Savannah in 1865, changed his name to Silva, and married Phoebe Van Dyk."

"Amos de Sylva's family lived in Philadelphia. And then Emanuel de Sylva changed his name to Silva and moved to Savannah?"

"Yes, the town where my ancestors lived and where I grew up. I am named for the two of them," she said. "Phoebe Emanuella Silva."

"Can't be," he exclaimed and then grabbed her arm, hurrying after the girls. "You mean we could be distant cousins?"

"No," she said. "Never."

"Daniel was devastated after being told his brother had died at Sint Eustatius."

"But he didn't die."

"Why didn't he contact his brother?"

"Amos was told that his brother's ship had gone down in a storm off the coast of France, with no survivors."

"The *Zilveren Maan* was lost, but not in a storm. By the way, that's *Silver Moon* in English."

"How come you know so much about this?"

"He's my ancestor, remember. Daniel was falsely

reported to have gone down with the ship. However, he was found on a beach near Brest in Brittany, France. He was severely injured, but he finally returned to Amsterdam, reporting that the ship was attacked and sunk by the British. While he was away, his father died of heart failure. My great-grandmother told me the story and made me promise to always tell my parents where I was at all times. That is why I remember."

"Oh, my. So, both brothers believed the other to be dead."

"Seems that way."

"So, Daniel de Sylva is your ancestor."

"And Amos de Sylva is yours." He turned to face her. "*Goede God*, woman, can you believe that? We are related!"

She didn't believe this turn of events. "Related? A very, very distant relationship." No, this obnoxious, arrogant, uppity man was not her cousin.

"Cousins," he challenged.

"Separated-by-several-hundred-years-ago-distant cousins," she grimaced and wrinkled up her face.

"I think it's sweet that we're cousins." Daan's face broke out into a big grin.

"Sweet, you say? Go eat a persimmon, Daan!"

She ran after her girls and jumped between them, grabbing their hands. She didn't know where she was going, but she would leave Daan de Sylva behind.

Cousins. My word.

He hurried after them. "Let's go this way. I want to show you the Portuguese Synagogue. It's the oldest synagogue in Amsterdam. It was finished in 1675

They rounded a corner, and he pointed to a large brick building.

"This is a synagogue?" Charlotte asked, and Daan nodded. "It's rather large."

"It's quite lovely inside," he said proudly. "It is where I had my *Bar Mitzvah*."

"Really?" Lucy said, pulling from Phoebe's grasp. "You had a *Bar Mitzvah* right here?"

"Yes, I did."

"Can we go inside?" Charlotte asked.

"It's locked. Terror attacks and all that," he said. "I'll see if I can organize a tour before you go home."

"Really," Phoebe remarked brusquely. "You can arrange a tour of this Synagogue but not the Anne Frank House?"

"That's not fair, Phoebe," he countered. "There are certain things I can do. A tour of the Portuguese Synagogue I just might be able to—how do you say it—ah, yes, finagle."

Phoebe said nothing.

"Mom, can we?" asked Charlotte.

"We'll see," Phoebe said.

Daan guided them past the Synagogue and towards the Opera House with the hotel in sight.

Suddenly, he laughed. "Cousins. Imagine." He looked at Phoebe. "Just think, Phoebe, we're family. Isn't that great?"

Charlotte was surprised at what he was saying. "Family? We're part of your family, Daan?"

He left Phoebe's, took the girls' hands, and began skipping down the walkway. "Can you believe that? We're family!"

"Very, very, very distant family!" Phoebe called after them.

"But family nonetheless," he yelled behind him.

"Come on, Cousin!"

They made it to the hotel faster than she and were sitting on a bench next to the canal, sharing cookies. He was laughing and talking to the girls when she came up.

"Join us, Cousin dear," he told Phoebe.

Daan was sitting between Charlotte and Lucy, and Phoebe dropped down on the other side of Lucy, pushing to make room for her. They were jabbering, but Phoebe didn't participate. She was watching the boats on the canal and still pondering the fact that they were—probably were—most likely were—distant relatives.

Daan had an idea. "Girls, let's take a river cruise tomorrow."

"Yes, yes." They sounded excited.

"That was already planned," Phoebe pointed out.

"Perfect." He was excited in spite of himself. He had taken the cruise so many times that he could be the tour guide. But not lately. "To see the city from the canals is the best way."

"Don't you have something else to do tomorrow?"

Daan didn't look at her, but he felt invisible knives being thrown his way with each word she spoke.

"Nope, my day is free so I can be with you," he smiled at her and noticed she wasn't happy with his answer.

Well, he promised himself, he wasn't going to play her game. His job was to protect the three of them and, surprisingly, he was quite enjoying himself doing it. And now, knowing that they were family, he felt more invested. More than that, he knew the Fiat guys were still watching them, and he was not going to allow them to get close to Phoebe and the girls. He wasn't sure whether

Phoebe would even recognize the two hooligans, but he didn't want to take a chance.

He wrapped his arms around the girls. "Tell you what," he said with a smile, "we'll go upstairs to rest so we can have a fun time tonight. Okay?"

"Must we?" Lucy asked.

"I'm okay with a rest," Charlotte said. "We've walked a lot today."

"Upstairs, we go," Daan pushed the girls up from the bench and reached over for Phoebe's hand. She refused to take it and hurried after the girls.

Daan took a deep breath. He was trying his best to act like a husband. But, oh, Phoebe was making everything so difficult. How could he take care of her if she didn't pretend with him? He shook his head and shrugged his shoulders. Maybe their audience would think the two of them just had a spat.

Daan hurried after Phoebe and the two girls because he was now afraid that her cold shoulder might unravel this make-believe show they were creating. He didn't see the Fiat guys, but someone else could be following them. He was glad he got to the elevator before the door closed on him. Didn't she didn't understand this play of theirs was to convince the Fiat guys and anyone else watching that they were married with two children? It was like she had forgotten the deal they had made this morning.

Then, a sudden thought occurred to him. Had he ruffled her feathers talking about her past? Perhaps that had brought up the memories of her deceased husband. Was she still in love with him as he was with Francine? That thought had not crossed his mind until right then.

Daan reprimanded himself and thought he must be more understanding with her. This escapade was bringing up memories of Francine for him, but he had not even considered Phoebe's feelings.

Looking over at Phoebe in the elevator, Daan saw what he believed to be hurt, not hate, in her eyes. Well, he would just need to persuade her and their watchers that this was real, the parts they were playing. Guess he would need to be more convincing.

Chapter 31

The caller dialed and, after a few moments, slammed his cell on the desk. Still no answer.

In the past, he had always been able to contact the assassin within twenty-four hours. Never had it taken so long to get in touch with Nick. He was probably on another job and was unavailable. After all, Nick was one of the best in the world. He had already come through for the caller time and time again.

The caller leaned back in his chair and, for a moment, allowed himself to think back when he first saw that beautiful face and long, silky, blond hair of de Sylva's wife. She had captivated his heart when he saw her waiting outside his colleague's office at the Kunstal Rotterdam and he strongly encouraged his colleague to hire her at the museum. Over the years, he had seen her numerous times, but she had ignored his advances which angered him.

His smile now became a glaring scowl. The bitch deserved to be punished for insulting him. Although he had a passing thought of saving her for himself, he decided against it. So, when the caller contracted Nick to kill the de Sylva family years ago, his instructions were to kill them all, de Sylva, his wife, and his children. The de Sylvas had tried to destroy the caller's family for centuries and it was best to get rid of them all in one swoop with no one left to hassle him.

The caller decided at the last moment to leave de Sylva alive. The man deserved to feel the hurt and pain of losing his family and the caller had relished that feeling of triumph over the last de Sylva all these years. But to find out that the sneaky bastard had tricked the caller and hidden his family away from him. Well, no one made a fool out of the caller and lived. NO ONE!

Since de Sylva's family arrived at the airport, the caller had them under surveillance. He was livid that de Sylva was parading them around town for all to see. Well, that was going to end soon. This time he would make sure that all four of them died.

The caller called again. No answer. He slammed his palm on the desk.

If I have to take care of this myself, you're a dead man, Nick!

There was a knock on the door, and his secretary poked her head in.

"Sir, they're waiting for you in the conference room."

"I'll be right there."

After the door closed, the caller picked up the phone and dialed again.

Chapter 32

On his way out of Amsterdam, Piers made a couple of phone calls to arrange for Daan, Phoebe, and the girls to be observed by a couple of police friends who knew Daan and him. Nothing official. He just acknowledged that Daan was being followed, and no one knew why.

Then, he made the trip to his home in Rotterdam. On the way, he made additional calls to put out feelers concerning the dilemma around Daan and Phoebe. Just before he made it home, he dialed a number on a different cell. After two rings, someone answered.

"Hey," Piers said into the phone.

"What's wrong?" the voice on the other end of the line asked.

"Someone's following Daan de Sylva."

"Daan?" The voice sounded concerned. "Why?"

"I have been asking around but have found nothing."

"You are sure?"

Piers stated, "I saw two guys in a black Fiat following him myself."

"Two men, you say?"

"Looked like they may have been from Morocco or Libya, maybe."

"I know nothing about this." The voice was calm. "Let me check into it."

"Tonight." And then Piers hung up. The conversation had taken less than a minute.

Going to his kitchen, Piers opened the fridge. Nothing but a milk container, a take-out box of Chinese food from last week, and a bottle of water. Piers laughed as he remembered chastising Daan about only having sour milk in the fridge after returning from his trip.

We're two peas in a pod, you and me, Daan.

Piers reached in and pulled out the milk and Chinese food, dumping both in the garbage. Pulling out the garbage liner, he headed out the back door to dispose of it in the outside trash can.

At the end of his kitchen counter, he opened a drawer and moved some papers around, uncovering his laptop computer. He pulled it out and placed it on the table. For the next hour or so, he checked out resources online, looking for anything that might lead him to information about Daan and Phoebe.

A while later , Piers pocketed his two phones and left his apartment. He meandered around for a couple of hours, talked to a few people, ate lunch with a police friend, and strolled up and down the waterfront.

A couple of his contacts asked how he was doing since he had called in sick today. So, the word was out that he was unwell. Just a bug, he told them. A walk and a little fresh air were helping him to feel better. He moved on and even went by Daan's place on the canal and waved at two policemen as he crossed the bridge.

Down by the docks, another informant walked with him for a few minutes, and Piers asked him if he had heard anything about Daan. No, but he'd let Piers know. They split at the end of the building where they met. Piers moved on and continued to stroll for another hour.

Then, he stopped by a market to replenish his kitchen. Bread. Cheese. Mustard. Gatorade. Water.

Cigarettes.

He had begun circling back towards his place when his special phone rang. Piers picked it up on the second ring.

"Found out that someone is interested in Daan and some woman that is his wife."

"Okay."

"I thought his wife was dead."

"Eight years ago in America," Piers explained. "So, what's going on?"

"He's going to the opera tonight with the woman and two children."

"That's true."

"Watch him. I'm still investigating."

Then the phone went dead.

Piers walked another block, turned a corner and, after taking out a pack of cigarettes, gave his bag of groceries to the homeless guy who was always sheltered in the doorway of an abandoned building. He'd buy groceries tomorrow. This was more important.

Piers crossed the street and hurried around another corner, then down an alley. The police station was only one more block away. He looked at his watch. It was 4:30 P.M., and the opera started at 7:00. He walked into the police station to alert everyone that he had just received a report that there might be a terrorist attack on Amsterdam's Opera House tonight and he was on the way.

Piers knew no one would question the validity of his report. But he also knew, if there weren't additional police at the Opera House, his best friend and his make-believe family might not survive the evening. Piers knew he had to return to Amsterdam.

Chapter 33

Wednesday afternoon Daan rested comfortably in the sitting room of the suite talking with Charlotte and Lucy. He felt he needed to get to know them better and, besides that, he told them they would discuss the opera together. Phoebe did not participate. She claimed to have a headache and went to lie down, shutting the bedroom door behind her without looking in his direction. The girls explained that their mother had periodic migraines and she was not fun to be around when she did.

At 4:00 o'clock, Daan sent the girls to their room to wash up for their early supper. Gently tapping on the door to the bedroom, he opened the door and shut it behind him. To his surprise, Phoebe didn't move so he figured she was asleep. Daan crossed the room and stood next to her at the bed, watching her sleep.

Phoebe had pulled the blanket from the end of the bed over her. This woman who had intrigued him so much was serene in her slumber as he crossed the room. Her lovely auburn hair was in disarray around her subdued face which seemed stressed and drawn in sadness. Her arms were wrapped across her chest as though she was protecting her heart. She did not look happy.

Today at the restaurant, he was trying to give her attention by pretending to be a caring husband. At first, she responded and then rebuked him. Had he brought on her migraine? He wasn't sure what he had done wrong but, as he watched her sleep, he played those moments over in his mind.

He thought for a moment. He gave her the ring, nibbled on her ear. What else? He said something about lovemaking and then she called him a bastard. The only other thing was the walk back to the hotel when they talked about her dissertation.

Wasn't it interesting that they were distant cousins? Dominik and Emanuel de Sylva were brothers who had expanded the family shipping business to the Americas. Daniel and Amos were the brothers who thought each other was dead. One family in Europe and the other in America. The families never knew about each other after the American Revolution. Now, Phoebe had enlightened him. But none of that would have caused her distress. She was a bit miffed when he mentioned that they were distant cousins. Part of the same family which were separated hundreds of years ago.

Hmmm. Daan hesitated for a moment. *No, there was more to this than that. It must be that you still love your dead husband. Is that why you never declared him dead?*

It was unimaginable that Daan had allowed this frustrating woman to stir something inside of him. Something he had not felt for eight years. Daan had not been celibate since he lost his wife. No way. He loved being with women. But he had walled off his heart from any emotions since Francine, and he had not let anyone close enough to even touch it.

Until today. Suddenly, in the café when he was with Phoebe, there was a little something that he thought was lost. A stirring inside. And he was sure she had felt it, too.

No, he told himself, shaking his head. This woman was a problem he had to solve. She had waltzed into his life without asking. Well, it had been more like she had crashed into his life like a bomb ready and waiting to explode without notice. He had to admit that Phoebe was a bit different, more tantalizing than any woman he'd met in eight years.

Daan gently sat down next to her, admiring the woman without the diversion of her sharp tongue to disturb him. All right, he'd concede that she could be a lovely distraction if he allowed it.

He remembered the kiss from this morning. He was being playful, but the kiss had been more than that when she responded. After releasing her, he had steadied her as much as he was steadying himself. This woman surprised him. They had just met on that transatlantic flight, yet he felt drawn to her like a magnet.

Daan carefully shifted a few strands of hair away from her face. She stirred. Her face relaxed. The sadness, gone. He had enjoyed nuzzling into her hair earlier as her aroma shrouded his senses. She smiled in her sleep and Daan found himself wanting to lay beside her, caressing her in his arms the rest of the afternoon. Lovemaking? Daan had told her that, when he made love to a woman, she would know that she was loved. Well, he'd show her lovemaking.

Then, he heard the girls in the sitting room.

Daan took a deep breath. *Alas, not this afternoon.*

He regretted having to up the sleeping beauty before him. But they had to get ready, so he gently touched her shoulder.

"Phoebe," he whispered her name.

She moved, and he shook her shoulder, saying her

name again, "Phoebe."

She slowly opened her eyes, and Daan found himself again envisioning the sharing of an afternoon with this woman. Then he noticed her eyes were bloodshot and swollen.

"Phoebe, what's wrong?" he questioned, knowing the moment was gone.

"I...I...," she began a little groggily, then realized where she was. She sat up and pushed him away. "What are you doing here?"

For a split second, he felt like he was a kid who had been caught with his hands in the cookie jar. Then, he relaxed. He had just surprised Phoebe.

Daan refused to move and asked, "Have you been crying?"

"That's none of your business," she barked.

"Hey," he finally stood up and responded in kind, "I was just trying to wake you. It's time to go downstairs for a quick supper before we get dressed for the opera."

Phoebe slowly dragged her legs out from under the blanket and set her feet on the floor. She tried to stand but fell back to the bed.

"Do you need some help?" His voice wasn't as harsh.

"No," she said. "Sorry, you just startled me. I'm not used to a man sitting on the side of my bed when I wake up."

In the back of his mind, he wondered about what would happen when a man sat next to her in bed. He smiled deviously for a moment and thought about locking the door, then joining her in the bed, sharing the rest of the afternoon with her. Then, he shoved the thought back.

"It's after 4:00, and we'll be late for the performance if we don't eat now." As she looked up at him, he knew she had been crying. He decided he would ask why, a little softer this time. "Phoebe, you've been crying?"

"No, my allergies have been bothering me. That's all," she lied, and he knew it. "Why don't you take the girls downstairs, and I'll take a shower to shake out the cobwebs." She let him help her up and walk beside her to the bathroom door. "I'll be ready when you get back. Then, you can have your turn in the bathroom while I help the girls."

"You're sure you're okay, then?"

"Don't worry about me, Bozo," she remarked, her voice sharp and brassy.

Daan was going to be just as curt as she was, but decided that, if something was bothering her enough to make her cry, he should be less disagreeable. He would back off.

"Sure," he responded as nicely as he could without the sugar coating. "Would you like for us to bring you back a salad or sandwich or something?"

"No, I'm not hungry."

You will be, he said to himself as he closed the bedroom door behind him. *I'll find out from the girls what to order.*

"Is Mom coming?" asked Charlotte as he entered the sitting room.

"It's just us, the Three Musketeers."

"That's what Mom says we are, silly," Lucy cackled. "So, we can't be any kind of musketeers."

"Okay," Daan racked his brain for a new character image for the three of them. "What about the three Bozos?"

175

Phoebe's going to kill me for this one.

"What's a Bozo?" Lucy asked. "I don't know what a Bozo is."

"It's the name of a clown," Charlotte answered before he could.

Daan opened the door to the hall, and the girls walked to the elevator.

"A clown? Why do you want us to be clowns?" Lucy said as she hit the down button.

"Well, we laugh a lot together and don't clowns laugh while making people laugh?"

"Okay," Lucy agreed. "We'll be the three Bozos."

Chapter 34

When they returned to the suite forty minutes later, the three were laughing. He suggested the girls hurry into showers, telling them he couldn't wait to see them in their beautiful dresses. He claimed that he only wanted spectacular women accompanying him to the opera tonight.

"You only have about thirty minutes to come out here looking fantastically spectacular!" he called to them as they closed their door.

He knocked on Phoebe's door and then opened it. "Are you decent?" he called before he entered the room with her salad.

"Please come in."

Daan walked in and closed the door behind him. "I brought you a salad with no tomatoes because the girls said you are allergic."

Her back was to him, but the floor-length black dress with the deep plunge in the back was very enchanting.

"Could you please zip me up? The zipper is just out of my reach."

"No problem," he said as he placed the salad on the dresser to his right and walked across the room to her.

He had not been asked to zip up a lady's dress since—he thought for a moment as he reached for the bottom of the zipper—since Francine had asked him in

San Francisco before she and his children were killed. He stopped and stood extremely still for a moment.

"Hey," Phoebe brought his thoughts back to her, "don't admire the view, just zip it up, please."

Daan shook himself and zipped her dress. Then she turned around.

"*Godverdomme*," he said and couldn't believe he said the comment out loud.

"What?" she asked, then made a 360° turn. "Do I have something on my dress?"

"No, nothing is on your dress."

Daan was stunned by how the dress hugged Phoebe's silhouette like a fitted glove. The tip of the V-neck plunge in front stopped just between her breasts, and there was a daring slit that reached her upper thigh. The dress had no detail, no sparkles, no sequins, no lace, no embroidery at all. It was amazingly simple and yet exquisite in showing off her figure. She had been wearing jeans, loose-fitting t-shirts, and baggy sweaters for the last two days, and he had not yet noticed her figure.

"Are you sure? You look a bit pale."

Daan noted she had pulled her hair up with a pearl hair brooch, and there were dangling pearl earrings in her ears that swayed when she moved her head. He looked into her eyes and decided that, given the chance, he might allow himself to get lost in them. But not now. It was all he could do to not drop his jaw in amazement.

Daan stood back a couple of steps. "Actually," he tried not to sound so overwhelmed, "you look rather nice in that dress."

"Really?" Phoebe turned around again. "I'm about ten pounds too heavy for this dress, don't you think? Is it too tight? Should I change? I only brought two evening dresses for the opera."

"No," he said almost too quickly. "You are perfect." He stopped as she faced him. "Ah, or maybe I should say the dress brings out the best in you."

Daan felt he was beginning to stutter, so he reached to grab her salad and pushed it into her hands. "Here. The girls didn't know whether you wanted...well which dressing you wanted...so I got you both blue cheese and ranch."

"The girls know that I don't like blue cheese."

"Sorry." Daan moved towards the bathroom. "I'll get ready now and be finished in about fifteen minutes."

He shut the door to the bathroom and leaned against it. He found himself taking a deep breath. Francine had worn evening dresses with lace and sequins and sparkles. She always looked beautiful, and he was delighted to have her on his arm whenever they went out to the opera or fancy parties. But Phoebe had rattled him. She was gorgeous in that simple dress, with her being the only detail.

There was a knock on the door. He tried to look casual as he opened it.

"You might need your evening wear to dress for the opera," she mentioned to him as she stepped back to allow him access to the room.

"You're right," he admitted, making his way to the closet to collect his things.

She waited for a moment, then told him, "When you're finished ogling at me, you might want to hurry if we're going to make it to the performance on time."

"Right."

He felt like a bumbling idiot as he took his shower.

When was the last time he was like this? He couldn't remember. Maybe, his first real date when he was a teenager?

As he shaved, he thought about how he was never befuddled around Francine. As he quickly dressed, he was still trying to figure out why he was so muddled. Well, thank goodness, this charade of theirs was only for a few days, and then she'd be gone.

Several minutes later, there was a knock at the bathroom door. "Daan, are you about ready?"

He opened the door and asked, "Can you help me with my tie? It's giving me trouble this evening." He tied a great bow tie, but tonight his fingers just wouldn't work properly.

"Come here." She motioned him forward. "I don't know how you men have such problems with tying bow ties. You can't see anything in that bathroom with all the steam you've built up in there."

He smiled at her. If she only knew how much steam he had built up because of her.

She continued, "...I always had to do my brother's bow tie for his proms, and my date's as well. Don't you go to a 'How to tie a bow tie class'? If not, you should."

She was rattling on and on as she tied the fabric easily.

When she stopped for a breath, he hurriedly commented, "I have been thinking about picking up a pre-tied one because I only wear this tux once or twice a year."

"Don't do that," she recommended. "A pre-tied bow tie just doesn't look professional, I think." She stood back from him. "There, all done."

He sat down on the bed right next to where she had

placed his shoes. She waited for him to tie his shoestrings and stand up.

"You look quite spiffy tonight, Mr. de Sylva."

"You look quite beautiful yourself tonight, Mrs. de Sylva," he couldn't help himself.

"Silva with an 'i,'" Phoebe remarked and then closed her mouth quickly.

"It is Mrs. de Sylva with a 'y' for a day or two," he reminded her in a low tone as he tried to be unconcerned. Then he noticed she had something in her hands. "What do you have there?"

"My pearls," she answered. "Would you please…?"

"I'd be happy to," Daan stopped just in time before he added 'Sweetheart.' He was really getting into this make-believe role being forced on them. He was a bit alarmed at how easy this transition was becoming. Only for a few more days, he promised himself. Then, she would return to America with those two lovely daughters of hers.

As he placed the pearls around her neck, the touch of her soft skin was as alluring as her lavender scent, captivating his senses. It was all he could do to snap the clasp of Phoebe's pearl necklace and not pull her to him.

"There you go, Mrs. de Sylva."

With a sound at the door, he spun around to see both girls peeking in the door. Daan tried to focus on the girls and not their mother.

"Did you just call Mother, Mrs. de Sylva?"

He had been thinking about this most of the day. So, before Phoebe could answer Charlotte's inquiry, he took the lead.

"Come here, you two," he led the girls into the sitting room and sat them down on the sofa. "You know how I'm here to protect the three of you because of some stuff going on."

They both nodded their heads.

He reached back for Phoebe's hand. "Well, to take care of you, I'm pretending to be married to your mother. That way, if anyone asks, you are part of my family and there is no question about our being together."

"Mom?" Lucy cocked her head to one side.

Phoebe let go of Daan's hand and sat next to her daughters. "This is the only way that Daan can protect us."

Charlotte looked confused, "This is really serious, then."

"Very serious," Daan admitted. "But I'm here to take care of you."

The girls looked at each other but didn't say anything for a full minute. Then Lucy questioned, "Do we have to call you, Daddy?"

"No, you can call me Daan just like you have been," he smiled at the two of them.

"But," Lucy continued, "how is anyone going to believe that you are married to Mom if we don't call you Daddy?"

"That doesn't matter, Luce." Phoebe was trying to uncomplicate things. "Daan is just pretending to be part of the family. It's only for a few days."

"Mom," Charlotte began, "didn't Daan say that we were part of his family because we are distant cousins?"

"Yes."

"Then, we really are family," Charlotte stated a fact, Phoebe realized.

Lucy jumped in, "And, Mom, I've never called anyone Daddy before. I think it might be nice."

Leave it to my girls to make things difficult. Now, how do we get out of this one?

Daan to the rescue. "Remember how we talked about the three of us being the three Bozos?" He pointed to the girls and himself,

They nodded.

"We'll just pretend to continue being the three Bozos."

"Okay, but what about Mom?" Lucy said.

Daan glanced at Phoebe and then smiled, "Well, now we must include your mother. So, we're the four Bozos."

"But I want to call you Daddy," Lucy cried and reached out for Daan's hand. "If you are pretending to be Mom's husband, then you must pretend to be our Daddy. Right, Char?"

"That sounds like the thing to do," Charlotte agreed.

"But little loves…" Phoebe began.

"No, Mom, this is how it is," Charlotte said seriously. "If Daan is going to protect us and we are pretending to be a family, then he is part of the family."

"He's not part of the family unless we can call him Daddy." Lucy was very specific about this. "And, you know how to treat daughters. You had two daughters like us, right?"

"Twin daughters."

Charlotte asked, "Do you miss your daughters, Daan?"

"Yes, I do," Daan admitted. "But they died a long time ago."

"How old were they when they died?" Lucy was the curious one now.

"They were six," Daan stated sadly.

It was Phoebe who spoke now. "Daan, I am so very sorry."

"Well, then, you must pretend that we are your daughters for the next couple of days." Charlotte had made the decision.

Neither Phoebe nor Daan knew exactly what to say, right then. The room was empty of sound except for the breathing of the four of them.

"Well," Charlotte finally said, "what's it going to be?"

"Yeah," Lucy added with her hands on her hips, and Daan had to admit she looked just like her mother.

Phoebe and Daan looked at each other and decided they didn't have a choice.

"Well, I guess I have just gained two daughters for a few days," he smiled at them, "and a beautiful wife."

Both girls twirled about the room in their satin and tulle dresses, Charlotte in purple and Lucy in pink.

"I think the three of you look delightful," he addressed them as he opened the door. "Come, Ladies, we will be late if we don't hurry. We still need to pick up the tickets, and we have a couple of blocks to walk."

"Maybe I shouldn't have worn high heels," Phoebe stated.

"That's okay, Phoebe," Daan said and grinned. "If you can't make it, we will carry you, right girls?"

They walked towards the Opera House hand-in-hand. Daan wanted to make sure the girls were in the middle with him and Phoebe protecting them on either side. If they really had been a family, that's how he would have organized them.

As they approached, Daan was quite amazed at all the police presence but said nothing to Phoebe. He just smiled at her periodically and, she smiled back.

Chapter 35

Piers was circling around the Opera House. He strolled along the canal, stopped, crossed in front of the modern building, walked over to the street, and then looped back to the canal. He was paying attention to his surroundings, to those making their way to the opera, to anyone standing in place. The area was crawling with police, and that was because of Piers' warning. And there was only one reason for that and why he was here at the Opera House, to protect his best friend.

Piers had always admired Daan, who was three years older than he. Daan came to the police after graduating from Cambridge and the law school at Oxford in England, then passed the Bar in England and the Netherlands. Originally, Piers thought Daan stupid to have chosen police work rather than going right into the law. After being Daan's partner for a few months, Piers knew Daan loved his work as a policeman. Piers smiled as he had to admit that Daan's police work now made him an even better prosecutor.

As Piers made a third trip from canal to Opera House and back, he thought about how he had made it to where he was. He hadn't been a good student in school and had bummed around after he graduated with little purpose or direction. About six months later, he was accused of selling pot and had to disappear. A friend of his knew the owner of a freighter and so Piers became a ship's mate. He stayed with the ship for a few years, but the ocean wasn't for him. Then, he picked up a job in a warehouse on the docks of Rotterdam where he had gotten to know a couple of policemen who suggested he apply for the police force. He passed the entrance exam just barely, and he ended up being partnered with Daan, which was the best thing that ever happened to him.

Piers now leaned against the canal railing and lit a cigarette as he watched Daan and his make-believe family make their way from the hotel to the Opera House. Daan was in his tuxedo, and his ladies were very well dressed in nice evening clothes. Piers smiled as he remembered the two times Daan had him dressed up in a similar tuxedo which Piers called a penguin suit. But Daan looked dashing and the ladies, rather lovely.

Piers knew Daan lived in a different world than he. Not that Daan had been born with a silver spoon in his mouth. No, Daan wasn't part of that crowd, although he could have easily been. Daan's family had money, old money. Daan could trace his family back five hundred years in world shipping and banking. Piers only knew who his mother and grandmother were. He never knew his father. That distinction, and the fact that he was black, mattered to some, but not to Daan de Sylva. Daan had always treated Piers as an equal to the chagrin of many fellow officers. No, better than that. Daan treated Piers as family.

"Hello, old friend," Piers greeted Daan as they came up to him and then looked at Phoebe. "How are you doing, Phoebe?"

"I'm really good, Piers," she said confidently. "And you?"

"Great!" Piers responded, fake smile intact.

"What brings you around, Piers?" Daan asked but Piers just shook his head.

"Girls, this is Uncle Piers," Daan introduced them. "Piers, this is Lucy and Charlotte."

"Are you Daddy's brother?" Lucy asked.

Piers was pleased that the children were involved with the family pretense. But he was shocked that Lucy would think he and Daan were related. He was black and Daan was white. No one had ever asked if they were brothers. This time his smile was genuine.

"Piers is a dear friend," Daan explained. "We were on the police force together. He's a chief inspector now."

"Lovely to finally meet you, Charlotte and Lucy." Piers took each of their hands and shook them.

"Did Daddy tell you about us?" Lucy asked.

"He sure did," Piers said. "But he didn't tell me how beautiful the two of you are."

Daan looked at Phoebe very intently and she took the hint.

"Daan, why don't we go in and pick up our tickets," she said. "We'll see you inside." She turned to her daughters. "Girls."

Piers waited for the girls to go inside and then had Daan walk with him to the railing at the canal. "Daan, that was quite a showing."

"Well, didn't you say that we needed to make-believe we're a family? And, for just a few days, we are."

"Be careful, Daan," Piers warned. "Still trying to find out who's doing the watching."

"We don't know who or why yet?" Daan leaned on the stair railing.

"Looking into it, Daan." Piers took out a cigarette and lit it, facing the crowd. "That's all I could find out today."

"And the police presence?" Daan asked.

"I reported that one of my informants said there might be a terrorist attack on the Opera House tonight."

"They believed you?"

"Of course," Piers smiled as he focused on opera patrons submitting to the security search, which had become the norm these days. "I lie with conviction when I must. Besides that, I couldn't let you die right in front of me without trying to save you, you know."

Piers turned back around and patted Daan on the back. "So, be careful, old friend."

Daan took a deep breath and almost asked Piers for a cigarette. He hadn't smoked in almost twenty years, but he was beginning to feel the urge right now.

"Got your gun?"

"Of course."

"Don't use it unless you must," Piers advised. "You cannot be involved if someone tries something."

"They could take me down right here in front of God and everybody, if they wanted to."

"Too many trees and too many people. You know that they'll try to take you down in a dimly lit hall inside or in a dark alley on the way back to the hotel."

Daan knew Piers was right.

"And," Piers continued, "I'm afraid to say that they might want Phoebe as well."

"Phoebe?" Daan stood up. "What's this got to do with Phoebe?"

Piers shrugged his shoulders.

Daan had promised he would put up with the pretense of marriage to this woman only for a little while. But he needed to know if his relationship with her, even for a few hours, had put her and her girls in danger.

"Do we know why?"

"Not yet, which is why I called in the *cavalerie* (cavalry)."

"Okay."

"Listen, be on your toes tonight."

"I will."

"By the way, your make-believe family looks pretty real tonight."

"Make-believe for only a few days, though, Piers." Daan's voice was so quiet that Piers could hardly distinguish what he was saying.

"And, Phoebe," Piers whistled, "she looks amazing."

"I know."

Piers looked at his friend and smiled.

"My pretending to be her husband is only for a few days. No more!"

"Okay. So, you'll only be married to this woman another day or so. Think you can handle that, my friend?"

Daan didn't respond, but Piers didn't expect him to. Piers knew his friend and knew this woman seemed to be getting to him. Daan and Phoebe were good for each other, but he could sense Daan's hesitancy. So, as a true friend, he would keep reminding Daan he had to let her go on Sunday. In the meantime, he would do his best to give Daan as much time with Phoebe as he possibly could. Daan would figure things out while he watched Daan's back.

Piers motioned towards the Opera House. "Go on, join Phoebe and the girls."

"Thank you, Piers, for having my back."

"You're my friend," Piers acknowledged as he put out his cigarette under his foot. "Isn't that what I'm supposed to do?"

Piers walked with Daan into the Opera House to clear him through security. Daan would not have made it with that gun of his. Then, Piers watched him join his make-believe family at the bottom of the stairs. He decided Phoebe had more going for her than Francine ever did. He wouldn't want Francine by Daan's side tonight in this situation.

After they had disappeared from his view, Piers meandered back to where he and Daan had been standing. He looked around, watching. No one stood out so he lit another cigarette and blew smoke into the air making his way back towards the Opera House. It was hard to determine who was doing the watching now. Too many people and not everyone was formally dressed these days.

"Hey, Vogel."

Piers knew the uniformed policeman coming up to him. He hadn't seen Kris Brinker in a while.

"Brinker."

"Was that Daan de Sylva I saw you with?"

"Uh-huh."

"Didn't think he was with the police anymore."

Piers blew smoke in the air. "He's not."

Brinker was very blond with fair skin. Not that it had anything to do with Piers not trusting him. Piers just didn't get a good feeling around Brinker. Never had. Instinct? Maybe.

"What's he doing here?"

Piers started walking away from the Opera House and allowed Brinker to keep in step with him.

"Who?" Piers asked, knowing exactly to whom Brinker was referring.

"De Sylva, of course."

Piers followed the sidewalk past a large tree and moved towards the canal, taking another puff. "Oh, you want to know about de Sylva?"

"The two of you were talking, weren't you?" Brinker seemed too curious for Piers.

"We used to work together, remember?" Piers stopped at the railing and looked across the canal.

"I remember," Brinker responded and stood next to Piers.

Piers turned around from the water and leaned on the railing, watching the parade of people before them. He took another puff of his cigarette and waited for Brinker's next comment. He didn't need to wait for long.

"So, why is de Sylva here?"

Wait, Piers said to himself. Just wait. Take a little longer than needed before you answer.

Brinker was moving his weight from one foot to the other in a nervous manner. "Vogel?" Brinker's voice was sharp.

Piers finally answered without haste. "Who?"

"De Sylva!"

Impatient asshole, Piers thought as he took another puff. *This is why I still smoke so that I can watch and listen carefully while everyone thinks I'm concentrating on my cigarette when what I'm really doing is drawing out conversations and learning more in the process.*

"Oh," Piers slowly responded. "Why is de Sylva here tonight?"

"Ja," Brinker said with annoyance, almost before Piers had finished his last word.

"0Mmmm…"

Piers decided to draw this out as long as possible. So many questions from someone he hadn't seen in years. He didn't think Brinker worked for Ziebach, but it wouldn't surprise him. He always thought Brinker was on the take with someone but couldn't prove it.

"He's here for the performance, Brinker. Didn't you notice his tuxedo?"

Piers looked directly at this over curious policeman and felt there was more on Brinker's mind. All he had to do was wait a couple more seconds. Piers took another drag on his cigarette.

"He's undercover, right?"

Piers smiled to himself then glanced around and pretended not to hear Brinker's comment.

"I mean," Brinker continued, "it would be a good thing to have someone undercover inside with the terrorist's threat and all."

Piers knew Brinker was just fishing for more information on Daan. Piers was happy to oblige but Brinker would find out only what Piers wanted him to know. While Brinker was with Piers, he wasn't releasing information to anyone, nor was he inside spying on Daan.

"So, he's undercover, right?" Brinker was getting antsy, now.

Piers could be extremely patient but wasn't sure how long Brinker's patience would hold.

"Undercover? Who? De Sylva?"

"Well?"

"Nah." Piers took another drag on his cigarette. "He has tickets to the Opera." He blew smoke in Brinker's direction. "This is his wife's favorite opera, you know."

Brinker's face lit up with a smile. "So, he took his wife to the Opera?"

"Who?"

Piers then watched Brinker take off with his phone in hand. Piers grinned and meandered slowly back to where he and Daan had been standing earlier. Very few people were in line now, and he looked at his watch, confirming that the opera had just started.

Let's see what happens now.

Piers watched Brinker speak into his phone, trying to hide behind a tree on the west side of the building. Piers kept Brinker in his sight as he nonchalantly walked to the front of the Opera House and dropped his cigarette in the garbage can there.

Just what I thought but didn't expect it to be Brinker who was the mole.

Piers wasn't usually a chain smoker, except when he was watching. So, he walked a few steps and lit another cigarette while taking note that Brinker was hurrying down the side of the Opera House to the back. So, Piers followed him while carefully dropping his newly lit cigarette in another garbage can down the way.

That's two. Maybe I ought to do another one just to make it look good.

Then, he continued to walk around the Opera House.

Chapter 36

As he walked into the lobby, Daan tried not to be obvious as he surveyed the area. His concentration was focused on others as he approached Phoebe and the girls. His gaze continued to scan, but then he realized Phoebe was telling him something which she felt was important.

"Your tickets are for my group of seats? Why does that not surprise me?"

"But Daan, I didn't know. I just went to the 'D' window first because the line was shorter, and the lady gave me six tickets for de Sylva. Four had our names on them, and the other two just had 'de Sylva.' I never went to the "S" window."

"It's okay," he told her and placed his arm around her waist. "It's what I expected."

"Daan, I'm trying to…"

He now pulled her close to him and gave her a long kiss. He had to shut her up because anyone could be listening to them.

"Did I tell you how beautifully exquisite you look tonight, Sweetheart?" The endearment slipped out without thinking as he praised her aloud for anyone who was listening. The girls were in front of them and started giggling.

"And us, Daddy?" Lucy was milking it for all it was worth.

Daan laughed. "And my lovely daughters, too."

Daan looked around without being too obvious.

God only knows why you are following me, watching me. So, I'm going to give you a show.

He did not release Phoebe as he guided his new family up the stairs and down the hallway to last door on his left, which opened into the section where his box seats were. For Francine, he had made sure to purchase tickets for the box seats closest to the stage on the right side of the theater. Four for his family and two for his parents. They usually were together for the opera. Even now, he purchased those same six seats when he came to the opera. He just didn't want to share his memories with anyone while he was here. No one.

Usually, he had five empty seats to his left when he came to the opera unless he could coax Piers to join him or the few times he brought a date. Tonight? Tonight, he had no control of things.

This wasn't my plan but...

"These are great seats, Daan," Phoebe announced to him as he placed the two girls closest to the stage with Phoebe next to them. He sat beside her with the two empty seats on his other side. He almost expected Ziebach to suddenly show up to occupy at least one of those seats.

"Only the best for you, Phe. I pay good money for the best." His voice carried to the ones behind them. "You and the children are worth it." He was curious why he had shortened her name. It had just come out, but it seemed appropriate at the time. It was interesting that she didn't argue about it.

She smiled at him and decided she liked the nickname he gave her. No one had ever called her 'Phe.'

Then the lights began to flicker, indicating the

performance was about to begin. He reached over and turned to Phoebe, giving her a wink. He took her hand and brought it to his lips and kissed it. "For our watchers," he told her quietly as the lights began to dim.

The orchestra started the overture, and he glanced around at the audience as though he could tell which of those many faces were their watchers. He decided he and Phoebe had to continue playing their parts until he and Piers could figure out what was going on.

Daan searched his memory to see what he had done to warrant being under surveillance. He had made enemies while as a policeman, but doubted it was any of them. Only Ziebach stood out as his worst foe and was the only one vindictive enough for this.

He also didn't believe he had made enemies as a prosecutor. His job in the prosecutor's office in Rotterdam dealt with immigration. He had hoped to be assigned to the criminal section because of his police background and had been promised that, soon enough, he would be transferred. But, for now, he had to bide his time. Till then, he felt he had been relegated to a pitiful looking office down the hall from where he wanted to be.

Right now, he decided he would not be surprised if he suddenly felt the sting of a bullet in his chest or his head. He didn't think that would happen, but it was what it was.

Then, Daan smiled.

He had not believed in God for many years, so he said to the Fates in his head, *If I die tonight, don't you dare take this woman and her children. They aren't part of this, so don't take Phoebe and her daughters with me. They are family. Distant family but still family.*

I will stand alone in this, so take me only. Just tell me what deal I must make to guarantee their safety, and I will do it.

He placed his arm around Phoebe and, when she turned around, he smiled at her. Then, the curtain opened to the first act of Wagner's Opera.

Chapter 37

The first night at the opera was more fun than Phoebe had envisioned it might be. The audience was bedecked in both evening wear and jewels of all sorts as well as eclectic daywear. The theater had chandeliers sparkling from the ceiling with a festive atmosphere. Phoebe felt her family fit in quite well in this foreign city.

The stage was set for a modern-day depiction of Wagner's play, rather than the antiquated robes and furs of the past. Actors wore contemporary clothing and up-to-date weaponry with backdrop scenery of city buildings and the use of cars, not horses, quite different from the past versions she had seen. Very few beards of ancient times adorned the men, and there were no Viking headdresses or elk's horns. Great music. Great presentation. Great acting.

The evening had gone quite well and ended with Daan between the girls and her in Daan's original seat. Phoebe smiled as Daan lifted Lucy in his arms, allowing her to rest her head on his shoulder. She took Charlotte's hand, guiding her out of the auditorium behind Daan.

Daan asked, "Lucy, do you remember the questions we talked about?"

Lucy lifted her head. "Uh-uh. There was a king who wanted the gold that the mermaids were protecting." She yawned and placed her head back down.

"That's right," Daan said.

"The King's name was Wotan," Charlotte responded.

"There were giants," Lucy whispered without raising her head. "I remember the giants."

Daan laughed. "You're right, Lucy, there were giants. And yes, Charlotte, the king's name was Wotan."

"But I thought the king of the Norse gods was Odin."

Phoebe responded to Charlotte, "Odin was the king of the Norse gods. But Wagner intertwined several mythical stories together to create *The Ring Cycle*."

"What about the rings, Charlotte?" Daan asked.

"The gold in the Rhine was taken by that ugly guy Al something, who made it into a ring," Charlotte said. "Everyone wanted the ring and the gold."

"His name was Alberich."

"Wait." Charlotte stopped. "That's kinda like *Lord of the Rings*, isn't it?

"Some people say so," Phoebe stated.

Daan balanced Lucy to his other shoulder, then asked, "What happened in the end?"

Charlotte smiled. "I liked the end the best because all the gods go to Valhalla, and a rainbow appeared."

"Good job!" Daan said. "I thought you might have fallen asleep for a while."

"But only for a few minutes," Charlotte assured him.

As they walked through the Opera House entranceway, people commented on how the opera was so different. Some liked it, some didn't.

Phoebe had watched the girls with Daan. She hadn't thought about the fact they had not had a father figure in a long time. She had lost Dominic six months after Lucy was born and she had never known him. Charlotte was only three, and he was just a faded memory to her. Her own father had been there for a while, but both of her parents had died, first one and then the other several years ago.

Daan was sweet to put up with so much from her children tonight. He never left them alone, except during intermission when she had taken the girls to the bathroom. Then, he waited for them in the hallway. He laughed with them, just like a real father. Then, Phoebe stopped herself. He was a real father or had been. If the accident had not happened, his twins would be fourteen, the same age as Charlotte. She felt sad for him to have lost his family so many years ago.

It was almost 11:00 when the four of them returned to the suite.

"Can we go to sleep in our clothes?" Lucy asked groggily as Daan sat her on her bed.

"You don't want to mess up your beautiful dress, do you?" He hesitated while Lucy shook her head. "So, you need to take off your dress so your mother and I can put it in a laundry bag. That way Mr. Lars downstairs can arrange for them to be dry cleaned."

Lucy took a deep breath and fell back on the bed, "I'm too tired."

"Luce, come on. I'll help the two of you."

Charlotte sat on her bed and began taking off her shoes. "I'm fourteen, Mother. I can undress myself!"

Daan waved as he closed the door to their room. Soon they were in bed and Phoebe gave them both kisses. She turned off the lights, taking their dresses with her.

Later when Phoebe entered the sitting room, Daan was lying on the sofa watching the news with his head under his left arm on top of a pillow at one end and his feet propped up at the other. Phoebe was surprised to see a gun next to his right hand. Daan had discarded his jacket and vest on the opposite chair, his shoes on the floor next to him. His tie was undone, leaving open the two top buttons of his formal shirt.

"It was a wonderful evening, Daan," she told him as she picked up his things and sat on the chair, placing the dresses and his discarded items in her lap. She gently pushed her shoes off her feet, and they landed on the floor next to his. She wasn't sure whether to mention the gun or to just let it go. It had not crossed her mind that he would have one. But then, that would make sense if he were protecting them as well as himself.

At the sound of her voice, he responded without even looking her way, "The girls?"

"If they are not asleep now, they will be in just a couple of minutes."

"Good," he said without ceremony.

He sat up and placed the gun in his back as he reached over to pick up the remote from the coffee table. As he was turning off the television, she noticed what looked like the Opera House with police and fire people hurrying around.

"What happened at the Opera House tonight?" she inquired.

"We shouldn't talk in here," he whispered. "Let's move to the bedroom."

He picked up their shoes, and she followed him with her cache of clothes. Only the bedside lamp was on as he shut and locked the bedroom door behind them. He dropped their shoes on the floor in front of the dresser. She did the same with the things in her hands.

"Sit down for a minute and rest yourself."

He watched her cross the room and sit on the bed. Now, he opened his side of the closet and retrieved his metal box, then placed it on the dresser, taking out the key from his pocket and unlocking the box.

"Phe, someone started fires in some garbage receptacles outside the Opera House, but we were safe inside." He went through the ritual of taking his pistol from his back and placing it carefully in the box, then locking the box and returning it on the closet shelf. He unhooked the holster and dropped it on the dresser. "Piers told me about it as I was waiting for you and the girls during intermission." He turned to face her.

"Should we be worried?" she questioned. To his surprise, she wasn't upset, nor did she mention his gun.

"No. But, I must be honest with you, Phe. I haven't told you everything." He sat next to her on the bed and took her hands in his. "I should probably do that now. Piers thinks you can handle it."

Phoebe took a deep breath. "Tell me what is really going on, then."

Daan wasn't her favorite person, but she felt she could trust this man, this Devil as she had called him. She was getting to know him better with each passing moment she spent with him. But now, he was hesitant, and she didn't know why.

"Daan, tell me," she urged and pulled her hands from his. "I am not some shrinking violet that you must be careful with. I can handle whatever you need to tell me."

He still waited to speak, and she wanted to slap him. "Daan, tell me!"

"I should never have gotten you involved with this,"

he sounded like he was tormenting himself.

"You didn't start this," she stated emphatically. "It started at the airport with Captain Vanderburg."

"Some of it did start then. Piers confirmed someone is watching us." He waited for her to respond to that, but she said nothing. "We don't know the reason, but Piers is looking into it." Again, he waited, but she didn't scream or yell or anything he expected. It was like he could feel the wheels turning in her head.

Finally, she said, "Okay. So, the main questions we need to be asking are: Why are we under surveillance? Why does someone think we are married? And what do we do now?"

She astonished him with her logical responses. He was really expecting a completely different reaction. Francine would have been freaking out by now. But this woman seemed to be taking it all in stride.

He stood up because he was getting antsy trying to figure this out and moved towards the window.

"It could just be a booking oversight, but I don't think so. I didn't expect the hotel mix-up with you and the girls being moved to my suite. That was totally unexpected." He looked at her as he leaned against the wall next to the window. "Your opera tickets being assigned to my personal seats with your names on them was half-expected."

"So, you know who's doing this?"

"Piers and I are not sure what I have done to cause this. And we don't know where you come in."

"So, it looks like whoever is after you is after me as well. Is that what you are saying?"

"No. Just me," He lied and shrugged his shoulders.

"So, what did you do?" she asked as she tucked her

feet under her.

"A police officer makes enemies, that's for sure. And being a prosecutor has its problems as well. But I deal with immigration cases, not criminal ones."

"So, you were a policeman for how long?"

"More than fifteen years."

"And a prosecutor?"

"A little over five, now."

"Okay, so it looks like someone in your past is keeping you under surveillance in order to—what do they call it in the movies? —oh yeah, 'snub' you out."

"I think they call it 'rub' you out." He smiled to himself and looked out the window into the night.

"Whatever. So, someone wants you out of the way. I can see that."

Daan chuckled. "Well, thank you for the analysis."

"You know what I mean. I'm not trying to put you down."

"Okay."

She waited for a minute. "So, if you've been out of the law enforcement business for over five years, why is someone following you around now?"

"We don't have all the details, so we don't know for certain."

"But you and Piers are pretty sure it has something to do with your being a policeman, not a prosecutor."

He faced her. "That's logical."

"So, that explains you," she nodded and took a deep breath. "But, what about me? What about my girls? Where do we fit into this? And why must we pretend that we are married?"

Daan was slow to answer. "I don't know. The only commonality that we have found is that our names are so similar." He wrinkled up his forehead. "Being distant cousins couldn't influence this. I didn't know that until today."

She pondered at what had been said and then replied, "So, you think that this started when we boarded the plane in Salt Lake? That makes no sense."

"Perhaps," he said. "Perhaps not."

"Really? You have no definite answer?"

"I need to think this through." He left the window and walked to the door. "Want a vodka to think with me?"

"Sure," she said. She really didn't want any alcohol to drink right now, but she would share a glass with him.

A few minutes later, Daan brought back napkins, two glasses filled with ice and two small bottles of vodka from the mini fridge in the sitting room. He placed the glasses and bottles on the bedside table and opened one of the napkins to produce curled lemon rinds. He rubbed the rim of both glasses with the rinds, dropping them on the ice. Daan shared one bottle between them and handed her a glass as she sat cross-legged on the bed, facing him.

"What's this?" Phoebe asked, pointing to the lemon rind.

"You've never seen a lemon twist?" He laughed. "Lars always stocks these for me."

"Don't laugh," she said. "Drinking is not my thing."

"I think you'll like this."

"Since it's you, I'll taste," she commented and took a sip. "Okay, not so bad."

He took a large gulp and then another.

"Hey, let's not get carried away like last night."

"I'm fine."

Then, Daan began pacing back and forth in front of

her. As she took another sip of her drink, Phoebe had to admit it was a nice difference. She stifled a yawn, realizing it had been a long day and she needed sleep but, first, wanted to help him work this out.

Phoebe was the first to speak, "Daan, does it have anything to do with that guy, Zayback?"

"Ziebach," Daan corrected her. "Luther Ziebach."

"Okay, Ziebach," she adjusted her pronunciation.

"Something's nagging at me. It's like there's a piece of the puzzle staring me in the face, but I just can't figure it out."

"Take your time, Daan. Relax. Be patient. It'll come to you." She watched him go from one side of the room to the other. She decided another approach might be beneficial. "So, there is nothing you and Piers have on him here in Amsterdam or Rotterdam, right?"

"Nope." He nodded his head. "European police agencies have tried to take down his organization for years. He's wanted for drug trafficking, human smuggling, money laundering. You name it, and he's been involved with it."

"And?"

He stopped for a moment and glanced at her. "No one's been successful. Every time someone's close, witnesses and evidence disappear into thin air." He threw his left hand dramatically in the air. "Ziebach's like Teflon, nothing sticks."

"So, he can't want you for what you don't have on him here, right?"

Daan stopped again and pointed to her with the forefinger of his hand holding the glass, "Maybe. That's a good point." Then, he started pacing again. "I'm missing something."

"Okay, so it's not about anything here in your country," she was trying to be logical. "So, it started with Ziebach yesterday. I mean Tuesday." It was, after all, past midnight on Thursday morning.

Daan didn't respond to her but kept pacing back and forth for a few minutes. She took another sip of her vodka and waited patiently.

"No, it didn't start on Tuesday." He took another gulp and emptied his glass. "No, it started many years ago in San Francisco." Daan stopped at the bedside table and poured the rest of the vodka from the other bottle into his glass.

"Daan, you're going to wear a hole in the carpet," she cautioned him. "Slow down."

It was as though he didn't hear her as he picked up his pacing again with his glass. "It started years ago in San Francisco. An acquaintance, Roy Sanderson, was with the San Francisco Police. He and several of his colleagues saw Ziebach kill someone, and they arrested him for murder. I was with them and saw what happened but wasn't needed to testify. Ziebach was convicted and sent to prison."

She listened with interest but didn't say anything. She just let him talk.

"All was well and good for a while until his case came up for appeal. I didn't know that at the time. If I had, I would not have and taken my family to San Francisco on vacation."

Daan stopped for a moment as though reflecting on his memory.

Finally, "We were going to *The Ring Cycle,* my wife's favorite opera. I had planned everything. We were spending a couple of days in San Francisco and then going to Napa to visit her parents."

Daan took another gulp of his vodka. "We wouldn't have been there eight years ago except for me."

He looked at Phoebe and she felt he was waiting for her to say something, but she remained silent, pondering his story and searching her brain for a connection. She took a sip from her glass and then remembered something.

"Wasn't that when the San Francisco Opera was doing *The Ring Cycle* in four installments over the course of four consecutive weeks?"

He nodded.

"I was there that evening." She hesitated.

"What?"

"Yeah, I was there with my friend, Vanessa," she said, smiling. "You were there, in San Francisco, for the fourth evening? I can't believe it. We were in the same theater."

Daan guzzled the last of his vodka and sat down next to her, slamming the glass on the table, allowing the last of his ice to jump out from his glass and scatter around. "No, we weren't in the theater."

"Not in the theater?" she questioned.

Suddenly, Phoebe was struck with a memory.

"Oh my God," she whispered in disbelief.

Chapter 38

The caller looked at his watch. He was furious and losing his patience with the assassin.

Is it possible that you were paid by de Sylva to leave his family alone and report to me that the job was finished?

He reached for his phone. If Nick didn't answer, he would find someone else to finish the job Nick had been paid to do years ago. No middleman, this time. He was going to handle it himself.

After the de Sylvas were gone, he would put a hit out on Nick, no matter how much it cost.

Last time, Nick. If you don't answer, I'll know you lied to me, you son-of-a-bitch.

Chapter 39

Phoebe's realization that she and Daan were in San Francisco at the same time to see the same opera so many years ago was mind-boggling.

"Daan, you lost your family in San Francisco that night?"

Daan didn't respond.

"That was the night they were killed in a car accident, wasn't it?" She pulled her legs out from under her and moved over next to him.

Daan murmured, his voice so quiet she had to lean forward to hear him, "No, that was the night that someone set off a bomb under my policeman friend's car." Tears had begun to stream down his face. "I should have stopped it!" He banged his fist on the table, knocking over his glass and scattering what was left of the ice. "They shouldn't have been there. Ziebach wanted Roy and me, not them."

"That night?" Phoebe was dumbstruck.

She thought back. Charlotte and Lucy were with her parents in Las Vegas so she and Vanessa could see the last segment of Wagner's Opera. They heard the explosion from far away. That was the explosion that had killed his family. His wife and children. His police friend. It was a coincidence she had been just a few blocks away.

Now, she looked at Daan crying next to her.

"Oh, Daan, I'm so sorry." she enveloped him into her arms. She said nothing else but just murmured into his ear that it was okay, that she was there.

He must have cried for about twenty minutes. She decided he probably had not shown any emotion about the incident since it happened. That would sound like the Daan she was coming to know. He would be strong and brave for his family and decide it was his fault that it had happened. She kept holding him and rocking him. Her back was hurting in that position, but she didn't move except to rock back and forth and run her hands over his head and down his back, massaging him. All she could think about was what she would want someone to do for her if she were in the same situation.

Finally, his sobbing ceased, and he pulled himself away from her. She then got up and went to the bathroom for a towel. She wanted to dry his tears and let him know she understood. She had cried her eyes out for Dominic, but that hadn't helped her. Nothing had helped her, but time.

"I'm okay," he mumbled, interrupting her thoughts. "Don't worry about me." He took the towel and covered his face with it.

"Daan, I am so sorry. I am so very sorry."

"Damnit," he remarked as he pulled the towel away from his face and stood up abruptly. "I should not have told you anything about that." He left and walked into the bathroom.

"Tell me why what happened tonight has anything to do with what happened to your family eight years ago."

He washed his face, dried off, and then turned around, drying his hands with the towel.

"I thought I had that all out of my system," he stated matter-of-factly.

Daan was holding onto the towel as he looked at her. Leaning on the door frame, he couldn't believe he had exposed his emotions to this woman, who was slowly seeping into his life like a lovely summer afternoon or a pleasant musical sonata. He had to stop this now.

"Sometimes, it takes a while to let grief run its course," she admitted.

"Like you?" He did not want to focus on him anymore and crossed his arms.

"Me? What do you mean, like me?"

"You were crying this afternoon. Want to tell me why?"

"Oh, that. I had a migraine, and it really hurt."

"You said it was your allergies."

"A migraine and allergies."

"Right."

"No, really."

She told herself he had no right to ask her about her feelings.

"So, why haven't you declared your husband dead yet?"

"What business is it of yours whether I declare my husband dead or not? What's it to you?"

"He's never coming home to you, again, is he?" Daan uncrossed his arms and stood straight, dropping them to his side.

"Of course not!" she yelled at him. It was like he had just slapped her in the face. Why had she waited so long to go to court and have Dominic declared dead? Was it easier this way?

"Well, Francine is never coming home to me

either!" It was like the realization had unexpectedly hit him.

They said nothing to each other for a long time. They were both tired, and the last hour had taken a toll on the two of them.

Phoebe didn't realize she had begun to cry until she felt tears sting her cheeks. He handed her the towel, and she wiped them away. "So, what does this have to do with what is going on now?"

"Phe, you have no part in this," he said. "I shouldn't have told you about my family."

"Tell me what else is going on."

"Nothing."

"Sorry, I'm in this all the way now. I mean, after all, there must be a reason Piers has us pretending to be husband and wife."

Daan was frustrated because he knew that he was the reason she was involved. He and Piers would figure out what to do. He didn't want to put her in any more danger because of him.

"I'm sorry you're involved with this. I'll contact Piers, and he will assign a police guard to protect you and escort wherever you go each day. I'll leave you and the girls right here. I'll pick up the tab for the room and return home right now. Then, I'll…"

"Daan, are you crazy? You can't just walk away and expect me not to try to figure this out on my own." She stood in front of him and got into his face. "Someone has thrown us together and you think it has something to do with the murder of your family, don't you?"

He backed away from her, "You are not involved, Phoebe." Again, he walked over to the window, and looked out into the night. "I thought you were, but you're not."

"What do you mean?"

He seemed to be concentrating on the lights out the window when she came up to stand beside him. "I really did think you were a plant from Ziebach when you boarded my plane in Salt Lake City. Piers said it was just coincidence, but I don't believe in coincidence." He looked at her now.

Now, she smiled. "No wonder you've been acting so strangely. You thought I was one of them!"

He hesitated for an entire minute and backed away from the window. "Yes, I did."

"You are such a fool sometimes." It was her turn to lean against the wall. "When your plane landed in Salt Lake for that medical emergency, we were waiting for our plane to Amsterdam which was due out a little over an hour later. One of my former students was being kind and put the girls and me on that flight in first class."

"Your student?"

"Yes, my student. She works for the airlines and was one of the gate agents. Our flight was overbooked, so she placed us on your flight. Our luggage didn't arrive until our original flight landed and then was delivered here."

"So, it was just one of those things." He shook his head back and forth. "And now I have involved you in this mess that is my doing."

"You know, Daan, I have only known you for just two days, and I do believe you are paranoid."

"Paranoid? I don't think so. Right now, I must be on my toes to take care of you and your girls. I wouldn't worry so much if it were just me."

"My God, Daan," she pushed him, and he fell back a bit. "You lost your family, and you blame yourself for

215

allowing them to be killed."

She pushed him, and he stepped back again. "You believe that this coincidence that threw us together is really a way for this bad guy to get back at you."

And again, she pushed him while he backed up a bit more. "I bet you've been trying to get back at this guy all these years, haven't you?"

"I…"

She went on. "And another thing. Quit thinking of me as a fragile, delicate little female who needs your protection. I am quite capable of taking care of myself!" She pushed him again.

Daan just looked at her in disbelief. He had never allowed anyone to push him like she just did. But who was she to think she knew him?

"You've only known me for two days. How would you know what's going on in my head?"

"Well," she pushed him one more time, and he landed against the wall on the other side of the room, "you are not hard to read, Bozo!" She stood in front of him with her arms crossed. "I am just tired of your telling me you must do this or that to take care of my girls and me."

Now, he knew she was angry with him but, for the life of him, he really didn't know why. She waited for him to respond. When he didn't, she dropped her hands and sighed. She turned and started towards the bedroom door.

"Why are you so angry with me?" He followed her and grabbed her arm, turning her to face him.

"Because…because you…you are so annoying and…" She jerked away. "And I need you to leave!"

She went to open the door, but he shifted in front of

her. "Don't you understand that I don't want the same thing to happen to you?"

"Really?" She was furious. "I'm not your real wife, and this Ziebach guy will figure that out. Nothing is going to happen to me. So go away!"

"Don't you realize I'm just trying to protect you?"

"Well, I can take care of myself."

He just looked at her and finally said, "But you are in danger."

"Because of you."

Daan didn't know what to say. He had already exposed more of himself to this woman than to anyone since his wife and children had been killed. Why?

"You need to leave, now." She pointed to the door.

"I shouldn't," he divulged and was trying to figure out what to do next. All he wanted to do was take care of Phoebe and her daughters, like he promised.

"Go away," she said softly.

Daan was suddenly aware of her lavender scent engulfing his senses. He looked into her eyes and realized she wasn't angry anymore. Her eyes teared up. That unsettled him.

"Phoebe," he began.

"Please go, Daan," she whispered.

"Do you know you are frustrating the hell out of me?" he murmured and reached out for her.

"You confuse me, Daan." Her voice was almost inaudible.

"I just can't leave you right now, Phe," he told her and brushed the tears from her cheeks with the back of his hand. "You confuse me as well."

Then, he drew her to him in a passionate kiss. To his surprise, she returned his kiss with as much passion as he was giving.

"Are you okay with this?" he asked softly.

She looked up at him and smiled.

Daan had not felt this way in a long time, had not wanted someone as much as he wanted her now. He began kissing her mouth, her neck, moving slowly to her ear. "Woman, you make my blood boil, you know."

"You are the Devil who is doing the same to me."

"No one's ever called me Devil. Should I be concerned?"

"Only if you stop." She dropped his tie and pulled his shirt open, kissing his neck.

"Oh, good God, woman." He was making his way back to her lips. "What are you doing to me? I haven't felt this way in a long time!"

"What were you saying to me about lovemaking earlier? Remember, in the restaurant?"

He stopped kissing her and picked her up in his arms. "I told you that when I make love to a woman, she knows that she is being loved," he murmured in her ear as he carefully laid her on the bed.

"Show me," she whispered, and she began unbuttoning his shirt. "It's just been so long, Daan. Please be gentle."

"I'll be gentle, I promise."

He was in the process of kissing her shoulders and pulling her dress down her arms when there was knocking at the door.

"Mommy." It was Lucy. "Mommy, I had a bad dream."

They both pushed away from each other, and Phoebe caught her breath before she called to Lucy, "Hold on a moment, little love. I'll be right there."

"It must be serious," she muttered to him, "she called me, 'Mommy.'"

Daan kissed her nose and then rolled off the bed, making his way across the room. Phoebe waited until he was in the bathroom before she unlocked the bedroom door and opened it.

"Come here, Luce," she knelt in front of her youngest. "Let me take you back to bed, little one."

"Mommy, why are you still in your dress?"

After she had gotten Lucy back to sleep , Phoebe yawned as she returned to the bedroom. Daan was already asleep in the bed, and she pulled the covers over his shoulder.

This man, this Devil had bewitched her. He had stirred up feelings inside her that she had buried after Dominic was gone. She had been with no one since Dominic. And, as she backed away from Daan, she knew she would have given herself to him without a moment's hesitation if Lucy had not interrupted them.

Moving over to the dresser, Phoebe pulled out her nightgown from the drawer and went into the bathroom to prepare for bed. When she came out, she dropped her dress on the floor with the other evening outfits.

Daan was sleeping just as she had left him. Phoebe wanted so much to crawl into bed next to him and feel his arms around her, telling her everything was wonderful because she was with him.

Trying to be as quiet as possible, Phoebe went over to Daan, standing next to him and listening to his breathing. The idea of waking him crossed her mind, but the girls were in the next room. Otherwise, she would probably fall into bed with him and enjoy every second of his lovemaking. But not tonight.

Phoebe smiled and turned to walk away when she felt him reach out to take her hand.

"Where are you going, Lover?" he questioned in a hoarse whisper and pulled her down next to him.

She was surprised at the word of endearment he used for her. 'Lover'? No one had ever called her Lover. Was she really ready for that?

"I'm going to Lucy. She had a bad dream, remember?"

"Ah, a mother's job is never done." He lifted her fingers to his lips as he caressed them with his tongue. "Go, take care of her. However, know that I am here waiting for you so that I can finish what we started."

She smiled at him. "I can't," she confessed, "not with the girls in the next room."

He sat up next to her and took her face into his hands, "I know." He kissed her and murmured, "Let me hold you for a few minutes before you go."

He drew her into his arms, and they cuddled for just a little while. Then, she said, "I must go."

He kissed her one more time, then released her. "I really do understand. But soon, we will finish this, I promise."

She stood up and walked away without looking back, closing the door behind her.

Chapter 40

Nick stepped out of the shower and realized his shaving kit was vibrating. His phone had been hidden there for ten days. But he recognized the number as he picked it up.

"Yeah?"

He listened to the irate voice at the other end of the line for a minute.

"My phone's been off. I'm on vacation."

He pulled the phone away from his ear as the caller yelled at him.

"I am not at your beck and call every minute of every day." Nick matched the caller's tone of voice.

He was ready to hang up the phone but listened more intently to what was being said.

"I did that job years ago. I was at the funeral. I know what happened."

A moment passed.

"Don't you dare question my integrity. I did the job that I was paid for. You wanted four dead, and that happened. You were very specific. The Chief Inspector was to be left alive."

Nick listened.

"No, your information is wrong. They are dead!"

Listening again.

"This must be a new family, I tell you."

He was silent as he listened.

"Sure, I'll finish this new job for you. But it'll cost you double. I don't like being called a liar."

He waited again and then interrupted the caller.

"You want to get someone else, go ahead."

Nick was trying to be patient as he listened.

"Saturday, I'll be there Saturday."

A shorter wait this time.

"Yes, I'm that far away. On vacation, remember."

He received instructions this time.

"Fine, I'll call when I get there."

Nick touched the disconnect button and threw the phone across the room, where it hit the wall, shattering into pieces.

The schmuck was wrong. His information was wrong. Nick knew de Sylva's family and the police officer were dead because he had triggered the bomb when all four were in the car, and he had watched it explode. He had made no mistake then, before, or since.

Nick walked to the sliding glass door of his rental cottage at the end of the beach. Opening the door, he breathed in the delightful sea air. His ten-day vacation was the longest he had ever taken. Feeling relaxed and rejuvenated, he was ready for his next job, but he was not prepared for that phone call. Being angry didn't help anything.

Nick dressed quickly and took a walk on the beach and allowed the ocean waves to lap across his feet as he sauntered along the shoreline thinking back. No, over the years he had made one major mistake. Not with a contract, but with his own life. He was hiding when he met her and married her on a whim, allowing him to disappear comfortably into the population where no one could find him. But he left quickly when he realized how close he was getting to her.

When he got back into the game, into his true calling, he never went back. Regret? Certainly not! Leaving the past in the past was where it belonged.

Nick knew he was good at what he did because he was calm, meticulous, and painstakingly thorough. He never left witnesses until that job eight years ago. That time, he followed instructions and left the Chief Inspector alive. This time, de Sylva and his new family would be just a memory in a few days.

Nick thought about the challenge he had with this new job. The slimy, cold-hearted employer would be looking to get rid of him for good now. Nick knew his time as an assassin would eventually come to an end. He had enough money stashed away so he could disappear forever where no one would find him. So, this would be his last job and he was sure that the old bastard had put a hit out on him already. Nick needed to be more diligent than ever in watching his own back before he vanished.

Nick returned to the cottage, shutting the door behind him. Walking to the landline phone, he confidently and precisely organized his trip back to Europe. It was already Thursday afternoon for him, and it would take almost thirty-six hours to fly to Europe via New Zealand. He would be there as promised late Saturday afternoon. After all, Fiji was a long way from Amsterdam.

Nick was in a much better mood after confirming his trip. He reached down to pick up his sim card from the broken pieces of his phone lying on the tile floor and pocketed it. He was whistling when he left the cottage.

Tomorrow, he'd pick up a new cell at the airport in Auckland. Tonight, he had a date with a beautiful raven-haired British flight attendant he met at breakfast this morning. He preferred redheads, but this one would have to do tonight.

Chapter 41

When Daan came out of the bathroom on Thursday morning, he was dressed in shorts and a t-shirt for his run. However, he heard the television in the next room and children's laughter. He took a deep breath. It seemed that children never changed. No matter what time you put them to bed, they were up bright and early the next morning, raring to go. He deduced that Phoebe must still be asleep in their room because she had probably been up all night off and on with Lucy.

Change of plans.

He returned to the bathroom, took a quick shower, shaved, and dressed for a day of sightseeing.

He pushed their evening wear into two laundry bags and opened the door to the sitting room. He dropped the bags on the floor next to the door so they could take them downstairs on the way to breakfast. Then, he turned to view two auburn-haired young beauties wrapped in each other's arms on the sofa.

Ah, how much you look like your mother.

"What are you watching?" he questioned aloud as he walked over to them.

"Cartoons in Dutch," Charlotte responded. "It's for Lucy. I would much rather be reading a book or walking next to the canal."

Lucy cackled, and Daan smiled.

"How's your mother?"

"Fine, I guess." Charlotte was still paying attention to the television. "She's still sleeping."

"Maybe we should wake her up?"

"Why was she sleeping with Lucy?" Charlotte turned to look at him.

"Your sister had a bad dream, and your mother went to be with her."

"You know, I'm not a baby anymore."

"Quite right. You're fourteen now and growing up fast."

"I'll be fifteen next month."

"Good for you," he said.

"I see how you look at my mother, you know."

He eyed Charlotte with concern. He knew she was now trying to be much older than her years and felt Phoebe certainly had her hands full with this one.

"Really?" He leaned on the chair. "So, how do I look at her?"

"Like they do in the movies."

Lucy was laughing again and jumping up and down on the sofa.

"How's that?"

"Daan, you like my mother. I know you do. I see how you watch her, how you smile at her."

"We've only known each other for a few days, Charlotte."

"And?"

He was afraid of where this was going but he had to be patient and try to answer her questions without sounding surprised or condescending. He knew children could smell fear from adults, and right now he certainly feared giving the wrong answers to Phoebe's daughter. "I do like your mother."

Charlotte scrunched up her face. "You more than like her and I expected the two of you to, well, you know."

"Know what?"

"You love her, don't you?" Charlotte blurted out. "I can tell."

Daan was silent.

Last night, when he had pulled Phoebe into bed next to him, he was ready to spend the rest of the night in ecstasy with her. Feelings? No feelings. Just a wish to have Phoebe share his bed for a few minutes. No, more than a few minutes, if he were honest with himself.

How did this little twerp of a girl know how he was struggling about what to do concerning her mother? Love? Nah, not love. Definitely not love. He had loved only one woman in his life, Francine. He had to admit, though, Phoebe had pushed some buttons.

Let's just go with that, shall we?

"Your mother is a very fine woman, and I admire her very much."

"Poppycock!" Charlotte shouted, and Lucy turned around.

"Hush! I'm trying to figure out what's going on!"

Me, too. Daan was upset with himself.

"Poppycock? Do you even know what that means, young lady?"

"Nonsense," she lowered her voice. "It means nonsense or ridiculous."

"I haven't heard that word in years." He smiled as he remembered the original Dutch old-fashioned word, *pappekak*. His grandmother used the word every time she knew he wasn't telling her the truth. "Who says that anymore?"

"Mom. She uses it all the time, but I don't think she's said it here, yet. But we've only been here a couple of days."

"Okay, so tell me what's nonsense."

"I thought you'd spend the night with Mom last night."

"That's what you thought?" *Out of the mouths of babes.*

"You wanted to, didn't you?"

Now, he was not prepared to answer that question. At least not to the fourteen-year-old daughter of—ah? What should he call her? His friend? His make-believe wife? His would-be lover?

"Well?" her question lingered in the air like a lead balloon.

Then, he decided to be truthful with her—or at least as truthful as he felt he could be.

He took a deep breath and said softly, "Your mother is more than fine. She is beautiful and intelligent and caring. And the way she watches out for you girls is quite extraordinary."

"And?"

He stopped and narrowed his eyes at this very astute teenager, who was just like her mother. Then, continued, "I believe that one day I might find a way to get her alone with me so we can talk."

"Talk?"

"Maybe just the two of us could go out for coffee or something."

"Coffee?"

"A nice dinner, perhaps. We must start with dating, I think."

"Daan, she—" Charlotte was trying to find the

words and then stopped.

"She, what?" Daan leaned in, curious.

Charlotte stood up and motioned for him to follow her to the window, away from her sister. "I have never seen my mother so happy with anyone. She smiles with you and laughs with you. Her face lights up when you walk towards her."

"Interesting."

"She gets angry at you, I think, because she doesn't know what to do around you."

"Well, thank you for telling me."

"You know something else?"

"What?'

"You seemed so angry when we first met you," Charlotte told him.

"I was?"

"Yes, but now, you're kinda different."

"How?"

"You smile a lot around her."

"I do?" He was going to have to watch that, he decided.

"Daan, the two of you just need a little romance in your lives."

"You don't say." He tried not to laugh.

"You haven't loved anyone since your wife died, I'm sure. That was eight years ago, right?"

"Yes."

"I suppose you've had a few girlfriends because you're not married yet."

Who are you, some ancient adult know-it-all soothsayer stuffed in a teenage body?

"A few."

"Well, I can tell you that Mom hasn't loved anyone

since my father died when Lucy was a baby."

"So, now you think we need romance in our lives?" Daan laughed.

"Don't laugh at me!" she exclaimed and crossed her arms in front of her.

Just like her mother, Charlotte was a mini-Phoebe.

"Oh, no, Charlotte, I'm not laughing at you. I am just surprised you are so intuitive." He reached out and held her shoulders as he kissed her on the forehead, then he stood back from her.

"Just to let you know, I care a great deal about your mother, and I care about you and your sister as well." He stepped back a little further. "But I must take care of you first, and then we can discuss getting to know your mother better."

Charlotte smiled at him. "Don't take too long because we will be gone on Sunday. So, don't waste precious time." She walked to the sofa and climbed over its back, crawling into her former place with her arms about her sister.

"Oh, and by the way," Charlotte said, looking back at him. "Why don't you go wake her up." She turned towards the television as Lucy cackled out again.

Daan stood for a moment by the window without moving, debating what to do now. This child was certainly acting like she was much older than fourteen. The girls were laughing at the television screen as he opened their bedroom door and closed it behind him.

Ah, Phoebe, if you only knew what your little ones were planning for us.

And there she was, lying in Lucy's bed on the other side of the room next to the window. He walked over and stood at the end of the bed, observing that she was snuggled down under the covers. Through the open curtains, the morning light was streaming in on Phoebe's face that was half-hidden by that luscious hair of hers. He wanted to pull back those soft curls and snuggle up next to her to wake her up with his kisses. Oh, how he wanted to do that. But her girls were in the next room, and he just couldn't.

Patience. I must have patience.

Without waiting any longer, Daan sat next to her on the bed. There was something about this woman that had him lusting after her despite himself. This beautiful angel of a woman. Maybe, this evening after the Opera, they might have a few minutes together. He smiled at the thought of spending the night with her. Although, it was funny how he understood her hesitation with the girls nearby.

Daan gently pulled the curls from her lovely face and kissed her forehead.

"What?" Phoebe started to question as she opened her eyes. Then, she saw him and smiled. "What was that all about?"

"Woman, it's time to wake up," he whispered, and kissed her nose. "We have a big day planned and it doesn't include sleeping until noon."

"Oh my gosh, it's noon? Already?"

"Not yet, Lover. If only we could spend the morning in bed together until noon." He reached down and kissed her lips, making his way to her ear. "If only."

There was a knock on the door.

He quickly jumped up and whispered, "And, again, another invasion from the little ones."

Phoebe smiled and said aloud, "Yes?"

Lucy came bouncing in the room before Charlotte

could stop her.

"Is she awake yet, Daddy?"

"Yes, I am awake," Phoebe sat up and pulled the covers up to her neck while Daan walked to the door.

"Good, the cartoon is over, and I'm hungry."

Phoebe laughed and announced. "Well, then, I guess I might as well take a shower and get dressed."

"Sounds like a good idea," Daan remarked as she passed him.

He followed her as she walked across the sitting room. "Need some help washing your back?" His whisper was only loud enough for her to hear.

"You Devil, that might start something," she said as she slowly began to close the door to the bedroom. Then she peeked out from the door. "See you downstairs for breakfast?"

He nodded as she shut the door.

Chapter 42

Daan took a deep breath as he turned to Charlotte and Lucy.

"Come on, girls," he said. "We have an errand to run, and then it's to breakfast for the three Bozos."

They marched out the door with bags in hand.

"What are these?" Lucy asked, struggling with her bag.

"These are our evening wear from last night," he pushed the elevator button. "You have our shoes, and Charlotte has all the dresses. I have my tuxedo and shirt here."

"And where are we taking them?"

"We're going to drop them off to Mr. Lars at the front desk. That way, he will make sure that everything is cleaned for tonight."

"Charlotte and I have another dress for tonight," Lucy said rationally. "Mine is yellow, and Charlotte's is royal blue."

"I only have one tuxedo outfit," Daan told the two of them as they walked out of the elevator on the main floor.

Charlotte smiled. "We only have two dresses each for the opera because Mom wanted us to pack light."

"Did you like Mom's dress?" Lucy suddenly asked but before Daan could answer she continued, "I thought she was the most beautiful lady at the Opera last night."

"Hello, Ty," Daan said to the kid behind the desk.

"Hello, Lucy. Hello, Charlotte," Ty said sweetly to the girls. "Do you want me to show you around Amsterdam while your parents do other things? There's a lot of stuff I can show you."

Suddenly, Daan felt a tinge of jealousy, or was it fatherly concern. What does Ty think he's doing? He was being overly charming and smooth talking to the two girls, his girls who were standing right here next to him.

"Excuse me."

Ty's eyes were focused on Charlotte. Daan slipped into Dutch to attract Ty's attention which wasn't working.

"Ty!" Daan said as he slammed his hand on the counter.

"Sorry, Mr. de Sylva," Ty jerked his head towards Daan. "Did you want something?"

Of course, I do, idiot! I want you to lay off Charlotte and Lucy. Especially Charlotte. They are with me.

"Would you get Lars for me?"

"I'm sure I can help you, sir."

"No, I need Lars," Daan was quite firm. "Now!"

Ty left the desk and went into the office beyond, and Lars appeared immediately. He sent Ty into the office and focused on Daan.

"How may I help you, Mr. de Sylva?"

"Hello, Mr. Lars," Lucy said.

Lars came out from behind the desk to shake her hand.

"It's good to meet you, Miss Lucy," Lars shook Lucy's hand and then Charlotte's. "And you as well, Miss Charlotte. Are you having a fun time here in Amsterdam?"

"Yep, but I don't think I liked the opera last night," Lucy was quite vocal about the evening before. "It was very long, and I was bored. But Daddy helped me with the German. There was a king and even giants!"

Lars gave a side glance to Daan, then moved back to Lucy.

"The opera is quite long, and I can understand why you were bored," Lars told her.

Lucy crinkled up her face.

Lars smiled. "Wagner is not my favorite musician."

"Mine either," Lucy said. "I like the Jonas Brothers."

"I prefer the Beatles and Boys II Men," Charlotte stated. "I am a more traditional girl."

"You have excellent taste, ladies," Lars remarked. Then, noticing the laundry bags on the floor next to the girls, he lifted them up.

"You will need these for tonight, yes?" Lars asked Daan.

"Please."

As he reached for Daan's bag, he said in a low voice, "You have friends in the lobby, I think."

"Not friends of mine."

"That's what I thought. I'll keep watch, don't you worry, sir."

Daan watched as Ty returned and asked, "When will they be ready?"

"They will be in your suite by 4:00 this afternoon, sir." Lars handed the bags to Ty and motioned him away.

"We appreciate your help."

"Ladies," Lars addressed the girls, "I thought you looked rather smashing when you left last evening with your parents."

"Thank you, Mr. Lars," Charlotte said and smiled.

Lucy waved as the three of them headed across the lobby.

"Daddy," Lucy asked as she placed her hand in Daan's, "what does 'smashing' mean."

Charlotte spoke up, "It means that we were beautiful, Luce."

"Then, why didn't he say beautiful?" Lucy asked innocently.

Daan beamed. "Because there is more than one way to say that someone is beautiful."

"Oh," Lucy said.

They walked into the restaurant and ordered the buffet breakfast. As Daan walked the girls down the steam tables and helped them select what they wanted, he casually glanced at the two Fiat guys in the lobby.

Chapter 43

Upstairs, Phoebe had taken her shower and had just finished dressing when the phone rang on the bedside table. She figured it was Daan telling her to hurry, so she almost didn't answer.

"Hold your horses. I'll be right down," she said into the receiver, expecting to hear Daan's voice.

"Phoebe, it's Piers Vogel. I need you to give a message to Daan."

"Why don't you join us for breakfast?"

"Phoebe," his voice was stern. "You must tell Daan to take a walk west behind the hotel. I need to talk with him, but I need the Fiat guys to pay attention to you, not him."

"They're here?"

"Yes, but don't worry. I've got your back."

"Piers, you know I trust you only because Daan trusts you, right?"

"Of course."

"And, if I ever find out that you have betrayed him in any way, I'll cut your heart out."

"I have no doubt."

"Now that we have everything straight, I'll give him the message."

"Thank you, Phoebe."

She hung up the phone and headed down to the lobby with her bag and Daan's camera. If they were going out together today, they needed to continue the guise of being a family on vacation.

Chapter 44

From his hiding spot along the canal railing, Piers watched Phoebe enter the hotel lobby and head towards the restaurant. She would deliver the message and Daan would join him in a few minutes, so he crossed the bridge, passing the hotel on the other side of the canal and heading west. He took the last puff of his cigarette and smashed it under his shoe in the concrete while he waited behind the hotel.

Phoebe's threat was not a surprise to him. He knew Daan and Phoebe were getting to know each other better. He heard it in Daan's voice when they talked about her. He could see it in her eyes as she interacted with him. Fate had brought the two of them together and Piers depended on Fate to help him take care of them.

Piers was smiling as he watched Daan leave the hotel from its rear entrance wearing those spiffy sunglasses of his.

"Hey, old friend," Piers greeted Daan as he lit another cigarette and walked west, away from the hotel.

"Phoebe asked me if I remembered the old friend I met last night on the west side."

"She's good, that pretend wife of yours. Gave the message, and the girls understood nothing."

Daan looked at his friend's troubled face. "What's wrong?"

"The Fiat guys didn't follow you?"

"No, I slipped out the back, through the kitchen."

"Well, then, we'd better hurry before they miss you."

Piers walked along the road rather than the canal. They had more privacy here.

"What's going on?"

"It's Ziebach who is having you followed."

"Not surprised," Daan admitted.

"No, you don't understand everything," Piers was explaining. "I found out the fool believes Phoebe is Francine, and the girls are Anya and Ilsa."

Daan stopped mid-stride. "That's it," he told Piers. "That's what I was missing. I don't believe it but that's why everything has been so quirky. That's the comparison. Francine and Phoebe. Anya and Ilsa, and Charlotte and Lucy." Daan grabbed Piers' arm. "But there's just no comparison. How has he gotten them mixed up? I don't understand."

"Keep walking, Daan. If someone is watching, we don't want to let them know."

"Everything does make sense now, and you were right." Daan reached over and took Piers' cigarette from him, taking a puff.

"Right about what?"

"It was a coincidence that Phoebe was on my plane and that she has a similar last name," Daan began to laugh. "Well, the joke's on Ziebach. He did kill my family eight years ago, and now he is grabbing at straws."

Piers lowered his voice, "Daan, he thinks his guys screwed up in San Francisco and that you have been hiding your family for all these years."

"Talking about paranoid," Daan shook his head.

"So, he believes I have waited eight years to bring my family home." He took another draw from Piers' cigarette then handed it back.

"Nah, you finish it." Piers pulled out another cigarette and lit it up, breathing the nicotine deep into his lungs.

They kept walking another few steps, then Daan stopped. "I don't get it. They look nothing alike. Francine and the twins were blonde. Phoebe and her girls have auburn hair. My girls were twins, Phoebe's are obviously not. Francine was taller than Phoebe. It makes no sense."

"Don't stop, Daan." Piers took his arm and pulled him forward. "I found out he is planning something to make you understand that he is serious."

"What does that mean?" Daan said.

"He wants to do something to hurt you. It's more than Phoebe and the girls. It's something else that I haven't found out yet."

"He's going to try to hurt Phoebe and the girls, Piers," Daan hissed. "I can't allow that.

"I know."

They meandered around to the back of the hotel so Daan could return to the restaurant.

"So, your plans today?" Piers questioned.

"We are on vacation, so we're taking the riverboat cruise."

"Why doesn't Uncle Piers join the family today?"

"You think I can't protect my family?" Daan hesitated and then continued, "I mean, Phoebe and the girls?"

"Daan, you're a fool. Don't you know this woman has fallen in love with you?"

"No, she hasn't. It's only been a couple of days."

"*Godverdomme*, man," Piers took another puff on his cigarette. "She just threatened to cut my heart out if I betrayed you!"

"You're kidding."

Piers shook his head, "So, there is no way you are going to go traipsing around Amsterdam on a river cruise because both of us are needed."

"Phe said that? I don't believe it."

"Well, believe it. So, off you go now, and I'll meet you at the boat landing." Piers looked at his watch, "Let's say twenty minutes."

Daan smiled. "She said she'd cut out your heart? Really?"

"Really," Piers confirmed. "So, I must be sure nothing happens to you because I'd like my heart to stay right where it is, thank you very much!"

Daan was walking away when Piers called him back.

"Daan, I have only two best friends, and you are one of them."

"I know, me and the kid you grew up with, Buddy."

"I'm telling you if you screw this up with Phoebe, I will never forgive you! She is your Helen of Troy, and you are her Paris, mind you."

Daan watch Piers walk away.

"She's my what? And why are we going to Paris?"

Chapter 45

Daan stood for a minute as he watched Piers disappear, then he shook his head and made his way back into the restaurant, sunglasses in hand.

"Are we ready to go?" he asked Phoebe and the girls. He picked up his camera from Phoebe and put on his sunglasses.

"I like your funny glasses, Daddy," Lucy said.

Then, Charlotte asked Phoebe, "Where are we going today?"

Phoebe smiled at her daughters. "We are taking a riverboat cruise and having lunch somewhere special, right?"

"That's right, so let's go!" Daan confirmed.

Daan placed the girls between him and Phoebe and led them along the canal towards the boat landing to pick up the cruise. As they walked, he pointed out several churches and museums, taking a few pictures along the way. Then they came up on a long line of people extending down the street and around a corner.

"Phoebe, this is the line of those with tickets to get into the Anne Frank House," Daan explained.

"That's a long line, Mom," Lucy said.

"And they all have tickets?" Charlotte asked.

"Yes," Daan said.

They crossed the canal and asked a policeman to take a picture of them with the Anne Frank House behind them. Daan took more pictures because he felt it was important to give the watchers a show.

As they approached the boat dock, the girls screeched, "Uncle Piers!" And took off running towards him.

Piers had already bought the tickets for a covered boat and sat between the girls on a padded bench at the bow, allowing Daan and Phoebe to sit together on a similar bench behind them under the covering. What surprised Phoebe was how noisy it was with various boats going to and from on the water, the cars traveling along the roads next to the canals, and people talking both in the boat and bustling along the canal way.

"So, what did Piers find out?" she asked.

He decided not to discuss anything with her yet. "Tell me about your teaching."

"Why?"

"I just want to know."

"Truly?"

"Uh-huh."

"I've always wanted to be a history and geography teacher so I could share knowledge. It was good practice to investigate historical data first-hand to present in class."

"I agree," he said smiling.

She looked at him intently.

"Continue."

"Well, pictures taken by me have always been received better than the pictures in books or on the Internet. I speak of first-hand experience with my slides of the United States and Australia. When we discuss American history, I show slides of battlefields and historical buildings taken by me or my parents. When discussing the famous Australian red Ayers Rock, Uluru is its ancient name, I have students who could not fathom how in the middle of nowhere there was this large red sandstone formation with only the flat outback surrounding it. In teaching the history of Egypt, Greece, and Rome, I enhance my lectures with my parents' slides from those places."

He was mesmerized by her passion for teaching as he listened. Her eyes lit up and her entire body swayed as she discussed how she taught about Europe and Asia during World War II and the current day, as well as the part the U.S. played and continues to play on the world stage.

"What about Wagner?" he asked.

"Wagner?"

"Why are you so enthralled with Wagner?"

"He just changed music."

"How?" was Daan's question.

She explained she was not a music professor by any means, but she felt music was a way to introduce subjects in another medium.

Discussing Richard Wagner and *The Ring Cycle* helped her describe the condition of the world in the mid-1800s. Italian opera tradition was to allow time after each aria for the audience to applaud their enjoyment. Wagner threw this tradition to the side and composed his music to move in a more continuous nature, so the composition flowed with the action, never stopping to allow the audience to breathe nor applaud until the end of the opera when the curtain fell. She told him Wagner was not her favorite opera composer. Verdi was. But Wagner did change opera and modern music.

Phoebe explained how she introduced her students

to other composers using Wagner's ideas. For example, John Williams for the *Star Wars* movies had created a distinctive theme for The Force, Darth Vader, and even Luke Skywalker. This was from Wagner. Then she would hit her students with how Wagner's *Ride of the Valkyries* was used in today's movies. Next, she would let them know *The Lord of the Rings* was taken from Wagner's *The Ring Cycle*.

To him, it sounded like she truly enjoyed hooking her students into her subject.

"I hope that the next time they see a movie, they will consider what they learned in my class. If this is the only thing my students remember, then so be it!"

She was in her element.

"Why put so much effort in teaching?"

She waited to answer and then said, "Daan, a college friend once told me he didn't understand my love of history. He slept through history class because he didn't like studying dead people and dead civilizations that made no difference anymore. So, it became my mission as a teacher to make those dead people and dead civilizations come to life for my students." She took a deep breath. "It's my job to figure out what will inspire a student to feel some excitement of being a part of history."

"Wow, such dedication from a teacher," he said admiringly. "However, I seem to remember someone saying that—how does it go—those who can, do; those who cannot, teach."

She sat up straight. "Bozo, that's from a play by George Bernard Shaw. I don't like him because of that. If I didn't know what to do, I couldn't teach!"

He laughed. "I love your eyes when you get angry."

"You are the Devil."

He laughed. "Come here and let me hold you. We have a show to put on." He pulled her to him, and she leaned into his shoulder. They were still for a few minutes watching the scenery slip by.

Then, he whispered in her ear, "It's Ziebach watching us, by the way. It looks like he is pulling the strings."

She tried not to look upset. "And?"

"Ah, Lover," he murmured and pulled her closer, "it looks like we are in this for the long haul." He didn't want to alarm her that Ziebach believed her and her daughters to be his deceased family. Not yet anyway. "We don't know everything, yet. So, we just need to be observant and pretend that we don't see."

"What do I do?"

"Well, the Fiat guys and probably others are following and watching," Daan told her. "You must smile and pretend you're enjoying yourself."

She started to say something, but he interrupted her.

"I promised you this is only for a few days, right?"

"True."

"I'm here to protect you, and Piers is here to help."

Lucy was suddenly next to them, hollering, "Look at all those crooked houses! They look so funny."

"I see, my little love," Phoebe pulled herself away from him. Then Lucy returned to Uncle Piers who pointed out Amsterdam's Floating Flower Market.

A few minutes later, Piers called out, "Daan, here comes the Magere Brug."

"What's that?" Phoebe asked.

"It's the Skinny Bridge," Daan said.

Piers laughed. "It's the Lover's bridge. They say a

kiss between two people under the bridge will insure forever love."

"Kiss Mom, Daddy," Lucy shouted.

Everyone on the boat began to call out, "Kiss her!"

Daan whispered in her ear, "It's just a legend. And doesn't really mean anything." Then he gave her a kiss as everyone on the boat clapped.

Phoebe's cheeks were red as they separated, he noticed.

They had taken one of the small, enclosed tour boats with room for only twelve. Either end was open, but it was mostly covered with plexiglass so passengers could see out and be protected from the elements. When they stopped at a boarding ramp, two couples left and the captain helped a family of four and an elderly couple into the boat, guiding them to seats.

The boat pulled into the canal again. Daan watched his little group for several minutes, smiling at those around him.

Then, something alerted his inner radar. Piers turned around as well. They sensed something, the two of them. Daan gently nudged Phoebe, but she had seen them tense up as they detected impending danger. Daan pulled the girls away from the bow of the boat and gently pushed them towards her.

"I want to see the crooked houses!" Lucy said with impatience.

"Luce let's order a drink. What do you want?" Phoebe moved to a table opposite them and picked up the colorful menu. "I think they have ice cream."

Charlotte loved ice cream. "Mom, may I have a scoop of vanilla and a scoop of chocolate?"

"Me too," Lucy cried.

Phoebe ordered from the waiter. She watched as the two men took up positions to protect them without anyone else noticing. A few minutes later, the girls were handed their ice creams and Phoebe took the five bottles of water. The waiter then moved away to other passengers.

Phoebe felt uneasy as Piers looked out one side of the boat while Daan concentrated on the other. Boats were passing back and forth in the open water, and then their boat moved down another canal.

She knew something was wrong but what?

Chapter 46

Phoebe was alert as she watched Daan and Piers surveying the area around them. To others, their little party looked like a happy family on vacation with hungry children. But something was wrong, and her job was to distract the girls. Her heart was beating faster than usual, but she felt safe with these two men.

She kept the girls jabbering about this and that so they wouldn't pay attention to Daan or Piers. Lucy, as usual, was hungry so looking at tourist brochures to find a good restaurant where they could have lunch after their cruise was how Phoebe drew the attention of both girls.

The boat now traveled down a different canal, where they went under several bridges. Phoebe now had her daughters counting bridges and towers. She laughed with them but watched the faces of Daan and Piers as they searched people on either side of the canal.

As the boat pulled up to a dock where the elderly couple disembarked and three more were getting ready to board, Daan suddenly picked up Lucy in his arms, heading for the gangway. Phoebe snatched Daan's jacket and grabbed Charlotte's hand, and they rushed from the boat with Piers bringing up the rear. Nothing had been said, only actions. Their group of five left the dock quickly and made their way down a side street into a residential neighborhood.

"Daddy," Lucy was saying. "I wasn't finished with

my ice cream."

Daan turned the corner of a building and came to a stop in front of at home with a decorative bright green door. He placed Lucy down on the door stoop.

"I'm sorry, Lucy but I thought you would want to see one of the crooked houses up close."

Daan directed Phoebe to move around him and she was followed by Piers and Charlotte.

"Look, Luce," Phoebe said. "This is one of the houses we saw from the canal. Over there is one with a red roof."

Piers asked, "Do you see the yellow one in the distance?"

Charlotte smiled. "I see the pink one we just passed, Luce. And there's a second pink one over there."

Suddenly, Daan jumped and clutched his left upper arm. He then darted towards them, standing in front of Phoebe. He asked Phoebe for his jacket, and he put it on as he fixed his eyes firmly on Piers.

In an instant, Piers pushed Charlotte closer to Phoebe, and both sat next to Lucy. She busied the girls with pointing out houses across the way. She then heard Daan and Piers speaking in Dutch, and Piers left them in a hurry.

Charlotte whispered, "Mom, what's going on?"

"We're playing a game, Charlotte. Just a game, little love."

"It's a game of who can find the most different colored houses," Daan said, leaning against the wall and giving a quick smile to Phoebe. Then to the girls, "Did you see the bright blue one?"

"Daddy, I saw that one before you did."

"You certainly did, Luce," Daan agreed with her.

"Charlotte, which one did you see first?"

"The red one."

"What color is the door of the blue one, Luce," Phoebe asked.

She kept the girls talking while she watched Daan's eyes darting back and forth, scanning the area. He looked around the corner of the building he was leaning on, and his furrowed forehead concerned her. He looked past her, and she felt he was a bit pale, but she said nothing.

A few minutes later, Piers pulled up in a small gray Mercedes. Daan opened the back door and the girls piled in. He leaped into the front passenger seat and Piers peeled off around the corner and out into traffic.

"Mom?" Charlotte asked.

"Don't worry, we're fine, little love," Phoebe said, patting Charlotte's hand.

Lucy began complaining that she wanted to be back on the boat because she had more room. Phoebe explained they were sight-seeing a new way now. Yesterday, they had walked. This morning they had started with a boat, now they had a car. Wasn't this fun? Again, she kept them talking about the houses, the boats on the canal, the bridge they had just crossed, and the bus they had just pulled up next to.

Daan and Piers were speaking Dutch in the front seat, so Phoebe had no idea what was going on. When they passed the bus, Piers pulled up two streets and parked the car in a driveway.

Daan turned around and looked at Phoebe. "Okay, ladies, we're taking a bus ride now."

"Why?" Lucy was complaining again.

"Come on, Luce," Phoebe encouraged Lucy out of the car. "We heard you when you said there was not enough room in the car, so now we're taking the bus."

Daan picked up Lucy and walked back to the bus stop just as the bus pulled up. Piers boarded the bus first to pay the fare, followed by Phoebe and Charlotte, then Daan and Lucy. Piers guided them to the back of the bus.

At Lucy's predictable question, Daan answered, "So, you can bounce on the bumps."

When Phoebe sat next to him on the aisle seat, he placed Lucy between them. Piers sat next to the window with Charlotte next to him across from Phoebe. Charlotte looked at her mother with concern, but Phoebe smiled at her reassuringly. Then she pointed out a statue and kept the girls talking about the scenery while the men watched their surroundings. Each time the bus stopped, Daan and Piers analyzed each passenger who boarded. Phoebe tried to have the girls speaking loudly so no one would come back to them.

They had been on the bus almost thirty minutes when Daan said, "This is our stop."

When the bus jerked to a halt, Phoebe took Charlotte's hand, and together they exited through the rear doors with Daan carrying Lucy and Piers last.

"Follow Uncle Piers, ladies," Daan directed as Piers sped past them to take the lead.

"Are we playing Follow the Leader, Daddy?" Lucy asked.

"Yes, Lucy, and Uncle Piers is the leader."

"I like this game, Daddy."

Chapter 47

Piers turned at the end of the block and crossed the street to a police station.

Inside, the large sergeant, who looked like a grizzly bear to Phoebe, came out from behind the desk and greeted them in Dutch, but the only words Phoebe understood were "Vogel! De Sylva!" He gave Piers a 'bear' hug and slapped Daan on the back. They spoke for a couple of minutes. Then, Daan introduced them, "Sergeant Smit, this is my wife, Phoebe, and Charlotte and little Lucy."

Lucy smiled. "My name is Lucy, but you can call me Luce."

"Hello, Miss Luce, Miss Charlotte, Mrs. de Sylva."

He turned back to the desk and shouted orders. Again, since he was speaking Dutch, Phoebe had no idea what was said.

Then, Daan told Phoebe, "Follow the Sergeant."

"Are we okay now, Mom?" Charlotte asked.

Daan responded, "Yes, Charlotte, we are just fine."

The sergeant showed them into what Phoebe assumed was an interrogation room. There was a table in the center with several chairs lined up along the wall. She noted these chairs were padded, unlike the chairs in that airport security room.

Daan sat Lucy in a chair and directed Charlotte to sit next to her. "Phe, sit here next to the door. We'll be right back." He gave her a reassuring smile.

"Daan?"

"It's okay, don't worry." He took her hand and squeezed it. "You're safe here."

Piers started down the hall, and Daan waved at the three of them before he disappeared after his friend. A minute later, the sergeant was back with treats for the girls.

"Miss Luce, Miss Charlotte," he said as he passed them cookies and cold drinks.

The girls chorused, "Thank you."

Then, he looked at Phoebe, "Coffee?"

"That would be fabulous."

Sergeant Smit disappeared, returning with a cup of steaming brew. "Not American coffee," he said.

"Sometimes, American coffee isn't very good," she admitted and took a sip, welcoming the warm liquid in her throat. "Thanks."

"I'm down the hall if you need me," he said to her. "They'll be back in a few minutes."

Sergeant Smit walked out and then turned to her before he shut the door, "So, you got de Sylva to the altar. That's great!" He shook his head and smiled. "That's really great," he repeated as he shut the door.

"Mom, why are we in a police station?" Charlotte asked after she took a taste of soda.

"Well," Phoebe was curious herself but addressed her daughters with a thoughtful explanation. "I think, it's because Daan and Piers wanted you to see how the police work here. You know, yesterday we toured Dam Square and this morning we took the river cruise, a car ride, and then rode the bus. We are seeing Amsterdam in different ways."

"I like the big policeman," Lucy was saying. "He's funny, and he gave us cookies."

"He sure did, little love," Phoebe agreed.

The sergeant came back with a deck of cards. "It's going to be a bit longer, Mrs. de Sylva, so I brought you something to entertain your girls."

"Thank you, Sergeant Smit," Phoebe replied. "Girls, what do you say to the sergeant?"

They replied in unison, "Thank you, Sergeant."

He smiled and then waved before he shut the door.

"Let's play, Go Fish," Charlotte said.

"Okay," Lucy agreed. "I want to be first."

Charlotte shuffled and dealt out seven cards each. About thirty minutes later, Piers showed up.

"Uncle Piers!" Lucy called. "Are you going to play with us now?"

Piers looked at Phoebe. "He's waiting for you down the hall."

"Okay," she replied.

He caught her arm as she went by, "Don't be alarmed. He's okay." He smiled at her as she left the room.

The sergeant was waiting in the hallway. "This way, Mrs. de Sylva."

He opened the last door on the right and shut it behind her as she walked in.

Chapter 48

Phoebe found herself in another room, smaller than where she had left the girls with Piers. It must have been their break room or something. There was a sink, cabinets, and a counter. Daan was sitting on the table in the center of the room with his jacket and shirt off. A police officer was bandaging his left shoulder.

"Daan," she cried as she ran across to him. She wanted to hug him, but she didn't want to hurt him. "What happened?"

"Hello, Lover," he smiled at her. "It is really not as bad as it looks." He reached for her with his free hand.

The officer spoke to Daan in Dutch and Daan asked that, for Phoebe's benefit, he use English.

He laughed and turned to Phoebe. "Mrs. de Sylva, I can't believe you were able to snag this old man into marriage."

"Dirk," Daan said.

"Right." Dirk turned to Phoebe. "Your husband's been shot, ma'am."

Phoebe's face was ashen white, Daan noticed. She looked genuinely worried.

"Someone was shooting at you?" Phoebe asked.

"I was just telling Daan, here, that he was very lucky. The bullet was lodged in his deltoid muscle, and I had to dig it out."

"I'm okay. Just a little prick. Dirk has done a good

job fixing me up."

"So, he'll be okay?" Phoebe looked at Dirk.

"Mrs. de Sylva, he needs to go to the hospital and have that stitched up properly," Dirk said to Phoebe as he gently placed Daan's arm in a sling. "I was a medic in the army and not a full-fledged doctor. His arm should stay in this sling for several days, and you need to watch that the wound doesn't open and start bleeding again. Or worse, get infected."

"See, I'm going to be just fine." He smiled at her.

"Daan, you are a moron!" She slapped him across the face. "That's not just a prick!"

"Wow." Dirk was surprised. "Did he deserve that?"

"He does when he didn't say anything to me."

"Phe, I'm okay. Really."

"Poppycock!" she screamed. "You should have told me!"

"Hey, no one else was hurt."

"When did it happen?" She couldn't believe he had been shot and didn't say anything.

"Mrs. de Sylva, please be careful. You really don't want to open up that wound."

"Why didn't you tell me, Bozo!" She started to slap him again, ignoring Dirk's comment, but Daan caught her arm with his right hand.

"Phe, let me explain."

"You should have told me!" Tears were rolling down her cheeks now.

"I'm going to leave the two of you to hash this out." Dirk quickly left the room.

"I didn't want to worry you." He pulled her to him. "I'm okay, honest."

"Daan," she said his name softly through her tears.

"You could have been killed."

He pulled her closer and whispered into her ear, "Lover, I'm right here. I'm not dead. And what's more important is that you and the girls are safe."

He could feel her tears as they cascaded down from her cheeks onto his bare chest.

Piers is right. I do believe you have feelings for me, Phoebe Emanuella Silva. Otherwise, you wouldn't have slapped me. Infatuation? Maybe. Love? Perhaps. And me? What am I feeling for you?

Daan didn't want to have this conversation right now because he knew he could have no feelings for this woman. This make-believe relationship of theirs was only for a couple more days, and then she'd be gone.

He kissed her forehead. "Could you help me with that borrowed shirt over there? Mine was cut off and I don't think I can button it up by myself."

Instead, Phoebe leaned in to press her lips to his. She had intended it to be just a simple kiss, but all her emotions flooded in, and she had to let him know she didn't want to lose him. She was suddenly not afraid of her passion for him, and she draped her arms around his shoulders.

He kissed her back and pulled her close to him with his free arm. Then, he gave a weak cry, "Ow."

She stopped and jumped back. "Oh, Daan, I'm sorry."

"I'm not," he whispered as he pulled her back to him and tucked her under his right arm. "Ah, Lover, what am I going to do with you?"

I don't think we're playacting anymore. But what AM I going to do with you, Phoebe Silva?

"Daan, I didn't mean to hurt you. I just wanted you

to know that—"

"Shh," he interjected before she could say any more, and slipped gingerly off the table. "I'm okay. You must be a little gentle with my left arm though."

She carefully drew herself back from him and picked up the towel the officer had left next to him and dried her tears off his chest. She picked up the shirt and was helping him into it when there was a knock on the door and Piers peeked in.

"I understand there may have been a few fireworks in here. So, I came to protect the injured man."

Daan laughed. "She was just expressing how upset she was that I had not told her someone had shot at me but missed."

"Missed?" she exclaimed. "The shooter hit you, Daan. He did not miss."

Piers shrugged his shoulders. "Phoebe, the shooter missed Daan's heart and his head."

"But, more importantly," Daan admitted as Phoebe stood in front of him buttoning up his shirt, "he missed you and the girls."

Phoebe stopped buttoning. "He was aiming for my girls and me? I must get back to them." Phoebe's voice was shrill. "Perhaps it's time we return home. I can't lose my girls, Daan. Not my girls."

"What I'm trying to say," Piers said, "is that the shooter was not successful." Then, he looked squarely at Phoebe. "I don't think you'll be able to leave, Phoebe. I don't think you'll be able to get a flight out of here. Ziebach will make sure of that."

"But we are American citizens," Phoebe protested. "He can't stop us."

"I have no doubt that Captain Vanderburg will stop

you at the airport and detain you," Piers said.

"But?" Phoebe was exasperated.

"Phoebe, this police station is the safest place for all of us to be right now." Daan took her hands in his. "That's why we came here. Piers and I know everyone in this station, and we trust them."

Piers tried to calm Phoebe. "Besides that, your girls have charmed old Smit out there, and no one gets a smile out of him. But Lucy and Charlotte did."

"If we can't leave, what do we do now?" Phoebe's question hung in the air for a moment.

"We must continue the game until we put together all the puzzle pieces," Daan said.

Piers pulled a light blue jacket from his side. "Throw this on. It's from the constable out front who says you'd better return it." Piers passed it to Phoebe. "It's a bit big, but that's good. It'll hide the sling."

"How are we going to keep this from the girls?" Phoebe asked as she helped Daan with the jacket.

"We carry on," said Daan, ready to leave. He was resting on Phoebe but felt a bit woozy and leaned back against the table. He had been given antibiotics and medication for the pain.

Piers was at Daan's side to help Phoebe steady him. "You okay, my friend?"

Daan breathed in. "I'll be fine."

"Good," Piers said. "We may have lost those watching us for a while. But when we get back to the hotel, we've got a lot of convincing to do so everyone knows you're not injured."

"It'll be a great performance with you and Phoebe by my side." Daan gave a faint laugh.

Piers walked to the door. "Give me a minute, and

then follow me."

Phoebe slipped under Daan's right arm to support him. Daan decided he couldn't pass out, not in front of Charlotte and Lucy. So, he concentrated on Phoebe and her luscious hair, her lovely hazel eyes, and her fabulous, kissable lips. That kiss she had just given him invited him to a wonderful evening if he could just make it to their room.

"Stay close, Lover," he whispered. "I need to lean on you."

"Don't worry, I'm here."

Chapter 49

Daan was leaning heavily on Phoebe as they walked down the hall towards the room where the girls were.

"Daddy," it was Lucy who grabbed his waist.

Charlotte noticed that Daan flinched. "What's wrong?"

Phoebe told the girls about how Daan had hurt his shoulder in all that traveling they had done today.

"And now we're taking the police van to the hotel," Piers added as he took over for Phoebe.

"Daddy, did you do that because you were carrying me?" Lucy sounded devastated.

Daan smiled as best he could. "I'm okay, Luce. It just means I shouldn't be picking up such a mature young lady."

"Okay, Daddy. I am big enough to walk by myself."

As they got into the police van, Piers whispered to Phoebe, "You stay with him. The pain meds are kicking in. We'll be at the hotel in a few minutes, and Lars will be waiting to help you take him upstairs. Just say he had a liquid lunch because we were celebrating his birthday."

Phoebe was surprised. "He didn't tell me his birthday was today."

"He's 103 today!"

"Am not," Phoebe heard Daan whisper.

"Looks pretty good for 103, don't you think?" Piers laughed and went to join the girls.

Debra Birdwell Winkler

"So, it's your birthday today, Daan de Sylva."

"Uh-huh." He leaned his head on her shoulder.

"That's another thing you didn't tell me."

As they arrived at the hotel, Piers told Phoebe, "You can trust Lars. He has been watching out for Daan for many years."

"Then, I guess I can't cut out your heart, Piers."

"Not yet." Piers smiled at her as he helped the girls out of the van. "He's still alive!"

Lars came over to Piers and Phoebe, taking Piers' place next to Daan. "I've got this Chief Inspector. You take care of those little ladies."

"Good," Piers said. "Phoebe, I'll take the girls to lunch, if that's okay with you."

"Uncle Piers," Lucy took Piers' hand, "can I have a hamburger?"

"Sure," Piers was saying as he took Charlotte's hand as well and walked them past the hotel.

Daan tried to stand up straight as they entered the lobby but slumped on Lars and Phoebe.

Lars said aloud for those in the lobby to hear, "So, Mrs. de Sylva, I see you were celebrating his birthday."

Phoebe racked her brain for an answer and then came up with, "He just couldn't wait for this evening."

"That sounds like Mr. de Sylva. So, let's see if he can sleep this off for a few hours and be ready for the opera tonight." Lars pushed the up button on the elevator, and they helped Daan in.

It was a little after 1:00 P.M. by the time Lars and Phoebe had Daan in the bedroom.

"Piers called before you left the police station," Lars told Phoebe as the two of them prepared Daan for bed. Then, he observed her worried face. "He'll be fine, Mrs.

de Sylva. He just needs rest."

"Thank you, Lars."

"The pain medicine will wear off in a couple of hours and he'll need another dose."

"We just won't go to the opera," Phoebe said firmly.

Lars looked at Phoebe with concern. "Oh no, Mrs. de Sylva. You must go tonight."

"Daan can't go in this condition!"

"All of you must go to the opera tonight. If you don't go, they'll suspect something is wrong. So, he must go."

"But next time, they may kill him, Lars!" Phoebe said.

"Mrs. de Sylva, they won't kill him because he has you by his side."

"I don't know what I can do to prevent another incident."

"You've given him a reason to hang around," he told her.

The two of them walked to the suite door.

"Lars, how can they not expect that Daan has been injured?"

"They won't believe he is injured if you are up here, and the children are with their Uncle Piers." Lars shook his head. "Why else would parents send their children off a couple of hours in the afternoon?" Then, he turned at the suite threshold. "Mrs. de Sylva, make sure to lock the door behind me."

"Lars, my name is Phoebe."

Lars smiled and walked to the elevator.

Piers had Daan's key to the suite, so Phoebe locked the door behind Lars. She walked into the bedroom and watched Daan sleep for a few minutes. She and Lars had taken off Daan's clothes except for his underwear and placed him on his back under the covers, so his wound did not show. God forbid the girls rush into the bedroom and see the bandages.

Fatigue overwhelmed Phoebe as she sat down on her side of the bed and took off her sweater, laying it next to her. She slipped out of her shoes and crawled under the covers herself.

She closed her eyes and was almost asleep when she felt Daan moving towards her. She turned over and saw him watching her.

"Hello, Lover."

"Hello, Devil."

"Come over to the other side of the bed so I might hold you. It hurts to lie on this side."

"You need to rest," she said to him.

"I can't rest until I know you're safe here next to me," he whispered. "We have so little time, and I don't want to waste it with you not in my arms."

"Shh," Phoebe said and moved to the other side of the bed. She crawled under the covers and helped him move over to make room for her. Then, she placed her head on his right shoulder. "Is that better?"

"Much," he said. "Now, kiss me like you mean it."

She gently placed a kiss on his lips.

"Like you mean it, Lover."

"I don't want to hurt you," she whispered.

"I can handle it."

They shared a long, passionate kiss and he murmured, "It's not fair that you're dressed and I'm not."

Phoebe snuggled under his right arm. Then, his body relaxed, and he slept. For a few minutes, she struggled to figure out how he had awakened a secret yearning inside of her heart. Lying here in his arms, she felt safe with him. Then, Phoebe cuddled closer to him, remembering there would not be enough time for them to share much together so she fell asleep appreciating the moments they shared.

Chapter 50

When Piers and the girls came in, Phoebe was immediately awake and looked at her watch. She couldn't believe it was almost 4:30 P.M. already. She carefully moved away from Daan so as not to disturb him.

Walking over to the dresser, she straightened herself in the mirror, glancing at Daan's reflection and smiled. She hated to wake him up but, if what Lars said was true, they had to attend the opera. How she was going to manage the girls and handle Daan, she didn't know.

She walked out into the sitting room and found the girls drinking cokes and playing 'Go Fish' with Piers.

"So, what's going on here?"

"Mom," Lucy exclaimed, "we had hamburgers, and then we went shopping."

"Uncle Piers had to get a tuxedo so he can go to the opera with us tonight," Charlotte remarked.

"We're going to be Uncle Piers' dates, Mom," Lucy said proudly.

"Remember, I told you that you couldn't date until you were sixteen," Phoebe tried to sound stern. "What's this about a date tonight?"

"Mom, it's just Uncle Piers," Lucy laughed.

Charlotte was concerned, "It's okay, right, Mom?"

"It sounds like fun, girls." It was hard for Phoebe to hide her joy of Piers' joining them tonight. "So, Piers, you purchased a tuxedo just so you could join us? I didn't think you liked the opera."

"Oh, I allowed the girls to talk me into it," Piers said. "I think they enjoyed helping me with my tuxedo."

"How were you able to pick one out so fast?"

"Mom," Charlotte said, "we just walked into this shop a couple of blocks away and they found a tux that was perfect!"

"Show her, Uncle Piers," Lucy was adamant the formalwear be taken out of its bag and displayed for Phoebe to see.

Piers unzipped the bag and took out a black tuxedo with shirt and tie. No vest like Daan's, but it would work for tonight.

"So," Phoebe directed her question to Piers, "a tux in a couple of hours?"

"Well, it's a rental. Daan made me attend the opera last year with him and then there was a fancy party we had to go to in December. The shop has my measurements, and this is probably the one I wore six months ago."

"It looks perfect," she smiled. She went up to Piers, kissed his cheek, and whispered, "Thank you."

"Come on, ladies," Phoebe addressed her daughters, "we don't have much time to get glamorous. So off you go to take showers and get ready. Charlotte, you shower first."

As she entered the sitting room, someone knocked on the suite door.

"I ordered you a sandwich from downstairs when we came in," Piers said as he opened the door.

Lars walked in, placed the sandwich on the coffee table, and told Phoebe she needed to eat quickly.

Piers asked in a low tone so the girls would not hear the conversation, "So, what's going on downstairs?"

"I chased off those gentlemen from the black Fiat after you came in this afternoon. I told them I would be happy to rent them a room except we were filled up for the weekend," Lars explained. "So, they are hovering around outside."

"What else?"

"There has been activity across the river with two men walking back and forth since you returned."

"I expected something like that," Piers remarked. "We have a major police presence because I confirmed this afternoon that the terrorist threat seemed pretty valid."

Phoebe began eating her sandwich, but she was nervous about Daan.

"So, are we sure Daan will make it to the Opera House without much help, tonight?" she asked.

"I'll be fine," Daan's voice came from the bedroom door. He was leaning on the door frame with a towel wrapped around his waist. "What did you do with my pants, Piers?"

Phoebe ran over to him. "How are you?"

"Great," he lied. "But you need to be getting ready and let me discuss business with Piers and Lars."

Piers helped Daan to the sofa. "Go, Phoebe," he told her. "Hurry, so we might get Daan ready. It's going to take both Lars and me to do that."

Giving a weak smile, Phoebe walked into the bedroom without looking back. She took a quick shower, dressed rapidly, and entered the bedroom to find Daan sitting on her side of the bed, his towel lying on the floor at his feet.

Phoebe did an about face, turning towards the closet. "Daan, cover up please."

She couldn't believe how much she was attracted to this man, how much his presence gnawed at her being, touching her inner feelings, her—dare she admit it—her heart.

"Fine," Daan said. "You may turn around now."

As she slowly moved to face him, Daan watched her with admiration. Like last night, he was mesmerized by her. She was dressed in a floor length black chiffon dress with an open back. The front was simple neckline and fitted bodice, unlike last night's plunge in the front. The dress delicately swayed as she moved, accentuating her—what, he was trying to find the word—her grace, her elegance. Again, no sparkles, no sequins, no embroidery, just plain and simple. The only decoration was her long lace sleeves.

She had surprised him in her 'simple' dress last night, so tonight he thought he would be prepared for her. Alas, he was wrong. The dress swirled as she turned back around to pick up her shoes from the closet. However, it wasn't the swirling that highlighted her figure which astonished him. No, he was astonished at how seductive the open back of this dress was.

"I figured you might need help with your zipper again," he announced, swallowing back the lust he felt, "so here I am."

"You are in no condition to zip my dress," she argued as she started towards him, trying to hold her dress together and juggle her shoes at the same time. "I'll go over to the girls, and Charlotte will take care of my zipper."

"There's not much of a zipper with that open back,

you know."

She dropped her shoes on the bed and turned her back to him. He fiddled with the zipper for a few seconds.

"See, I told you," she said.

"Don't move," Daan said and slowly stood up, so he had a better hold on the zipper. "I like your dress, by the way." He zipped her up and then slowly ran his fingers along her back.

"Hey," she said.

"You are pretty seductive, you know." He began to cover her bare back with kisses.

"Daan, don't start something you can't finish, especially in your condition."

"I think we have time," he whispered as he drew her close to him and felt her bare skin against his. Then, he began to slowly pull the dress off her shoulder.

"Leave it to a man to think a few minutes is all a woman needs."

"Mmmm…" He stopped, then pulled the back of the dress together to hook the top. "I guess we do have someplace to be in a few minutes. Later we will continue; mark my words."

She turned around to face him. "Why didn't you tell me today is your birthday?"

"It's not important. Just another day on the calendar." He began to caress her face with his right hand.

"For some," she said sadly.

He pulled her face towards him, "Wait, it's not your birthday, too, is it?"

"No." She drew back and carefully pushed him down on the bed. "It's Dominic's birthday."

"You are kidding."

"Nope."

"That's a little strange, don't you think?"

"Like a lot of things involving us. Coincidence?"

"I don't believe in coincidence. I thought you knew."

"Oh, you've told me." She put her hands on her hips. "But there's no denying how we have had several definite similarities involving us. It's like there are forces beyond our control which have thrown us together, no matter how you look at it."

"Ziebach," was his only comment.

"Ziebach didn't cause your plane to land in Salt Lake City. Ziebach didn't sit me next to you on that same plane. Ziebach didn't cause this electricity between us."

"But he is involved."

"Oh, come on, Daan," she argued. "Your paranoia is rising to the surface. Ziebach is not the controlling factor. Not with this thing between us."

"The Fates are involved, perhaps."

She laughed.

"You know, like in Wagner's *Ring Cycle*. The gods are trying to control people who don't realize it. Maybe we are being controlled by the Fates. Who knows?"

"Ziebach is just stimulating your paranoia." She turned to pick up her shoes on the bed.

He grabbed her hand. "It's my paranoia that has kept me alive for so long."

"Maybe."

"And it's my paranoia that originally told me you were with Ziebach. Now I know differently."

"One point for you, Daan." She licked her right forefinger and drew a number one in the air. "Welcome to the real world."

"Sit here next to me, Lover, because you are part of the real world." He tapped the bed, and she sat down. He leaned over and began kissing her. "Why, oh why, when I get near you, do you do this to me, woman?" he questioned her as he pulled his lips away and started down her neck. "You are driving me crazy."

"Daan," she said his name softly with tears in her eyes and gently pushed him back. "You need to get your head on straight and get dressed. We're going to be late."

He ignored her. "This dress should be outlawed," he whispered in her ear.

There was a knock on the door. It was Piers reminding them of the time.

"Damn," Daan said under his breath. "If it's not a child, it's an adult!"

"Saved by the knock," she responded, wiping her eyes with her hands, but he didn't notice. Then, she grabbed her shoes and stood up. "Coming."

She unlocked and opened the door and headed towards the girls' room. Piers was already dressed, and Lars followed him into the room.

"Friend," Piers declared, "I don't think I have seen you quite like this in many years."

"She's intriguing. What can I say? A quick romp in the hay would have been nice."

"Hmmm," Piers said. "I'm sure it would not have been very quick."

"And we need to dress you for the opera now." Lars took out Daan's tuxedo from the closet along with his shirt and vest.

"Guys, I don't know what it is about her, but she fascinates me." Then, Daan stopped.

"She is doing more than fascinating you, my friend."

Daan took a deep breath and proceeded to stand up. "I can't get involved with this woman, Piers. There is too much going on to get involved."

"Remember what I told you, Daan," Piers said.

Daan's voice almost sounded sad, now. "She'll be gone on Sunday anyway, so it really doesn't matter." He looked at his friend and then headed towards the bathroom. "Business first. Besides that, you two know there is no time for me to even begin to enjoy being with her."

"Who are you trying to convince?" Piers remarked.

Chapter 51

Lars and Piers had discussed the chain of events surrounding Daan and Ziebach's determination to believe that Phoebe was Francine. It was obvious that the two women were nothing alike. Both felt Ziebach's vengeance against Daan was more than San Francisco. But, what? Neither knew.

Even though Lars had run off the Fiat guys, they were still watching. He was also suspicious of a woman with short, curly, blonde hair and her heavy-set husband. This couple were guests at the hotel who said they were going to the opera, but they had asked Ty about the de Sylva family when Daan and Phoebe had left for the boat tour this morning. Ty had started talking with them, but Lars had been able to thwart the questioning by sending Ty on an errand and telling the couple he knew nothing about the family. When Lars checked on them through the Dutch police, nothing came up.

Lars and Piers would do anything to protect Daan de Sylva. Thwarting Ziebach's vendetta against Daan and Phoebe had become their priority. Piers had arranged additional police around the Opera House on the pretense of a terrorist attack. Lars was intently watching the comings and goings of those in the hotel as well as the de Sylva suite upstairs.

These two protectors had made phone calls concerning leads, but nothing had come to fruition. It was unfortunate, but Lars and Piers could do nothing right now but watch and wait. That was the hardest thing to do at this point. Even in Daan's condition, he was there with Phoebe and the girls which allowed them to focus on Ziebach's cronies.

One thing was for certain. That wasn't a stray bullet that had struck Daan earlier. Luckily, Piers had been with the family, today. Lars knew that things would have been different if Piers had not been there. Ziebach's men may have gotten Daan and the three innocents.

Still pondering the facts at 6:30 P.M., Lars watched as Piers walked out the hotel doors holding Lucy's and Charlotte's hands. Following close behind was Daan with his right arm around Phoebe. Daan could not use his sling tonight and was leaning on Phoebe for support. Lars thought they just might pull the evening off. Phoebe's dress helped because it looked like there was a reason for Daan to not keep his hands off her as he ran his fingers along her back.

Lars smiled at himself as he thought about how he had taken on watching out for Daan de Sylva. For thirty years, he had managed the hotel, and before that he had been a beat cop in this area of Amsterdam. Lars had known Daan's parents, Dominik and Ina, who were good people. The de Sylvas were from ancient stock like him with the de Sylva family living in Amsterdam for almost five hundred years and his family, longer than that.

Lars had watched Daan grow up here in the hotel. And, it had been a pleasure to keep an eye on him after his parents passed away. Dominik died of cancer a while ago and his mother just a little over a year after Daan's family had died in the explosion in San Francisco.

Daan's wife, Francine, and the twins had been the

center of Daan's existence. But he was not the same after he lost them. Over the last eight years, Daan did his job well both as a police officer and a prosecutor, but he seemed to have cut himself off from the world. Daan was conscientious, honorable, and excellent at what he did. However, Lars felt that Daan had become like a robot with no feelings for anyone except for his friend and former partner, Piers, and maybe himself.

It was not a chore to watch over Daan who had grown up to honest, trustworthy, and respectable man. A kind man who deserved a second chance at a good life. Perhaps, the last couple of days was Daan's second chance.

This woman, Phoebe Silva, had touched something in Daan's being. Lars knew that Daan kept his feelings buried and would never admit it, but she made him smile, made him care again. After so much tragedy, Daan de Sylva deserved to have a little bit of happiness in his life.

When Lars walked to the hotel's front doors and took a look around, the Fiat guys were not in sight. The blonde woman and her husband made their way past him through the doors and joined others walking towards the Opera House. But Lars saw no one suspicious hanging around out of place. He spotted several police officers, which gave him reassurance that Piers' warning was being taken seriously.

Lars walked into the hotel, heading towards the restaurant. He wanted to confirm the small birthday cake he had ordered for Daan was going to be delivered to their suite. That would put them in a good mood when they returned from the opera.

As he made his way across the lobby, he noticed Ty was paying more attention to Daan and his entourage walking to the Opera House than he was to the customers standing in front of him at the desk. Lars decided Ty was attentively watching Charlotte and Lucy and not the adults.

Ah, young love.

He changed his direction and moved to the front desk. Standing between Ty and the window that looked out toward the Opera House, Lars quietly reminded Ty that he had customers before him.

Chapter 52

Earlier, when Piers redressed his wound, Daan had refused more pain medication because he wanted to be as alert as possible tonight, forcing himself through the pain. His whole arm throbbed as his mind ran through all those movies where the hero acted as though nothing was wrong after an injury and was back into normality almost immediately.

Damn, but my arm and shoulder are annoyingly sensitive. Sensitive? Hell, it damn well hurt! Thank goodness Phoebe is here to lean on.

He tilted his head and kissed her cheek and continued to touch her back. With her to focus on, the pain subsided a bit.

He was pleased Piers had taken over handling the girls. He was their date, and they were elated with his attention and were both actively discussing things with him. Daan didn't remember ever seeing Piers so involved with children.

They joined the line of patrons as they approached the Opera House doors. They could pass through without inspection because Piers showed his ID and vouched for the family. With the girls repeatedly calling him, Uncle Piers, there was laughter among the security team.

Phoebe started to let go of Daan to head for Will Call for the tickets, but he held her back. "Let Piers get them with the girls," he told her.

Daan allowed his right hand to make circles on her bare back. "Ah, but this helps me concentrate on you and not the pain," he said. "Also, it allows me to whisper sweet nothings into your ear so that everyone must try to imagine what I am saying to you."

She turned to him. "And what sweet nothings are you saying to me so that I can respond for our watchers?"

He laughed out loud and then brought her as close to him as he could. His voice was soft and seductive as he nuzzled near her ear. "The women are admiring you because your dress is delightful and shows every curve which has caught the eyes of men all over the lobby. The men are wishing they were me because they know I am telling you what we are going to do when I get you to bed tonight."

"And our watchers?"

"We are confirming for them and everyone that you are my wife and lover."

Phoebe just smiled and tried to look pleased.

A minute later, Piers and the girls met them at the elevator. Daan swayed a bit as he leaned on the elevator doors, but Phoebe was right there at his elbow. Then he laughed as Lucy hugged him. Phoebe allowed Daan to use his right hand to hold Lucy's while she used her arm to support his left side. She knew the wound in his shoulder was painful; she could feel him flinch when Lucy grabbed him. But she kept smiling and supporting him as best she could.

When they were seated, Daan looked around and smiled like he was pleased with his family. Piers sat between the girls in the seats closest to the stage. They were talking and laughing together.

He focused on Phoebe and she smiled.

"You know these last two days have been pretty special to me."

"Me, too," he responded. "Except for this little scratch which prevents me from holding you like I want."

She smiled mischievously. "You can be a real Devil, you know."

"Come closer, Lover, and let me kiss you for our audience. The performance should win us an Emmy."

She leaned over to him, and they lightly kissed as the lights were blinking to notify theater patrons that the opera was about to begin. Then, the overture filled the auditorium.

Daan laid his left arm in his lap and draped his right arm around Phoebe, letting it rest there for a while as he kissed her shoulder. When the curtain rose, she took his hand off her shoulders and placed it in her lap because he was distracting her.

She wasn't watching the opera now but was trying to figure out exactly what had happened in the last few days. First, she felt Daan was an obnoxious European, then an unconcerned Devil, then a drunken intruder, and finally a reluctant bridegroom being chased by some unknown villain. Now he was acting like the attentive husband in this charade of theirs. The Devil had captured her heart and she didn't realize it until it was too late. She looked around to Daan and saw that he was watching her instead of the stage.

"Is everything okay?" she asked softly.

"Everything is perfect."

She smiled and felt his hand move to stroke her leg. "What are you doing?"

"Reminding you that I am here, sharing this moment

with you."

She placed his hand in hers so he would stop massaging her leg. To her surprise, he pulled her hand to his lips, then leaned in and nibbled on her ear, "Much more of this, and we are going to excuse ourselves so we can return to the hotel."

"And what about the children?" she whispered.

"Uncle Piers can handle them while I take care of you."

"And what about our watchers?"

He smiled. "They're just envious."

On stage, the second story unfolded to the heavy music of Wagner.

Phoebe whispered to Daan, "Wagner's story is almost as complicated as ours."

"In what way?"

"Well, Wagner tells the story of the value of love and how some people are willing to abandon love when it fits their needs," she explained.

"I see. And who am I? The one who values love or the one who is throwing it away?"

She thought for a moment and then said, "It's like you're Wotan trying to control everything, Daan."

"No, I'm not king of the gods."

She said nothing and wouldn't even look at him.

"Okay," Daan said, draping a loose curl behind her ear. "If I'm king of the gods, then you are Fricka, my queen."

Phoebe leaned over and murmured in his ear, "But we're not actually married, remember?"

"That's true." He nodded. "Then, I guess we're Sigmund and Sieglinde."

"No, we're not siblings."

"Ah," he said. "Then, I am Siegfried, and you are Brünnhilde trying to save me."

"But Brünnhilde doesn't save Siegfried, and he dies anyway, Daan."

"Shhh," he finally said. "Watch the opera. You came almost 5,000 miles to see it, so you need to pay attention."

As Act II closed, the house lights came on and the two girls were discussing the last scene with excitement. Piers stood to stretch.

Daan said, "Now I must stretch. I've been sitting too long."

Phoebe helped him stand and laughed as she wrapped her arm around him.

"Ah, Lover," he whispered, "that was not as effortless as I wanted it to be."

She kissed his cheek. "Does that help?"

"More than you can imagine." He smiled at her and watched the lady in the next set of seats grin at them and turn away.

He took Phoebe's hand as they walked toward the hallway, "I do think I am a little older than the last time I was shot."

"And when was that, pray tell?"

"A long time ago," he said, "maybe a lifetime ago."

The girls filed past them, and Piers walked next to them.

"And, I was there to help," Piers interrupted. "He took it in his hip because he wasn't where he was supposed to be."

Daan laughed. "So, he says."

"Such a rascal," Piers told Phoebe. "I was perfectly happy doing what I do best. Then, he stepped between me and the perp, taking the bullet meant for me."

"And, again, you were being the hero," Phoebe commented.

"What can I say? My job is to protect family and friends."

"Mom, I gotta go to the bathroom," Lucy was now saying.

"Then, let's hurry, ladies." Phoebe took the girls' hands.

"We're bringing up the rear," Piers said with Daan in tow.

"Mom, can we see the violin guy, again?"

The group made its way to the main hallway with others and there was the bronze statue of a man playing the violin coming right out of the floor. Lucy and Charlotte had been fascinated by the statue.

"Who did it, Uncle Piers?" Charlotte asked.

"It is by an anonymous sculptor," Piers related. "There are statues like this in several places in Amsterdam. Perhaps tomorrow we can go see the Running Man and the Harmonica Man. There was a Man with a Saw in a tree, but he disappeared."

Daan said, "No one really knows who did the sculptures."

"No one?" Phoebe asked.

Piers explained, "They just suddenly appeared in various places in Amsterdam at different times." He motioned for the girls to come over near him. "Some say our former Queen Beatrix is the creator of these pieces of art. She is a great sculptress."

"But no one really knows who created them?" Charlotte was curious.

"No," Daan answered. "But they are unique, don't

you think?"

Lucy laughed. "This one coming out of the floor is funny."

"Come on, Luce, Charlotte," Phoebe was calling now, "Intermission is almost over, and we are coming up on my favorite piece of music in the whole opera."

"Yeah, we know, Mom, *The Ride of the Valkyries*," Charlotte said with not much enthusiasm.

"It's my favorite piece as well, girls," Daan reminded them as they headed down the hall where there were few people.

"We'll only be a couple of minutes," Phoebe told Daan and Piers as they went into the ladies' room.

Daan leisurely made his way to the men's room while Piers waited in the hall. A couple of minutes later, Daan slowly walked out, and they switched places.

This way the two of them could protect the women. Daan leaned against the wall listening, waiting. Suddenly, he sensed something. His inner radar was alerted, a prickle of uneasiness at the base of his neck, like on the boat earlier. He looked around, observing, but there was no one in the hall right now.

Piers has made sure there are plenty of police around. A pair will be coming this way in a minute or so. Nothing to worry about.

Chapter 53

Inside the ladies' room, the girls were taking their time. Phoebe was the first out of the stall and said to them, "Hurry, girls."

At the sink was a blonde curly-haired lady who Phoebe had not noticed when they walked in. There was something about this woman that nagged at Phoebe's memory as she washed her hands. Then, she remembered and was uneasy.

"Didn't we see each other yesterday in the restaurant near Dam Square?"

"Oh, yes," the German woman admitted. "It was your husband who was ravishing you at the table."

"Wow, it sure is a small world."

The girls joined Phoebe. As they dried their hands, the lights blinked, indicating intermission was over and the third act was about to begin.

"Let's go, girls." Phoebe was trying to hurry them out.

"Yes, a small world, Mrs. de Sylva."

Phoebe knew in her heart this blonde German had been one of their watchers and felt a sudden feeling of terror.

"You know my name?"

"Oh, yes. And these are your daughters, Anya and Ilse."

"No, you must have us mixed up with someone

else," Phoebe commented with a confused look for the woman's benefit.

Phoebe tried to reach for her daughters but, suddenly, a stall door jerked open and there was the man she had seen at the restaurant with this woman. He pushed a gun into her side, out of sight of the girls.

The woman spoke in a serious tone, "You must understand, Mrs. de Sylva, we are just following orders."

"Whose?" Phoebe tried to act innocent but now felt everything was moving in slow motion.

As the lights began blinking, Phoebe noticed pieces of the duct tape lined up on the edge of the counter. In one swift motion, the woman strapped one piece across Lucy's mouth. Just as Charlotte screamed, her mouth was covered as well. Phoebe gasped.

"Do not scream, Mrs. de Sylva, or we will shoot you and then your husband as we leave. Do you want your girls to be orphans?"

Then, duct tape was pressed across Phoebe's mouth.

Chapter 54

When the lights began blinking, Daan was alert but leaning against the wall across from the ladies' room. Phoebe and the girls were taking a long time.

Where in the hell are you, Piers?

Daan jumped as he heard Charlotte's beginning scream and was rushing across the hall when someone came up behind him.

"Daan de Sylva?" The voice was deep and low.

Daan felt the muzzle of a gun poked into his side and his left shoulder was squeezed tightly. He was being forced into submission but smothered a cry of anguish.

"Don't move."

"What do you want?" Daan asked, trying not to acknowledge the agonizing pain.

Before him, a blonde woman emerged from the ladies' room leading Lucy and Charlotte down the hall. Both had their mouths covered with duct tape and their eyes were big with fear as they looked at him.

A heavy-set man shoved Phoebe to follow them. She too was at gun point, her wrists and mouth restrained with duct tape. She looked at Daan with angry eyes that pleaded for him to intervene, tears streaming down her cheeks. She struggled with her abductor, but he held her tight.

Daan's heart was racing, and a heavy despair formed in the pit of his stomach. He moved towards them, but his attacker clamped down tighter on his wound as the gun was rammed into his ribs.

Daan frantically looked around, analyzing their predicament. Police officers were conveniently absent, and there were no other witnesses. Phoebe and the girls were being forced down the hall by unknown kidnappers. He was imagining the worse had happened to Piers. He tried to free himself but was impotent to help.

"One more move and your wife is dead, then you," the man hissed. "Tell you what, we'll shoot you all."

The guy waved his pistol at Daan's make-believe family. "Bang! Bang! Bang!" Then, he raised the pistol to Daan's temple. "Bang!"

From the auditorium came the sound of the orchestra playing *The Ride of the Valkyries*. Daan jerked around to attack his assailant but felt a sharp pain in the back of his head. He was falling to the floor as he watched Phoebe and the girls being dragged off in the distance as black nothingness engulfed him with the *Ride of the Valkyries* echoing in the background.

Dah, dah dah, da dah, dah; dah, dah, da dah, dah; dah, dah, da dah, dah; dah, dah, dah, dah.

Chapter 55

"Daaaaaan? Daaaaaan?"

Daan slowly dragged himself from the depths of darkness and gradually opened his eyes.

"Daan?" It was Piers calling his name and shaking him.

"Yeah," Daan finally responded roughly.

"Thank God," Piers sounded relieved. "Come on, friend. Let's try to find out where they've gone." Daan noticed Piers had blood running down the side of his head.

Piers helped Daan slowly get up. "Which way?"

Daan reached back and touched his head oozing blood. It was like he was coming out of a groggy dream, and his body was racked of pain. He had only been down a couple of minutes at the most because *Valkyries* was still playing.

"Piers, they went down the hall and out the side door." He pointed where the kidnappers had taken Phoebe and her daughters.

Unexpectedly, a phone began ringing. The ringing sound was coming from Daan's jacket pocket.

"Someone is calling you," Piers told Daan.

Daan shook his head, "That's not my phone. Mine is in my back pocket."

Piers reached into Daan's jacket and withdrew the ringing phone. "Hello?"

After a few seconds, "Daan, the phone is for you."

"De Sylva," Daan said into the phone.

"Daan de Sylva?" A deep, aged voice said. "It's good to finally meet you."

"Who are you?"

"This is Luther Ziebach."

"Ziebach?"

"We need to talk, de Sylva."

"What do you want?"

"Well, I want you to know I'm really sorry I didn't get your wife and children eight years ago. I thought they were eliminated in the explosion in San Francisco. I originally thought I would only go after you. But I got so much more pleasure watching you stumbling around without your beloved family since then."

Ziebach laughed.

Daan bit his tongue in disgust, falling back on his hostage negotiation training.

"You know, de Sylva, I left you alone after that because I knew you'd be utterly broken without them. It was much sweeter watching you wallow in misery and knowing you were the one responsible. But you slowly dragged yourself up, and you were like a little dog nipping at my heels, trying to destroy me, like so many before. But I am untouchable. I thought you knew that."

Another heavy laugh echoed through the phone.

Daan was angry beyond words, but he needed to listen, needed to find out where Phoebe and the girls were.

Ziebach continued, "Changing professions only took you farther away, being bogged down with immigration cases. Again, you found nothing because I'm invincible."

Daan knew he could not be confrontational and asked in a level tone, "What do you want, Ziebach?"

The old man ignored Daan's question. "How do you think I felt on Tuesday when I found out you were bringing your family home? I have eyes and ears everywhere. Did you think I wouldn't find out you were sneaking them into the country?"

Ziebach's laughter rang out.

"Did you think a little bit of hair dye and fake curls could disguise your three lovelies?"

Daan was trying so hard not to say anything. His pain was intense, and he could feel the shoulder wound and his head bleeding. He ignored the pain and forced himself to concentrate on Ziebach's words. He needed to be patient, composed, and professional, but most importantly, listen and draw out information to find Phoebe.

"And to find out you had hidden your family in the wilds of southern Utah in America?" Ziebach paused. "You know, I had to look Utah up on a map. It is a faraway place where there are not a lot of people. BORING. I compliment you on hiding them in such a remote area."

The opera music had changed in the auditorium. Now, Daan was counting the minutes in his head since Phoebe and her daughters had been kidnapped. Maybe nine or ten had passed. They could be almost anywhere by now. Daan's head was pounding, his left arm and shoulder were throbbing, and he was conversing with the evil who had caused him to be in the predicament he was in. He commanded his brain to focus!

"So, Ziebach, I ask again, what do you want?" Daan asked, trying to detach himself from his personal feelings.

"I have you where I want you, de Sylva. I have your family."

Daan could only imagine what Ziebach would do with Phoebe and her girls. He had to do something but reaching into the phone and choking the bastard was not going to happen.

"Now," Ziebach jeered, "what I want you to do is to listen carefully and pay attention to what I am going to do to you." Ziebach's laughter seeped into Daan's consciousness. "I remember a story told by my father and his father before him and several generations back to hundreds of years ago. A story of how your family tried to destroy mine by sinking our livelihood. You tried to destroy us then, and my ancestor promised yours that we would take you down, and now we are. A pledge is a pledge."

"Hundreds of years ago?" This was a story Daan had never heard.

"But, the Ziebachs have long memories, de Sylva. Eye for an eye and all that."

"That was a long time ago, Ziebach."

Racking his brain around what Ziebach was saying, Daan searched his mind for any clue of what was being related about the past. His family had been involved with banking and shipping in the Netherlands for hundreds of years. But the Ziebachs? Where did they come in?

Ziebach was now saying, "So, you see, it has taken a long time to have your family under our control. I just want you to know I am enjoying this immensely."

Patience, my boy, Daan could hear his father's voice whispering in his ear. *Patience will win the day.*

"Why is this so important, Ziebach?" Daan asked,

patiently listening to the ravings of this old man.

"Because we must wipe you and all Jewish vermin off the face of the earth. You've ruined everything for the Dutch. Your bank is finally finished, your shipping company extinguished, and now I will have the rest of your financial holdings."

"I see." Daan tried to make his voice firm. Obviously, Ziebach and his family were taking credit for natural disasters, wars, stock market failures, the general ups and downs of history and life. Let him. Daan needed to bide his time for a few more minutes. The police would surely be here soon.

"Now, we come to another fork in the road to your destruction, and you are the only one left. You, your beautiful wife, and these luscious girls of yours. You are the last of your line, and now I am going to destroy you and yours for all time."

It was then that Daan lost his patience. "Ziebach, you prick!" Daan screamed into the phone. "Don't take them. Take me. Leave them. They are not my family. This woman and her children are innocent. Take me!"

"Ha! Ha!" Ziebach was laughing. "You can't lie yourself out of this, de Sylva. You and your kind will be wiped off the face of the earth and no one will care. No one will mourn your passing. No one!"

Daan believed this was it. He had screwed up royally, this time. He had been unable to help Francine and his girls. And now, he had led Phoebe and her daughters to the same fate.

"Ziebach!"

"I have destroyed you, de Sylva!" Ziebach was laughing as the phone disconnected.

"Ziebach!" Daan was screaming into the silenced

phone.

"Daan," Piers was trying to calm him down. "Daan."

"Don't touch me, Piers!"

Daan slammed the phone into the floor when he saw someone knocking on the glass door at the end of the hall. He took off running in spite of his pain. He knew that someone. It was Phoebe.

"Phoebe, my love," he pushed open the door, and she fell into his arms. "Phoebe." He kissed her forehead and held her as tight as he could.

Phoebe was crying and screaming at him, "They've taken my babies, Daan!" Her hands were still bound, and she was bleeding from a scrape on her head and her elbow, her lace sleeves were ripped, and she was covered in dirt, leaves, and twigs.

Daan didn't know what had happened to her but was just glad she was back in his arms. He tried to hold her close to him, but she pushed him into the wall and dropped on the floor with a mangled piece of duct tape hanging from her cheek and what looked like a yellow fuzzy rat held between her fingers.

"They shoved us into a white van and there was a policeman helping to push us in and then he took off!"

"In a uniform?" Piers asked.

Phoebe nodded to Piers. "Must have been an imposter of some sort."

Piers dialed his phone and spoke quickly into the receiver.

Phoebe continued, "The van skidded out of the parking lot, and then they threw me into the bushes. I screamed out, but no one was there. No police! No people! No one! You weren't there to help, Daan! You weren't there!" She was pounding on his chest. "I grabbed at the woman who threw me out but all I got was her blonde wig." Phoebe continued to hit his chest. "They have my babies! Why did you let them take my babies?"

Phoebe was still pounding on Daan's chest and crying hysterically when Piers pulled her off Daan, who sank down to the floor in a heap. He was bewildered. He was hurting. He was bleeding from his wounds. As he watched Phoebe crying, he felt her pain and knew he was to blame for Lucy and Charlotte being kidnapped. He felt useless.

Suddenly, there were people all around them. He was being dragged onto a gurney and then to the ambulance outside. Piers was following him with Phoebe.

Daan had failed to protect Phoebe and her girls and had lost her beautiful daughters. He had failed Phoebe as he had Francine.

"*Oh, minj God*, Phoebe," he whispered in Dutch. "*Het spijt me zo* (I'm so sorry)."

Chapter 56

A couple of hours later, the three of them walked out of the hospital. Daan's left arm had been re-stitched and was resting in a sling while the back of his head was bandaged. Piers, too, had his head bandaged. Phoebe's wound on her forehead had been dressed along with the scrapes on her right elbow and arm. A police officer took them to the hotel.

Lars met them at the door and thought they looked like a sorry lot. The three had the semblance of coming home from a party that had been raided by the police. Daan and Piers were in their tattered, bloody tuxedos and shirts, and Phoebe's beautiful black gown had been torn up the side, her lace sleeves were hanging in shreds, and the dress was covered in dirt. Phoebe was holding the guys' jackets while Piers was helping Daan. No one said anything as Lars got them in the elevator and into the suite on the hotel's top floor.

Phoebe headed for her bedroom and then stopped at the door. "I'm taking a shower in here, and the two of you can go into the girls' room. I just can't." And then she burst into tears and slammed the door behind her. They could hear her sobbing even through the closed bathroom door.

Daan crossed over and dropped down on the sofa. "How did I let this happen?" he asked. It was rhetorical because he knew how it happened. He had not done his job, had not been diligent, not been focused. He had allowed himself to be distracted, to be compromised.

"It wasn't you," Piers said as he found his way to the chair. "I found out the police contingent at the Opera House was called away for a multiple automobile accident around the corner, and there was a house fire on the other side of the canal."

"It was a series of unfortunate events," Lars chimed in. "It wasn't your fault, Daan."

"But it was my fault!" Daan shouted. "I knew it was Ziebach. He knew we were going to the opera. We made no secret of that. He knew what to do to get to me. He knew!"

"Of course, he knew. I just never thought he would be so bold as to take the girls in public. We were always together, and it was—" Piers' voice trailed off.

"Stupid!" Daan completed Piers' sentence. "Just stupid on my part."

"Stop talking about it and do something," Lars admonished them both. "Clean up and get yourselves together. I need to make a few phone calls, and you two put a plan together. I'll be back in about thirty minutes or so." Lars left the suite without fanfare.

Daan stood up and told his friend, "You take a shower in the girls' bathroom. I'll go into Phoebe's bedroom and get your clothes."

"Great," Piers said. "You only have a few minutes before Phoebe attacks you, so be careful. You don't need that wound opened up again."

"She has good reason to be angry, Piers." Daan opened Phoebe's bedroom door. "I wasn't doing my job, and now Ziebach has her daughters."

"Shit, Daan, you can't be everything to everyone."

"No, but I could have done a better job of taking care of the three of them." He closed the bedroom door behind him.

Daan listened to Phoebe still crying in the shower. He slowly walked over to the closet and gathered Piers' things. Since Piers was in the shower, Daan left them on Charlotte's bed. When he returned to the bedroom for his clothes, Phoebe opened the bathroom door.

She had draped a towel around her body and was silhouetted in front of the light behind her. "What are you doing here?" Her eyes were swollen from crying.

"I need my clothes," was all he said as he crossed over to his side of the closet.

"What are you going to do to get my babies back?" she demanded as she backed against the doorframe. "You are the great Daan de Sylva who can do anything and everything, right?"

He didn't answer but took out a shirt which he laid across his shoulder. He was concentrating on each article of clothing with only one arm.

"Well?" she blurted out as she crossed over to him. "You promised we would be safe with you, and now they are gone!"

He still said nothing and tried to ignore her. That was all he could do.

She came up behind him. "You and your insinuation that Ziebach was after you and you only! You and your paranoia! You and your hoity-toity attitude that you know what's best for everyone. You and your belief that the great and powerful Daan de Sylva can do anything. You and your inability to keep my babies safe from that evil, evil man!"

He slowly turned around to face his accuser. "You

are one hundred percent correct, Phe. Everything you say is true. It was stupid and idiotic to bring you into all this."

"But you did and, now he has my babies!" she yelled at him and drew back her hand.

"Go ahead, Phe, slap me," he murmured. "I deserve it. Go ahead, get it out of your system."

She just looked at him and then fell to the floor sobbing. He dropped down next to her and tried to pull her to him with his right arm, leaning against the wall.

"Phoebe, I'm sorry," he whispered as she leaned against his chest. "I'm so sorry." He began kissing her forehead and ran his fingers through her hair.

She cried and cried, and he just held her close to him for a long time. He didn't move and just let her cry.

Finally, she pulled herself back. "Your shirt is still covered with blood, Daan."

"I know."

"You need to take a shower and change."

"I know."

"You must get my babies back."

"I know."

"Well?"

"Well," he began, "I can't unless you move away."

"Close your eyes," she said. "My towel has come loose."

"Right," he tried not to smile as he closed his eyes.

She said nothing as she pushed herself up and secured her towel.

"May I open my eyes and get up, now?" he questioned.

"Sure," she said and stepped back. "But I'm not helping you."

"Fine," he said as he struggled to his feet.

"Now, take your shower and decide the best course of action for us to find Lucy and Charlotte."

He watched as she moved back from him. He picked up his things off the floor and started towards the bedroom door.

"Hurry," she said. "We are wasting precious time."

Twenty minutes later, the three of them were in the sitting room discussing what had happened. Phoebe was on the sofa with Daan and Piers in the two chairs.

Piers was explaining how he had made some telephone calls while they were changing. The security cameras throughout the Opera House building had been disabled right before the intermission. No one knew how that happened. He also announced the Dutch police were looking for the girls.

"An Amber alert has been issued throughout Europe because we know Ziebach will not be bound by our border."

Phoebe asked surprised, "You have Amber alerts in Europe?"

"We do," Piers said proudly. "And the police, working together, have found many missing children. There was a Czech child found a month ago. In February a Polish child was returned to her mother."

"What about those who weren't found?" Phoebe groaned. "What about those children?"

"It's pretty much the same as in the United States," Daan told her. "We just keep looking until they are found."

She glanced at Daan. "How could this have happened, Daan? How could you have let this happen?"

"Phoebe, that's not fair," Piers stated. "Daan and I were supposed to be taking care of the three of you, and it just happened. If you blame him, you must blame me as well. Remember, it was my idea that you keep up the pretense of being a family."

No one spoke for a few minutes. The calm was broken by a knock on the door and then Lars used his key to come in.

"I called in a few favors," Lars let them know. "And, found out Ty was feeding Ziebach information about you two.

"Why would he do that?" Phoebe asked.

"Money. I interrogated him, but the little pipsqueak was only passing information and knew nothing else. I let him go. But not before I told him, if I found out that he was involved in the physical kidnapping of the girls, I would kill him myself, and no one would ever find his body. I turned him over to the police."

"What else did you find out?" Daan requested.

"That blonde German woman and her husband were guests here in room 632," Lars turned to Phoebe. "That was your original room, Phoebe."

"My room?"

"Ziebach." Daan cursed under his breath.

Lars nodded. "She and her companion have disappeared. The police are searching through the room now to see if they can find any evidence of where they've gone."

Phoebe said, "She was wearing a wig and, when I grabbed it, I saw she had dyed red hair underneath. I hope the wig was taken by the police for a DNA test to find out quickly who she is and then how she's involved with Ziebach."

"Phe, this isn't one of your American CSI television shows where DNA results are available in less than an hour," Daan warned her. "Things don't happen that fast. It will take time for us to track her down."

Daan got up and walked over to the window.

Piers interjected, "They found the van several blocks from the Opera House at a canal boat dock, but we couldn't trace the boat they took."

"They won't get far," Lars assured Phoebe.

"So, what do we do now?" Phoebe questioned.

"We hit Ziebach where it hurts," Daan started. "I have been tracking him from information in those immigration files. He has a network of drug operation and human trafficking safe houses we can raid."

"And the docks, you must hit the docks as well," Lars confirmed.

"That's already in the works," Piers disclosed. "There are a series of raids beginning at 4:00 A.M., both here and in Rotterdam."

"That's in an hour." Phoebe was looking at her watch.

Lars commented, "It'll be like watching rats leaving a sinking ship."

"We've wanted to do a wide sweep for a while," Piers continued, "but we never had firm, solid leads. Now we do."

"These raids involve both Ziebach and his competitors," Lars stated.

"How long before we find Lucy and Charlotte?" Phoebe's voice was shaky.

There was silence. Then Phoebe screamed at them, "How long?"

Finally, Piers answered her question, "It could take several hours or several days. No one knows, Phoebe, but we will find them, have no fear."

"Several days?" she yelled at them. "What do you mean several days?"

Lars tried to console her, "Phoebe, we are dealing with organizations that bring in illegal drugs and humans for sale in thousands of containers at the docks. You must be patient."

"Daan, they are only eleven and fourteen," she said and was crying again. "They're scared and worried, and they don't know what to do!"

Daan had been quiet for a few minutes. Now, he turned from the window and moved slowly to the sofa. "We know, Phe, we know." He sat next to Phoebe and took her hand. "We will find them, I promise."

She jerked her hand from him. "You lost them, Daan. You promised me they would be safe! You promised!"

He said nothing. Neither did Piers nor Lars. What could they say?

"I hate you, Daan de Sylva," she cried. "I hate you for allowing this to happen. I wish I had never met you!"

"I know," he stated softly.

Piers said, "It will take time, but we will find them, Phoebe. We're going to hit Ziebach where he is the most vulnerable. His docks. His warehouses, His infrastructure. Don't worry. We'll find Charlotte and Lucy."

She looked directly at Daan. "You'd better find my babies, bastard!" Then, she left the room, slamming and locking the bedroom door behind her.

Chapter 57

An hour later, the raids began. Piers, Lars, and Daan left to be part of the search. Phoebe wanted to go with them but was told she could be taken again and needed to stay safe.

Afraid Phoebe might try leaving the hotel, Daan and Piers left her with a policewoman while they searched for her daughters . Police were stationed around the hotel as well, just in case Ziebach tried to take her by force.

Although she screamed at them, especially Daan, she dutifully stayed in the suite, waiting for them to return with her daughters.

Hour after hour, Phoebe paced from one room to the other. Fenna, the policewoman, was in her early twenties, short blond hair, blue eyes, and a nice smile. She tried to calm Phoebe with conversations about the Netherlands and her trip to New York with some friends of hers a couple of years ago, but she didn't listen.

Phoebe then tried to watch television, but she could n 't concentrate. Food was brought up to them along with coffee, tea, and water. Phoebe hardly ate or drank anything.

By Noon, another policewoman, Maud, relieved Fenna. She was an older lady with gray hair and a stern look, who was even more a talker than Fenna, driving Phoebe near-crazy. Phoebe's only reprieve was a phone call at three. She excused herself and went into the bedroom with her cell. It was Daan.

"My babies?" she asked.

"We're still searching, Phe."

"How much longer, Daan?"

"As long as it takes."

After the phone call, Phoebe returned to the sitting room to look out the window. Finally, she did eat a little of a sandwich and drank a cup of coffee. Then she paced some more while Maud discussed the problems of the European Union and how the weather was affecting the tulips. Phoebe knew Maud was just trying to help, but she wasn't interested in politics or financial information or the weather or tulips. Phoebe continued to walk back and forth while Maud droned on and on.

At 6:00 P.M. Maud left when another policewoman named Annie joined Phoebe. Annie was also in her early twenties, about Phoebe's height but heavier, mousy brown hair, brown eyes, not much of a smile. She was a reader and stayed on the chair next to the couch engrossed with her book. Phoebe continued to pace back and forth, up and down from room to room. She sat periodically, but mostly she paced.

It was a little before 10:00 P.M. when there was a knock on the door. Annie opened it to a short man with a ski mask over his head. Annie moved to the side and the man rushed in, brandishing a gun around.

"Who are you?" Phoebe asked in a shaky voice.

The man began speaking in Dutch and then looked at Annie, who Phoebe saw was also holding a gun on her as well.

"Don't scream or Niels here will shoot you."

Phoebe took a deep breath and then said, "I have no intention of screaming as long as you take me to my

Debra Birdwell Winkler

children."

"I'll check."

With her eyes on Phoebe, Annie spoke to the man, who responded in a harsh tone.

"Mrs. de Sylva, it looks like you *are* going with us. You will call your husband to come to you. Then, we will take you both to our employer."

"I promise to not scream if you take me to my children," Phoebe said frantically.

The hooded man grunted and said something in Dutch.

"Mrs. de Sylva," Annie began. "Niels, he is a very good shot, and he will kill you if you don't call your husband now."

Annie moved around behind Phoebe and pushed her gun into Phoebe's back. "Now, Mrs. de Sylva. Now!"

Phoebe was reaching for her phone on the table when the elevator door dinged. Phoebe was hoping against hope it was Piers or maybe even Daan.

"What's that?" Annie questioned.

Phoebe was quick to answer. "Oh, that elevator does that every night. Constantly going up and down, dinging as it opens on every floor. It's broken." She took a breath and continued. "You should hear it in the wee hours of the morning because it is constantly doing that. Such a nuisance it is, that dinging. Maintenance was supposed to fix it today."

The man turned as the suite door opened and was surprised as Daan rushed in, tackling him to the floor with the gun flying under the sofa. Phoebe quickly pressed back against Annie, pushing her to the floor. Annie's gun went off and put a hole in the ceiling above them. Phoebe elbowed Annie down, then Phoebe jumped on top of her knocking the air out of the woman. Daan pulled the arm of the man behind him and angrily said something to him in Dutch.

"Phoebe, take my phone and dial 3. That's Piers ."

Phoebe did as she was told, and two uniformed police officers appeared at the door in a few minutes, taking Niels and Annie into custody. Piers showed up right after.

"What's going on here?" he asked.

"I really don't know. I think they were going to take me to the girls," Phoebe said and looked at Daan. "They wanted me to call my husband."

"Thank goodness I sent Daan to relieve the policewoman with you."

"That policewoman was no policewoman on your force," Daan stated emphatically. "I think she's one of Ziebach's people."

"Well, Phoebe is fine now," Piers said, then turned to go. "Daan, you are to lock this door and let no one in, do you understand?"

"Those were my plans before I interrupted Phoebe's kidnapping."

"Remember, you are no longer a policeman, so call me if anything else happens."

"Isn't that what we did?"

Piers said, "Phoebe, I'm glad you're okay. Now try to get some rest."

"I can't rest till my children are with me and out of the hands of that monster!" she shouted.

Piers ignored her and slammed the door closed.

Phoebe leaned against the wall for support, her adrenaline waning.

"Are you okay?" Daan asked softly. "I'm sorry I

didn't get here sooner."

"If you hadn't come, they might have taken me to my children, and I would have been fine."

" You believe that?"

She said nothing but just looked at the floor.

"What are you doing here?" she finally asked irritably.

"I was relieving the policewoman."

"Piers couldn't send someone else?" she asked arrogantly.

"Please sit down, Phe." He gestured towards the sofa.

Phoebe glared at him, then slowly made her way across the room.

Daan walked to the chair and leaned on the back for support, placing his left arm back into the sling. The medication was wearing off and his shoulder and head were hurting. He watched Phoebe for a minute and reasoned she might not be so upset if she knew what they were doing.

"Phe," he began, "Piers and his team and other teams are beating the bushes and rattling the cages of Ziebach and his competitors. Finding the girls will take time."

Daan would much rather be in the field than dealing with Phoebe right now. During his years with the police department, he had dealt with distressed parents involving kidnapping cases. Most times, the children were found. Only once were he and Piers involved with a case where the child had disappeared never to be found and twice when the child was found dead. In all three cases, the parents were beside themselves. One mother even committed suicide because of the death of her child by an unknown assailant. Even so, he believed they had a good record of finding missing children.

Phoebe was doing better than any other parent he had dealt with in such a situation. The case was young, yet he knew the first forty-eight hours were the most critical. However, his personal involvement was nagging at him, and he realized he was as distraught as Phoebe. He looked over at the auburn-haired woman smelling of lavender before him and tried to remain objective as if this case meant nothing to him. He had to concentrate only on the facts.

She said nothing for at least an eternity. Then started to say something but stopped.

"I'd like to tell you what's going on. Are you ready to listen, now?" he asked sharply.

She took a deep breath and dropped onto the sofa.

He sat down in the chair and began to discuss what had taken place during the day. The raids started at 4:00 A .M . She knew that. The police had searched warehouses and dock facilities during the day. They had found two containers in Rotterdam full of people being brought into the Netherlands illegally. These containers were allegedly Ziebach's. The raids also produced illegal weapons, drugs, and stolen computer parts. Most were from Ziebach's docks and warehouses, some from his competitors. But no Charlotte or Lucy.

She was silent at first and then said, "Okay, you've told me. Anything else?"

"I've told you all I know."

She stood up and bellowed, "Good, n ow get your lazy ass out of that chair and go find my babies!"

"Phoebe, I need you to calm down and sit." He stood to face her.

311

"Daan," she shrieked at him, "my daughters mean more to me than life itself! You know that! Now go find them!" She pointed to the door.

"Phoebe, shut up!" he stormed at her and grabbed her elbow with his free hand. "Shut up and sit down!" He shoved her down onto the sofa.

He surprised her with his raised voice and the force which he used to push her down, and she stopped.

"I can't go after the girls!" he roared. "They kicked me out, Phe! They kicked me off the investigation team! Don't you understand?"

"They what?" Phoebe's voice was cracking.

"Phoebe, they sent me away, okay?" His voice was hollow. "Lars was ordered to drag me back here—carry me if necessary."

"Why?"

"Piers said I'm too close to the case, and I was ordering everyone around," Daan admitted sadly. "But all I want to do is find your daughters."

The silence between them was deafening. Daan slowly moved to sit next to her.

Phoebe was softly crying now, and she leaned over and placed her head on his right shoulder. His other shoulder and head hurt and every muscle, sore. But he thrust his feelings into the darkness of his mind. Phoebe was the one he should be concentrating on. And that's what he did for a long while.

Daan was still holding her when his phone rang after midnight.

"De Sylva," he answered as he gently pushed her away.

He listened and then said, "Yes, she's with me."

He listened again and responded, "I'll tell her.

Thanks, Piers."

Daan hung up the phone and told Phoebe, "Piers said the police are still looking for the girls. He wanted me to tell you that there is nothing new, but he will call us with an update in a few hours."

"Daan," Phoebe was so quiet he had a hard time hearing her. "What am I going to do if we can't find Charlotte and Lucy ?"

"We'll keep looking, Phoebe."

"What am I going to do?" Daan could see she was close to hyperventilating. "I can't return home without them. I must stay here for as long as it takes to find them. I'll sell everything I own to stay in Amsterdam until my babies are found." She began crying again. "I can't leave without my girls! I just can't!"

"Shhh," he pulled her close to him. "Don't worry. I'll take care of you, Phe ."

She pulled herself back from him, tears still streaming down her cheeks. "No, no, no. I've heard enough of this I'll-take-care-of-you stuff."

"Phoebe, don't cry."

"I am not your responsibility, your burden. I am responsible for myself," she stated adamantly. "I'll do what I must to hang around until my girls are found."

Neither said anything for a few moments.

"What did Piers and Lars say?" Phoebe finally asked.

He smiled at her. "They told me to pass on a message to you, and I quote, 'Tell her we'll find those beautiful daughters of hers no matter how long it takes.'"

"But, what if they don't—"

"We will," he interrupted her.

She stood up now, "But, what do I do in the

313

meantime?"

"G et ready for bed and try to get some sleep. I'll be out here on the sofa," he assured her. " Piers has the hotel surrounded by police, so you are safe."

She walked towards the bedroom and then turned around.

"Daan, I just remembered something."

"What?"

"I told you there was a policeman with us, trying to get us in the van? You thought it might have been an imposter."

"Uh-huh ."

"The man's name, I saw his name tag," she had wrinkled up her forehead. "It had something to do with skates."

"Skates?" Daan asked. "His name was Skates? I don't know any police officer whose last name is Skates."

"Wait," she said to him and thought for a few minutes. "*Hans Brinker and the Silver Skates*. The man's name was Brinker."

"Brinker," Daan thought. "He was in a policeman's uniform?"

"Yes," Phoebe acknowledged. " He had light skin."

"You're sure?" Daan pulled out his phone.

"Very ."

"Blond ish white hair, very straight, almost looking unkempt?"

"Yes," she confirmed. "Daan, I kicked him in the shins with my heel. I may have hurt him."

"Piers," Daan said when his friend answered the phone. "Phoebe just remembered that it was Kris Brinker who was involved with the kidnapping."

Piers responded, "But, Brinker was on duty in the auditorium."

"Was he limping?"

"You know, now that you mention it, he was. He told me he had slipped on the concrete steps going into the Opera House."

"That was Phoebe. She kicked him with her high heel ."

"That woman is really good, you know."

"I don't know who hit me on the head, and I didn't recognize the voice, either. Could it have been Brinker?"

"I wouldn't be surprised ," Piers told him. "There was a policeman in the john when I went in, but I didn't notice who it was. I was hit over the head by someone behind me. I just never thought it was a policeman."

"A policeman came out after you went in, but I was paying attention to the Ladies Room," Daan remarked. "It very well could have been Brinker."

"We'll check it out."

"Great."

"Tell Phoebe that she's a good observer."

"I will."

He closed the phone and looked at her, grinning. "Good girl. Piers is looking into this new development and will get back to us."

She sadly smiled at him, "I'm sorry it took me so long to remember."

"Sometimes, you just need to allow your mind to relax after a trauma," he replied. "Go rest, now."

She turned from him and walked into the bedroom, closing the door behind her. Then, he heard her turn the lock.

Leaning back on the sofa, Daan tried to get

comfortable. His body ached all over, and the raging headache wouldn't quit as he pulled his gun from his back and sat it next to him. He wasn't going to take any medication for his throbbing arm because he wanted to be alert.

H e propped himself on one of the pillows and pulled his knees up without taking off his shoes. His watch confirmed it was past midnight and he realized he hadn't slept in more than thirty-two hours . He closed his eyes, but all he saw were images of Phoebe and the girls being dragged away from him. Obviously, sleep wasn't in his immediate future.

Daan reached over and picked up the remote control from the coffee table. There would be nothing on the news about the kidnapping because the police were keeping that under wraps right now. Flipping through the channels didn't help, so Daan dragged himself up, replaced the gun behind him, and walked towards the window. Looking out into the night, he kept going over in his mind what he could have done to avert the disaster of losing Phoebe's daughters.

Daan looked at his watch again. It was after one. He decided he was dealing with another sleepless night. Then, he heard a door open and whipped out his gun, facing the sound.

He relaxed when he saw Phoebe at her bedroom door and replaced the gun in its holster.

"What's wrong, Phe?" he asked as he moved towards her.

"I think I've cried all my tears out," she murmured, "and there's nothing else I can do.

"Try to get some sleep," he said as he stopped in front of her. "When we find them tomorrow, you'll want to be the perfect mom for them. You can't do that if you're up all night, again."

She took his hand, "I can't be alone. Please lie down with me."

He followed her into the bedroom. "Are you sure?"

"I can't believe it," she smirked and turned to him as she got to the bed. "You've been trying to get me into bed for two days and now you're backing off?"

"I shouldn't."

"You won't," she informed him. "You are an honorable man, Daan de Sylva, no matter how much of a hard-ass you try to make yourself out to be or how angry I am with you." She crawled onto the bed. "I need you to hold me because I don't want to be alone."

"Well, there's not much I can do anyway with only one arm."

"In different circumstances, I'm sure you'd figure out a way."

He smiled at her and walked back into the sitting room. After checking the locked door, he went through the suite and turned off all the lights, except for the lamp in the sitting room. Then, he returned to the bedroom and asked again, "Are you sure?"

"Daan, you can't be out there in the night looking for my little loves because Piers says you 're too involved. You told me yourself."

"And?"

"I'm worried about my girls, and I'm upset we lost them," she murmured. She looked up at him with her pleading eyes that once he had said he could get lost in. "I need someone to hold me, and you are here."

"I think it was that 'honorable' comment that worries me, now," he remarked. "That means—

"That means you need to stop talking and get in bed."

She propped up the pillows and allowed him to get comfortable. Then, she pulled up the covers and snuggled into his right side.

"Phe?"

"Uh-huh," she said.

"I am so sorry I lost the girls and I promise we will find them tomorrow." He kissed the back of her head.

"I know," she yawned. "I know."

She was soon asleep because he could feel her relax, followed by her slow, rhythmic breathing.

In his mind, Daan was still reprimanding himself for his behavior the night before. If he had been more conscientious, he may have seen this whole incident coming. He should have never involved Phoebe to begin with. Then he thought about what Piers had told him about Ziebach being determined to kill Phoebe because he believed she was Francine.

Daan agreed. Ziebach could have chosen any night to take them. He could have chosen Sunday, the day they're booked to go back to the States. He could have waited until Phoebe and the girls returned home to Utah. And, in America, Daan couldn't protect them at all.

He had been irrational today and nothing Piers and Lars said could drag his ass out of the pit he had dug for himself. He was angry when they forced him out of the operations center.

They were right. He was too involved, and he never realized it until now. As he looked back at last night's fiasco, he knew there was nothing he could have done to stop Ziebach. Except for one thing. He shouldn't have gotten infatuated with the woman in his arms.

Infatuated? The word hung in the back of his mind. Was he infatuated?

Oh, mijn God, but this woman still makes my blood boil.

He kissed her head again, and she snuggled closer into him and sighed.

Daan looked at his ring on Phoebe's finger and thought of his mother, who said to him so long ago, "One day you will realize your heart no longer belongs to you alone."

Daan held Phoebe closer to him and knew when they found her girls — and they would find her girls — he had to let her go. Because that is what one does when one has overstepped one's bounds, and he knew he had gone overboard with this woman. This lovely, captivating woman. This woman had stolen his heart. Stolen? Maybe not stolen. He only knew that his heart didn't belong to him alone. How did his mother know?

Then he said to the Fates in his head, *Help us find Lucy and Charlotte and let them be unharmed. If you do, I promise I will say goodbye to Phoebe and her daughters and never see them again.*

"Ah, Lover," he whispered softly to the sleeping Phoebe, "I had no idea the chain of events which brought us together would touch us and mean so much." He allowed himself to nuzzle into her hair. "If I had not lost your beautiful daughters, we could have spent so many precious moments together. I thought I had more time with you, to pretend with you, to share with you until Sunday. Ah, but that is not to be." He gently kissed her head one more time.

So, now, he was just going to enjoy holding her and being enraptured by her because they only had a few more hours together.

As he drifted off to sleep, he could hear the music from *The Ride of the Valkyries* and in the distance, he could see Brünnhilde riding across the sky with Lucy and Charlotte straddling the saddle in front of her. But Phoebe? Where was Phoebe?

Dah, dah, da dah, dah; dah, dah, da dah, dah; dah, dah, da dah, dah; dah, dah, da dah....

Chapter 58

When Phoebe woke up, she was alone in the bed with the covers draped over her shoulders. Daan was gone. She quickly got up and looked around for his things, but everything was gone. His side of the closet was empty. Not even a note to let her know about her girls.

She rushed out into the sitting room to find Fenna sitting on the sofa watching television.

"Mrs. de Sylva, may I get you something?" Fenna asked, startled.

"Have we heard anything about my daughters?" Phoebe asked.

"Not yet, Mrs. de Sylva. I'm sorry."

"Daan?"

"Mr. de Sylva left when I came in."

Phoebe returned to the bedroom. Daan had left no word about what was happening with the search for Lucy and Charlotte. And he was gone.

In the shower, she let the hot water cascade down her back and thought about the man she had called the Devil. She had been angry with him for losing her daughters and called him horrible names, accusing him of not being diligent. Now, she had to admit to herself he had been more than diligent, he had been attentive and caring, he had watched out for them and, in protecting them, he had been shot. He did not cause her to lose her daughters. Not in the least.

Phoebe now acknowledged she was in love with Daan. She knew that on Thursday night during the opera before the kidnapping . For the first time in years, she was in love.

You're a stupid fool, Phoebe Silva. This man is not in love with you. You were his pretend wife just so he could take down his nemesis. Just like in The Ring Cycle, *love is a commodity to be valued and abandoned when it fit someone's needs. She was the commodity.*

Phoebe took a deep breath. She had told Daan he was an honorable man, and she knew he was. Now, she told herself, he was still in love with his real wife, his deceased wife. Daan had no feelings for her, not at all, although she had fallen hard and fast for him.

She finally stepped out of the shower and prepared for the day. Daan had promised they would find Lucy and Charlotte. It was Saturday already, and they were supposed to leave tomorrow.

She kept herself busy going through her things and packed everything but what she would need for tonight and tomorrow. She then went into the girls' room and did the same for them, anticipating their return.

By this time, it was noon.

"Mrs. de Sylva, what would you like for lunch?" Fenna asked, and for the first time in two days, Phoebe felt she'd better eat something.

About twenty minutes later, Lars brought up a couple of sandwiches.

"Phoebe, it was good you remembered about Brinker. He disappeared after the opera on Thursday evening and called in sick yesterday. He must believe he is in the clear because he hasn't turned off his police phone, and they are tracking him now."

"Thank you, Lars," she said and hugged him.

"We haven't found Lucy and Charlotte, yet, but we know we're close."

Lars smiled at her and left.

"Mrs. de Sylva, you must eat," Fenna urged. "They will find your children, believe me."

Fenna led Phoebe to the sofa, and she ate a little.

At 2:00 P.M., Fenna was relieved by Maud. Phoebe was not in the mood to listen to Maud and her list of the Netherlands' achievements. But she tried hard to be engrossed with Maud's stories of Dutch fame and glory but was failing miserably. She leaned her head against the back of the couch and felt she was drifting in time as it crawled by in slow motion on and on, minute by minute. As she waited for Daan and the others to find her daughters, Phoebe was fading into a shadowy deep sleep on a mountaintop like Brünnhilde.

Chapter 59

It was just before four in the afternoon as Daan and Piers were sitting in the control center at the police station in Amsterdam reviewing the case. Daan was only allowed back into the center after he promised to curb his temper. The police were pleased with what had been accomplished so far. They felt like they had made several major busts and were continuing the incursion on Ziebach and his competitors, concentrating mainly on Ziebach.

However, the girls were still missing. Daan was begging to be put in the field to follow up on several leads. He had promised Phoebe the girls would be found today, so he had to initiate additional ways of delving into Ziebach's network. Piers shook his head at Daan's suggestion and refused to allow him out of the control center unless he wanted to go back to the hotel.

That was when Piers received a phone call. He walked out of the room, down the hall, and into the parking lot.

"Yes?"

"The girls are being released soon," a voice on the other end of the phone was saying.

"Where?"

"It will be a little bit because there are things I must do."

"When?"

"You must call off your dogs."

"Not until the girls are returned. I told you that was the deal." Piers was firm. "You have one hour."

Piers listened as the connection was broken, and he wondered if he had pushed too hard. He turned and Daan was standing next to him.

"Well?" Daan asked.

"Soon, Daan. Soon."

"Who was on the phone, Piers?"

"Nobody important ."

"Piers, I love you like a brother, but I'll only give you one hour. If those girls aren't returned in one hour, all hell will break loose. I will call the American Embassy, the media, anyone I can think of. This will end!"

Piers put his hand on Daan's right shoulder. "One hour." And then Piers walked back into the building, leaving Daan alone in the parking lot.

Piers had been Daan's best friend for over twenty years. Now, Daan didn't know if he could trust him anymore.

Exactly one hour later at 5:00 P.M. on the dot, the door opened to the police station where Sergeant Smit was operating the front desk. He looked up to see the two missing girls, Lucy in yellow and Charlotte in royal blue. They looked very out of place in evening wear in the late afternoon. But here they were after two days of being missing.

The sergeant raced out from behind his desk. "Ladies, we have been so worried about you."

"Sergeant," they both called in unison and then ran into his arms.

He picked them both up simultaneously and barked

the order, "You, you, and you," he pointed to three colleagues. "Go and find out who just dropped these ladies off." Then, he took the girls down the hall, yelling to the next officer, "Call Daan de Sylva, immediately. Tell him we have his girls."

Twenty minutes later, Daan ran into the police station with Piers following directly behind. They were taken to the room where the girls were playing cards with Sergeant Smit.

When the girls saw Daan entering through the door, they both jumped up and ran to him, yelling, "Daddy!"

"Hello, little loves." All three of them fell on the floor, crying in relief, then smiling in delight at being reunited. Daan ignored his shoulder as he began kissing them.

Then, Lucy saw Piers. "Uncle Piers! " A nd she rushed into his arms.

"Where's Mom?" Charlotte asked, looking around at the door.

"We are going to take you to see your mother," Daan declared with joy. "She is so worried. We all were!"

Piers said, "We have been looking everywhere for you two."

Charlotte reached into her pocket and handed Daan a small envelope that had his name typed on the outside. "Oh, Daddy," Charlotte said, "this is for you."

"Who gave this to you?" he asked as he quickly ripped open the envelope.

"The man who dropped us off," she affirmed.

"What did he look like?" Piers questioned.

"I don't know," Charlotte wrinkled up her nose. "He was not as tall as you, Uncle Piers, and he wasn't dark." She turned back to Daan. "He wore a Yankees baseball cap, had kinda blonde hair, and wore sunglasses all the time. They were like yours, Daddy. When he took off our blindfolds in front of the police station, he told me I had to give that to you as soon as I saw you."

Daan was still on the floor as he unfolded a typed sheet of paper:

"I am sorry that my father has made your life miserable all this time. I guarantee he will cause no one else distress. This will never happen again. "

Daan handed Piers the note. "What does this mean?"

Piers read the words. "The girls have been returned, and Ziebach will no longer bother us."

The sergeant helped Daan up from the floor and assisted him to a chair.

"Girls," Daan looked at Phoebe's children and smiled, "please go with Sergeant Smit and wash your face and hands so we can go to see your mother."

"But, Daddy, we've already washed up," Lucy said.

Sergeant Smit said to Lucy, "Miss Luce, Miss Charlotte, I think we can find a brush for you to take care of your hair. Then, your dad and Uncle Piers will take you to your mother. Besides, I think I can find a few more cookies."

The girls waved and went with the sergeant down the hall.

"Alright Piers," Daan began as soon as the door was closed, and they were in the room alone. "What happened?"

"It looks like someone returned the girls without Ziebach's knowledge."

"Piers?"

Piers looked up at the monitoring devices in the room. "Daan, let's get the girls to their mother as soon as possible. I've already signed the paperwork."

Daan followed Pier's eyes as he viewed the corners of the ceiling where the surveillance cameras were. "Let's go then. The girls need their mother."

Daan wanted to call Phoebe and let her know that they were on the way. However, he decided that they would surprise her.

After they stepped off the elevator on the top floor, Daan used his key card to open the suite door. When Phoebe saw Charlotte and Lucy, she ran across the room and opened her arms to embrace them. The three of them fell to the floor as she smothered them with kisses as tears poured down her cheeks.

Phoebe looked up at Daan and smiled. He turned and made his way to the elevator. Phoebe pulled herself from the girls and rushed after him, but the elevator doors were closing as she ran out into the hall.

"Thank you, Daan," she said as the doors closed. "Thank you for returning my little loves to me."

Chapter 60

Daan met Piers outside of the hotel, and the two of them walked along the canal. Piers had been chain-smoking since the girls had been kidnapped on Thursday evening.

"You know that the cigarette hanging out of your mouth for days on end makes you look like an old man," Daan told him.

"I feel like I've aged twenty years in the last two days," Piers admitted as he took the last drag on his current cigarette, lit a new one with its remnants, and then stuffed the old one out in the sand bucket hooked on the trash receptacle they were passing.

"Me too," Daan agreed.

They walked almost a block without talking and then Piers said, "Daan, you deserve an explanation."

Daan grabbed Piers' arm with his right hand and threw Piers against the canal railing with all his might. "You're damned right. How involved were you with the kidnapping? How deep are you with Ziebach?"

"I had nothing to do with the kidnapping, Daan! Nothing, I tell you!" He jerked away from Daan's grip.

"Who were you speaking to on the phone?" Daan was insistent. "One of Ziebach's cronies or someone else?"

Piers took a deep drag on his cigarette and released the smoke towards the canal. He leaned on the railing, avoiding his friend's eyes. "I don't know where to begin."

"Probably at the beginning. Although you may find out I know a lot already, but not as much as I thought."

Daan's voice was coarse and frigid. His black mood had been brought on because he was convinced Piers was involved with this whole affair. Daan had lost his wife and children to Ziebach. Now, he had almost lost Phoebe and her daughters as well. As he stood next to the man he thought was his best friend, Daan was close to taking out his gun and shooting Piers, then pushing him into the canal in front of them and walking away with no regrets.

"Well, it all began in school," Piers told him and related the fact he had known Caro Ziebach many years. It was Caro, who he had taken the rap for with the dope back after high school. It was Caro, who had found him the job on the freighter which had gotten him out of the Netherlands for a couple of years. It was Caro, who had found him the job at the warehouse in Rotterdam, his father's warehouse.

Daan interceded, "I knew you went to school with Caro, but there was never a thread of evidence connecting the two of you except that you worked in Luther Ziebach's warehouse."

"You knew that?"

"Of course."

"Why didn't you tell me?"

"Why should I?"

"You mean I've been hiding this from you, but you already knew it?"

"Piers, we were put together as partners because the police brass didn't believe you could be trusted . I didn't at first either," Daan told him and started walking again.

"But I watched you, and I began to have confidence in you. Why not? You were my partner and had proved yourself more than once ."

"Ah, so you took me under your wing for observation."

"At first, but I began to trust you. I have put my life in your hands more than once, Piers, my life! That's what partners do. We were a great team, you and me. The higher ups believed me that you were worth your weight in gold. And you became my best friend in the process."

Daan watched Piers take out another cigarette and light up.

"That was, until today."

"Like I said, I need to explain a lot to you."

"I'm waiting."

As they meandered through the streets of Amsterdam, Piers went into great detail about how Caro and he had watched out for each other all those years ago. After Piers joined the force, they continued to watch each other's backs.

"But I never betrayed you, Daan. Not you, not the force!"

"Until today, Piers."

"No, not even today."

"Then what was the phone call I overheard?"

"Daan, you know I have two best friends, you and—"

"Yeah, me and Buddy," Daan interrupted. "Over the years, I figured out 'Buddy' was probably 'Caro.' Now, I see I didn't know the depth of your relationship."

"Another secret I kept for no reason."

"A secret I told no one," Daan confessed. "No one."

"That's a good thing," Piers stammered. "But you

don't know the half of it. Caro kept us out of trouble on more than one occasion."

"When? "

"Remember the time we caught up with those two idiot car thieves? Remember the yelling we heard around the corner, and we lost the perps?"

"Yeah, it took us another week to catch them. What's that got to do with anything?"

"That was Caro. His father was funding that stolen car ring. He had several things going on, and Caro found out we were targets that night. That's why he yelled to warn us and then ran."

"Okay."

"Daan, there have been several times we have been on the verge of being in deep trouble or blown up or shot, you name it, and Caro has gotten us out of jams."

Piers watched Daan's repugnant expression. "There have been a few times I've let him know how close we were to him—not his father, mind you—him."

"Piers, how could you?"

"It was like paying for protection."

"And now you owe him?" Daan felt betrayed. "I should arrest you right now, Piers! For your lying! For your fraternizing with the enemy! For your part in the kidnapping of Lucy and Charlotte! For your betrayal!" Daan could no longer control his anger, and he reached back for his gun.

"You're no longer a police officer, Daan ." And he began to walk away with his back to his friend.

"I'm not going to shoot you in the back, Piers."

"Good, because I'd rather you didn't."

Daan started after Piers. "But you allowed him to take the girls, right? He and his father were involved and—"

"No!" Piers stopped and faced Daan. "I didn't allow any of this to happen, Daan! Neither Caro nor I were involved! But he has been my eyes and ears in finding out what Ziebach wanted from you."

"Me? I haven't done anything to Ziebach except accumulate information so we, the two of us, could take him down."

"I know. But Ziebach thinks differently."

"As he so graciously pointed out Thursday evening on the phone, Ziebach has been after my family. My entire family. After me, not just because of the murder in San Francisco, just because I am a de Sylva!"

"What was he saying about ancestors?"

"We're Jewish, Piers."

"I know that," Piers said. "What does that have to do with anything?"

"It looks like Ziebach's family has had it out for Jews and my family ."

"Makes no sense to me."

"Seems like Ziebach's family has been trying to take us down for a long time because of some ancient curse one of his ancestors put on us."

"Maybe there is a curse, and the Fates are manipulating us all."

"Please, Piers. There's no such thing as curses."

"Maybe."

"Life happens, Piers. Just life. My family has survived in spite of what life gives us."

"Remember, we keep talking about coincidences?"

"As you know, I don't believe in coincidences, either."

"Well, every time we get involved with Ziebach, it's

more of a coincidence, an accident, a happenstance. It's like the Fates have it out for us."

"How so?"

"Well," Piers continued after he lit up another cigarette. "That car theft ring thing, you're witnessing the murder in San Francisco, and a handful of other incidents over the years. Ziebach sees you attacking him directly and has been targeting you . Caro had tried his best to keep us out of Ziebach's way."

"And Caro? Where does he fit in?"

The two of them were now walking in Dam Square. Piers went over the years he and Caro had been comparing notes, protecting each other and Daan as well. But the most important information that Piers related to Daan was that, over the last few years, Caro had been slowly moving Ziebach's holdings into legitimate businesses.

"According to Caro, Ziebach had felt his son didn't appreciate the business opportunities provided for him. It had taken time, but Caro finally has his father's confidence. In the meantime, he has been doing his best to take the Ziebach Corporation out of illegal activities slowly, one business at a time, right under the nose of his father. I have been trying to help Caro as much as I could."

"By providing information to him from police files?" Daan snapped. "How could you, Piers?"

"No, nothing like that! Don't throw me under the bus, yet!"

"What then?"

"Since you've been in the prosecutor's office, you've come across prospective immigrants, who have stated how they came into this country through Ziebach's organization, right?"

"Right. But you haven't been very excited about what I have provided."

"Well, as soon as you give me information, I take it to Caro, who supplies me with more feasible evidence to catch his father on illegal enterprises. We've been working this chain of operation, the three of us. But you didn't know it. We kept you out of the loop so you wouldn't be implicated. You know the old saying, 'plausible deniability.'"

"Caro?"

"Yes, Caro. He wants the illegal stuff gone."

"What about his father? Hasn't he been catching on? It makes little sense that Ziebach wouldn't know what Caro was doing."

"Not until Tuesday when you came in with Phoebe Silva in tow."

"But Phoebe had nothing to do with me. She wasn't involved."

"You and Caro and I knew that, but his father went off the deep end. Ziebach began investigating how your family could have come to Amsterdam without his knowing it. Remember when Ziebach told you he had eyes and ears everywhere?"

Daan nodded his head, yes.

"It was reported to him that you were flying in from San Francisco after a detour to Salt Lake City to pick up your wife and children. He didn't see a coincidence that Phoebe and her girls were on your plane. At first, you didn't see the coincidence either." Piers took a deep drag on his cigarette. "He only saw that you were bringing your family home. He really did think Phoebe was Francine."

"But, Piers, it was so obvious they weren't the same people."

Piers grinned at him. "It took Caro a couple of days to figure that one out. Caro tried everything he could to point out discrepancies between Francine and Phoebe, your children and hers. Ziebach wouldn't hear of it because he was convinced you were able to change the records due to your relationship with the police."

"I couldn't do that."

"He believed you could, my friend. He's more paranoid than you."

Daan walked in silence.

Piers continued, "By the way, Caro didn't know about the kidnapping of Lucy and Charlotte until I called him."

They were slowly strolling around the main part of old Amsterdam and were on their way back to the hotel, the long way.

"Caro didn't know until you told him?"

"Daan, it was Caro who convinced his father he would take the girls off his father's hands and get them out of his way so he could concentrate on the raids. Caro lied to his father that he had the perfect harem to send them to and that the money would be good. It was Caro who was able to sneak the girls out yesterday and hide them until he could drop them off at the police station today."

"So, it was Caro who saved them?"

"They arrived at the police station unharmed, Daan," Piers reminded him. "Ziebach had them scheduled to fly out in a private jet last night to parts unknown. Caro stepped in."

"And what do you owe Caro for protecting the

girls?"

"Nothing, nothing at all."

Daan couldn't believe Caro didn't want something. "Convince me."

"Who do you think gave me the information about which of Ziebach's warehouses to hit and containers to choose in the harbor?"

"Caro?"

"Caro."

"Why?" Daan thought for a moment. "No, don't tell me. We took down his father's illegal businesses, and Caro is left with the legal ones."

"Bingo."

They walked for ten minutes without saying anything.

Then, Piers said, "By the way, I came close to killing Caro myself yesterday. I didn't realize how much those girls meant to me until they were gone. Caro was the first call I made as soon as I was away from you. Let me just say that I was ready to wring his neck."

Daan said nothing.

"Caro promised it wasn't him, and he would prove he wasn't involved . That's what he did, Daan. He found the girls and separated them from his father." Piers lit a new cigarette with his last one. "*Miji God,* Daan, those girls crept into my heart."

Daan smiled because he understood. Not only had Phoebe reached his inner soul, so had those two daughters of hers. And, he had to admit he enjoyed having them call him, 'Daddy.'

"So, what now?"

Piers looked at his watch and relaxed a little. "Well, just to let you know, Ziebach is gone."

"Gone where?" Daan figured this was a legitimate question. Had Ziebach fled the country? Where would he go?

"Gone, gone."

"Gone, as in dead gone?"

"Just accept the fact we shall never hear from him again."

"Caro?" Daan couldn't imagine the son taking out the father.

"Let's just say Caro is supposed to be innocent in this. He needs to be innocent so he can take over what's left of his father's businesses."

"Okay, so who is supposed to have eliminated Ziebach?"

Piers took a drag on his cigarette and looked squarely at Daan. "You."

Chapter 61

Caro Ziebach had been standing with his father on a dock in Rotterdam. Few lights, no cameras. The isolated dock belonged to the Ziebach Corporation and was where Luther Ziebach discussed things with his son when he wanted no other eyes and ears present.

"Well, son, I have new plans for us to continue our businesses," Ziebach said as he looked across the river and out to the North Sea beyond. "First, we must find the snitch. Only someone on the inside could have set us up so completely."

"Your plans aren't needed, Father," Caro said as he pointed a gun at Ziebach.

"You don't have the courage to shoot your own father, boy."

"Watch me," Caro said. "I learned from the best. You."

Caro pulled the trigger twice, and his father fell in a heap at his feet. Caro spit on the corpse.

"The bullet in your heart is from my mother, who you destroyed with your hatred," he hissed. "The bullet in your head is from me, Old Man. I regret nothing."

It took Caro a few minutes to roll his father off the pier into the shallows of the River Maas. He dropped the gun in the bushes nearby, easy to find. Tomorrow, an anonymous phone call to the police would alert them where the body could be discovered. The gun would be found soon enough, the owner's fingerprints intact since Caro had worn gloves.

Later, as he let himself into his father's office with the keys he had removed from the body, Caro looked at his watch. Everything was going as planned. This next part would only take another hour or so. Then he could begin finalizing the strategies he had arranged for the new Ziebach Corporation.

He opened his father's computer and began his work.

Chapter 62

Daan stopped and grabbed Piers' arm. "I did what?"

"You killed Luther Ziebach, my friend."

"Me?" Daan was surprised. "Why me?"

Piers started walking again. "You are the obvious one who did it. Ziebach killed your wife and children eight years ago. Ziebach has been after you for some time. And then when you had a new love interest, Ziebach tried to take this new wife of yours and her kids."

"We both know I didn't kill him, although I would have been happy to do it and go to prison for the crime."

"Daan, you don't remember how out of control you were when the girls disappeared?" Piers reminded him. "You were foaming at the mouth! Why do you think I had to send you away last night? You were shouting and screaming how you wanted to do away with Ziebach."

"I did use the word 'kill,' if I'm not mistaken. I was going to shoot him in the head myself with my own gun. And, you know, I meant it."

"Everyone in that room, in the whole police station and probably a block away, knew you meant it." Piers took another drag on his cigarette. "By tomorrow morning, the whole world will know Ziebach has disappeared and, when his body is recovered, you will become the number one suspect to have put that bullet in his head."

"How did you pull that off?"

"That gun in your holster is not yours. It looks just like yours, but it's not." When Daan reached for it, Piers shook his head. "Don't. Believe me."

They were now sitting on a bench a block behind the Opera House, watching the boats traveling on the River Amsel with street lights reflecting in the water . No one was around them, so they were not going to be overheard.

"So, now I am wanted for a murder I didn't commit."

"Not yet. But in the morning. We'll try to make it late morning to give you a head start."

"So, what's going to happen now? Is Caro going to put me on a freighter for a couple of years because, let me tell you, I'm too old for that, my friend."

Piers grinned. "Something much more sophisticated. Caro and I have devised a special plan to send you away."

"Send me where?"

"You must disappear tonight." Piers chuckled.

"And how is that going to happen?"

"We have it all taken care of. How does Iceland sound?"

"You know that ice and snow are not my thing."

"Germany and Italy are too close. How about South Africa?"

"Never been there."

"India?"

"No."

"Australia?"

"Perhaps."

"There are a couple of islands in the Caribbean that

we might be able to send you to. Maybe the Pacific."

"Possibly that would work." Daan thought for a minute. "I think I might like some place warm ."

"Daan, you must leave everything . You can take nothing with you."

"But, what about my life here?"

"Your life in the Netherlands is gone ."

"Piers, I can't just disappear," Daan was trying to be practical. "Wouldn't that be too much of a coincidence?"

"No. You killed Ziebach and someone in Ziebach's organization—his old organization—does you in." Piers smiled, "It's perfect."

"Maybe for you."

"No, you will have a new identity, and no one will come looking for you because you will be dead."

"Fingerprints? What about fingerprints? Records of my fingerprints are on file. What are you going to do with that?"

"Like usual, you worry too much. Things are in the works already."

"International intrigue at its worst, I see. This must be costing a pretty penny."

"It is, my friend, but you are worth it!" Piers popped Daan in his right shoulder with his fist.

"Hey, watch it, injured man here."

"Could have hit you on the other side, but we don't want you showing any injury to give you away as you leave the country ."

Daan sighed. "You know, shooting me would be the best thing. Just put me out of my misery."

"Can't do that, my friend."

Daan tried to be nonchalant. "So, who am I going to be?"

"I was thinking about using your middle name. Would that work?"

"Piers, I hate my middle name ."

"It's a name that has been passed down through your family for 500 years, right?" Piers was smiling at his friend. "Your mother told me that story."

"It is true that the eldest son of each generation has been given that name to remind us of our heritage and why we had to leave Spain during the Inquisition." Daan's face was void of expression. "I'm the last of my family , you know. So, it looks like Ziebach got his wish if I die, real or not. He will have destroyed my family."

"The sacrifice is necessary to protect you."

Daan turned to Piers, and with a smile, said, "Did you know Phoebe and I are distant cousins?"

Piers laughed. "Cousins, you say?"

Daan shrugged his shoulders. "Very, very distant cousins."

"Family is family."

"I suppose."

"Don't worry. Everything is falling into place . I owe you that much."

"So, how will I die?" Daan felt a shiver run up his spine. He always thought he'd die in police service or in bed of old age now that he was a prosecutor . But this? Not what he had in mind.

"Leave your death to me, and don't worry about it. I just need a few hours to finalize everything."

"I didn't know you had that kind of talent."

"I needed help, but your papers will be in excellent condition. No one will question who you are."

"But what if I meet someone who knows me before I leave the country?"

"You won't," Piers said.

"What if I say no."

"You can't, my friend. This is the only way I can save you," Piers confided.

"The only way?"

"Yeah."

Daan stood up from the bench and stretched. He was preparing to walk back to Piers' car.

"So, take me home so I can pick up a few things and disappear."

"No, Daan," Piers told him as he walked next to his friend. "You can't go home."

"So, I'm going to leave and can't take anything? No pictures? No reminders?"

"Nothing," Piers stopped him.

It was late and their shadows passed under the streetlights from one side to the other. Daan decided he had nothing to live for anymore, so why not start another life. He had already lost his two loves, one eight years ago and one a few hours ago. He was finally able to admit he was in love with Phoebe.

"Piers, you know I was so angry with you that I felt like killing you a little while ago."

"I know. Why didn't you?"

"Because you're my best friend and I needed to know the truth and I was waiting to hear your side of the story."

"If you had killed me, I would not have been able to tell you everything," Piers chuckled.

There was silence between them as they walked. Piers' car was parked at the rear of the hotel. Daan looked up to the penthouse where Phoebe and the girls were. Now, standing by the passenger door, he waited for Piers to unlock it.

"No, Daan ," Piers said as he looked at his watch.

"What now, Piers?"

Piers smiled at him. "Fool, you're going to see Phoebe. She's in love with you and you are in love with her. Saying goodbye is the least you can do." Piers looked at is watch. "You only have eighteen minutes, so hurry.

"I've already told her goodbye. Last night."

"But, not today, my friend."

"What will I say to her since I'm never going to see her again."

"Oh, you'll think of something."

Daan walked around the car.

"You must use the back door and go up the freight elevator." Piers grabbed his arm as he went past. "Lars is waiting for you at the back door, and you must give him your wallet and ID, your phone, your jacket, your sunglasses. Everything that can identify you as Daan Dominik de Sylva."

"You need my clothes, too?"

"Don't be daft," Piers said softly. "I can't have you arrested for public indecency. We'll take those in a little while, just not now."

Chapter 63

Instead of renting a car at the Brussels Airport, Nick searched long-term parking for a suitable vehicle. In a dimly lit corner with a broken surveillance camera, he picked up a simple dark sedan and hid his face under his hat as he left the garage. In Amsterdam, he parked along the street in front of the multi-storied building with the name, Ziebach, in neon lights on the roof.

He observed the area for a few minutes, then dialed a familiar number. The voice that answered was not his employer, so he hung up quickly. Then, he dialed again.

"Hello."

Nick was cautious. He never mentioned the name of his employer on a telephone call. But he didn't have a choice. His life was at stake.

"I'm looking for Luther Ziebach."

"I'm sorry but he is unavailable," was the answer he received.

"Well pull him away from whatever whore he's with and tell him Nick's on the phone."

"What's your business with Luther Ziebach?"

"Listen to me," Nick snapped. "I have a contract with him and must confirm the deal."

"What deal?"

"I'll only speak to Luther Ziebach."

"Who are you?"

Debra Birdwell Winkler

"Nick none-of-your-business who."

"My father is dead," Caro Ziebach stated firmly.

Nick wasn't surprised at the information. He had thought about doing the bastard in himself several times, but the money was better leaving him alive.

"So, who took your father out?"

"No one knows."

Nick decided he would try a different tactic. "Have anything to do with Daan de Sylva?"

Caro wasn't ready to release anything about Daan yet. "Daan de Sylva? The name's not familiar."

"Don't toy with me, kid. You know exactly who de Sylva is if you are Ziebach's son."

Caro waited. It had taken him over an hour to decipher his father's imbedded passwords and the information being revealed was encouraging since he was taking over. But he had found nothing on any 'Nick' doing a job for his father. Not even the name 'Nicholas' or 'Nikolas' came up.

"Well?"

Caro had a hunch Nick was the assassin his father hired to take out Daan. He was stalling to find out as much as he could.

"I don't know you, and I can't find a connection to you with my father and Daan de Sylva." Caro was clicking computer keys, looking for the code that he knew Nick wanted. "If you truly know my father, you know how secretive he was about all things."

"The code, please. If you're Ziebach's son, you'd have it."

Frantically searching his father's phone, Caro said, "You must understand, Nick, that I just found out about my father's death, and everything is in disarray. Give me

348

a minute."

Caro knew his father hated Daan and his family. Something about an ancient curse or some such nonsense and his father's discrimination against Jews was a double whammy for Daan. Right now, one thing Caro knew was, if he didn't give Nick the code, he would have no control of the situation.

"It's been a madhouse around here, and my dad was very cautious about his business. Let me double-check his records." Caro placed his father's cell on the desk. "I'll need to put you on speakerphone while I continue to search."

Nick's voice echoed in the room. "Check them fast, because I'll not do anything until there is money in my account."

Caro knew no one did anything for his father without money. At that moment, Caro remembered one of his father's rules which was to never, ever trust an assassin. Assassins had their uses, but it was important to get rid of them when you were through with them. He wondered how long Nick had been employed by his father.

Another piece of advice his father had given him was to always have security nearby. Never be alone and unprotected. Caro could almost feel the closeness of Nick and speculated he was nearby watching their building. Caro was alone because he didn't trust his father's security men. He had only one person he could trust, Piers. And Piers was nowhere around. He quickly touched a button on his own phone and left the phone on the desk next to the computer keyboard. His father's phone was on the other side.

"Nick, I'm checking. One moment please."

Caro was a computer whiz, but he could not find Nick in the records. He knew he was running out of time and had to find a way to get rid of this assassin.

"There's no Nick listed here," Caro stated firmly as he saw that Piers had answered his phone. "It's gotta be under another name. Last name, perhaps?"

Nick was getting antsy. Ziebach never used last names, and neither did he. He had promised this would be his last job with Luther Ziebach and he wanted his money. Would Ziebach's son pay him in his father's stead ? Or should he just walk away?

Nick decided to take the chance. "Try DT in caps." Those were his real initials. Only Ziebach knew his real initials.

Caro placed his father's phone closer to the computer keyboard so Nick could hear the clacking of the keyboard better. "Sounds like initials. But there's no 'N' for Nick."

"Just try it."

"Okay," Caro said. "DT in caps as you said."

Caro knew Piers was listening so he was giving as much information as he could. Ten seconds later, the name appeared on the computer screen. "Ah, there you are." And now Caro had Nick's full name. He was definitely surprised. "I see your name is— "

"The code," Nick interrupted. "That's all I need to complete my job."

Caro was reading through the information and was surprised to see how long Nick had worked for his father.

"Come on, kid," Nick said, interrupting Caro's thoughts. "I just flew in from Timbuktu and want to do this job quickly so I can leave on an early morning flight."

"Where are you going?" Caro tried to sound innocent while he continued to clack the computer keys. His father always used 'Timbuktu' when he didn't want anyone to know where he was coming from or going to. So, this assassin was using the same tactics which he must have learned from Luther Ziebach.

Caro prided himself on knowing out-of-country flights and ventured another question to stall. "So, you're on your way to South America, from Amsterdam, right?"

"You have thirty seconds, kid."

Caro decided he couldn't delay Nick much longer. "Wait another minute."

"Fifteen seconds or I'll need to go in there and give you what your father got."

That was when Caro knew he had to leave his father's office immediately after this phone call. He hoped he'd have enough time before Nick came barging in.

Then he found what he needed. "The code is 1653LZDT."

"That wasn't too hard, was it?" Nick said.

" My father was a very secretive man. He encrypted everything."

"Secretive and smart," Nick agreed and wondered how de Sylva had been able to get close enough to murder the great Ziebach. Only de Sylva could have mastered that with his connections. "The targets are still Daan de Sylva and his family, right?"

Going back to the last entry on the screen, Caro confirmed that, three days ago, his father had contracted Nick to kill Daan, Francine, Ilsa, and Anya de Sylva. His father was a sick bastard, and now he had an assassin ready to murder Daan, Phoebe, and those girls. However,

Caro speculated that his father had, for some reason, gotten impatient, kidnapping Phoebe's girls. Now the assassin was here to kill the whole family anyway.

"Tell you what, Nick," Caro reached forward and slammed his hand on his father's desk. "I am furious that de Sylva killed my father right under my nose. I want to be in on his demise. So, I'm going with you." Caro sounded incensed, which he was—but not at Daan, at his father.

"I work alone, Ziebach," Nick said.

"Not tonight. Weren't you responsible for killing de Sylva's family years ago?" Caro had remembered how furious his father was the other day. He thought he'd take the plunge here and blame Nick. "You botched that up, didn't you?"

"When your father told me de Sylva's family was still alive, I was a bit confused. I placed a bomb under that car and was at their god-damned funeral. De Sylva must be a magician to have pulled that switch-er-roo. I never suspected him at all."

Caro wanted to laugh out loud. This guy was very good at his job and Caro knew Nick was a very dangerous man. His father was the one who questioned that the assassin hadn't done his job.

Caro said to Nick and tried to sound excited, "I'm going with you. I'll transfer the money only when I know the de Sylvas are gone."

"Aren't they together?"

Caro looked at his watch. "No, de Sylva is sending them home to America tomorrow afternoon. He's at his home in Rotterdam finalizing his departure. I'll meet you there and after de Sylva is dead, I'll give you the address where his family is so you can finish the job."

"Transfer half now, and then the rest when de Sylva and his family are dead."

"No problem."

"If you wish." Caro clicked computer keys for show. "Sorry, the bank won't accept the transfer, Nick."

"Of course, it will."

"No," Caro lied very persuasively. He was again stalling so he could delay Nick as long as possible to give Piers a chance to back him up. "I must say that another transfer I was making to the same bank an hour ago was stopped until I gave them the account owner's special password. They said there was a glitch in the system, maybe from a hacker. So, in order to make the transfer, the client had to give me his password. As soon as I added that in, the transfer went through like a breeze."

Caro waited and, when Nick didn't immediately respond, he said, "You can change your password right after I forward the rest of the money. All I can say is this is what happened earlier with one of my father's clients."

"I've never had a problem like that." Nick was skeptical.

"If you want your money, give me your password. Or not. It's your decision," Caro said matter-of-factly.

Nick said nothing.

Caro said, "I want to kill the son-of-a-bitch who murdered my father. Then, I'm going to kill his security team who allowed it. So, no password, no deal."

"Fine, but if anything happens, I'll come after you, kid."

"Agreed."

Nick reminded himself to add one more to his contract with Ziebach. The son was being a prick, just like his old man. But the Ziebach kid was making one mistake. Meeting an assassin in person was not very smart.

Caro said, "I have the account number logged in, but I now need the password. You want to get paid, give me the password."

A minute later Nick confirmed the money transfer as agreed.

"Good," Nick told Caro. "Where is de Sylva? I want to finish this tonight so I can move on to the rest of the family. I'm booked on a morning flight to Rio."

Rio? So, the bastard was faking a flight from Amsterdam to Rio. Caro knew the flight to Rio was midnight tomorrow.

"I understand Rio is a nice place to visit."

"Perhaps." Nick sounded impatient.

Caro gave the address.

"I'll meet you in Rotterdam."

Then, Nick disconnected the phone.

Caro was shutting off the computer and his father's phone when he heard footsteps in the hall. Two men in black attire entered the room, guns drawn but at their sides.

"Mr. Ziebach?" the first one asked, and Caro nodded. "Chief Inspector Vogel sent us."

Caro picked up his cell and spoke to Piers. "Thanks, Piers."

"Caro, I can't get to Rotterdam before Nick. What about you?"

"I have a helicopter at my disposal, so I'll beat you there."

"Hurry, Caro. We need to nip this in the bud and fast."

Caro ordered a helicopter on his father's desk phone,

and he left the office with the two undercover police officers Piers had sent following. Caro had tried to act unsure of himself and unprofessional to Nick. But Caro was very professional, much like his father but he prided himself in not being a criminal. This act he was about to do was what his father had taught him. But this was the last such act he would do, and it was only for Piers that he was doing it.

Nick waited patiently for about ten minutes, waiting for Caro. Then he heard the blades of a helicopter and opened the car door to observe it landing on the roof. Caro entered with two bodyguards. Then, the copter flew away.

Nick had never trusted Ziebach, and he certainly didn't trust his inept son. However, the helicopter was something unexpected. So, Nick started his car and headed for Rotterdam. The address had better be legit because, if not, it was going to be a pleasure to kill them all.

Chapter 64

A few minutes after he left Piers outside, Daan de Sylva was softly knocking on the suite door on the top floor of the *Inn on Amstel*. There was no sound coming from the other side, so he knocked one more time. No answer. He moved back to the elevator and swore under his breath. He was hoping to say goodbye to Phoebe, but he'd missed his opportunity.

Viewing his reflection in the elevator doors, Daan didn't look his usual self. He thought of Roy Sanderson and felt a bit disheveled. Daan's wrinkled shirt was pulling under the sling holding his left arm in place, and his rumpled slacks looked like they'd just come out of a cold dryer. No, he wasn't himself, that was for sure.

He was standing at the freight elevator when he heard her door open.

"Daan," Phoebe exclaimed, welcoming him in.

His heart began to race as he moved towards the auburn-haired woman he'd known only a few days. "I can't go in, Phe. I only have a few minutes."

She turned the dead bolt to lock position so the door wouldn't close as she walked out into the hall. "I was afraid I wouldn't be able to tell you goodbye. The airlines called to say our flight was switched to early tomorrow morning."

"That's good," he said. "You and the girls need to

get home to — well — to — "

She interrupted him, "Why did you just leave after you brought the girls back to me." She leaned into him and took a quick breath.

"I had fulfilled my promise." He tried to sound nonchalant.

"Do you know what you are doing to me right now?"

"I'm not doing anything to you."

"I know. Don't you think it's about time you did?"

"I can't." His voice sounded tormented as he ran his fingers slowly up and down her arm, "even though you are standing out here in the hallway leaning against me in your nightgown, your very silky, lacy, pink nightgown." He gently touched her gown straps. It would be so easy for him to drop them off her shoulders and kiss her.

"Then, come in," she said softly. "You still haven't shown me the lovemaking you promised me the other day."

"And the girls?"

"They are in bed, sound asleep."

"You must remember I only have one arm."

"And this is my last night in town."

"I remember."

He brought her to him with his one good arm and kissed her passionately. "Ah, but you do make my blood boil, Lover," he whispered softly in her ear. "Do you know I've never told anyone that?"

"No one?"

"No one," he kissed her again.

She pulled herself away from his mouth. "Well, I've never called anyone Devil before."

"Lover, you can call me Devil anytime you wish," his voice was hoarse as he grabbed her and embraced her with his entire soul.

"Oh, Daan," her words were lost as he crushed her to him, and she wrapped her arms around his neck.

He kissed her neck and moved his lips to her earlobe, caressing her face in his hands, ignoring the sling. "I never knew what heaven felt like," he murmured. "Now I know this is heaven."

He continued to kiss down her neck, over her shoulder, and followed the slow tilt of her gown towards her heart. There, he stopped and pushed her away from him. Those eyes of hers. He was captivated by those beautiful, delightful eyes and her luscious, delicious lips, and her

"I was hoping to God that I could make love to you before you headed home." He pulled her back to him and crushed his mouth on hers. They were lost in each other for a few minutes.

Finally, he slowly released her. She took a deep cleansing breath.

"I have never asked this of anyone, Daan," she whispered, taking his hand in hers. "Please stay the night with me."

"Woman, we have been good together these last few days. God knows, we would have been better together with time."

He leaned into her, and they were kissing each other more passionately than before. But a couple of minutes later, he tore himself away.

"I can't, Lover, I must go." He kissed her cheek and hated himself.

"You can't leave me now," she complained softly.

"Not now."

"If I didn't have to be somewhere, I would stay here with you and suffer the consequences in the morning." He kissed her nose.

"Then, promise you'll visit us in Utah if you're ever in the neighborhood. My door will always be open to you, Daan de Sylva."

"I can't, Lover."

"Daan?"

"Phoebe, my love, I want you to always remember *The Ring Cycle* brought us together," he whispered, and he focused on her lovely face, etching every detail of it to his memory.

"I thought it was a medical emergency that flew your plane into Salt Lake City," she said teasingly.

He laughed. "You have a point, dearest one."

She reached up and brushed her lips against his. It was all he could do not to pick her up and take her to the bedroom no matter how much it would hurt for him to use both arms. But he stopped himself.

He gently stroked her face with the back of his good hand. "You know Piers said you were my Helen, and I was your Paris. I think maybe he's right." When she wrinkled up her forehead, he continued, "It's from Homer's tragedies…"

"I know where it's from, Daan." She looked lovingly up at him. "Do you think this is a tragedy?"

"I don't want it to be. "

He pulled her to him and kissed her one more time. Then, he nibbled on her ear and engulfed himself in her hair so he might take her lavender essence with him for a while. From here on out, to the end of his days, he would remember the smell of her lavender. On that distant island or faraway spot, wherever he was to end up, he would make sure to have lavender plants all around his new home. Then, whenever the wind blew, he would be surrounded by thoughts of her.

Now, he backed away, keeping her in his sight while he reached out and touched the freight elevator button behind him.

"When will I see you again?" she asked desperately.

He wouldn't answer that question. He couldn't tell her he would never see her again. Never hold her in his arms. Never.

He heard the elevator approaching.

"One more time." He rushed over to her and held her tight for what he knew was the very last time. "One more kiss, and then I must go!" He pulled her so close she could hardly breathe as he gave her his last, emotional kiss.

This must last forever till the end of my lifetime!

Daan heard the freight elevator ding, and he pushed her away. Before the elevator door closed, she heard him say, "I do believe you have my heart, Lover!"

And then he was gone.

"But Daan," she called after him as the elevator was making its way to the bottom floor at the back door. "Your ring?"

Phoebe stood very quietly for a long time without moving a muscle. Daan was gone and she knew from his last embrace, his last kiss that he was saying goodbye. The idea she would never see him again consumed her. That idea was much too hard for her to fathom.

Slowly returning to the suite, Phoebe unhooked the latch, closed the door, and then locked it. In the girls' room, she gave each another good night kiss. She walked over to the window in her room and pulled the curtain back to look out at the city.

Daan had stood right here not too long ago. Standing in this exact place, looking out into the night just as she was doing now. The lights of the city were almost mesmerizing, holding her interest, keeping her there, not wanting to move. They had been through a lot together these past few days. She smiled. A lifetime of memories flooded through her mind.

Finally, she let the curtain drop and ambled across the room.

In just a few hours, she would wake up Charlotte and Lucy and, while they were getting ready, she would finalize everything and pull their suitcases next to hers at the door of the suite.

Lars had promised he would give her a wake-up call so she wouldn't oversleep. Then, he would have a taxi waiting to take them to the airport and breakfast sandwiches and drinks for the trip. He told her not to worry because he had arranged everything. Now that she thought about it, she believed he already knew Daan would not be with her when she left.

Ultimately, she climbed into bed and pulled the covers tightly around her. She looked at her left hand, where his ring still graced her finger.

It's not fair that this part of my life should end on a tragic note like Brünnhilde's.

She held her left hand to her face and realized that this ring was the only thing she had left of him and might as well be as cursed as the one from *The Ring Cycle*.

"I hate *The Ring Cycle*," she said aloud and buried her head in her pillows, crying herself to sleep.

Chapter 65

Lars had been waiting for Daan to return downstairs from his visit with Phoebe so he could wish Daan luck in his new life. Then, he caught sight of the Fiat as it pulled up and parked across the street along the side of the hotel. The occupants were the same guys who had been watching Daan and the family for the last few days.

Now, Lars backed into the shadows of the hotel behind the bushes, focusing on the Fiat. He carefully pulled out his gun and attached a silencer expecting trouble. Daan stepped out of the hotel and strolled towards Piers who was smoking next to his car. Lars didn't move but waited.

The two Fiat guys slowly got out of their vehicle with guns raised at Daan. Lars knew he wasn't as quick as he used to be, but he was able to shoot the closest one before he left the door of the car. The other one coming around the back of the Fiat was surprised enough that Lars got off another round before the guy had a chance to respond. Neither had made a sound except for the plop their bodies made on the pavement.

Lars stepped back into the shadows, so neither Piers nor Daan noticed anything had happened as they drove away. Lars watched Piers' car turn the corner at the next street and disappear.

"Goodbye, my friend," Lars whispered after the car.

"I just hope we've got them all and no one will be following you to the airport in the morning."

Now, he unscrewed the silencer from the gun and dropped it into his pocket, tucking the gun itself into his back. He pulled each body into the canal where the current would take them both out to sea before anyone would see them. This time of night, no one saw him do his duty to the de Sylva family.

The Van Dyk family had been watching over the de Sylvas for five hundred years, from when Solomon Dominick de Sylva had loaned money to Jan Lars Van Dyk to buy property when no one else would. The de Sylvas had been kind to them over the years. When Van Dyk land had been flooded when dikes broke in that storm a couple hundred years ago, the de Sylvas had welcomed them into their home right here on this property.

But the de Sylvas were kind to many and trusting, extremely trusting. Therefore, his family had always been there to watch over and protect them. To keep them safe. Lars had been assigned to take care of Daan by his father, and he had taken care of the boy as directed.

Lars smiled. In the morning, he would resign as manager of the *Inn on Amstel.* Now, his job as watcher and protector of Daan Dominik de Sylva, the last of the de Sylvas, had come to an end. The Van Dyk family debt was paid in full.

Chapter 66

In the elevator, Daan had to admit saying goodbye to Phoebe was the hardest thing he had ever done. He was not in a good mood as he left the building via the back door and headed for Piers' car.

Piers didn't ask anything when Daan joined him except to double-check that he had given everything to Lars.

"You told me to, didn't you?" Daan was curt.

"Hey, friend, don't bite my head off."

"Sorry," Daan apologized and turned his head, watching the city lights go by.

Piers headed south from Amsterdam and Daan continued to look out his window. Piers knew he was hurting. Piers was hurting for Daan. But Daan had to disappear before he was arrested. Sending Daan away was the best thing for his friend. Tomorrow, Daan would agree.

After a while, Piers questioned his friend, "Are you okay?"

"Sure." Daan tried to sound confident and then said nothing for fifteen minutes or so as Piers continued to drive south.

Finally, Daan turned to Piers and said, "I need a favor from you, Piers."

"Anything."

"The airlines changed Phoebe's flight to the

morning."

"I know. It was to protect her."

Daan smiled at his friend. "Well, could you please make sure Phoebe and the girls have first-class tickets home. Is that possible?"

"For you, just about anything's possible right now," Piers claimed. "Let me see what I can do." He dialed the phone from his pocket.

It wasn't his regular phone, Daan noticed. It was the one Piers had used earlier to talk to Caro. At this point, Daan didn't care. He wanted Phoebe's flight home to be in comfort. Before they got to Piers' flat in Rotterdam, everything had been handled. Phoebe and the girls were going back to Salt Lake City first-class.

"Thank you, Piers," Daan told him. "I owe you."

"You owe me nothing, my friend," Piers let him know. "Nothing at all, except your friendship."

Daan didn't notice Piers had not lit up a cigarette the entire trip to Rotterdam. For the first time in years, Piers was too involved, making plans for Daan's well-being, and smoking was not on the agenda.

Chapter 67

Daan had crashed at Piers' place for a couple of hours. When Piers woke him, Daan took a shower and prepared to dress in the outfit Piers had for him.

"What's this?" Daan asked as he picked up the dark casual shirt, sweater, jeans, ball cap, and sneakers. "This isn't me."

"You're right," Piers said. "You can't be you anymore."

While they drove to the airport. Daan was slowly trying to convince himself this was the best option he had, given the circumstances. According to Piers, his death would be on the news soon. His old life was gone. Daan de Sylva no longer existed.

Piers told him they had to finalize a few things before Daan boarded his plane for his new life. As they went through the back hallways of the airport, Daan drew the ball cap low over his face so no one would recognize him. Now, in security, the two passed the infamous interrogation room Daan knew so well.

Was it only just a few days ago she had sat across from him? That was when he thought she was with Ziebach. He closed his eyes and envisioned for just a second that she was there with him, and he could smell lavender.

Piers took him one more door down, and they entered a dark room which showed the double-sided mirror. "We know this room isn't bugged."

"Vanderburg?"

"He no longer works here, Daan," Piers confirmed. "The police have cleaned house since Vanderburg's name along with several others were found on documents in one of Ziebach's warehouses in Rotterdam Friday afternoon. The raids did more than just render to the police stolen weapons and computer parts along with human beings. The filing cabinets were full of information. It'll take us a while to get all his underlings, but we will."

The door opened from the hall, and an officer dressed in a captain's uniform came in. "Sir," he said to Piers.

"Daan, you may remember Lieutenant Voss?"

How well, indeed, Daan remembered Voss. He had worked for Vanderburg.

Piers saw Daan's puzzled look. "He's been our eyes and ears in Vandenburg's domain. Now, he's our new captain of airport security, taking Vanderburg's place."

"Sir," Captain Voss acknowledged Daan.

"Captain," Daan responded.

"Chief Inspector," the captain addressed Piers and handed him a manilla envelope. "We don't have much time."

"Right," Piers took the envelope and looked at Daan.

"Thank you, Captain," Piers said. "Give us a few minutes, please."

Voss nodded and left the room.

"Daan, remember you cannot return to The Netherlands, or you will be arrested."

Piers knew how angry Daan had been a couple of

days ago. He had never seen Daan lose his temper, never! Daan didn't realize that his performance was all that was needed to convince the world he was capable of and justified in killing Ziebach.

"The bullets that killed Ziebach will be traced to your gun, confirming police suspicions," Piers reminded Daan. "Remember, you're dead, so no one will come looking for you. Therefore, you must never return."

"Got it."

"And Daan, another thing."

"What?"

"Those stupid sunglasses of yours with the reflective lenses are your signature."

"And?"

"Give them to me. You were supposed to pass them to Lars last night. "

"Great." Daan reluctantly handed his sunglasses over to his friend. "I think you have now taken everything that would identify me as Daan Dominik de Sylva."

"Good." Piers smiled and handed him a cheap pair that was common for tourists. "And now to get you on your way to your new identity, you have brand new clothes and shoes, nothing of the old you any longer. Nothing flashy, nothing you."

Daan looked at himself, knowing Piers was enjoying this part. "Okay, already."

"Hand me your sling."

"My sling?"

"You are no longer Daan de Sylva with the bullet hole in your shoulder."

"I was supposed to wear that for a few days more and not open up this stupid wound."

"Here's your new trench coat. Plain. Simple. Non-descript beige."

"You're kidding, right ?"

Piers ignored the comment. "Do you see me placing your sling in the trench coat? You can wear it after you're in the air. And in the other pocket is your new phone. You can't activate it until your plane lands at your new location."

"I've always hated trench coats, Piers. You know that."

"Everyone who knows you, knows that as well. So, get used to it."

"Fine." Daan took a deep breath as Piers helped him draw it up his left arm.

"Now, to top off your new look," Piers took Daan's ball cap and handed him a fedora hat, which matched the trench coat.

"That might be a bit much, Piers."

"Daan, you need something to hide your face as you go through security and down the concourse to your flight. I didn't make plastic surgery part of the deal."

"Fine, what else?"

"Incidentally, thank you for your house, your car, and your bank account."

"My what?"

"Remember years ago, while you and Francine were still married, the two of us had our wills drawn up?"

"Vaguely."

"You were my beneficiary, Daan."

"And you were mine if something happened to my family and me."

"Well, you are now officially dead, and you never changed your will."

"I guess I didn't," Daan paused. He'd lost everything now. Family. Home. Bank account. And he reminded himself, even Phoebe. "Take it. Take it all, Piers. I really don't care."

"I won't take advantage of you, dear friend. That's just the way the world sees it so we could confirm the charade."

"Great. Now, my only problem is where am I going and what do I live on?"

"Your new wallet with sufficient money is in your ID envelope."

"You mean the one you are still holding?"

"Yes, but this is the best so far, my friend," Piers seemed very pleased with himself. "Your money has been secretly transferred into a Cayman Island account. You have over $5 million in that account."

"Piers, my accounts had much less than that. Even the accounts my parents had left that I held for my twins."

"This is Caro's way of saying 'thank you,' and there's no more discussion on that." Piers tapped the manilla envelope he held. "By the way, do you remember your camera?"

Daan nodded.

"Well, I had that roll of film developed. They're here for you to remember your final days in Amsterdam."

Daan reached for the envelope, but Piers still held it to his chest.

"Oh, and by the way, I understand Phoebe and her girls live in a rented large Victorian home across the street from her university."

"So?"

"Well, when Phoebe gets home tonight, she'll find the deed to that house in an envelope in her mailbox," Piers informed him. "It's a gift from Caro and me."

"Thanks." Daan nodded his head. "She deserves so much more, Piers."

"There's no way to trace the funds, I promise," Piers said. "Don't ask how it was done on a Saturday evening. I won't tell you."

Daan took a deep breath and smiled. *At least Phoebe will have a house in her name and her memories of the week. And I have her etched into my being.*

Now, Daan said aloud, "Piers, I've lost my country, I've lost her." Daan had a look of melancholy as he stared at Piers for a long moment. "And you, what am I going to do without you?"

"My friend, you know we can never see each other again. I'll be watched like a hawk while you slip away to your new reality. You must remember that Daan Dominik de Sylva is dead."

There was a knock on the door, and Captain Voss stuck his head in. "If we don't leave now, he may not make his flight."

"Before I forget," Piers said, "you're going to need to learn to write your name with a 'c' and not a 'k.' And don't forget to drop the 'd-e'?"

"What?" Daan asked.

"Ziebach didn't win, my friend. You did because you're here, and he's not." Piers grabbed Daan and hugged him. Then, he stepped back and handed him the envelope, pulling Daan's hat low over his face. "I love you so don't get into any trouble, got it?"

"I'll try my hardest." Daan was irritated.

"Bye, my dear friend," Piers whispered and watched

the captain and Daan hurry down the hallway.
And then his friend was gone forever.

Chapter 68

From behind him, Piers recognized a friendly voice. "How did it go?"

"Good." Piers turned to Caro and pushed open the door allowing them to enter the large airport corridor which was bustling with people.

"Does he know where he's going?" Caro asked.

Piers lit a cigarette and said, "No ."

"Does he know his name yet?"

Piers grinned. "No, I didn't tell him that either. He'll find out soon enough."

"I'm glad Nick came along when he did."

Piers shrugged his shoulders and took a drag on his cigarette.

"Who knew that Nick was short for Dominic?" Caro asked. "And that Dominic Thompson, alias Dominic Thompson Silva, Phoebe's dead husband, was Ziebach's assassin?"

"I'm just glad you had that helicopter available, and you beat him to Daan's."

"Using him prevented us stealing a cadaver from the morgue to substitute for Daan. It was easy enough to switch the identities."

"That's because, when the two of us work together, Caro, we are great."

Caro looked at Piers and smiled. "Well, did you tell him about us?"

"No, Hon, I didn't want to enlighten him on that front."

"See you tonight at your place or mine?"

"We should probably lay low for a few weeks," Piers said. "Then, we'll go to Paris."

Piers smiled as he thought about spending a few days in Paris with the man he loved. He and Caro had cared about each other for a long time. A very long time.

As they stood next to each other on the way down the escalator to the trains, Piers leaned over to Caro and whispered, "I don't care how much I love you, just remember I'm watching you and the first time I see anything illegal come out of the Ziebach Corporation from here on out, I'll take you in myself. That I promise!"

They didn't look at each other as they moved apart when the escalator ended.

Well, dear friend, Piers whispered to Daan under his breath as he stood on the train platform. *You are on your way to a new life, and so am I. We shall never meet again because we can't. Please take care of yourself. Goodbye and good luck to both of us!*

Two trains arrived at the station below the Amsterdam-Schiphol Airport facing opposite directions. There were lots of people vying to board them. Two men nodded to each other as strangers will do in a train station. One was the new CEO of the Ziebach Corporation, who boarded the train for Amsterdam, and the other was a Chief Inspector with the Dutch Police on his way to Rotterdam.

BOOK 3: The Future

Chapter 69

When Phoebe and her daughters had checked in for their flight, Phoebe was surprised they had been bumped up to first class.

"Are you sure?" Phoebe asked the agent.

"Doctor Silva, you were upgraded."

As they boarded the plane, the girls were excited to see Sally, the flight attendant from their last flight.

"It looks like you have the same seats as before, Doctor Silva," she told Phoebe. "The only difference is you have the window seat this time."

"Thank you, Sally."

"I will make sure your girls have their cokes. What about you?"

"Just water," Phoebe told her softly.

When Sally brought their drinks, she asked Phoebe, "Will Mr. Silva be joining you?"

"What?"

"Your husband?" Sally indicated the empty seat beside Phoebe.

"No ." Phoebe was much too curt and was sorry immediately after. Why question her about her husband. Then, she looked down at Daan's ring. Perhaps she noticed the ring. That made sense, she supposed.

When Phoebe checked on the girls in front of her, both gave her their thumbs up then went back to their television monitors. She shook her head as she moved back to her seat.

All seems fine with them. No arguments. No hassles. What a change from a few days ago. Have they grown up while I wasn't looking?

When they returned home, Phoebe would have Dr. Goodman from her school's psychology department talk to her daughters about the kidnapping. It seemed the right thing to do. She needed to make an appointment for herself because she was dealing with a lot as well.

Charlotte and Lucy had told Piers and Daan all about what happened to them. The trip in the van with that horrid redheaded lady and her two companions, the big Andre the Giant type guy and the thin little Peewee guy driving the van, were not nice at all. The first night they were held in a small room with only blankets which Charlotte wrapped around the two of them.

The next morning, the nice man had taken them on a car ride blind-folded to a beautiful bedroom with food and drink. There were two twin beds where they could sleep and a great bathroom with fluffy towels and lovely smelling soaps. He treated them well and gave them pizza and hamburgers. He promised to take them to their daddy, and he did. They were excited to see Daan when he collected them at the police station.

This morning on the way to the airport, both girls asked if 'Daddy' would be coming with them to fly home. Phoebe explained that their pretend 'Daddy' had to go home to his house in Rotterdam.

"That's not fair, Mommy," Lucy had said.

"He was good to us, Mom," Charlotte confided in her. "You're in love with him, you know."

"I am?"

Charlotte said, "I saw the way you looked at him

and, by the way, I think he's in love with you too, Mom."

"We were just playacting," Phoebe told Charlotte.

Now, Phoebe closed her eyes but all she could see was the news report on the television at the gate. It was in Dutch, so she didn't know exactly what was going on. On the screen was a five-story brick house on a canal in Rotterdam from which a body was being removed. In the corner was a picture of Daan. She asked the man next to her to translate. He explained that the man in the corner of the screen was Daan de Sylva who had died due to a gas leak in his Rotterdam home. The man explained that the police believed it to be a very tragic accident.

Phoebe was stunned by the news. She had just seen Daan last night. Now, he was dead, and she hadn't even told him she was in love with him. She raised her fingers to her lips. She could still feel the warmth of his kiss and his arm around her. She reprimanded herself for falling in love with the Devil in less than a week. Her heart was broken, and she admitted it might never heal after Daan.

Just before they sealed the door for takeoff, someone had taken the seat next to her, but she didn't pay attention because she didn't care and was trying hard not to cry.

The plane slowly made its way through the clouds into the sky and leveled off. The pilot told everyone they were approaching cruising altitude and were running on time. Phoebe glanced over at the man next to her. His newspaper was in the way, so she couldn't see his face at all.

Phoebe moved closer to her window as tears rolled down her cheeks and she could not control herself anymore. She grabbed the napkin Sally had brought with her water, but it was soaked through in no time. She had to stop crying but she just couldn't.

It's going to be a long flight home and an even longer lifetime without love. Might as well make the best of it.

But Phoebe Silva wasn't doing a very good job of making the best of it and she tried to focus on the clouds outside the window, while letting her tears fall.

Chapter 70

The plane had been at cruising altitude for a while now. Phoebe didn't know how long because she wasn't paying attention. She was numb with grief and wiped the last of her tears with the back of her hand.

Was she going to be fine now? Of course! She had her daughters and her job. The last few days had been trying, but she was fine.

Phoebe took a deep breath, but it wasn't helping much. She was tired and unhappy, and all she could think about was what would have happened if she had told Daan how she felt. Then, he would have stayed with her at the hotel and not returned to Rotterdam, succumbing to the gas!

Oh, Daan, I am so very sorry. If only you had stayed with me...

Her tears began cascading down her cheeks again. This time they were more like a waterfall that wouldn't stop, even with her eyes closed.

Finally, Phoebe's seatmate moved. But she wasn't paying attention as he slowly closed his paper and began to fold it carefully and meticulously. She didn't see him place it in the seat pocket in front of him. She had no idea that he reached up and took something from the flight attendant. Her eyes were closed, and she didn't see the napkin being offered to her.

Then, she heard a familiar voice say to her, "Hello,

Lover."

Phoebe was afraid to move. Had she imagined his voice calling her? She slowly opened her eyes and turned towards the voice.

"Please dry your tears. I'm here now."

Was it just her imagination that he was sitting there beside her, just an apparition that she had conjured up?

"I see you still have my ring on your finger." He reached out his very solid hand and pulled her fingers to his lips. "Ah, Lover, I'm so glad we're still married. That's good, you know, since officially we're going to spend the rest of our lives together."

He slowly pulled her face to his, kissing her tears away and then gently her lips. He whispered in her ear, "You know what I'm thinking about right now?"

She shook her head.

"I'm thinking about what we're going to do when we get home. I can't wait to show you the lovemaking I promised you in Amsterdam."

"Are you really here?"

"Yes." He kissed her again.

"So, sir, who am I addressing if Daan de Sylva is dead?" Phoebe asked softly.

"Officially, I'm your husband, my love."

"My husband?"

"Quiet," he whispered softly. "You know that I don't believe in coincidences, but coincidence brought us together."

"What?"

"Phe, don't ask questions. Everything's good, and Piers sends his love."

Her eyes widened. "Piers?"

"Shh. Everything is as it should be." He smiled at

her. "Oh, and call me Dom, okay?"

"Dom?"

"Yes, my love," said the reborn Dominic Silva.

"How?"

"The past is in the past, now," he said, brushing away a missed tear on her cheek. "You know you saved me, Lover. You are my Brünnhilde."

She wrinkled up her forehead. "But, Brünnhilde died at the end of the opera, as did her lover."

"Well, we just re-wrote the story, and you are taking me off to Valhalla."

Phoebe giggled. "I've never heard Utah called Valhalla."

"Call it what you will."

She started to say something, but he placed his finger on her lips.

"Remember the Skinny Bridge?"

"You mean the Lover's Bridge?"

"Uh-huh."

"Are you saying the legend doesn't matter?"

He kissed her nose. "All that matters is that we are together now. The four of us." He nodded toward the girls. "So, let's celebrate a new life together."

"Can this be really happening?"

"Don't think about it, my love. I have a vodka on the rocks for you." He handed a glass to her. "Sally created lemon twists for us. But I'll do it better when we get home."

She gave him an endearing smile, and he touched his glass to hers in a toast.

"So, Lover, I understand the weather in southern Utah is rather nice this time of year."

A word about the author...

My name is Debra Birdwell Winkler, and I am a writer who is passionate about sharing my stories.

A writer's job is to take a reader into another reality where the reader can experience wonderful adventures in the reader's imagination guided by the writer's words. This is my goal for my readers.

I was born and raised in the South, and now live in the West. Never thought I'd end up here, but life has moved me from one moment to the next without clearing my destination with me. Things don't always end up the way I've planned, but my children and my grandchildren make it all worthwhile.

My writing career started when I won an award in fifth grade for a poem I wrote about my sister. Since that time, I have craved becoming part of the writing world. But life got in the way as I took care of my family and my writing dream fell to the wayside. Don't get me wrong, I love my family and my teaching. I've been writing pretty much all my life. It wasn't until I retired that I was able to fully concentrate on my writing dream and writing became my focus, my job, my joy.

I have written novels, short stories, and poems. Most are fiction, a couple are non-fiction. In the Spring of 2021, I felt comfortable enough to finally begin submitting stories to writing contests. Although I didn't win a contest, one of my stories was "published" online. I was so thrilled to type my name into Google and find the story there for all to see.

Since then, several of my stories are available online and one was selected to be published in an international literary journal. On 14 February 2022, my short story, NEVER IN A MILLION YEARS, was published in the anthology, SECOND CHANCE, A ROMANCE ANTHOLOGY. On 1 July 2022, I was nominated for the award BEST OF THE NET NONFICTION CATEGORY for my short story, WHEN I WAS TEN.

Each of my stories are attached to a piece of music which inspired me to create my narratives and I have intertwined historical events in my stories. I hope you enjoy what I have written for you.

For more information, please check out my website: DBWinklerWrites.com